ANTHOLOGIES BY
WRITTEN BACKWARDS

PELLUCID LUNACY

International Book Awards – Winner
USA News Best Book Awards – Winner

CHIRAL MAD

Eric Hoffer Awards – Grand Prize Finalist
ForeWord Reviews Book of the Year – Finalist
Halloween Book Festival – Honorable Mention
Indie Book Awards – Finalist / Silver Medal
International Book Awards – Winner
London Book Festival – Winner
Anthology of the Year by This is Horror – Runner-up
USA News Best Book Awards – Finalist

CHIRAL MAD 2

Bram Stoker Awards ® (Horror Writers Association):
Superior Achievement in Short Fiction – Nomination: "The Geminis" by John Palisano
Superior Achievement in Long Fiction – Winner: "The Great Pity" by Gary A. Braunbeck
ForeWord Reviews Book of the Year – Finalist
Independent Publisher Book Awards – Finalist / Silver Medal
Indie Book Awards – Winner / Gold Medal
International Book Awards – Winner
Paris Book Festival – Runner-up
Publishers Weekly – Starred Review

THE LIBRARY OF THE DEAD

(coming soon)

QUALIA NOUS

QUALIA NOUS

| EDITED BY MICHAEL BAILEY |

WWW.NETTIRW.COM

PUBLISHED BY WRITTEN BACKWARDS

Cover artwork by Michael Bailey.

FIRST EDITION

ISBN: 978.0.578.14646.1

QUALIA

| qua·li·a / kwɑliə / quālis |

instances of subjective, conscious experience; the internal and
subjective component of sense perceptions arising from
stimulation of the senses by phenomena; the way it
feels to have mental states

NOUS

| noōs / naʊs / nu |

intellections; awareness; perception; understanding; reason;
thought; intuition; the faculty of the human mind; having
the ability to understand what is true or real;
practical intelligence

0 - 1

| MICHAEL BAILEY |

THE SPACE BETWEEN 0 AND 1 is a whole number (one), or a pool of infinite partial numbers, which can be represented by the symbol ∞. 0 can represent nothing, or it can signify something; 1 can be a single something, or an infinite amount of anythings.

Let's make this even more confusing. 1 can be represented as a single digit of 1, for example, or four fourths (4/4), or any number divided by itself (196/196, 87/87, whatever/whatever), and is often used in mathematics to solve complex equations. 1 can therefore represent any number imaginable, even partial numbers divided by the same partial numbers (.196/.196 = 1); similarly, 0 can represent all things null when dividing any number imaginable by 0 (78/0 = *error?*), or can return a product of 0 when multiplying any number of somethings by 0 (87 x 0 = 0).

Despite their simplicity, 0 and 1 are complex. Still with me?

We know there's enough space between 0 and 1 to fit a single whole number, but how many *partial* numbers exist between 0 and 1? *An infinite amount* is the answer. We know that 0.1 exists, as does 0.01, 0.001 and 0.0001. What about 0.000000196? Yes; the amount of zeroes can go on forever, giving us an infinite amount of possibilities. If the italicized answer above is true, and there are an *infinite* amount of partial numbers between 0 and 1, then how many partial numbers exist between 1 and 2? The answer must also be *an infinite amount*. This presents a conundrum...

Is anything greater than ∞? No. And *yes*. If an infinite amount of numbers exist between 0 and 1, and an infinite amount of numbers exist between 1 and 2, then the infinity between 0 and 1 must equal the infinity between 1 and 2. Theoretically, wouldn't these 'infinities' (individually) be smaller than the combined infinity that exists between 0 and 2? These 'smaller' infinities *should* be twice as small, or perhaps *half* as infinite. Can one ∞ be larger than another ∞? Apparently, yes. And *no*, because it's the same damn thing.

But back to the ones and zeroes, the whole number variations. Why are these two numbers important? What is their significance? And why do we have a mathematical language called binary, which is sometimes referred to as 'the universal language'? *Binary* literally means *'composed of two pieces or two parts.'* (Meaning a hydrogen atom is technically 'binary' since the composition is a positively charged proton and a negatively charged electron bound to a nucleus by what is called the *Coulomb* force. Is this significant? Hydrogen is the first on the periodic table of elements and has an atomic weight of 1, so perhaps; maybe there's an invisible element with an atomic weight of 0 waiting to be discovered.) In binary code, the language of computers, 0's and 1's represent processor instructions to help hardware and software communicate (on devices designed to assist *our* technologically-evolved lives to communicate, no less) with seemingly endless strings of 'off' and 'on' commands: 0's and 1's.

The binary numeral system (also known as *base two*) is a mathematical representation for numbers using two digits: 0 and 1; as opposed to the decimal numeral system (known as *base ten*, or *denary*), which is a mathematical representation for numbers using ten digits: 0 through 9. When counting in decimal, a single digit in the right-most placeholder increments from 0 to 1, and then 2, 3, 4, 5, 6, 7, 8, and finally 9; when rolling over to 10, a hidden placeholder on the left (previously an invisible 0) flips to 1, and the single-digit placeholder on the right returns to 0 (resulting in the decimal number 10) before repeating the next ten-digit cycle of numbers. The numbers on the right count over again: 1, 2, 3, 4, 5, 6, 7, 8, 9, 0, before the 1 that previously 'flipped' on the left increments to a 2, at which point the digits on the right recursively increment one whole number at a time. Visualize a tachometer in a car. The 'tens' placeholder increments every ten clicks, the 'hundreds' placeholder every hundred, the 'thousands' every thousand, and so on. The numbers continuously increment and shift to the left by powers of ten (hence the *dec* in *decimal*). The decimal number 4,884 can thus be represented (and computed) as follows:

$$4 \quad\quad 8 \quad\quad 8 \quad\quad 4$$
$$4\times10^3 + \quad 8\times10^2 + \quad 8\times10^1 + \quad 4\times10^0$$
$$4000 + \quad 800 + \quad 80 + \quad 4 \quad = \quad 4{,}884$$

Binary is a similar numeral system, but with two numbers to consider (0 - 1) instead of ten (0 - 9). When counting in binary, numbers in the placeholder flip every two digits (not ten). Counting in binary to a decimal equivalent of ten, for example, would be 0, 1, 10, 11, 100, 101, 110, 111, 1000, 1001, 1010, with each digit in the placeholder represented by a power of two instead of a power of ten (as represented in decimal). '10' in binary (one-zero, not ten), represents a combination of *1 x 2 to the 1st power* (2) and *0 x 2 to the 0th power* (0), which gives you 2 … '0' in binary is equivalent to the decimal number 0, '1' in binary is 1, '10' is 2, '11' is 3, '100' is 4, '101' is 5, '110' is 6, '111' is 7, '1000' is 8, '1001' is 9, and '1010' is ten (or a combination of *2 to the 3rd* (8) and *2 to the 1st* (2), which gives you 10). Here's how it looks compared to the example above:

$$1 \quad\quad 0 \quad\quad 1 \quad\quad 0$$
$$1\times2^3 + \quad 0\times2^2 + \quad 1\times2^1 + \quad 0\times2^0$$
$$8 \quad + \quad 0 \quad + \quad 2 \quad + \quad 0 \quad = \quad 10$$

You may not understand binary, 'the universal language' or the 'digital language' understood by computers and the various technological devices in which we have immersed our lives, but you may have heard of bits and bytes. A *bit* is a portmanteau of 'binary' and 'digit,' and can have only one of two values: 0 and 1. So, 0 is a bit, and 1 is a bit. A *byte* is simply eight of those bits strung together. In the example above (1010), the byte equivalent would be 00001010, or eight bits of information (also known as a bit string). Each string of binary represents 'something' to a computer, like ASCII characters, such as *a*, *b*, or *c*. An uppercase *N*, for example (for *Nous*), can be represented by a bit string of 01010001, which, if converted from binary, is 78 in decimal. The binary on the front cover of this book converts to 'qualia' and 'nous' in lowercase text.

Interesting, but where does this leave us?

After we are gone, after our species ceases to exist, proof of humanity will remain in a potentially infinite collection of 0's and 1's (unless destroyed). Our existence will outlive us, detailed in bits and bytes. We live digitally, take pictures and videos and document ourselves doing anything and everything with gadgets that speak binary, and we post these 'things' to an etherweb of apps and websites and online social gatherings that have become digital representations of our being. Fragments or puzzle pieces of our memories are saved on portable 'memory' (irony at its finest) cards and sticks, on laptops, cameras, cellphones, hard drives, solid state drives, and other various internal and external computer devices, Mylar discs, redundant arrays; we upload ourselves and replicate to data farms capable of surviving nuclear blasts (making our digital exhibitions the new cockroach).

We have quickly become binary. We have translated humanity to bunch of 0's and 1's as a means of living in the infinite. Within this binary, we can represent nothing, or can signify something; we can be a single something, or an infinite amount of anythings. We can replicate, like a virus. We can be copied. And with a simple addition or subtraction of a bit (0 or 1), one complex number, we can be *changed*, or *erased*, which is a science fiction nightmare.

Which brings us to this book...

Qualia Nous is a collection of fiction that deserves to outlive humanity, with words that express the blend of science fiction and horror our kind has created. This anthology will someday be converted from paper to digital, the twenty-eight stories and two poems within, along with this introduction (of sorts) will be translated to binary… and will be left behind long after we are gone, which is the purpose for this book; the purpose for *all* books. Every author in *Qualia Nous* will die. Yes, that is blunt, and a horrifying thought, but their words and the worlds they have created will survive (perchance in the infinite). Their ideas will exist in the space between 0 and 1, and that is a beautiful thought. As long as the binary makeup remains in order, as long as every bit goes unchanged (and *unformatted*), perhaps the stories within *Qualia Nous* (which represent 'something' special) and their creators (who are each extraordinary in his or her own way) can exist indefinitely, if only in a digitized, binary sense, waiting for translation.

Is anything greater than ∞? Can one ∞ be larger than another ∞? As the stories and poems in this anthology progress (counting from 00000000 to 00011110 in binary), they will offer possible solutions, and may perhaps pose new challenges, although the answer t0 b0th quest10ns 1s

01110100 01101000 01100101 01110010 01100101
00100000 01100001 01110010 01100101 00100000
01100001 01101110 00100000 01101001 01101110
01100110 01101001 01101110 01101001 01110100
01100101 00100000 01100001 01101101 01101111
01110101 01101110 01110100 00100000 01101111
01100110 00100000 01101001 01101110 01100110
01101001 01101110 01101001 01110100 01101001
01100101 01110011 00101110

00100010 01001001 01101110 01100100 01101001
01110110 01101001 01100100 01110101 01100001
01101100 00100000 01110011 01100011 01101001

THE JAUNT

| STEPHEN KING |

THIS IS THE LAST CALL for Jaunt-701," the pleasant female voice echoed through the Blue Concourse of New York's Port Authority Terminal. The PAT had not changed much in the last three hundred years or so—it was still grungy and a little frightening. The automated female voice was probably the most pleasant thing about it. "This is Jaunt Service to Whitehead City, Mars," the voice continued. "All ticketed passengers should now be in the Blue Concourse sleep lounge. Make sure your validation papers are in order. Thank you."

The upstairs sleep lounge was not at all grungy. It was wall-to-wall carpeted in oyster gray. The walls were an eggshell white and hung with pleasant nonrepresentational prints. A steady, soothing progression of colors met and swirled on the ceiling. There were one hundred couches in the large room, neatly spaced in rows of ten. Five Jaunt attendants circulated, speaking in low, cheery voices and offering glasses of milk. At one side of the room was the entranceway, flanked by armed guards and another Jaunt attendant who was checking the validation papers of a latecomer, a harried-looking businessman with the New York *World-Times* folded under one arm. Directly opposite, the floor dropped away in a trough about five feet wide and perhaps ten feet long; it passed through a doorless opening and looked a bit like a child's slide.

The Oates family lay side by side on four Jaunt couches near the far end of the room. Mark Oates and his wife, Marilys, flanked the two children.

"Daddy, will you tell me about the Jaunt now?" Ricky asked.

"You promised.

"Yeah, Dad, you promised," Patricia added, and giggled shrilly for no good reason.

A businessman with a build like a bull glanced over at them and then went back to the folder of papers he was examining as he lay on his back, his spit-shined shoes neatly together. From everywhere came the low murmur of conversation and the rustle of passengers settling down on the Jaunt couches.

Mark glanced over at Marilys Oates and winked. She winked back, but she was almost as nervous as Patty sounded. *Why not?* Mark thought. First Jaunt for all three of them. He and Marilys had discussed the advantages and drawbacks of moving the whole family for the last six months—since he'd gotten notification from Texaco Water that he was being transferred to Whitehead City. Finally they had decided that all of them would go for the two years Mark would be stationed on Mars. He wondered now, looking at Marilys's pale face, if she was regretting the decision.

He glanced at his watch and saw it was still almost half an hour to Jaunt-time. That was enough time to tell the story…and he supposed it would take the kids' minds off their nervousness. Who knew, maybe it would even cool Marilys out a little.

"All right," he said. Ricky and Pat were watching him seriously, his son twelve, his daughter nine. He told himself again that Ricky would be deep in the swamp of puberty and his daughter would likely be developing breasts by the time they got back to earth, and again found it difficult to believe. The kids would be going to the tiny Whitehead Combined School with the hundred-odd engineering and oil-company brats that were there; his son might well be going on a geology field trip to Phobos not so many months distance. It was difficult to believe…but true.

Who knows? he thought wryly. *Maybe it'll do something about my Jaunt-jumps, too.*

"So far as we know," he began, "the Jaunt was invented about three hundred and twenty years ago, around the year 1987, by a fellow named Victor Carune. He did it as part of a private research project that was funded by some government money ... and eventually the government took it over, of course. In the end it came down to either the government or the oil companies. The reason we don't know the exact date is because Carune was something of an eccentric—"

"You mean he was crazy, Dad?" Ricky asked.

"Eccentric means a little bit crazy, dear," Marilys said, and smiled across the children at Mark. She looked a little less nervous now, he thought.

"Oh."

"Anyway, he'd been experimenting with the process for quite some time before he informed the government of what he had," Mark went on, "and he only told them because he was running out of money and they weren't going to refund him."

"Your money cheerfully refunded," Pat said, and giggled shrilly again.

"That's right, honey," Mark said, and ruffled her hair gently. At the far end of the room he saw a door slide noiselessly open and two more attendants came out, dressed in the bright red jumpers of the Jaunt Service, pushing a rolling table. On it was a stainless-steel nozzle attached to a rubber hose; beneath the table's skirts, tastefully hidden, Mark knew there were two bottles of gas; in the net bag hooked to the side were one hundred disposable masks. Mark went on talking, not wanting his people to see the representatives of Lethe until they had to. And, if he was given enough time to tell the whole story, they would welcome the gas-passers with open arms.

Considering the alternative.

"Of course, you know that the Jaunt is teleportation, no more or less," he said. "Sometimes in college chemistry and physics they call it the Carune Process, but it's really teleportation, and it was Carune himself—if you can believe the stories—who named it 'the Jaunt.' He was a science-fiction reader, and there's a story by a man named Alfred Bester, *The Stars My Destination* it's called, and this fellow Bester made up the word "jaunte' for teleportation in it. Except in his book, you could Jaunt just by thinking about it, and we can't really do that."

The attendants were fixing a mask to the steel nozzle and handing it to an elderly woman at the far end of the room. She took it, inhaled once, and fell quiet and limp on her couch. Her skirt had pulled up a little, revealing one slack thigh road-mapped with varicose veins. An attendant considerately readjusted it for her while the other pulled off the used mask and affixed a fresh one. It was a process that made Mark think of the plastic glasses in motel rooms. He wished to God that Patty would cool out a little bit; he had seen children who had to be held down, and sometimes they screamed as the rubber mask covered their faces. It was not an abnormal reaction in a child, he supposed, but it was nasty to watch and he didn't want to see it happen to Patty. About Rick he felt more confident.

"I guess you could say the Jaunt came along at the last possible moment," he resumed. He spoke toward Ricky, but reached across and took his daughter's hand. Her fingers closed over his with an immediate panicky tightness. Her palm was cool and sweating lightly. "The world was running out of oil, and most of what was left belonged to the middle-eastern desert peoples, who were committed to using it as a political weapon. They had formed an oil cartel they called OPEC—"

"What's a cartel, Daddy?" Patty asked.

"Well, a monopoly," Mark said.

"Like a club, honey," Marilys said. "And you could only be in that club if you had lots of oil."

"Oh."

"I don't have time to sketch the whole mess in for you," Mark said. "You'll study some of it in school, but it *was* a mess—let's let it go at that. If you owned a car, you could only drive it two days a week, and gasoline cost fifteen oldbucks a gallon—"

"Gosh," Ricky said, "it only costs four cents or so a gallon now, doesn't it Dad?"

Mark smiled. "That's why we're going where we're going, Rick. There's enough oil on Mars to last almost eight thousand years, and enough on Venus to last another twenty thousand ... but oil isn't even that important, anymore. Now what we need most of all is—"

"*Water!*" Pattie cried, and the businessman looked up from his papers and smiled at her for a moment.

"That's right," Mark said. "Because in the years between 1960 and 2030, we poisoned most of ours. The first waterlift from the Martian ice-caps was called—"

"Operation Straw." That was Ricky.

"Yes. 2045 or thereabouts. But long before that, the Jaunt was being used to find sources of clean water here on earth. And now water is our major Martian export ... the oil's strictly a sideline. But it was important then."

The kids nodded.

"The point is, those things were always there, but we were only able to get it because of the Jaunt. When Carune invented his process, the world was slipping into a new dark age. The winter before, over ten thousand people had frozen to death in the United States alone because there wasn't enough energy to heat them."

"Oh, yuck," Patty said matter-of-factly.

Mark glanced to his right and saw the attendants talking to a timid-looking man, persuading him. At last he took the mask and seemed to fall dead on his couch seconds later. *First-timer*, Mark thought. *You can't always tell.*

"For Carune, it started with a pencil ... some keys ... a wristwatch ... then some mice. The mice showed him there was a problem ..."

Victor Carune came back to his laboratory in a stumbling fever of excitement. He thought he knew how Morse had felt, and Alexander Graham Bell, and Edison ... but this was bigger than all of them, and twice he had almost wrecked the truck on the way back from the pet shop in New Paltz, where he had spent his last twenty dollars on nine white mice. What he had left in the world was the ninety-three cents in his right front pocket and the eighteen dollars in his savings account … but this did not occur to him. And if it had, it certainly would not have bothered him.

The lab was in a renovated barn at the end of a mile-long dirt road off Route 26. It was making the turn onto this road where he had just missed cracking up his Brat pickup truck for the second time. The gas tank was almost empty and there would be no more for ten days to two weeks, but this did not concern him, either. His mind was in a delirious whirl.

What had happened was not totally unexpected, no. One of the reasons the government had funded him even to the paltry tune of twenty thousand a year was because the unrealized possibility had always been there in the field of particle transmission.

But to have it happen like this … suddenly … with no warning … and powered by less electricity than was needed to run a color TV … God! *Christ!*

He brought the Brat to a screech-halt in the dirt of the door-yard, grabbed the box on the dirty seat beside him by its grab-handles (on the box were dogs and cats and hamsters and goldfish and the legend I CAME FROM STACKPOLE'S HOUSE OF PETS) and *ran* for the big double doors. From inside the box came the scurry and whisk of his test subjects.

He tried to push one of the big doors open along its track, and when it wouldn't budge, he remembered that he had locked it. Carune uttered a loud "Shit!" and fumbled for his keys. The government commanded that the lab be locked at all times—it was one of the strings they put on their money—but Carune kept forgetting.

He brought his keys out and for a moment simply stared at them, mesmerized, running the ball of his thumb over the notches in the Brat's ignition key. He thought again: *God! Christ!* Then he scrabbled through the keys on the ring for the Yale key that unlocked the barn door.

As the first telephone had been used inadvertently—Bell crying into it, "Watson, come here!" when he spilled some acid on his papers and himself—so the first act of teleportation had occurred by accident. Victor Carune had teleported the first two fingers of his left hand across the fifty-yard width of the barn.

Carune had set up two portals at opposite sides of the barn. On his end was a simple ion gun, available from any electronics supply warehouse for under five hundred dollars. On the other end, standing just beyond the far portal—both of them rectangular and the size of a paperback book—was a cloud chamber. Between them was what appeared to be an opaque shower curtain, except that shower curtains are not made of lead. The idea was to shoot the ions through Portal One and then walk around and watch them streaming across the cloud chamber standing just beyond Portal Two, with the lead shield between to prove they really were being transmitted. Except that, for the last two years, the process had only worked twice, and Carune didn't have the slightest idea why.

As he was setting the ion gun in place, his fingers had slipped through the portal—ordinarily no problem, but this morning his hip had also brushed the toggle switch on the control panel at the left of the portal. He was not aware of what had happened—the machinery gave off only the lowest audible hum—until he felt a tingling sensation in his fingers.

"It was not like an electric shock," Carune wrote in his one and only article on the subject before the government shut him up. The article was published, of all places, in *Popular Mechanics*. He had sold it to them for seven hundred and fifty dollars in a last-ditch effort to keep the Jaunt a matter of private enterprise. "There was none of that unpleasant tingle that one gets if one grasps a frayed lamp cord, for instance. It was more like the sensation one gets if one puts one's hand on the casing of some small machine that is working very hard. The vibration is so fast and light that it is, literally, a tingling sensation.

"Then I looked down at the portal and saw that my index finger was gone on a diagonal slant through the middle knuckle, and my second finger was gone slightly above that. In addition, the nail portion of my third finger had disappeared."

Carune had jerked his hand back instinctively, crying out. He so much expected to see blood, he wrote later, that he actually hallucinated blood for a moment or two. His elbow struck the ion gun and knocked it off the table.

He stood there with his fingers in his mouth, verifying that they were still there, and whole. The thought that he had been working too hard crossed his mind. And then the other thought crossed his mind: the thought that the last set of modifications might have . . . might have done something.

He did not push his fingers back in; in fact, Carune only Jaunted once more in his entire life.

At first, he did nothing. He took a long, aimless walk around the barn, running his hands through his hair, wondering if he should call Carson in New Jersey or perhaps Buffington in Charlotte. Carson wouldn't accept a collect phone call, the cheap asskissing bastard, but Buffington probably would. Then an idea struck and he ran across to Portal Two, thinking that if his fingers had actually crossed the barn, there might be some sign of it.

There was not, of course. Portal Two stood atop three stacked Pomona orange crates, looking like nothing so much as one of those toy guillotines missing the blade. On one side of its stainless-steel frame was a plug-in jack, from which a cord ran back to the transmission terminal, which was little more than a particle transformer hooked into a computer feed-line.

Which reminded him—

Carune glanced at his watch and saw it was quarter past eleven. His deal with the government consisted of short money, plus computer time, which was infinitely valuable. His computer tie-in lasted until three o'clock this afternoon, and then it was good-bye until Monday. He had to get moving, had to do something—

"I glanced at the pile of crates again," Carune writes in his *Popular Mechanics* article, "and then I looked at the pads of my fingers. And sure enough, the proof was there. It would not, I thought then, convince anyone but myself; but in the beginning, of course, it is only one's self that one has to convince."

"What was it, Dad?" Ricky asked.

"Yeah!" Patty added. "What?"

Mark grinned a little. They were all hooked now, even Marilys. They had nearly forgotten where they were. From the corner of his eye he could see the Jaunt attendants whisper-wheeling their cart slowly among the Jaunters, putting them to sleep. It was never as rapid a process in the civilian sector as it was in the military, he had discovered; civilians got nervous and wanted to talk it over. The nozzle and the rubber mask were too reminiscent of hospital operating rooms, where the surgeon with this knives lurked somewhere behind the anesthetist with her selection of gases in stainless-steel canisters. Sometimes there was panic, hysteria; and always there were a few who simply lost their nerve. Mark had observed two of these as he spoke to the children: two men who had simply arisen from their couches, walked across to the entryway with no fanfare at all, unpinned the validation papers that had been affixed to their lapels, turned them in, and exited without looking back. Jaunt attendants were under strict instructions not to argue with those who left; there were always standbys, sometimes as many as forty or fifty of them, hoping against hope. As those who simply couldn't take it left, standbys were let in with their own validations pinned to their shirts.

"Carune found two splinters in his index finger," he told the children. "He took them out and put them aside. One was lost, but you can see the other one in the Smithsonian Annex in Washington. It's in a hermetically sealed glass case near the moon rocks the first space travelers brought back from the moon—"

"Our moon, Dad, or one of Mars's?" Ricky asked.

"Ours," mark said, smiling a little. "Only one manned rocket flight has ever landed on Mars, Ricky, and that was a French expedition somewhere about 2030. Anyway, that's why there happens to be a plain old splinter from an orange crate in the Smithsonian Institution. Because it's the first object that we have that was actually teleported—Jaunted—across space."

"What happened then?" Patty asked.

"Well, according to the story, Carune ran…"

Carune ran back to Portal One and stood there for a moment, heart thudding, out of breath. *Got to calm down*, he told himself. *Got to think about this. You can't maximize your time if you go off half-cocked.*

Deliberately disregarding the forefront of his mind, which was screaming at him to hurry up and do *something*, he dug his nail-clippers out of his pocket and used the point of the file to dig the splinters out of his index finger. He dropped them onto the white inner sleeve of a Hershey bar he had eaten while tinkering with the transformer and trying to widen its afferent capability (he had apparently succeeded in that beyond his wildest dreams). One rolled off the wrapper and was lost; the other ended up in the Smithsonian Institution, locked in a glass case that was cordoned off with thick velvet ropes and watched vigilantly and eternally by a computer-monitored closed-circuit TV camera.

The splinter extraction finished, Carune felt a little calmer. A pencil. That was as good as anything. He took one from beside the clipboard on the shelf above him and ran it gently into Portal One. It disappeared smoothly, inch by inch, like something in an optical illusion or in a very good magician's trick. The pencil had said EBERHARD FABER NO. 2 on one of its sides, black letters stamped on yellow-painted wood. When he had pushed the pencil in until all but the EBER had disappeared, Carune walked around to the other side of Portal One. He looked in.

He saw the pencil in cut-off view, as if a knife had chopped smoothly through it. Carune felt with his fingers where the rest of the pencil should have been, and of course there was nothing. He ran across the barn to Portal Two, and there was the missing part of the pencil, lying on the top crate. Heart thumping so hard that it seemed to shake his entire chest, Carune grasped the sharpened point of his pencil and pulled it the rest of the way through.

He held it up; he looked at it. Suddenly he took it and wrote IT WORKS! On a piece of barn-board. He wrote it so hard that the lead snapped on the last letter. Carune began to laugh shrilly in the empty barn; to laugh so hard that he startled the sleeping swallows into flight among the high rafters.

"Works!" he shouted, and ran back to Portal One. He was waving his arms, the broken pencil knotted up in one fist. "Works! Works! *Do you hear me, Carson, you prick? It works AND I DID IT!*"

"Mark, watch what you say to the children," Marilys reproached him.

Mark shrugged. "It's what he's supposed to have said."

"Well, can't you do a little selective editing?"

"Dad?" Patty asked. "Is that pencil in the museum, too?"

"Does a bear shit in the woods?" Mark said, and then clapped one hand over his mouth. Both children giggled wildly—but that shrill note was gone from Patty's voice, Mark was glad to hear—and after a moment of trying to look serious, Marilys began to giggle too.

The keys went through next; Carune simply tossed them through the portal. He was beginning to think on track again now, and it seemed to him that the first thing that needed finding out was if the process produced things on the other end exactly as they had been, or if they were in any way changed by the trip.

He saw the keys go through and disappear; at exactly the same moment he heard them jingle on the crate across the barn. He ran across—really only trotting now—and on the way he paused to shove the lead shower curtain back on its track. He didn't need either it or the ion gun now. Just as well, since the ion gun was smashed beyond repair.

He grabbed the keys, went to the lock the government had forced him to put on the door, and tried the Yale Key. It worked perfectly. He tried the house key. It also worked. So did the keys which opened his file cabinets and the one which started the Brat pickup.

Carune pocketed the keys and took off his watch. It was a Seiko quartz LC with buttons that would allow him to do everything from addition to subtraction to square roots. A delicate piece of machinery—and just as important, a chronometer. Carune put it down in front of Portal One and pushed it through with a pencil.

He ran across and grabbed it up. When he put it through, the watch had said 11:31:07. It now said 11:31:49. Very good. Right on the money, only he should have had an assistant over there to peg the fact that there had been no time gain once and forever. Well, no matter. Soon enough the government would have him wading hip-deep in assistants.

He tried the calculator. Two and two still made four, eight divided by four was still two; the square root of eleven was still 3.3166247...and so on.

That was when he decided it was mouse-time.

"What happened with the mice, Dad?" Ricky asked.

Mark hesitated briefly. There would have to be some caution here, if he didn't want to scare his children (not to mention his wife) into hysteria minutes away from their first Jaunt. The major thing was to leave them with the knowledge that everything was all right now, that the problem had been licked.

"As I said, there was a slight problem..."

Yes. Horror, lunacy, and death. How's that for a slight problem, kids?

··· — — — ···

Carune set the box which read I CAME FROM STACKPOLE'S HOUSE OF PETS down on the shelf and glanced at his watch. Damned if he hadn't put the thing on upside down. He turned it around and saw that it was a quarter of two. He had only an hour and a quarter of computer time left. *How time flies when you're having fun*, he thought, and giggled wildly.

He opened the box, reached in, and pulled out a squeaking white mouse by the tail. He put it down in front of Portal One and said, "Go on, mouse." The mouse promptly ran down the side of the orange crate on which the portal stood and scuttered across the floor.

Cursing, Carune chased it, and managed to actually get one hand on it before it squirmed through a crack between two boards and was gone.

"*SHIT!*" Carune screamed, and ran back to the box of mice. He was just in time to knock two potential escapees back into the box. He got a second mouse, holding this one around the body (he was by trade a physicist, and the ways of white mice were foreign to him), and slammed the lid of the box back down.

This one he gave the old heave-ho. It clutched at Carune's palm, but to no avail; it went head over ratty little paws through Portal One. Carune heard it immediately land on the crates across the barn.

This time he sprinted, remembering how easily the first mouse had eluded him. He need not have worried. The white mouse merely crouched on the crate, its eyes dull, its sides aspirating weakly. Carune slowed down and approached it carefully; he was not a man used to fooling with mice, but you didn't have to be a forty-year veteran to see something was terribly wrong here.

("The mouse didn't feel so good after it went through," Mark Oates told his children with a wide smile that was only noticeably false to his wife.)

Carune touched the mouse. It was like touching something inert—packed straw or sawdust, perhaps—except for the aspirating sides. The mouse did not look around at Carune; it stared straight ahead. He had thrown in a squirming, very frisky and alive little animal; here was something that seemed to be a living waxwork likeness of a mouse.

Then Carune snapped his fingers in front of the mouse's small pink eyes. It blinked...and fell dead on its side.

"So Carune decided to try another mouse," Mark said.

"What happened to the first mouse?" Ricky asked.

Mark produced that wide smile again. "It was retired with full honors," he said.

Carune found a paper bag and put the mouse into it. He would take it to Mosconi, the vet, that evening. Mosconi could dissect it and tell him if its inner works had been rearranged. The government would disapprove his bringing a private citizen into a project which would be classified triple top secret as soon as they knew about it. Tough titty, as the kitty was reputed to have said to the babes who complained about the warmth of the milk. Carune was determined that the Great White Father in Washington would know about this as late in the game as possible. For all the scant help the Great White Father had given him, he could wait. Tough titty.

Then he remembered that Mosconi lived way the hell and gone on the other side of New Paltz, and that there wasn't enough gas in the Brat to get even halfway across town...let alone back.

But it was 2:03—he had less than an hour of computer time left. He would worry about the goddam dissection later.

Carune constructed a makeshift chute leading to the entrance of Portal One (really the first Jaunt-Slide, Mark told the children, and Patty found the idea of a Jaunt-Slide for mice deliciously funny) and dropped a fresh white mouse into it. He blocked the end with a large book, and after a few moments of aimless pattering and sniffing, the mouse went through the portal and disappeared.

Carune ran back across the barn.

The mouse was DOA.

There was no blood, no bodily swellings to indicate that a radical change in pressure had ruptured something inside. Carune supposed that oxygen starvation might—

He shook his head impatiently. It took the white mouse only nanoseconds to go through; his own watch had confirmed that time remained constant in the process, or damn close to it.

The second white mouse joined the first in the paper sack. Carune got a third out (a fourth, if you counted the fortunate mouse that had escaped through the crack), wondering for the first time which would end first—his computer time or his supply of mice.

He held this one firmly around the body and forced its haunches through the portal. Across the room he saw the haunches reappear... just the haunches. The disembodied little feet were digging frantically at the rough wood of the crate.

Carune pulled the mouse back. No catatonia here; it bit the webbing between his thumb and forefinger hard enough to bring blood. Carune dropped the mouse hurriedly back into the I CAME FROM STACKPOLE'S HOUSE OF PETS box and used the small bottle of hydrogen peroxide in his lab first-aid kit to disinfect the bite.

He put a Band-Aid over it, then rummaged around until he found a pair of heavy work-gloves. He could feel the time running out, running out, running out. It was 2:11 now.

He got another mouse out and pushed it through backward—all the way. He hurried across to Portal Two. This mouse lived for almost two minutes; it even walked a little, after a fashion. It staggered across the Pomona orange crate, fell on its side, struggled weakly to its feet, and then only squatted there. Carune snapped his fingers near its head and it lurched perhaps four steps further before falling on its side again. The aspiration of its sides slowed ... slowed ... stopped. It was dead.

Carune felt a chill.

He went back, got another mouse, and pushed it halfway

through headfirst. He saw it reappear at the other end, just the head...then the neck and chest. Cautiously, Carune relaxed his grip on the mouse's body, ready to grab if it got frisky. It didn't. The mouse only stood there, half of it on one side of the barn, half on the other.

Carune jogged back to Portal Two.

The mouse was alive, but its pink eyes were glazed and dull. Its whiskers didn't move. Going around to the back of the portal, Carune saw an amazing sight; as he had seen the pencil in cutaway, so now he saw the mouse. He saw the vertebrae of its tiny spine ending abruptly in round white circles; he saw its blood moving through the vessels; he saw the tissue moving gently with the tide of life around its minuscule gullet. If nothing else, he thought (and wrote later in his *Popular Mechanics* article), it would make a wonderful diagnostic tool.

Then he noticed that the tidal movement of the tissues had ceased. The mouse had died.

Carune pulled the mouse out by the snout, not liking the feel of it, and dropped it into the paper sack with its companions. *Enough with the white mice,* he decided. *The mice die. They die if you put them through all the way, and they die if you put them through halfway headfirst. Put them through halfway butt-first, they stay frisky.*

What the hell is in there?

Sensory input, he thought almost randomly. *When they go through they see something—hear something—touch something—God, maybe even smell something—that literally kills them. What?*

He had no idea—but he meant to find out.

Carune still had almost forty minutes before COMLINK pulled the data base out from under him. He unscrewed the thermometer from the wall beside his kitchen door, trotted back to the barn with it, and put it through the portals. The thermometer went in at 83 degrees F; it came out at 83 degrees F. He rummaged through the spare room where he kept a few toys to amuse his grandchildren with; among them he found a packet of balloons. He blew one of them up, tied it off, and batted it through the portal. It came out intact and unharmed—a start down the road toward answering his question about a sudden change in pressure somehow caused by what he was already thinking of as the Jaunting process.

With five minutes to go before the witching hour, he ran into his house, snatched up his goldfish bowl (inside, Percy and Patrick swished their tails and darted about in agitation) and ran back with it. He shoved the goldfish bowl through Portal One.

He hurried across to Portal Two, where his goldfish bowl sat on the crate. Patrick was floating belly-up; Percy swam slowly around near the bottom of the bowl, as if dazed. A moment later he also floated belly-up. Carune was reaching for the goldfish bowl when Percy gave a weak flick of his tail and resumed his lackadaisical swimming. Slowly, he seemed to throw off whatever the effect had been, and by the time Carune got back from Mosconi's Veterinary Clinic that night at nine o'clock, Percy seemed as perky as ever.

Patrick was dead.

Carune fed Percy a double ration of fish food and gave Patrick a hero's burial in the garden.

After the computer had cut him out for the day, Carune decided to hitch a ride over to Mosconi's. Accordingly, he was standing on the shoulder of Route 26 at a quarter of four that afternoon, dressed in jeans and a loud plaid sport coat, his thumb out, a paper bag in his other hand.

Finally, a kid driving a Chevette not much bigger than a sardine can pulled over, and Carune got in. "What you got in the bag, my man?"

"Bunch of dead mice," Carune said. Eventually another car stopped. When the farmer behind the wheel asked about the bag, Carune told him it was a couple of sandwiches.

Mosconi dissected one of the mice on the spot, and agreed to dissect the others later and call Carune on the telephone with the results. The initial result was not very encouraging; so far as Mosconi could tell, the mouse he had opened up was perfectly healthy except for the fact that it was dead.

Depressing.

"Victor Carune was eccentric, but he was no fool," Mark said. The Jaunt attendants were getting close now, and he supposed he would have to hurry up ... or he would be finishing this in the Wake-Up Room in Whitehead City. "Hitching a ride back home that night—and he had to walk most of the way, so the story goes—he realized that he had maybe solved a third of the energy crisis at one single stroke. All the goods that had to go by train and truck and boat and plane before that day could be Jaunted. You could write a letter to your friend in London or Rome or Senegal, and he could have it the very next day—without an ounce of oil needing to be burned. We take it for granted, but it was a big thing to Carune, believe me. And to everyone else, as well."

"But what happened to the mice, Daddy?" Rick asked.

"That's what Carune kept asking himself," Mark said, "because he also realized that if *people* could use the Jaunt, that would solve almost *all* of the energy crisis. And that we might be able to conquer space. In his *Popular Mechanics* article he said that even the stars could finally be ours. And the metaphor he used was crossing a shallow stream without getting your shoes wet. You'd just get a big rock, and throw it in the stream, then get another rock, stand on the first rock, and throw *that* into the stream, go back and get a third rock, go back to the second rock, throw the third rock into the stream, and keep up like that until you'd made a path of stepping-stones all the way across the stream ... or in this case, the solar system, or maybe even the galaxy."

"I don't get that at *all*," Patty said.

"That's because you got turkey-turds for brains," Ricky said smugly.

"I do *not!* Daddy, Ricky said—"

"Children, don't," Marilys said gently.

"Carune pretty much foresaw what has happened," Mark said. Drone rocket ships programmed to land, first on the moon, then on Mars, then on Venus and the outer moons of Jupiter ... drones really only programmed to do one thing after they landed—"

"Set up a Jaunt station for astronauts," Ricky said.

Mark nodded. "And now there are scientific outposts all over the solar system, and maybe someday, long after we're gone, there will be even another planet for us. There are Jaunt-ships on their way to four different star systems with solar systems of their own ... but it'll be a long, long time before they get there."

"I want to know what happened to the *mice*," Patty said impatiently.

"Well, eventually the government got into it," Mark said, "Carune kept them out as long as he could, but finally they got wind of it and landed on him with both feet. Carune was nominal head of the Jaunt project until he died ten years later, but he was never really in charge of it again."

"Jeez, the poor guy!" Rick said.

"But he got to be a hero," Patricia said. "He's in *all* the history books, just like President Lincoln and President Hart."

I'm sure that's a great comfort to him ... wherever he is, Mark thought, and then went on, carefully glossing over the rough parts.

The government, which had been pushed to the wall by the escalating energy crisis, did indeed come in with both feet. They wanted the Jaunt on a paying basis as soon as possible—like yesterday. Faced with economic chaos and the increasingly probable picture of anarchy and mass starvation in the 1990's, only last-ditch pleading made them put off announcement of the Jaunt before an exhaustive spectrographic analysis of Jaunted articles could be completed. When the analyses were complete—and showed no changes in the makeup of Jaunted artifacts—the existence of the Jaunt was announced with international hoopla. Showing intelligence for once (necessity is, after all, the mother of invention), the U.S. government put Young and Rubicam in charge of the PR.

That was where the myth-making sound Victor Carune, an elderly, rather peculiar man who showered perhaps twice a week and changed his clothes only when he thought of it, began. Young and Rubicam and the agencies which followed them turned Carune into a combination of Thomas Edison, Eli Whitney, Pecos Bill, and Flash Gordon. The blackly funny part of all this (and Mark Oates did not pass this on to his family) was that Victor Carune might even then have been dead or insane; art imitates life, they say, and Carune would have been familiar with the Robert Heinlein novel about the doubles who stand in for figures in the public eye.

Victor Carune was a problem; a nagging problem that wouldn't go away. He was a loudmouthed foot-dragger, a holdover from the Ecological Sixties—a time when there was still enough energy floating around to allow foot-dragging as a luxury. These, on the other hand, were the Nasty Eighties, with coal clouds befouling the sky and a long section of the California coastline expected to be uninhabitable for perhaps sixty years due to a nuclear "excursion."

Victor Carune remained a problem until about 1991—and then he became a rubber stamp, smiling, quiet, grandfatherly; a figure seen waving from podiums in newsfilms. In 1993, three years before he officially died, he rode in the pace-car at the Tournament of Roses Parade.

Puzzling. And a little ominous.

The results of the announcement of the Jaunt—of working teleportation—on October 19th, 1988, was a hammerstroke of worldwide excitement and economic upheaval. On the world money markets, the battered old American dollar suddenly skyrocketed through the roof. People who had bought gold at eight hundred and six dollars an ounce suddenly found that a pound of gold would bring something less than twelve hundred dollars. In the year between the announcement of the Jaunt and the first working Jaunt-Stations in New York and L.A., the stock market climbed a little over a thousand points. The price of oil dropped only seventy cents a barrel, but by 1994, with Jaunt-Stations crisscrossing the U.S. at the pressure-points of seventy major cities, OPEC had ceased to exist, and the price of oil began to tumble. By 1998, with Stations in most free-world cities and goods routinely Jaunted between Tokyo and Paris, Paris and London, London and New York, New York and Berlin, oil had dropped to fourteen dollars a barrel. By 2006, when people at last began to use the Jaunt on a regular basis, the stock market had leveled off five thousand points above its 1987 levels, oil was selling for six dollars a barrel, and the oil companies had begun to change their names. Texaco became Texaco Oil/Water, and Mobil had become Mobil Hydro-2-Ox.

By 2045, water-prospecting became the big game and oil had become what it had been in 1906: a toy.

"What about the *mice*, Daddy?" Patty asked impatiently. "What happened to the *mice?*"

Mark decided it might be okay now, and then drew the attention of his children to the Jaunt attendants, who were passing gas out only three aisles from them. Rick only nodded, but Patty looked troubled as a lady with a fashionably shaved-and-painted head took a whiff from the rubber mask and fell unconscious."

"Can't Jaunt when you're awake, can you Dad?" Ricky said.

Mark nodded and smiled reassuringly at Patricia. "Carune understood even before the government got into it," he said.

"How *did* the government get into it, Mark?" Marilys asked.

Mark smiled. "Computer time," he said. "The data base. That was the only thing that Carune couldn't beg, borrow, or steal. The computer handled the actual particulate transmission—billions of pieces of information It's still the computer, you know, that makes sure you don't come through with your head somewhere in the middle of your stomach."

Marilys shuddered.

"Don't be frightened," he said. "There's never been a screw-up like that, Mare. *Never.*"

"There's always a first time," she muttered.

Mark looked at Ricky. "How did he know?" he asked his son. "How did Carune know you had to be asleep, Rick?"

"When he put the mice in backwards," Rick said slowly, "they were all right. At least as long as he didn't put them *all* in. They were only—well, messed up—when he put them in headfirst. Right?"

"Right," Mark said. The Jaunt attendants were moving in now, wheeling their silent cart of oblivion. He wasn't going to have time to finish after all; perhaps it was just as well. "It didn't take many experiments to clarify what was happening, of course. The Jaunt killed the entire trucking business, kids, but at least it took the pressure off the experimenters—"

Yes. Foot-dragging had become a luxury again, and the tests had gone on for better than twenty years, although Carune's first tests with drugged mice had convinced him that unconscious animals were not subject to what was known forever after as the Organic Effect or, more simply, the Jaunt Effect.

He and Mosconi had drugged several mice, put them through Portal One, retrieved them at the other side, and had waited anxiously for their test subjects to reawaken ... or to die. They had reawakened, and after a brief recovery period they had taken up their mouse-lives—eating, fucking, playing, shitting—with no ill effects whatsoever. Those mice became the first of several generations which were studied with great interest. They showed no long-term ill effects; they did not die sooner, their pups were not born with two heads or green fur and neither did these pups show any other long-term effects.

"When did they start with people, Dad?" Rick asked, although he had certainly read this in school. "Tell that part!"

"I wanna know what happened to the *mice!*" Patty said again.

Although the Jaunt attendants had now reached the head of their aisle (they themselves were near the foot), Mark Oates paused a moment to reflect. His daughter, who knew less, had nevertheless listened to her heart and asked the right question. Therefore, it was his son's question he chose to answer.

The first human Jaunters had not been astronauts or test pilots; they were convict volunteers who had not even been screened with any particular interest in their psychological stability. In fact, it was the view of the scientists now in charge (Carune was not one of them; he had become what is commonly called a titular head) that the freakier they were, the better; if a mental spaz could go through and come out all right—or at least, no worse than he or she had been going in—then the process was probably safe for the executives, politicians, and fashion models of the world.

Half a dozen of these volunteers were brought to Province, Vermont (a site which had since become every bit as famous as Kitty Hawk, North Carolina, had once been), gassed, and fed through the portals exactly two hand-miles apart, one by one.

Mark told his children this, because of course all six of the volunteers came back just fine and feeling perky, thank you. He did not tell them about the purported *seventh* volunteer. This figure, who might have been real, or myth, or (most probably) a combination of the two, even had a name: Rudy Foggia. Foggia was supposed to have been a convicted murderer, sentenced to death in the state of Florida for the murders of four old people at a Sarasota bridge party. According to the apocrypha, the combined forces of the Central Intelligence Agency and the Effa Bee Eye had come to Foggia with a unique, one-time, take-it-or-leave-it, absolutely-not-to-be-repeated offer. Take the Jaunt wide awake. Come through okay and we put your pardon, signed by Governor Thurgood, in your hand. Out you walk, free to follow the One True Cross or to off a few more old folks playing bridge in their yellow pants and white shoes. Come through dead or insane, tough titty. As the kitty was purported to have said. What do you say?

Foggia, who understood that Florida was one state that really meant business about the death penalty and whose lawyer had told him that he was in all probability the next to ride Old Sparky, said okay.

Enough scientists to fill a jury box (with four or five left over as alternates) were present on the Great Day in the summer of 2007, but if the Foggia story was true—and Mark Oates believed it probably was—he doubted if it had been any of the scientists who talked. More likely it had been one of the guards who had flown with Foggia from Raiford to Montpelier and then escorted him from Montpelier to Province in an armored truck.

"If I come through this alive," Foggia is reported to have said, "I want a chicken dinner before I blow this joint." He then stepped through Portal One and reappeared at Portal Two immediately.

He came through alive, but Rudy Foggia was in no condition to eat his chicken dinner. In the space it took to Jaunt across the two miles (pegged at 0.000000000067 of a second by computer), Foggia's hair had turned snow white. His face had not changed in any physical way—it was not lined or jowly or wasted—but it gave the impression of great, almost incredible age. Foggia shuffled out of the portal, his eyes bulging blankly, his mouth twitching, his hands splayed out in front of him. Presently he began to drool. The scientists who had gathered around drew away from him and no, Mark really doubted if any of them had talked; they knew about the rats, after all, and the guinea pigs, and the hamsters; any animal, in fact, with more brains than your average flatworm. They must have felt a bit like those German scientists who tried to impregnate Jewish women with the sperm of German shepherds.

"What happened?" one of the scientists shouted (is reputed to have shouted). It was the only question Foggia had a chance to answer.

"It's eternity in there," he said, and dropped dead of what was diagnosed as a massive heart attack.

The scientists foregathered there were left with his corpse (which was neatly taken care of by the CIA and the Effa Bee Eye) and that strange and awful dying declaration: *It's eternity in there.*

··· — — — ···

"Daddy, I want to know what happened to the *mice*," Patty repeated. The only reason she had a chance to ask again was because the man in the expensive suit and the Etrna-Shine shoes had developed into something of a problem for the Jaunt attendants. He didn't really want to take the gas, and was disguising it with a lot of bluff, bully-boy talk. The attendants were doing their job as well as they could—smiling, cajoling, persuading—but it had slowed them down.

Mark sighed. He had opened the subject—only as a way of distracting his children from the pre-Jaunt festivities, it was true, but he *had* opened it—and now he supposed he would have to close it as truthfully as he could without alarming them or upsetting them.

He would not tell them, for instance, about C.K. Summers's book, *The Politics of the Jaunt*, which contained one section called "The Jaunt Under the Rose," a compendium of the more believable rumors about the Jaunt. The story of Rudy Foggia, he of the bridge-club murders and the uneaten chicken dinner, was in there. There were also case histories of some other thirty (or more … or less … or who knows) volunteers, scapegoats, or madmen who had Jaunted wide awake over the last three hundred years. Most of them arrived at the other end dead. The rest were hopelessly insane. In some cases, the act of reemerging had actually seemed to shock them to death.

Summers's section of Jaunt rumors and apocrypha contained other unsettling intelligence as well: the Jaunt had apparently been used several times as a murder weapon. In the most famous (and only documented) case, which had occurred a mere thirty years ago, a Jaunt researcher named Lester Michaelson had tied up his wife with their daughter's plexiplast Dreamropes and pushed her, screaming, through the Jaunt portal at Silver City, Nevada. But before doing it, Michaelson had pushed the Nil button on his Jaunt board, erasing each and every one of the hundreds of thousands of possible portals through which Mrs. Michaelson might have emerged—anywhere from neighboring Reno to the experimental Jaunt-Station on Io, one of the Jovian moons. So there was Mrs. Michaelson, Jaunting forever somewhere out there in the ozone. Michaelson's lawyer, after Michaelson had been held sane and able to stand trial for what he had done (within the narrow limits of the law, perhaps he was sane, but in any practical sense, Lester Michaelson was just as mad as a hatter), had offered a novel defense: his client could not be tried for murder because no one could prove conclusively that Mrs. Michaelson was dead.

This had raised the terrible specter of the woman, discorporeal but somehow still sentient, screaming in limbo ... forever. Michaelson was convicted and executed.

In addition, Summers suggested, the Jaunt had been used by various tinpot dictators to get rid of political dissidents and political adversaries; some thought that the Mafia had their own illegal Jaunt-Stations, tied into the central Jaunt computer through their CIA connections. It was suggested that the Mafia used the Jaunt's Nil capability to get rid of bodies which, unlike that of the unfortunate Mrs. Michaelson, were already dead. Seen in that light, the Jaunt became the ultimate Jimmy Hoffa machine, ever so much better than the local gravel pit or quarry.

All of this had led to Summers's conclusions and theories about the Jaunt; and that, of course, led back to Patty's persistent question about the mice.

"Well," Mark said slowly, as his wife signaled with her eyes for him to be careful, "even now no one really knows, Patty. But all the experiments with animals—including the mice—seemed to lead to the conclusion that while the Jaunt is almost instantaneous *physically*, it takes a long, *long* time mentally."

"I don't get it," Patty said glumly. "I knew I wouldn't."

But Ricky was looking at his father thoughtfully. "They went on thinking," he said. "The test animals. And so would we, if we didn't get knocked out."

"Yes," Mark said. "That's what we believe now."

Something was dawning in Ricky's eyes. Fright? Excitement? "It isn't just teleportation, is it, Dad? It's some kind of time-warp."

It's eternity in there, Mark thought.

"In a way," he said. "But that's a comic-book phrase—it sounds good but doesn't really mean anything, Rick. It seems to revolve around the idea of consciousness, and the fact that consciousness doesn't particulate—it remains whole and constant. It also retains some screwy sense of time. But we don't know how pure consciousness would measure time, or even if that concept has any meaning to pure mind. We can't even conceive what pure mind might be."

Mark fell silent, troubled by his son's eyes, which were suddenly so sharp and curious. *He understands but he doesn't understand,* Mark thought. Your mind can be your best friend; it can keep you amused even when there's nothing to read, nothing to do. But it can turn on you when it's left with no input for too long. It can turn on you, which means that it turns on itself, savages itself, perhaps consumes itself in an unthinkable act of auto-cannibalism. How long in there, in terms of years? 0.000000000067 seconds for the body to Jaunt, but how long for the unparticulated consciousness? A hundred years? A thousand? A million? A billion? How long alone with your thoughts in an endless field of white? And then, when a billion eternities have passed, the crashing return of light and form and body. Who wouldn't go insane?

"Ricky—" he began, but the Jaunt attendants had arrived with their cart.

"Are you ready?" one asked.

Mark nodded.

"Daddy, I'm scared," Patty said in a thin voice. "Will it hurt?"

"No honey, of course it won't hurt," Mark said, and his voice was calm enough, but his heart was beating a little fast—it always did, although this would be something like his twenty-fifth Jaunt. "I'll go first and you'll see how easy it is."

The Jaunt attendant looked at him questioningly. Mark nodded and made a smile. The mask descended. Mark took it in his own hands and breathed deep of the dark.

The first thing he became aware of was the hard black Martian sky as seen through the top of the dome which surrounded Whitehead City. It was night here, and the stars sprawled with a fiery brilliance undreamed of on earth.

The second thing he became aware of was some sort of disturbance in the recovery room—mutters, then shouts, then a shrill scream. *Oh dear God, that's Marilys!* he thought, and struggled up from his Jaunt couch, fighting the waves of dizziness.

There was another scream, and he saw Jaunt attendants running toward their couches, their bright red jumpers flying around their knees. Marilys staggered toward him, pointing. She screamed again and then collapsed on the floor, sending an unoccupied Jaunt couch rolling slowly down the aisle with one weakly clutching hand.

But Mark had already followed the direction of her pointing finger. He had seen. It hadn't been fright in Ricky's eyes; it had been excitement. He should have known, because he knew Ricky— Ricky, who had fallen out of the highest crotch of the tree in their backyard in Schenectady when he was only seven, who had broken his arm (and was lucky that had been all he'd broken); Ricky who dared to go faster and further on his Slideboard than any other kid in the neighborhood; Ricky who was first to take any dare. Ricky and fear were not well acquainted.

Until now.

Beside Ricky, his sister still mercifully slept. The thing that had been his son bounced and writhed on its Jaunt couch, a twelve-year-old boy with a snow-white fall of hair and eyes which were incredibly ancient, the corneas gone a sickly yellow. Here was a creature older than time masquerading as a boy; and yet it bounced and writhed with a kind of horrid, obscene glee, and at its choked, lunatic cackles the Jaunt attendants drew back in terror. Some of them fled, although they had been trained to cope with just such an unthinkable eventuality.

The old-young legs twitched and quivered. Claw hands beat and twisted and danced on the air; abruptly they descended and the thing that had been his son began to claw at its face.

"Longer than you think, Dad!" it cackled. "Longer than you think! Held my breath when they gave me the gas! Wanted to see! I saw! I saw! Longer than you think!"

Cackling and screeching, the thing on the Jaunt couch suddenly clawed its own eyes out. Blood gouted. The recovery room was an aviary of screaming voices now.

"Longer than you think, Dad! I saw! I saw! Long Jaunt! Longer than you think—"

It said other things before the Jaunt attendants were finally able to bear it away, rolling its couch swiftly away as it screamed and clawed at the eyes that had seen the unseeable forever and ever; it said other things, and then it began to scream, but Mark Oates didn't hear it because by then he was screaming himself.

01100101 01101110 01100011 01100101 00100000
01100110 01101001 01100011 01110100 01101001
01101111 01101110 00100000 01110011 01110100

THE VAPORIZATION ENTHALPY OF A PECULIAR PAKISTANI FAMILY

| USMAN T. MALIK |

1

THE SOLID PHASE OF MATTER is a state wherein a substance is particulately bound. To transform a solid into liquid, the intermolecular forces need to be overcome, which may be achieved by adding energy. The energy necessary to break such bonds is, ironically, called the *heat of fusion*.

On a Friday after jumah prayers, under the sturdy old oak in their yard, they came together as a family for the last time. Her brother gave in and wept as Tara watched, eyes prickling with warmth that wouldn't disperse no matter how much she knuckled them, or blinked.

"Monsters," Sohail said, his voice raspy. He wiped his mouth with the back of his hand and looked at the sky, a vast whiteness cobblestoned with heat. The plowed wheat fields beyond the steppe on which their house perched were baked and khaki and shivered a little under Tara's feet. An earthquake or a passing vehicle on the highway? Perhaps it was foreknowledge that made her dizzy. She pulled at her lower lip and said nothing.

"Monsters," Sohail said again. "Oh God, Apee. Murderers."

She reached out and touched his shoulders. "I'm sorry." She

thought he would pull back. When he didn't, she let her fingers fall and linger on the flame-shaped scar on his arm. *So it begins*, she thought. *How many times has this happened before? Pushing and prodding us repeatedly until the night swallows us whole.* She thought of that until her heart constricted with dread. "Don't do it," she said. "Don't go."

Sohail lifted his shoulders and drew back his head, watched her wonderingly as if seeing her for the first time.

"I know I ask too much," she said. "I know the customs of honor, but for the love of God let it go. One death needn't become a lodestone for others. One horror needn't—"

But he wasn't listening, she could tell. *They would not hear nor see nor smell once the blood was upon them, didn't the Scriptures say so?* Sohail heard, but didn't listen. His conjoined eyebrows, like dark hands held, twitched. "Her name meant a rose," he said and smiled. It was beautiful, that smile, heartbreaking, frightening. "Under the mango trees by Chacha Barkat's farm Gulminay told me that, as I kissed her hand. Whispered it in my ear, her finger circling my temple. *A rose blooming in the rain.* Did you know that?"

Tara didn't. The sorrow of his confession filled her now as did the certainty of his leaving. "Yes," she lied, looking him in the eyes. God, his eyes looked awful: webbed with red, with thin tendrils of steam rising from them. "A rose God gave us and took away because He loved her so."

"Wasn't God," Sohail said and rubbed his fingers together. The sound was insectile. "Monsters." He turned his back to her and was able to speak rapidly, "I'm leaving tomorrow morning. I'm going to the mountains. I will take some bread and dried meat. I will stay there until I'm shown a sign, and once I am ..." His back arched, then straightened. He had lost weight; his shoulder blades poked through the khaddar shirt like trowels. "I will arise and go to their homes. I will go to them as God's wrath. I will—"

She cut him off, her heart pumping fear through her body like poison. "What if you go to them and die? What if you go to them like a steer to the slaughter? And Ma and I—what if months later we sit here and watch a dusty vehicle climb the hill, bouncing a sack of meat in the back seat that was once you? What if…"

But she couldn't go on giving name to her terrors. Instead, she said, "If you go, know that we as we are now will be gone forever."

He shuddered. "*We* were gone when *she* was gone. We were shattered with her bones." The wind picked up, a whipping, cha-dor-lifting sultry gust that made Tara's flesh prickle. Sohail began to walk down the steppes, each with its own crop: tobacco, corn, rice stalks wavering in knee-high water; and as she watched his lean farmer body move away, it seemed to her as if his back was not drenched in sweat, but acid. That his flesh glistened not from moisture, but blood. All at once their world was just too much, or not enough—Tara couldn't decide which—and the weight of that unseen future weighed her down until she couldn't breathe. "My brother," she said and began to cry. "You're my little brother."

Sohail continued walking his careful, dead man's walk until his head was a wobbling black pumpkin rising from the last steppe. She watched him disappear in the undulations of her motherland, helpless to stop the fatal fracturing of her world, wondering if he would stop or doubt or look back.

Sohail never looked back.

Ma died three months later.

The village menfolk told her the death prayer was brief and moving. Tara couldn't attend because she was a woman.

The villagers helped her bury Ma's sorrow-filled body, and the rotund mullah clucked and murmured over the fresh mound. The women embraced her and crooned and urged her to vent.

"Weep, our daughter," they cried, "for the childrens' tears of love are like manna for the departed."

Tara tried to weep and felt guilty when she couldn't. Ma had been sick and in pain for a long time and her hastened death was a mercy, but you couldn't say that out loud. Besides, the women had said *children*, and Sohail wasn't there. Not at the funeral, nor during the days after. Tara dared not wonder where he was, nor imagine his beautiful face gleaming in the dark atop a stony mountain, persevering in his vigil.

"What will you do now?" they asked, gathering around her with sharp, interested eyes. She knew what they really meant. A young widow with no family was a stranger amidst her clan: at best an oddity, at worst a ripe seductress. She was surprised to discover their concern didn't frighten her. The perfect loneliness of it, the inadvertent exclusion—they were just more beads in the tautening string of her life.

"I'm thinking of going to the City," she told them. "Ma has a cousin there. Perhaps he can help me with bread and board, while I look for work."

She paused, startled by a clear memory: Sohail and Gulminay by the Kunhar River, fishing for trout. Gulminay's sequined hijab dappling the stream with emerald as she reached down into the water with long, pale fingers. Sohail grinning his stupid lover's grin as his small hands encircled her waist, and Tara watching from the shade of the eucalyptus, fond and jealous. By then Tara's husband was long gone and she could forgive herself the occasional resentment.

She forced the memory away. "Yes, I think I might go to the City for a while." She laughed. The sound rang hollow and strange in the emptiness of her tin-and-timber house. "Who knows I might even go back to school. I used to enjoy reading once." She smiled at these women with their hateful, sympathetic eyes that watched her cautiously as they would a rabid animal. She nodded, talking mostly to herself. "Yes, that would be good. Hashim would have wanted that."

They drew back from her, from her late husband's mention. *Why not?* she thought. Everything she touched fell apart; everyone around her died or went missing. There was no judgment here, just dreadful awe. *She could allow them that*, she thought.

2

The Liquid Phase of Matter is a restless volume that, by dint of the vast spaces between its molecules, fills any container it is poured in and takes its shape. Liquids tend to have higher energy than solids, and while the particles retain inter-particle forces they have enough energy to move relative to each other.

The structure therefore becomes mobile and malleable.

In the City, Tara turned feral in her pursuit of learning. This had been long coming and it didn't surprise her at all. At thirteen, she had been withdrawn from school; she needed not homework but a husband, she was told. At sixteen, she was wedded to Hashim. He was blown to smithereens on her twenty-first birthday. A suicide attack on his unit's northern check post.

"I want to go to school," she told Wasif Khan, her mother's cousin. They were sitting in his six-by-eight yard, peeling fresh oranges he had confiscated from an illegal food vendor. Wasif was a Police hawaldar, and on the rough side of sixty. He often said confiscation was his first love and contraband second. He grinned when he said that, which made it easier for her to like him.

Now Wasif tossed a half-gnawed chicken bone to his spotted mongrel and said, "I don't know if you want to do that."

"I do."

"You need a husband, not—"

"I don't care. I need to go back to school."

"But why?" He dropped an orange rind in the basket at his feet, gestured with a large liver-spotted hand. "The City doesn't care if you can read. Besides, you can housekeep for me. I'm old and ugly and useless, but I have this tolerable house and no children. You're my cousin's daughter. You can stay here forever if you like."

In a different time she might have mistaken his generosity for loneliness, but now she understood it for what it was. Such was the way of age: it melted prejudice or hardened it. "I want to learn about the world," she said. "I want to see if there are others like me. If there have been others before me."

He was confused. "Like you how?"

She rubbed an orange peel between her fingers, pressing the fibrous texture of it in the creases of her flesh, considering how much to tell him. Her mother had trusted him. Yet Ma hardly had their gift and if she did Tara doubted she would have been open about it. Ma had been wary of giving too much of herself away—a trait she passed on to both her children. Among other things.

So now Tara said, "Others who *need* to learn more about themselves. I spent my entire childhood being just a bride and, look, I am left with nothing. No children, no husband, no family." Wasif Khan looked hurt. She smiled kindly. "You know what I mean, Uncle. I love you, but I need to love me too."

Wasif Khan tilted his head back and pinched a slice of orange above his mouth, squeezed it until his tongue and remaining teeth gleamed with the juice. He closed his eyes, sighed, and nodded. "I don't know if I approve, but I think I understand." He lifted his hand and tousled his own hair thoughtfully. "It's a different time. Others my age who don't realize it don't fare well. The traditional rules don't apply anymore, you know. Sometimes, I think that is wonderful. Other times, it feels like the whole damn world is conspiring against you."

"I understand." She rose, picking up her mess and his. "Thank you for letting me stay here."

"It's either you or every hookah-sucking asshole in this neighborhood for company." He grinned and shrugged his shoulders. "My apologies. I've been living alone too long and my tongue is spoilt."

She laughed loudly; and thought of a blazing cliff somewhere from which dangled two browned, peeling, inflamed legs, swinging back and forth like human pendulums.

··· — — — ···

She read everything she could get her hands on. At first, her alphabet was broken and awkward, as was her rusty brain, but she did it anyway. It took her two years, but eventually she qualified for F.A examinations, and passed on her first try.

"I don't know how you did it," Wasif Khan said to her, his face beaming at the neighborhood children as he handed out specially prepared sweetmeat to eager hands, "but I'm proud of you."

She wasn't, but she didn't say it. Instead, once the children left, she went to the mirror and gazed at her reflection, flexing her arm, making the flame-shaped scar bulge. *We all drink the blood of yesterday*, she thought.

The next day she enrolled at Punjab University's B.Sc program.

In Biology class, they learned about plants and animals. Flora and Fauna, they called them. Things constructed piece by piece from the basic units of life: cells. These cells in turn were made from tiny building blocks called atoms, which were bonded by the very things that repelled their core: electrons.

In Physics class, she learned about electrons. Little flickering ghosts that vanished and reappeared as they pleased. Her flesh was empty, she discovered, or most of it. So were human bones and solid buildings and the incessantly agitated world. All that immense loneliness and darkness with only a hint that we existed. The idea awed her. Did we exist only as a possibility?

In Wasif Khan's yard was a tall mulberry tree with saw-like leaves. On her way to school she touched them; they were spiny and jagged. She hadn't eaten mulberries before. She picked a basketful, nipped her wrist with her teeth, and let her blood roast a few. She watched them curl and smoke from the heat of her genes, inhaled the sweet steam of their juice as they turned into mystical symbols.

Mama would have been proud.

She ate them with salt and pepper, and was offended when Wasif Khan wouldn't touch the remaining.

He said they gave him reflux.

3

The Gaseous Phase of Matter is one in which particles have enough kinetic energy to make the effect of intermolecular forces negligible. A gas, therefore, will occupy the entire container in which it is confined.

Liquid may be converted to gas by heating at constant pressure to a certain temperature.

This temperature is called the *boiling point*.

The worst flooding the province has seen in forty years.

Wasif Khan hadn't confiscated a television yet, but if he had, Tara was sure, it would show the same cataclysmic damage to life and property. At one point, someone said, an area the size of England was submerged in raging floodwater.

Wasif's neighborhood, in the northern, hillier part of town, escaped the worst of the devastation, but Tara and Wasif witnessed it daily when they went for rescue work: massive upchucked power pylons and a splintered oak tree smashing through the marketplace stalls; murderous tin sheets and iron rods slicing through the inundated streets; bloated dead cows and sheep eddying in shoulder-high water with terrified children clinging to them. It pawed at the towering steel-and-concrete structures, this restless liquid death that had come to the city; it ripped out their underpinnings and annihilated everything in its path.

Tara survived these days of heartbreak and horror by helping to set up a small tent city on the sports fields of her University. She volunteered to establish a nursery for lost or displaced children and went with rescue teams to scour the ruins for usable supplies, and corpses.

As she pulled out the dead and living from beneath the wreckage, as she tossed plastic-wrapped food and dry clothing to the dull-eyed homeless, she thought of how bright and hot and dry the spines of her brother's mountains must be. It had been four years since she saw him, but her dreams were filled with his absence. Did he sit parched and caved in, like a deliberate Buddha? Or was he dead and pecked on by ravens and falcons?

She shuddered at the thought and grabbed another packet of cooked rice and dry beans for the benighted survivors.

The first warning came on the last night of Ramadan. *Chand raat.*

Tara was eating bread and lentils with her foundling children in the nursery when it happened. A bone-deep trembling that ran through the grass, flattening its blades, evaporating the evening dew sitting on them. Seconds later, a distant boom followed: a hollow rumbling that hurt Tara's ears and made her feel nauseated. (Later, she would learn that the blast had torn through the marble-walled shrine of Data Sahib, wrenching its iron fence from its moorings, sending jagged pieces of metal and scorched human limbs spinning across the walled part of the City.)

Her children sat up, confused and scared. She soothed them. Once a replacement was found, she went to talk to the tent city administrator.

"I've seen this before," she told him once he confirmed it was a suicide blast. "My husband and sister-in-law both died in similar situations." That was not entirely true for Gulminay, but close enough. "Usually one such attack is followed by another when rescue attempts are made. My husband used to call them 'double tap' attacks." She paused, thinking of his kind, dearly loved face for the first time in months. "He understood the psychology behind them well."

The administrator, a chubby short man with filthy cheeks, scratched his chin. "How come?"

"He was a ranger. He tackled many such situations before he died."

"Condolences, *bibi.*" The administrator's face crinkled with sympathy. "But what does that have to do with us?"

"At some point, they will use the double tap as decoy and

come after civilian structures."

"Thank you for the warning. I'll send out word to form a volunteer perimeter patrol." He scrutinized her, taking in her hijab, the
bruised elbows, and grimy fingernails from days of work. "God
bless you for the lives you've saved already. For the labor you've
done."

He handed her a packet of boiled corn and alphabet books.
She nodded absently, the charred bodies and boiled human blood
swirling up from the shrine in her head, thanked him, and left.

The emergency broadcast thirty minutes later confirmed her
fear: a second blast at Data Sahib obliterated a fire engine, killed a
jeep-ful of eager policemen and vaporized twenty-five rescuers.
Five of these were female medical students. Their shattered glass
bangles were melted and their headscarves burned down to unrecognizable gunk by the time the EMS came.

Tara wept when she heard. In her heart was a steaming shadow
that whispered nasty things. It impaled her with its familiarity and a
dreadful suspicion grew in her that the beast was rage and wore a
face she knew well.

4

When matter is heated to high temperatures, such as in a flame,
electrons begin to leave the atoms. At very high temperatures, es-
sentially all electrons are assumed to be dissociated, resulting in a
unique state wherein positively charged nuclei swim in a raging 'sea'
of free electrons.

This state is called the Plasma Phase of Matter and exists in
lightning, electric sparks, neon lights, and the Sun.

In a rash of terror attacks, the City quickly fell apart: the Tower of
Pakistan, the Shrine of Jinnah, Iqbal's Memorial, Shalimar Gardens,
Anarkali's Tomb, and the fourteen gates of the walled City. They
exploded and fell in burning tatters, survived only by a quivering

bloodhaze through which peeked the haunted eyes of their immortal ghosts.

This is death, this is love, this is the comeuppance of the two, as the world according to you will finally come to an end. So snarled the beast in Tara's head each night. The tragedy of the floodwaters was not over yet, and now this.

Tara survived this new world through her books and her children. The two seemed to have become one: pages filled with unfathomable loss. White space itching to be written, reshaped, or incinerated. Sometimes she would bite her lips and let the trickle of blood stain her callused fingers. Would touch them to water-spoilt paper and watch it catch fire and flutter madly in the air, aflame like a phoenix. An impossible glamor created by tribulation. So when the city burned and her tears burned, Tara reminded herself of the beautiful emptiness of it all and forced herself to smile.

Until one morning she awoke and discovered that, in the cover of night, a suicide teenager had hit her tent city's perimeter patrol.

After the others had left, she stood over her friends' graves in the twilight.

Kites and vultures unzipped the darkness above in circles, lost specks in this ghostly desolation. She remembered how cold it was when they lowered Gulminay's remains into the ground. How the drone attack had torn her limbs clean off so that, along with a head shriveled by heat, a glistening, misshapen, idiot torso remained. She remembered Ma, too, and how she was killed by her son's love. The first of many murders.

"I know you," she whispered to the Beast resident in her soul. "I know you," and all the time she scribbled on her flesh with a glass shard she found buried in a patrolman's eye. Her wrist glowed with her heat and that of her ancestors. She watched her blood bubble and surge skyward. To join the plasma of the world and drift its soft, vaporous way across the darkened City, and she wondered again if she was still capable of loving them both.

The administrator promised her that he would take care of her children. He gave her food and a bundle of longshirts and shalwars. He asked her where she was going and why, and she knew he was afraid for her.

"I will be all right," she told him. "I know someone who lives up there."

"I don't understand why you must go. It's dangerous," he said, his flesh red under the hollows of his eyes. He wiped his cheeks. "I wish you didn't have to. But I suppose you will. I see that in your face. I saw that when you first came here."

She laughed. The sound of her own laughter saddened her. "The world will change," she said. "It always does. We are all empty, but this changing is what saves us. That is why I must go."

He nodded. She smiled. They touched hands briefly; she stepped forward and hugged him, her headscarf tickling his nostrils, making him sneeze. She giggled and told him how much she loved him and the others. He looked pleased and she saw how much kindness and gentleness lived inside his skin, how his blood would never boil with undesired heat.

She lifted his finger, kissed it, wondering at how solid his vacant flesh felt against her lips.

Then she turned and left him, leaving the water and fire and the crackling, hissing earth of the City behind.

Such was how Tara Khan left for the mountains.

The journey took a week. The roads were barren, the landscape abraded by floodwater and flensed by intermittent fires. Shocked trees, stripped of fruit, stood rigid and receding as Tara's bus rolled by, their gnarled limbs pointing accusatorially at the heavens.

Wrapped in her chador, headscarf, and shalwar kameez, Tara folded into the rugged barrenness with its rugged people. They were not unkind; even in the midst of this madness, they held onto their deeply honored tradition of hospitality, allowing Tara to scout for hints of the Beast's presence. The northerners chattered constantly and were horrified by the atrocities blooming from within them, and because she too spoke Pashto they treated her like one of them.

Tara kept her ears open. Rumors, whispers, beckonings by skeletal fingers. Someone said there was a man in Abbottabad who was the puppeteer. Another shook his head and said that was a deliberate shadow show, a gaudy interplay of light and dark put up by the real perpetrators. That the Supreme Conspirator was swallowed by earth soaked with the blood of thousands and lived only as an extension of this irredeemable evil.

Tara listened and tried to read between their words. Slowly, the hints in the midnight alleys, the leprous grins, the desperate, clutching fingers, incinerated trees and the smoldering human and animal skulls—they began to come together and form a map.

Tara followed it into the heart of the mountains.

5

When the elementary particle boson is cooled to temperatures near absolute zero, a dilute 'gas' is created. Under such conditions, a large number of bosons occupy the lowest quantum state and an unusual thing happens: quantum effects become visible on a macroscopic scale. This effect is called the macroscopic quantum phenomena and the 'Bose-Einstenin Condensate' is inferred to be a new state of matter. The presence of one such particle, the Higgs-Boson, was tentatively confirmed on March 14th, 2013 in the most complex experimental facility built in human history.

This particle is sometimes called the *God Particle*.

When she found him, he had changed his name.

There is a story told around campfires since the beginning of time: Millennia ago a stone fell from the infinite bosom of space and plunked onto a statistically impossible planet. The stone was round, and smaller than a pebble of goat shit, and carried a word inscribed on it.

It has been passed down generations of Pahari clans that that word is the *Ism-e-Azam*, the Most High Name of God.

Every sect in the history of our world has written about it. Egyptians, Mayans. Jewish, Christian, and Muslim mystics. Some have described it as the primal point from which existence began, and that the Universal Essence lives in this *nuktah*.

The closest approximation to the First Word, some say, is one that originated in Mesopotamia, the land between the two rivers. The Sumerians called it *Annunaki*.

He of Godly Blood.

Tara thought of this oral tradition and sat down at the mouth of the demolished cave. She knew he lived inside the cave, for every living and nonliving thing near it reeked of his heat. Twisted boulders stretched granite hands toward its mouth like pilgrims at the Kaaba. The heat of the stars they carried in their genes, in the sputtering, whisking emptiness of their cells, had leeched out and warped the mountains and the path leading up to it.

Tara sat cross-legged in the lotus position her mother taught them both when they were young. She took a sharp rock and ran it across her palm. Crimson droplets appeared and evaporated, leaving a metallic tang in the air. She sat and inhaled that smell and thought of the home that once was. She thought of her mother, and her husband; of Gulminay and Sohail; of the floods (did he have something to do with that, too? Did his rage liquefy snow-topped mountains and drown an entire country?); of suicide bombers, and the University patrol; and of countless human eyes that flicked each moment toward an unforgiving sky where something merciful may or may not live; and her eyes began to burn and Tara Khan began to cry.

"Come out," she said between her sobs. "Come out, Beast. Come out, Rage. Come out, Death of the Two Worlds and all that lives in between. Come out, Monster. Come out, Fear," and all the while she rubbed her eyes and let the salt of her tears crumble between her fingertips. Sadly she looked at the white crystals, flattened them, and screamed, "Come out, ANNUNAKI."

And in a belch of shrieking air and a blast of heat, her brother came to her.

They faced each other.

His skin was gone. His eyes melted, his nose bridge collapsed; the bones underneath were simmering white seas that rolled and shimmered across the constantly melting and rearranging meat of him. His limbs were pseudopodic, his movement that of a softly turning planet drifting across the possibility that is being.

Now he floated toward her on a gliding plane of his skin. His potent heat, a shifting locus of limp time-space with infinite energy roiling inside it, touched her, making her recoil. When he breathed, she saw everything that once was; and knew what she knew.

"Salam," she said. "Peace be upon you, brother."

The *nuktah* that was him twitched. His fried vocal cords were not capable of producing words anymore.

"I used to think," she continued, licking her dry lips, watching the infinitesimal shifting of matter and emptiness inside him, "that love was all that mattered. That the bonds that pull us all together are of timeless love. But it is not true. It's never been true, has it?"

He shimmered, and said nothing.

"I believe in existing, in *Ex Nihilo Nihil Fit*. If nothing comes from nothing, we cannot return to it. Ergo life has a reason and needs to be." She paused, remembering a day when he plucked a sunflower from a lush meadow and slipped it into Gulminay's hair. "Gulminay-jaan once was and still is. Perhaps inside you and me." Tara wiped her tears and smiled. "Even if most of us is nothing."

The heat-thing that her brother was slipped forward a notch. Tara rose to her feet and began walking toward it. The blood in her vasculature seethed and raged.

"Even if death breaks some bonds and forms others. Even if the world flinches, recedes, and becomes a grain of sand."

Annunaki watched her through eyes like black holes.

"Even if we have killed and shall kill. Even if the source is nothing if not grief. Even if sorrow is the distillate of our life."

She reached out and gripped his melting amebic limb. He shrank, but didn't let go as the maddened heat of her essence surged forth to meet his.

"Even if we never come to much. Even if the sea of our consciousness breaks against quantum impossibilities."

She pressed his now-arm, her fingers elongating, stretching, turning, fusing; her flame-scar rippling and coiling to probe for his like a proboscis.

Sohail tried to smile, and in that smile were heat-deaths of countless worlds, supernova bursts, and the chrysalis sheen of a freshly hatched larva. She thought he might have whispered sorry. That in another time and universe there were not countless intemperate blood-children of his spreading across the earth's face like vitriolic tides ready to obliterate the planet. That all this wasn't really happening for one misdirected missile, for one careless press of a button somewhere by a soldier eating junk food and licking his fingers. But it was. Tara had glimpsed it in his *nuktah* when she touched him.

"Even if," she whispered, as his being engulfed hers and the thermonuclear reaction of matter and antimatter fusion sparked and began to eradicate them both, "our puny existence—the conclusion of an agitated, conscious universe—is insignificant, remember ... remember, brother, that mercy will go on. Kindness will go on."

Let there be gentleness, she thought. *Let there be equilibrium, if all we are and will be can survive in some form. Let there be grace and goodness and a hint of something to come, no matter how uncertain.*

Let there be possibility, she thought, as they flickered annihilatively and were immolated in some fool's idea of love.

THE SHAKING MAN

| GENE O'NEILL |

"Beware; for I am fearless, and therefore powerful."
– Mary Shelley, *Frankenstein*

Although the cause of Tourette syndrome is unknown, current research points to abnormalities in certain brain regions (including the basal ganglia, frontal lobes, and cortex), the circuits that interconnect these regions, and the neurotransmitters (dopamine, serotonin, and norepinephrine) responsible for communication among nerve cells. Given the often complex presentation of Tourette syndrome, the cause of the disorder is likely to be equally complex.
– MedicineNet.Com

1

EAST OAKLAND
JULY 4TH, 14 YEARS AGO

THE EIGHT-YEAR-OLD BOY could barely contain himself as dusk settled. His mother was off early from her nursing assistant job at Serenity Seniors Living Center—a rare treat. The young boy raced his older brother to their Escort, parked in front of the 97th Avenue bungalow near Elmhurst Park, even though their single mom forbade either of them being on the dangerous East Oakland streets after dark. He jumped into the back seat, his brother up front. "C'mon, Mama, hurry up," the young boy shouted out the open car window.

They were going over to Jack London Square to get an unobstructed view of the Independence Day fireworks display that night over the greater San Francisco Bay.

"I'm coming, Eugene, I'm coming just as fast as I can," his chubby mother replied, as she waddled around the front end of the little Ford.

But at that moment a wide-bodied, pink Cadillac convertible careened around the corner from the direction of the park and slammed into the unprotected woman. It flipped her over the top of the car to a spot another thirty feet down the street, as the Cad smashed in the entire front of the Escort. Then, the huge automobile backed up, and left behind a trail of steam as it fishtailed on up 97th Avenue, swerving around the downed and bleeding woman.

Moments later multiple sirens were *screaming* like animals protesting in the night.

The young boy awakened at Oakland Children's Hospital later that night in ICU. He was very groggy, disoriented, and had a terrible headache, the result of a badly lacerated forehead and a concussion. The emergency room staff, after running their preliminary assessment protocols, didn't think there was any serious internal cranial damage; but they decided to keep the boy overnight in ICU for another twenty-four hours of observation and more tests.

He found himself hooked up to several monitors and a hand drip in the funny-smelling, noisy, and scary place. He didn't know it then, but his mother and older brother had been killed instantly by the driver of the pink convertible, who would remain unidentified. The boy was given a pill by a nice-smelling nurse, and soon drifted back to sleep.

Early the next morning the hospital staff began administering more extensive and sophisticated testing, including a CAT scan and an EEG; the humming sound and inanimate, metallic look of both machines frightening the young boy, who still had a terrible headache. Later that same day he experienced the first involuntary symptoms of early onset Tourette's syndrome. The staff did not believe the Tourette's was necessarily a direct result of the head trauma. But the boy believed the involuntary limb tremors and uncontrolled facial tics and twitching were the result of the tests and being hooked up to all the weird machines. *No* one ever explained anything different to him. Distrustful now of even the nice-smelling nurse, he withdrew deeply into himself.

The boy, who in the past had been joyful and outgoing, was released from the hospital several days later, his Tourette's syndrome symptoms even more pronounced, his behavior and attitude severely altered. Mourning the death of his brother and mother, and with no living relatives, he found himself in the custody of total strangers, consigned to the bureaucratic and impersonal guardianship of Alameda County Department of Child Support Services.

At his first foster home placement, the other kids began teasing him and calling him *Shake*, after they were first exposed to the bizarre symptoms of his Tourette's. The nickname would stick with him for life; but the accompanying teasing and bullying terminated quickly. Shake was big for his age, and others around him soon found that the involuntary shaking episodes of his disease were often followed by rage and a ferocious physical acting out of punching, kicking, biting—recipients left bloody, bruised, and broken, but wiser.

Over the years, shuttled from foster home to foster home, Shake grew into a muscular teenager. He became even more taciturn, morose, quick-tempered, and ruthless—striking out at even the slightest hint of disrespect. Not someone others dared to pick on, even in the tough East Oakland neighborhoods where he lived. A wise forewarning offered by those who had encountered him: *Man, tha boy start shakin be pass time to getta hat, ya unnerstan?*

Surprisingly for a youngster afflicted with Tourette's syndrome, he did well in the several different schools he attended, especially in reading and math. He sat quietly in class, despite all the disruption around him, and at home he doggedly did his homework assignments. No kids dared make fun of his classroom achievements, like they did the few other nerdy students.

But at the end of Shake's junior year, he dropped out of school after he found a well-paying job that suited his skillset, street smarts, and temperament. At six-foot-two, two hundred ten pounds, and completely fearless, he became a collector and *arm* for Big Henry, a nefarious East Oakland bookmaker and major employer of many girls cruising *The Track* on International Boulevard. You didn't pay off your weekly gambling debt, or you tried to recruit one of Big Henry's female street employees, then you could expect a visit from Shake—one brief visit, enough to loosen up pockets or discourage employee raiding. He didn't have to carry a concealed weapon other than two rolls of nickels in his pockets; his reputation, size, and cold-blooded gaze were usually enough to slow down travelers in the fast lane.

2

SAN QUENTIN STATE PRISON MAIN YARD
A YEAR AND A HALF AGO

The invisible boundaries across the main yard were as well defined as barbed wire fence lines separating Northern California cattle ranches. These borders defined race/gang turf, and outsiders *never* crossed a line uninvited ... except for twenty-two-year-old Eugene Jefferson, #152536. It was his first day back on the yard after being locked down 24/7 for another three months in the maximum segregation unit.

Of course no one on the yard would recognize the young man's given or family name; he was known by almost everyone as

The Shaking Man because of the occasional involuntary wild movements associated with his Tourette's syndrome—bizarre movements often followed by sudden, ferocious, and frightening violence. But directly to his face everyone called him *Shake*, and always in a polite manner. He tolerated this nickname survivor from his boyhood.

Earlier that day, at the mess hall, Shake had lightly brushed against Lil Abner when they were both scraping their trays into the garbage cans after lunch. The nickname, Lil Abner, was intentionally ironic, as the man was almost as tall as Shake, who was a muscular six-four.

Lil Abner turned, and in a threatening manner said: "Hey, *Smoke*, watch where the fuck ya going, ya hear me?" Of course Smoke was racist, intended to demean a black. And it was a derogatory term often used by Lil Abner and his cohorts in the dangerous white supremacist prison gang, the Aryan Brotherhood—the ABs.

But Shake kept his cool, even smiled and shrugged apologetically at the heavily set AB, who outweighed him by at least forty pounds. He slipped away, avoiding any real confrontation, which would have been broken up too quickly by the nearby COs on mess hall duty. Shake thought as he walked away: *Not yet, big boy, I'll see your ass out on the yard.*

Later, on the main yard, Shake shuffled along all by himself, looking like he'd been addled by his last ninety days locked down in dark max-seg, and now acting dazed out in the bright summer sunshine. He was even bundled up in a navy-blue prison jacket as if he'd anticipated a foggy wintery day. He stumbled inside the far corner of the separation border where white guys were pumping iron—a handful of biker dudes along with seven or eight Aryan Brotherhood.

Lil Abner and a smaller AB, called Double J, were standing guard closest to the invisible boundary Shake had just violated.

Both immediately went into *red alert* mode, and held up their muscled and blue-tatted arms and hands in the stop gesture. Lil Abner moved closer and in a tone heavy with threat ordered: "Hold it right there, Smoke! Don't you dare fucking move!"

Shake, his features dancing now with an assortment of disconcerting ticks, jerks, twitches, and winks, whispered: "We meet again, *Fat Albert*. Call it!" Then, he flipped a round plastic washer high into the air as if it were some denomination of coin...

The surprised giant AB reacted naturally, looking up, following the path of the tumbling washer as it neared its apex—

Shake planted his right leg, sat on a right cross, and with maximum force hit the white man with a crunching blow in his exposed, tattooed throat, dropping the tall AB like a felled tree.

Double J went into instant attack mode, pulling a shank from the back of his pants, rushing at the huge black man, and plunging the short blade into his stomach. But Shake had carefully taped magazines around his entire mid-section under his jacket, which protected him from any serious damage by the thrust of the thin four-inch blade.

He grabbed the AB's extended right wrist, brought his other hand forcefully under Double J's elbow, and snapped one of the bones in the lower arm like a twig. Then, with a loud grunt, Shake dropped the smaller AB with a devastating head-butt to the face. As the two downed white men lay groaning in agony, the huge black man planted a vicious kick into the side of each one's head.

Shake's disabling attack of the two AB sentinels had taken all of five seconds, at most.

By then weights were being grounded, the lifters all initially taken by surprise by the lightning strike inside their territory on two armed perimeter guards by *one* black man. Simultaneously, whistles were *blowing* and a siren was *blaring*, the earsplitting alerts momentarily followed by a dozen COs charging across the yard from all directions toward the white weightlifting area. Overhead, the armed tower guard along that section of wall yelled through a megaphone:

"Everyone down, *now*. Down." Inmates, including the weightlifters, were quickly assuming the prescribed prone positions all over the main yard.

Order was soon established as The Shaking Man was whisked away before any whites could get close enough to retaliate.

But the two unconscious ABs were rushed by ambulance to a nearby Marin County hospital, both suffering serious injuries—Lil Abner had a crushed larynx and bad concussion and would forever after speak in a raspy whisper; his smaller cohort had a fractured radius, a badly broken nose, and a severe concussion, but he would eventually fully recover, although facing life a bit uglier.

In less than ten minutes, Shake found himself back in his old tiny cell in the 24/7 lock-down unit.

Later that afternoon, at a quickly assembled staff meeting, the CO shift Captain in charge of maximum segregation summarized the prisoner's incarceration history: "Eugene Jefferson came here on a three-year sentence for felony assault in Oakland, with a juvenile rap sheet, mostly involving minor crimes. I remind staff that he came out of intake with a psychological diagnosis stating he was suffering from an antisocial personality disorder. A sociopath who could be violent and required careful handling. Since then he's had numerous write-ups for physical altercations, requiring four stays in max-seg, which have added an additional nine months to his original sentence. And after these four stays in isolation, we think he may now be suffering from delusions, perhaps even brief psychotic episodes. What black inmate in his right mind—by himself—would cross into AB weight-lifting territory in broad daylight?"

After a brief discussion, the correctional, medical, and psychological staff all agreed that Eugene Jefferson had—in addition to having a history of being violent—exhibited signs of psychotic behavior. Dr. Czyz, the young psychometrist, sighed and said: "What a pity, because this man tests very high on all our IQ examinations, including a 150 on the revised Stanford-Binet."

Shortly thereafter, the consensus decision of the prison staff meeting was to assign Eugene Jefferson for an indefinite period to Napa State Hospital as a PCP—a Penal Code Patient—for extensive observation, testing, diagnosis, and treatment.

Shake was transferred from San Quentin Prison the next day, thirty-five miles northeast to Napa State Hospital.

3

NAPA STATE HOSPITAL, MAXIMUM SECURITY WARD
TEN MONTHS AGO

Eugene Jefferson had been transferred from San Quentin State Prison to Napa State Hospital as a PCP after busting up a pair of Aryan Brotherhood members on the main yard. He'd been in constant trouble during his almost four years of State Prison and State Hospital incarceration, including a series of violent assaults, some in self-defense, but all ending in serious injury to the other party. The medical staff at the State Hospital initially focused on controlling his Tourette's syndrome. But the psychological staff was mostly concerned with the aggressive, violent behavior often accompanying the outbreaks of his Tourette's physical symptoms—episodes of uncontrollable rage. His formal psychological/medical diagnosis was now: paranoid schizophrenia with delusions of grandeur, behavior complicated by the Tourette's syndrome.

So, Shake was in the last two months of his original three-year sentence plus nine months of add-ons, serving all of his Napa State Hospital time in the Maximum Security Ward for PCPs.

The Maximum Security Ward at the State Hospital resembled a wing at San Quentin, a long gray corridor lined on both sides with cells. Except, perhaps more so than the State Prison, it could be a dangerous place, even medicated cellmates exhibiting aggressive behavior, including numerous cases of aggravated assaults and attempted murders. There were a few patients passing through who wore the distinctive blue uniforms and a music player earplug, indicating they were from Atascadero State Hospital for the Criminally Insane. Most were convicted of bizarre sexual crimes like murder accompanied by necrophilia. They were housed in Napa State Hospital while waiting for subsequent Bay Area court hearings.

During the past eight months, the staff at the Hospital had tried different treatments to control Shake's symptoms, especially the accompanying violent rages, with very minimal success. Recently, they'd tried a series of three electro-shock treatments. Still, his involuntary physical symptoms and the rages prevailed.

Monday morning, Dr. Jones had called Shake into his office.

"Sit down, please, Eugene. How are you feeling today?"

"I'm fine, Doctor," he answered in his usual guarded manner, his dark eyes alert and watchful.

"That's good," Doctor Jones said absently, opening the file in front of him. "Well, we haven't helped you much, Eugene. So, the patient review board has decided that, with your permission, we would like to try something different. A relatively new version of *Deep Brain Stimulation*. Now *DBS* has been around for quite some time. It involves an insertion of a permanent electrode into the cerebral cortex, like a pacemaker. It has proven to be very effective with patients exhibiting a number of serious disorders, including a high degree of success with those suffering from various psycho-motor seizures related to diseases such as Parkinson's disorder and epilepsy. In addition, there has been some limited success with a much smaller subject group diagnosed with Tourette syndrome."

Shake didn't say anything. He nodded and raised his eyebrows indicating his interest.

"But DBS is very invasive, a major surgical procedure requiring the removal of a quarter-size piece of skull, and then deep implantation of an electrode. It requires constant medical monitoring, including frequent battery replacement. But we'd like to try a new, less invasive, experimental treatment with you, *Temporary Deep Brain Stimulation*," Dr. Jones continued. "TDBS involves inserting a very thin, almost microscopic, wire into the cerebral cortex of your brain, specifically into *Brodmann Area 25*. And then over a short period of time stimulating the neurons in this area with six electrical surges, which would be about triple the magnitude of the battery shocks of DBS. The procedure is designed to eliminate or at least reduce your involuntary psychomotor movements. The tremors, tics, blinking, and such."

Shake held up his hand as if a student and asked: "Why does this TDBS work?"

"Good question," Dr. Jones said, and then shrugged slightly as he continued: "Well, we *think* the probe and electrical shocks may have a direct effect on one or more psychomotor neurotransmitters. Similar to Parkinson's syndrome, the involuntary movements in your case may be caused by the defective operation of several neurotransmitters—dopamine, serotonin, epinephrine, and perhaps acetylcholine. That's the theory anyhow. Regardless, we *know* TDBS effectively reduces or completely eliminates the symptoms of Tourette syndrome..." Dr. Jones paused for a response.

"Okay ... So it suppresses the sudden onset of shaking and twitching," Shake said, unable to stifle a bit of a wry smile. For years he had felt he was different from other people, brighter, more gifted physically, and absolutely fearless. He knew that was part of the reason why he'd been so effective working as an *arm* for *Big Henry*—he obviously scared the shit out of his boss's customers. Only occasionally having to hurt someone.

But Shake had grown up reading comics and daydreaming about the abilities of superheroes. Then, in high school, after reading a recommended science article on evolution and the different stages of man, he suspected he might be much more than just different than other people around him. He might be the next stage in human evolution. The only thing keeping him from becoming a true *superman* was the Tourette's syndrome. In fact, he was convinced the first symptoms had originated in the hospital after he'd been brought in with head injuries suffered in the car accident when he was eight years old. *They* must have recognized his potential super abilities even back then, and somehow caused the disease in order to contain him. But, now, *they* were going to try and suppress his Tourette's.

Shake appreciated the irony and almost chuckled with glee.

Dr. Jones smiled back and continued: "We are sure it will have a good effect on the involuntary movements. But more important, we are hoping it will also help you control your irrational aggressive outbursts. If we are right, you will be able to soon return to a normal life back in the community. Be a positive asset to society with your high intelligence … So, we would like your permission to do a TDBS probe."

Shake paused for a few moments. It sounded too good to be true … He finally asked: "This probing inside my head is completely safe … and there is no physical danger to me?"

"Yes, it's safe, but not one hundred percent localized. We can shock the specific neurons in *Brodmann Area 25*. But the tiny wire also may touch and shock other neurons during the procedure. No harmful side effects have shown in any of the research studies reported in the literature. Whatever secondary effects you may experience will be minimal, I'm sure. I can confidently recommend this TDBS procedure. But it is your call, Eugene."

"And it's a no big deal, the surgery? You said non-invasive? Which must mean a quick recovery, too, right?"

"Yes, you will actually be completely awake during the entire procedure, a minor local anesthetic required on your shaved scalp. We'd first stabilize your head. Then a microscopic wire will be inserted through a tiny hole precisely drilled in your skull using a *stereotactic frame* positioned over your head. You will experience absolutely no pain. Nor will there be a loss of consciousness. And a very slight chance of post-insertion infection. If everything goes well, as I anticipate, you will have minimal hospital stay—a day or perhaps two. I'm convinced this will really be beneficial for you, Eugene."

"Man, if it gets rid of all the involuntary Tourette's movements, it's worth whatever risk, Doc. Where do I sign?"

The next morning they inserted the temporary wire into his cerebral cortex and shocked *Bodmann Area 25* six times ... along with over a hundred thousand non-targeted neurons.

Shake was released back to his ward less than two days later on Wednesday evening, apparently fully recovered from the minimally invasive probe. He felt fine.

During the next three weeks, Shake didn't experience any of his Tourette's syndrome symptoms—not even the hint of an out-of-control eyelid twitch.

I'm cured, I really am, he decided, feeling an overwhelming surge of elation. He was ready to take his rightful place in the world. And he had some *definite* plans for accomplishing that after his release and return to East Oakland.

In the small recreation room, Shake described his euphoric state to his domino playing buddy, Ahmaad. "Man, I think Doc Jones done worked some magic. I'm cured of all that twitching and jerking shit."

Ahmaad nodded and smiled thinly, spreading out the dominoes. The husky Black Muslim was shirtless, an indigo crescent and star tattooed over his heart. "That's great news, man. Maybe I can get a decent *tell* from your face now, without all that diabolical twitching and blinking."

But that evening in the showers, Shake had a recurrence of some of his Tourette's symptoms.

One of the Atascadero State Hospital temporary PCPs had a new young guy backed into the far corner of the shower room on his knees, and was trying to force the boy into performing oral sex. Unusual, because the Atascadero patients were normally so loaded with medication that they were never aggressive, moving about with the characteristic zombie-like *thorazine shuffle.*

Shake didn't experience any moral outrage at this sexual assault, just a sense of annoyance at the tranquility he liked when showering, being disturbed.

"Hey, man, let the boy go," he said to the rapist.

The guy, almost as tall and well-built as Shake said: "Mind your own fockin business, *Boog.*"

The old-time derogatory expression, a shortened form of *boogie-woogie,* pissed off Shake.

And in a threatening tone, he said: "I guess I didn't make myself clear, *whitey.* I wasn't asking you."

The naked Atascadero visitor frowned, and then doubled his fists and crouched to face the threat.

Shake glared unwaveringly into the man's eyes, his fists relaxed at his sides. Then, suddenly, he felt the overwhelming onset of a mass of assorted facial quivers, twitches, and tics. But the partial onset of his Tourette's symptoms left his stern glare unfazed. And it commanded the attention of the aggressor.

Out of the side of his mouth, Shake ordered the victim: "Get your ass dressed and out of here."

The boy snatched his clothes from a wall hook and left.

Then, Shake heard a metallic *click* deep inside his head like a microswitch being tripped; and he simultaneously felt a sudden overwhelming chill that made him shiver violently and almost buckled his knees—

The white man immediately *seized* up with an exhaling grunt as if he had been probed by something physical by the suddenly icy stare . . . His eyes glazed over, as a thin trickle of blood ran down his nostril onto his upper lip.

Then, the man collapsed on the shower's tiled floor into a heap like a discarded huge rag doll...

No question, Shake thought, *this guy is* gone.

But he was confused by the rapid sequence of events leading to the death. *I didn't touch him*, he thought, but knew he was somehow responsible. And then he glanced back at the entryway into the six-unit shower room.

Ahmaad was standing there, a towel around his waist; and beside him was Irvin Robinson, one of the ward's psychiatric technicians—a good guy.

Ahmaad turned and in a low-pitched but persuasive voice said: "Mr. Robinson, Shake never even touched that white dude, ya hear. Just stared him in the eye. That's all."

After a moment, the psych tech nodded slowly and agreed: "Yeah, from what I saw, that's exactly what happened. *No* one touched anyone."

As it turned out, there were no written charges filed over whatever happened in the shower between the PCP from Atascadero State Hospital and Shake.

There was an autopsy performed. And later during the formal hospital inquiry it was determined the visiting patient died, while taking a shower, of *sudden cardiac arrest*—an unexplained electrical stoppage of his heart.

During the next month, Shake quietly finished his sentence at Napa State Hospital and left formal custody after completing a little over four years of being locked up, but still facing another two years of supervised parole. Which made little difference to him, because he was leaving incarceration with an awareness of an amazing secret super power.

There was *no* doubt: he was the next step in human evolution.

And this realization fit perfectly with his new plans for taking over all of East Oakland's lucrative crime business.

4

EAST OAKLAND
THREE WEEKS AGO

Shake met with his old boss, Big Henry, and suggested he be given back his old job, and then put in line for a quick promotion, like maybe helping to manage one of the operations.

Big Henry thought it over, smiled, and agreed, holding his right fist out for a bump.

"Ya got it, man. Start collectin again, I moves ya up inna three or four weeks. Take over *The Track*. Baby Junior raggedy ass comin off bail then, goin back down, ya unnerstan."

"Sounds good."

Shake was staying at the Starlight Motel off of I-880, on the way to the Oakland Airport. Big Henry had driven out there to see him. After the brief business discussion, Shake walked his boss back out to his car—a customized 1959 pink El Dorado convertible.

Shake stopped short, surprised by the sight—a car he'd seen often in his dreams and would never forget, along with the animal-like screaming sirens.

"Say, hold up there a minute, Bigs."

Big Henry turned to face him.

"New car?"

"Nah, jus bringin it back outta bein inna a barn sittin foh years, ya unnerstan. Cool ride. Hoes dig it."

Shake didn't say anything, feeling himself harden.

Big Henry looked into Shake's suddenly dancing face, and a mesmerizing icy stare.

Click.

Shake felt like he'd stepped into a meat reefer...

And Big Henry looked like he'd stepped into that deep freeze with him.

6

OAKLAND TRIBUNE
THIS MORNING

Four Mysterious Deaths

Oakland Police found Henry Williams dead in his vintage Cadillac late last Saturday night in the Oakland Airport long-term parking lot. Cause of death has just been determined.

Mr. Williams is probably the first in a recent wave of mysterious deaths involving alleged East Oakland crime kingpins.

The four bosses have been linked to heading gambling and prostitution rings, and are responsible for the bulk of both China White and Mexican Tar heroin sold in the greater East Bay Area. All four of the alleged crime bosses are relatively young men, their ages ranging from 29 to 49.

According to Alameda County Medical Examiners, there is absolutely no evidence to render a verdict of death by foul play. Despite their relative youth and good health, each man suffered from a sudden cardiac arrest. A strange coincidence to say the least.

But the Tribune staff has just learned that the homicide division of the Oakland Police Department is continuing the investigation of the odd deaths further, despite Alameda County Medical Examiner opinion.

The authorities had no clue as to what had happened. But, the four deaths and the subsequent consolidation of power caused a shockwave to rumble through the entire Bay Area underworld. They soon knew *who* was responsible for the deaths.

··· — — — ···

7

STARLIGHT MOTEL
PRESENT

Shake finishes reading the article in the Tribune and smiles. These four are just the beginning, he thinks. He is going to finish consolidating his reign over the East Bay crime structure this afternoon by placing his three hand-picked lieutenants in charge of each newly defined accounting division—*Betting*, *Broads*, and *Dope*. Tonight, he has a meeting scheduled over in the Tenderloin in San Francisco with three Peninsula and North Bay top crime lords.

Before being driven over to the 'loin, he takes a quick shower.

Standing in front of the mirror admiring his nude, godlike image, he glares and asks himself: Who can stop me now from taking over all of NorCal bidness, and then very shortly LA and So Cal? "No one!" he answers with a dry chuckle—

But Shake is badly mistaken.

There is *one* person who can stop him immediately, *BigTime*, and Shake will recognize him instantly.

As he stares into his own eyes in the mirror, his face begins to dance, and he hears a familiar metallic *click* deep inside his head, and he feels the excruciating pain of an icicle being driven deeply into the sinus cavity behind his eyes; but he is unable to turn his gaze away...

01101111 01110010 01101001 01100101 01110011
00100000 01101101 01100001 01111001 00100000
01110011 01100101 01100101 01101101 00100000

DYSCRASIA

| ASHLEE SCHEUERMAN |

SHE LIVES IN THE CARAVAN. I might have let her stay in my two-bedroom house—more of a bungalow, really—except for our differences. They are insurmountable. I know this. I still suffer. I grieve for the distance, physical and emotional.

We meet on what passes for my porch, a protrusion of wood and metal with two low and greying couches facing one another. Dust clings so thickly to the flyscreen that the golden desert sands are a blurred mirage even in the cool morning. She always smiles. I have come to resent the glitter of her too-white teeth peeking between cracking lips. There is a tint of silver showing on her expression, and I wonder, not for the first time, if this is a symptom of her otherness breaking through.

The machine in her soul.

I hear her words like the quiet pitch of something mechanical. A buzz, a whirr. All in careful timing, repetitive, and somehow soothing in spite of the grating nature of her sonance. The content of her speech is what burns. She is gifting me with agony, and sometime amidst the litany of her vicious truths—what she believes is her honesty—she leans forward to kiss me. Her mouth tastes of disregard, and I wish the moisture on my tongue could turn this into something slick and easy, but in the end, we are sapped dry by the endless sands and her degraded humanity. I cannot exist with her, not on this plane, yet we still embrace.

I understand our being together is the proverbial blessing and curse. The salvation, and the bitter destruction. Our personal end-times. I let her press our hungry mouths together and find my thoughts straying, imagining probing tendrils growing from be-tween our lips, contorting and writhing, a Creation once within my power. Something critical wonders if this is the result of a bored mind. These... notions of genetic manipulation, scientific theories of harvesting and re-coding the function of cells, both regenerative and immunological. I am unsure if reality is a construct formed by an overactive imagination. Or, if our world had really become so much nano-alloy and microprocessors; silica, diamond, and light. All we could salvage after the side effects came on too swiftly. The violent damage control.

We part, and she cannot stay for coffee. She will return, never to enter my abode. The fruits of her roaming will be taken to the back of her caravan. I'm curious how she finds room to store eve-rything she brings in from the desert, but I dare not look inside for fear of becoming what she wants.

She tells me there is someone else, someone new. The way she speaks her name is with the same sensual familiarity of running a hand along the curve of a lover's bare hip and across the deepening warmth of their waist. The syllables linger in her mouth, cupped in the dip of her tongue where she shapes her sounds.

I hear myself ask, "Does your woman Create?"

The one thing I have lost. What I can no longer do.

I feel neither satisfaction nor relief when she says, "No." In-stead I mourn, unexpectedly, for this person I have not met. She does not know the treasured moment of godliness when shaping reality to her vision.

But if I were her, and I could do all that, would I lay blame on the external world or square on my own sagging shoulders? Would I doubt my own goodness and believe I was responsible?

I had the foresight. God knows, I saw the way we were losing the race to fill the cracks before the next, and the next, could spring into being. Before everything crumbled.

I emerge from my reverie and shatter imaginings of the other woman. There are just the two of us ensconced here.

She is already aware I am not interested in meeting other people, yet she asks all the same, wearing the smile I love and hate. I
wonder then, in the shadow of my previous musings, if I was the
one to mold the turn of her lips? Did my hands manipulate the clay
of her flesh in hopes of making a saint to abate my sins? Did I turn
her into the resulting sinister cynicism through the faults of my
mortal failings?

"I'm not in the mood to meet your friend," I had already muttered in the middle of my overwrought ideas. She nodded, understanding. The machination of her answer drives another wedge
between us, another shard into my heart. She kisses me as she always kisses me, dry, clinging, and leaves to fulfil her wanderings.

I do not watch her pass through the doorway, or flinch when
the metal screen clatters closed. My eyes do not follow her swaying
form or the thin dust cloud lifting from each footstep, yet I still
know the exact moment she has crested the rise and left the shallow bowl in which we live. When she is gone, I go inside. A grinding pulse, an artificial heartbeat welcomes me as I step into the second room. I did not even notice the journey through lounge and
hallway to get here, though the grease and ichor now painting my
limbs tells me I caressed the guns and stakes and knives lining the
walls on the way in to meet my destiny.

Violence is promised in the contraption, in the way it shudders
and the metal shines with a polished finish. I never clean; the surfaces devour any dust which tries to settle. Prints made in oil secreted from my skin are accepted and absorbed with the same zeal
of the machine's primary purpose.

I shed my shirt. My face is already drooping to blankness. The
drain over my heart is clogged from abuse and mutilations. I clear
away the detritus with a blade I discover in my hand, one taken
mindlessly from the passageway wall, sloughing away layers of scar
tissue and other unidentified matter until I am free to take up the
cold hose and connect the machine to my thankless body. True to

its design, the pistons and tubes suck away the emotions, the scars, the slurs, until blood and clots run through the silvered sewers of its construct, adding a bouquet of metal to the stifling air. When had the day's heat become unbearable? I gaze down at the raw port in my chest and wonder, when had I stopped being human?

She has brought me a new arm. Once, I would have believed her beautiful when the passion took her, even if I could have never understood the light in her eyes, the animation of her guarded face. She has so much strength of faith in the new ways of the world and tries, oh does she try, to convert me. I am an unwilling parishioner, not ready to turn my back on the analogue, the original, all the while the lies in my chest linger in the shadows of everything un-spoken. Her voice slows. Stutters. She has realised I am not buying, and for the first time this seems to pain her.

I look at my left arm with a detached sense of misery where it hangs by my side, useless, atrophied. The flesh is blackened. I am burnt, as we all are.

She is speaking again, saying the name of her woman in rever-ent tones. "She thought this one would work for you, if you'll but try."

"You said she doesn't Create," I accuse, with self-righteous condemnation ready to fling back into her lovely, frightening face.

"No, it's not like that. They're not medical. Not clinical. I don't understand all the details, I'm not clever like the two of you… But this is different. Something new."

The spectre inhabiting the metal hidden under her flushed, supple skin projects all the right amounts of emotion to try and appeal to my better nature. My attachment to the organic, and the person I used to be. But I hear the grind and sirens underlying her words, the pips and clicks begging me to restructure my reality to mesh with the rest. I sense the self-deception I battle daily, ready to trap me, to make me another casualty of this war.

"I won't become mechanised."

"You won't," she agrees. She has this purposeful way of mishearing my tone.

"I haven't been the same lately."

I think she is startled by the admission.

"I've stopped remembering."

I see her fingers tighten, a thread of tension creeping into her shoulders and up her neck until her slender jaw is taut and losing colour. I find myself imagining what her entire body would look like bloodless and dangling. She breaks my morbid daydream with drawn-out, overly cautious words: "Remembering what, exactly?"

I realise there is no need to answer her.

I no longer try to bring up the memories of what we could have done to prevent all this. We great men and women of science. Before we were forced to turn to machines. I allow the passage of time to shear away the sharpened edges of my guilt. I do not force myself to recollect the bright visions for the future which we nursed, or the muttered justifications we laid between ourselves to reassure the entire team that our intentions were good and every next step, every line crossed, would be worth it in the end.

We would eradicate suffering.

We would be the end of death.

I leave her alone on my porch with the appendage I cannot keep, dust settling into her hair like flakes of gold leaf upon brittle paper. I am all too ready to retire, to drain the bile bubbling inside me before all the hurts of our meddling in humanity drag me to destruction. I strip the clothing and overhanging flesh away from the gleaming port embedded between my nipples, the one concession I make toward the new way of surviving.

My parched lips crack when an ancient expression crosses my face. The wry twist of a smile.

01100001 01110011 00100000 01110100 01110010
01101001 01110110 01101001 01100001 01101100
00100000 01100001 01110011 00100000 01100101

THE RONDELIUM GIRL
OF RUE MARSEILLES

| EMILY B. CATANEO |

THE RONDELIUM GIRL performed at the Exposition Universelle in the first year of the new century. Maybe you saw her there.

She wore black velvet, and as she sang, her silk-and-cheese-cloth wings rose above her head, shimmering in turquoise and azure, magenta and ochre. The glow from the wings played over her smooth forehead, the delicate moles on her cheeks. The audience held its breath and I squeezed Andrei's smooth hand.

As she crescendoed into the song's finale, she closed her eyes, bent her knees, then rose into the air. Her velvet shoes floated two, three, four feet above the stage's wooden floor. The tops of the wings soared above her head, while the bottoms coiled around her ankles. The audience gasped, and she rose higher, pointing her toes and raising her arms as she hit that final note.

I didn't know what that moment would mean to me someday, that I would return to it again and again throughout my life: that sensation of sitting in the dark watching the Rondelium Girl fly.

Because I never saw her fly again. That night, she disappeared.

You still see rondelium girls once in a while, around the city. Some of them dance for coins in Montmartre, their wings ripped from years of pounding rain. One of them begs outside Notre Dame, her wings limp on the pavement around her.

You also see people who remember the rondelium girls, but who hate to admit to any involvement with them. Last August, as I ordered a drink in a basement café off Rue Mouffetard, an elbow jostled me. A portly man swiveled around: Gustav, who I'd known before his bald spot and broken veins, when we studied at the Sorbonne together, when Andrei and I first began our rondelium experiments.

He snorted. "Can I get a drink?" he shouted at the bartender.

I gripped his forearm, about to blurt out questions. Have you seen the original Rondelium Girl who flew at the Exposition Universelle ten years ago? Can you help me and Andrei?

He jerked back and knocked a glass off the bar. It shattered on the sticky floor.

"Don't you dare touch me," he snarled. "You're poisoned, aren't you? Don't deny it, you look like death. Serves you right, after what you—"

"So pious for a man who sat in the front row at the exposition, Gustav," I said. I hated him for that, him and all the students and professors who had once devoured our research on rondelium, who had clamored for more information about the rondelium girls after the exposition.

That night, in our flat in Rue Marseilles, Andrei curled in his bed like an empty sack.

"I saw Gustav tonight," I told him.

"I don't want to hear about it."

"He wouldn't speak to me, smug—"

"Katerina. I said no."

My lamplight fell on the shiny white warts limning his arms, his swollen finger-joints. He squinted his cataract-clouded eyes. "I don't want to hear about any of those people anymore. I'd rather forget them."

"But what if . . . what if *she* comes back?"

Andrei turned away.

"She would, if she knew how much we needed her. She probably doesn't know." The warts on my own arms tingled. "She probably hasn't seen the query I put in the Journal, or—"

"Give it up." Andrei draped his arms over his face.

I retreated into our parlor, where our rondelium had once gleamed in glass tubes. We had sold it long ago, to pay for the bread and wine that we needed through these long brittle years, before the current generation of researchers discovered that rondelium cures rondelium poisoning.

I knelt at the window, peered through the wrought-iron box overflowing with dead geraniums, at the empty street below. I rested my cheek on the lumpy warts on my left arm.

Someday, I imagined, the Rondelium Girl would return. She would appear on the cobblestones beneath that window, her wings glowing brighter than any streetlight. She would shout, "Katie, the keys, if you please," and I'd throw the keys to her as I always had before, in that long-ago spring and summer.

Andrei and I met the Rondelium Girl when she was just an ordinary girl, when we were just two students who had traveled west to study chemistry at the Sorbonne. We scrounged together enough francs to take a bus to the Bois de Vincennes, where a Ferris wheel cut through the sky across the lake, and my stocking scraped against cold pavement through my cracked saddle shoe. Andrei hummed the chickens and cows song, the one Mama had always sung when she'd churned butter. The smell of chestnuts wafted from one of the vendors.

"Chestnuts," I sighed. I rummaged in my pocket, pulled out a handful of lint and a button.

"Need to borrow some coins?"

A girl lounged on a bench near us. Cherry juice stained her white gloves and a pretty line of moles extended across her plump cheek.

"I'm sure I have some francs here somewhere." I patted my pockets.

"My dear sister has the endless capacity for hope," Andrei said.

"I'll buy you some chestnuts," the girl said, and before I could protest she had sashayed off to a vendor. Andrei stared at the curve of her shoulder blades above the back of her dress.

"Oh Andrei, what would Mama say? She's *French*," I joked. "Shall I pray the rosary for you?"

"Shh." Andrei jabbed me in the ribs.

The girl returned, handed me a paper packet of chestnuts. "I'm dreadfully bored; you'll have to forgive me for accosting strangers in the park. Mama and Papa are off with my siblings and I'm left all alone."

I bit into one of the chestnuts. "Come with us, then. Andrei and I were going to ride the Ferris wheel."

"No, you said you wanted to ride the Ferris wheel. I said I wasn't going anywhere near that death trap."

"You'll miss out on your first chance to fly? Come on."

"I ... I'm game." The girl lifted her chin. "It looks rather dangerous, doesn't it?"

We cajoled Andrei into joining us. The girl paid for our tickets and we crowded together three to a seat—we were all slender-hipped and lanky in those days. As we reached the wheel's apex and the trees and hazy roofs of Paris spread before us, with the brand-new Eiffel Tower puncturing the clouds, the girl emitted a tiny delighted laugh.

There are some days, moments, memories that play in our minds as though we are watching a motion picture. When I close my eyes now, I can see the girl's cherry-stained gloves, as though I could reach out and touch them. I can feel the pavement scraping against my foot and taste the meaty chestnuts on my tongue.

As August crept into autumn, the cataracts clouded Andrei's eyes.

"Look, I'll find one of your favorite books," I said, rummaging through the stack piled next to his bed. "Here, Crime and Punishment."

"No."

"What about this?" I pulled out a yellowed newspaper, its edges crumbling. "The article you wrote about how rondelium promotes weightlessness and the—"

"No." Andrei jerked up in bed, his cloudy eyes focused on a spot three feet to my left. "She's gone. Even if she did come back, I wouldn't be able to see her."

"Unless she cured—"

Andrei's swollen fingers clamped into the warts on my wrist. "She's not coming back." He dug harder into my skin and I ground my teeth. "I'm sick of protecting you. Chickens and cows, chickens and cows, well, you're not a little girl anymore. She's not coming back. And you know what, Katerina?"

The clock ticked.

"You don't believe it either."

"Yes I—"

"No, you don't," Andrei said. "Because you haven't tried very hard to find her, have you?"

Andrei dropped my wrist and wrapped himself in dirty sheets.

I fled the apartment. Out of breath, I emerged on the embankment and raced past the shuttered-tight bouquanistes, towards Notre Dame's glowing jewel windows.

The truth is, Andrei was correct. Yes, I had placed the ad in the Journal. I had spent long nights dreaming about her return. I had tried to ask Gustav if he had seen her.

But in the ten years since the exposition, I hadn't done more than that.

Because I clung to the theory that she didn't know we were poisoned, that she had no idea I watched the street every night dreaming of chestnuts and Ferris wheels. If I found her and she refused to help us, it would destroy me.

But Andrei needed her, and so I approached the plaza that sprawls before the cathedral. Most of the beggars had left for the night, but against the stones of the cathedral, blue glimmered, like a moth in the dark.

I charged forward. It wasn't her, of course: this rondelium

girl's nose curved hawkish. Her wings trailed bedraggled around her, ripped, glowing.

"Please, alms for the—" Her eyes rose to my face, and her lips curled back.

My stomach churned. I remembered her. Victoire. She had screamed loudest of all of them. Then she had written that article, about the pain, about how she had become poisonous, about how she could hover above the ground, but not truly fly. It had turned everyone against us.

"Have you seen her?" I said.

"Why should I tell you that?" Victoire unfolded, rose. "Why in God's name would I help you?"

She whipped around. Through the hole in her ripped dress, her wings protruded from a maw in her back, fresh blood gleaming on the metal stitches.

"It never healed," she said. "It never healed."

The sound of an accordion trailed from one of the bridges. Someone laughed loud, by the water. I wrapped my arms tightly around my chest.

We hadn't meant to hurt them. I hadn't meant for the wing-wounds to remain raw forever, or for the flying experiments to falter and fail. I hadn't meant for them to poison their beaux and mothers and brothers with the rondelium. I thought the eager girls who visited Andrei's and my flat to receive their wings, after they saw the Rondelium Girl at the exposition, would soar over Paris' rooftops, shining effervescent, not wilt begging before Notre Dame.

"I am sorry," I said to her bloody back. "I am. I really am. But Andrei is dying. I know your wings can heal us, because only rondelium can heal—"

"I will tell you where *she* is, if you'd like," Victoire said. "Do you know the Bois de Vincennes? She's there. She lives under an abandoned Ferris wheel. Oh, you think I've had a change of heart? Don't. Go see her. You'll find out. She despises you too."

She grinned, feral, and melted into the shadows.

I walked down the embankment, over glittering bridges and broken sidewalks, limping through the pain in my hip that's sprung up in the past five years. I stopped at a vendor and bought a packet of chestnuts, but they tasted dusty, as though the shells had gotten mixed up with the meat.

I leaned over the railing at the Pont Alexandre, my heart pattering with the knowledge that I knew where she was, that I could go see her right then, if I wanted to.

I stared at the Eiffel Tower around the bend of the river. From that distance it was easy to pretend it was still new, a shining gleaming symbol of possibility, instead of just a metal tower, vandalized with chewing gum and rusting against the night sky.

"Rondelium. It promotes weightlessness on objects and people in close proximity." Andrei closed his eyes and kissed the side of the Rondelium Girl's head. We browsed in a bookstore by the river, brushing shoulders with other Parisians wearing cotton in the July heat. "The scientific applications..."

"Weightlessness? So it could cause objects to simply blow away like feathers?" The Rondelium Girl's heavy pale eyebrows rose.

"Not exactly," I said, "It decreases a person's weight enough to promote flight." In those days, I spent so much of my time in the laboratory with rondelium that I felt rather weightless myself: I could see all my veins like handmade lace through my paper-thin skin, and I could leap down Rue Marseilles with my feet barely touching the ground.

"Ah, yes." Andrei picked up a book off a table: that copy of Crime and Punishment, the cover slick and the pages unfolded. "The rondelium girls."

"Girls with rondelium-infused wings," I said. "Andrei and I have been working on the prototype all year, and we're preparing an article for the academy. We think we'll make the wings of linen, a layer of rondelium, then a thin coating of glass."

"In the cities of the future, the rondelium girls will be integral as—" Andrei said.

"They'll be able to fly, soar like … like beacons of tomorrow," I said. "Beautiful."

Our Rondelium Girl grinned, and under the glow of her smile, the rest of the bookstore dimmed into dust.

Andrei and the Rondelium Girl may have been engaged, involved in that kind of love, but I've always believed that she and I truly knew each other, deep inside of ourselves. For example, that night, Andrei stayed at the café late, and the Rondelium Girl and I climbed the rickety fire escape behind the building on Rue Marseilles and sat on the roof, deep in the throes of a July night, as we did so many times that summer.

"I've been thinking about what you told me earlier, about the rondelium girls." She wrapped her arms around her knees, tilted her head to the glowing sky. "I can imagine, in just five years, us sitting up here and watching them soaring through—"

"I think about that all the time."

"Do you think it would be dangerous? Like the Ferris wheel?"

She cocked her head so the lights from the city leapt over her cheekbones. She had lost weight since she came to live with us on Rue Marseilles.

"Of course, but—"

"The best things always are, right?"

"It could be you." The words tumbled out of me. I knew Andrei had thought it too.

"Sorry?"

"You could be the first rondelium girl."

"What … me? You think I could?"

"Of course. You'd be perfect for it. You're charming and you can sing and carry yourself."

"You … you think so?" She turned to me, grinning. "I could be the one flying, out there. Why, I could—"

"You'd make history. You'd be the most beloved girl in Paris."

"Katie, I can't imagine how wonderful it would be—you think I...When can we begin?"

"Well, Andrei and I are still conducting experiments on the best ways to make the wings and the best ways to attach them, but we should be finished by early autumn."

"The best ways to attach them." Her brow creased. "Will this ... will it hurt?"

"Of course not," I said, and I had no reason, back then, to believe otherwise.

"Hmm."

She shot me a strained smile, and I continued to describe how the world would adore her once she became a rondelium girl. But she answered me curtly, and soon after she said she was tired, and retreated downstairs to the flat, while the first autumn wind blew and blew and blew off the clouds above me.

Andrei and I had not spoken since our quarrel. I sat on the bed beside him, stroked his hair off his forehead. His stomach bloated under his shirt.

Rondelium. The element that promotes weightlessness and we thought would promote flight ... after Andrei and I left the Sorbonne in disgrace, the next generation of researchers discovered that exposure to rondelium and then lack of exposure to rondelium disturbs all the body's systems, as the bones hollow and then refill, as the skin thins, then grows tough and warty.

I stroked Andrei's forehead, wishing we had never sold our rondelium, wishing she would return to us, wrap him in her wings. I sang him the song about the chickens and the cows. I had never sung it to him before. I imagined his lips moving, his voice chiming in before the chorus, bellowing about the chicken that tried to fly.

But he didn't even open his eyes. So I shrugged into my woolen coat, left the flat and hurried down Rue Marseilles while rain whipped against my face.

··· — — — ···

"You're sure it won't hurt?"

She studied her stained gloves, instead of the two pieces of silk, cheesecloth, and glass that dangled from metal rods in the corner of the room. Autumn rain lashed the windows outside and we hadn't lit our lamps, so the wings glowed the colors of the rain.

"After it's done, you'll be able to fold them up or extend them at will, see, because of these." I ran my fingers over the steel supports that trisected the wings. We had already tried strapping the wings onto her back using a harness, but she had failed to achieve the proper control that way. It had been Andrei's idea to try alternative methods in our own laboratory, away from the watchful eye of the academy.

"Do we have to do it tomorrow?" she said.

"You need time to learn to fly before the exposition."

"I'm not sure I—"

"I think you should sing while you fly. Something modern, none of that old-fashioned nonsense, and it'll be—"

"I'm not sure I want to do it."

Rain against the windows. How could she not want this opportunity? This was the chance of a lifetime, and I told her so.

"What if I decide I don't like them in a few months? What—"

"I promise you'll like them. Everyone will want to be like you."

"Why don't you do it?"

Why didn't I do it? I can't remember now. I must have had a good reason. I must have been needed for the procedure. I must have known she would make a better rondelium girl than I would.

My reason couldn't have been fear. When I was young I was fearless. That's why she and I first became friends, on the Ferris wheel. I told her as much, that I had thought she wasn't afraid of anything, and we quarreled until dusk fell outside.

Then she left. She didn't come back all night, and I paced the laboratory in the dull glow of the wings while Andrei sat in the corner with his head in his hands.

But at dawn she appeared in the sun-washed, rain-slick street below. I found out later that she had spent the night riding the Ferris wheel, staring at the city lights until they burned into her retinas.

"Throw down the keys, Katie," she shouted. "I'm ready."

Blood speckled the backs of my hands. She didn't scream. Her face was buried in a pillow, and besides, we had pressed an ether mask over her mouth, so the pain must have been dulled. It must have. Her shoulder blades contracted and Andrei pressed down on them, keeping her still, while I dug the curved metal needle through her skin, binding the steel rods against her spine with metal stitches. A line of soft moles dotted the skin of her back. I inserted a needle through one of them.

Andrei hummed the chicken and the cow song, and I snapped at him, "Don't distract me, Andrei, I need to concentrate," and he said, "I'm not singing it for you."

Did we deserve what she did to us? I sliced a needle through her back, turned her into poison. But then she abandoned me for ten years—on the night of our greatest triumph—leaving me to these warts creeping over my arms, leaving me to wonder whether she's alive, what she thinks about on summer nights without me. We loved each other, but we hurt each other so much.

And yet, I clutched onto hope that someday, if she knew I still loved her, still needed her, she would return to us and heal Andrei and everything would be the same as when we were young.

I nursed that hope as I disembarked at Bois du Vincennes and struck out across the park, my hip aching. I walked and walked, wending my way past the ghostly serpentine to the skeleton of the Ferris wheel. Half its yellow seats had been stripped away and chestnut trees twined around its frame. I wrapped my hand around the metal. It chilled my hand through my glove.

"I know you're here," I shouted. "Where are you?"

On the other side of the Ferris wheel, light fluttered.

Velvet whispered.

I don't know if you've ever stood outside under a canopy of trees searching the night around you for someone you once loved. I don't know if you stared until the planes of the night resolved into a person, or if you gave up and returned to your empty house.

But that night, as I stared, the shadows beneath the ripped yellow seat became a girl. Wings stuck jagged out of her back and their silvery glow illuminated a black velvet cape, a line of moles on a gaunt cheekbone.

I faced her from the other side of the Ferris wheel. I whispered her name, her real name: Juliette.

"Andrei's sick," I said. "He's sick and dying, and if you ever cared about him at all, you'll come with me now to Rue Marseilles and help him."

The lights from her wings shifted over the packed dirt.

Then she turned and ran.

I wobbled beneath the ruined Ferris wheel. I had seen her. I had told her. I had dreamed of this moment for ten years. She knew everything now.

And she had run away. Victoire had been right. All these years, she had stayed away because she hated us.

The worst had happened, I thought, and I walked home hours later with a very different poison spreading through me, a black cloud of the cold disappointment that comes from believing in someone, and having them let you down.

But the worst had not happened yet, because by the time I returned to Rue Marseilles, as you might have already guessed, Andrei was dead.

I sat by the window in my shabby black dress after the public cemetery funeral. I tried to eat a chestnut that I had purchased from a vendor but it tasted ashy, rotten.

Do you know what it's like to attend your brother's funeral alone? To read his obituary detailing his role in a cruel experiment that ruined so many lives? To sit by the window knowing you will never again hear him—or anyone—sing *the cow told the chicken, you'll never fly*.

At first, I thought she was an apparition on the street beneath my window. I had imagined the moment when she would appear there so many times, so many different ways, that when she walked down Rue Marseilles in her black velvet cape, her wings glowing behind her, milkmen and ladies alike shrinking away from her … I turned away from the window and bent to sort the stack of books on the floor.

But then the front door jiggled, and she stepped into the flat.

I stood up slowly, clutching a stack of books to my chest.

Crow's feet creased the space around her eyes. Her hips had widened and her face had resolved into something older, harder. Her skin was so pale it was almost translucent. The moles looked angry and black, and thin hairs grew out of each of them.

"An old man let me in." Her voice had grown thicker and throatier. "I suppose Monsieur Jacques doesn't live here anymore?"

I didn't speak.

At last she said, "It's good to see you, Katie."

My cup of coffee shook in my hands; hers stayed untouched on the wooden folding table between us.

"You've been in the papers," she said.

"We were," I replied. "But that was years ago."

What do you say to someone when so much time has passed, so many years filled with so much triumph and pain? I told her that, and she twisted a smile.

"I feel the same."

"So why? Why did you leave when you did? And Andrei … if you had come back earlier, he …"

I think I truly did despise her in that moment, just as I despised Gustav, and all the pious people of this city—you perhaps—who turned against us. After all, if she had emerged from under the Ferris wheel that night, she could have saved Andrei.

But how could I despise her when behind the crow's feet, the girl from the Bois de Vincennes still glimmered?

"I didn't want to see you, after everything," she said. "But I'm so sorry that Andrei...you know how much I loved—"

"Then why didn't you—"

"Don't interrupt me." She pursed her lips. "I'm here now."

She was. She had come back. She would heal me and stay with me and I told her as much, told her that we would set everything right back on track, but she shook her head.

"I'm not staying."

"What?"

"We can never go back to that first summer. The innocence..." She shook her head.

"No. It can be—"

"Katie. I don't think you understand what you and Andrei did to me."

"Yes, but you abandoned—"

"Will you listen?" She had never shouted at me before. "You grafted wings onto my back, permanently. You turned me into a monster, a not-human. Do you know how I've lived these past ten years? Financially?"

"No," I whispered.

"My family has paid me to stay away from them. Katie...you and Andrei destroyed me."

You destroyed me. I bowed my head and allowed myself to acknowledge for the first time that she was right, that my young carelessness had broken the girl I loved. Yes, she had left me, but only after I had ripped her apart.

At that moment, I wished she hadn't returned just to glow in my living room, just to remind me that she still existed and had stayed away for all those years, just to tell me that I had no one to blame but myself.

"I know," I whispered. "I'm sorry. I shouldn't have done it. I should never have done it. I know you can never forgive me, but—"

When I looked up, she loomed close to me. She extended her wings so they scraped against the ceiling and dragged against the floor, as they had at the exposition. She clamped her arms around me and her wings ensconced both of us. The linen touched cool against the back of my neck, the metallic smell of rondelium filled my nose, and the warts on my arms burned.

I closed my eyes and pressed my head against her shoulder. My skin tingled and the poison drained away and in that moment, so did the past ten years, the years of gray hairs and sickness, of loneliness and disappointment. I held that spring and summer in my hands, that day in the Bois de Vincennes, those nights whispering with her on the roof. I cupped it and blew on it as though it were a candle that would shimmer forever.

At some point the pressure of the arms and wings left me, and I sank to the floor.

When I opened my eyes again, the flat no longer glowed soft silver. She was gone.

That was last autumn. I haven't seen or heard from her since. My warts have come back, crawling over my arms, and my hair clogs the drain when I wash it in the sink.

But she came for me once, listened to my apology, restored my faith.

And what else do I have?

So I wait at my window every night, rubbing salve on my arms. Any day now, she'll cross the cobblestones. She'll wave at me, and I'll throw her the keys, and she'll wrap me in her wings and my skin will become smooth again. Maybe we won't ever fly, but we'll climb to the roof and her wings will flutter in the wind, and we'll stand with our toes over the edge of the roof and hold hands and feel as though we're soaring.

She will bring me chestnuts, and this time, they won't taste like ash on my tongue.

01110110 01100101 01110010 00100000 01110100
01101111 00100000 01110100 01101000 01100101
00100000 01100010 01101100 01101001 01101110

THE ANGEL CHASER

| ERIK T. JOHNSON |

"Every angel is terrifying."
– Rainer Maria Rilke

HAD HE CRASHED THE CAR? Didn't everything twist, shatter, dazzle? Yes, but his hands remained firmly on the wheel; he was disoriented, but still driving along the road. It hadn't been a crash. It was some other awesome, instantaneous event. How galaxies and afterlives begin.

But it had started like any other Sunday. Archie Mitchell had been taking Elsie and his Sunday school kids toward Gearhart Mountain for an afternoon of picnicking and fishing in Sprague River. In the next instant the Angel appeared, hovering just ahead of the Plymouth. A switch in his brain had been not so much flicked as ripped out of him, so it couldn't ever be reset.

DF-11...I take it the project's gone wrong.

Yes.

How bad, DF-11?

You and I probably won't recognize each other by the end of the week.

Isn't that the opposite of bad?

Listen, it wasn't my idea to redeploy on a global scale.

You're the lead scientist.

And you're the lead, DF-12. So what now?

I don't know. Any ideas?

I think we should go over the original, 1950 experiment, step-by-step.

Twist, shatter dazzle...

The dirt road was uneven, choppy as the New Testament; Archie's eyes pointed skyward. He drove fast and the car rumbled, shaking everyone up and down like newly sprung jack-in-the-boxes. Tall Oregon wilderness rushed by the open windows like great, green waves coalescing in aftershock. It was Weyerhaeuser land far from battlefields, where trees once milled for 1944 wars waited to become 1951 textbooks and jury duty summons and grocery receipts, suicide notes, love letters, spitballs and speeding tickets, and newspaper headlines for who knows how many more decades.

HAPPY NO YEAR!

TIMES SQUARE EMPTY, QUARANTINED FOR 2020!

Through his half open window, Pacific wind buffeted Archie's graying hair.

"Where are we going?" Elsie asked. "This isn't the way to Gearhart."

"Quiet," he cautioned.

She lowered her voice to a considerate whisper that made him feel she was talking down to him:

"What's wrong? Where are we going?"

All right. Where is the critical starting point?

You know as well as I do, the first mistake was delivery to subject.

Via compass needle?

Correct.

That's been a matter for debate for—

—Sixty-nine years, I know, I know. But I've done some new studies.

OK DF-11, go ahead.

The Angel was spherical and erratically sped parallel to the choppy road. It was blue, as perfectly matched to the sky as a stray drop of paint to its can. It had the hermetically sealed curves of the O in Only and was the size of remembered childhood trampolines, storybook illustrated moons. It was a sign that pointed to itself and then, when you followed it, you… he didn't know.

It was difficult to explain.

Or rather, it didn't *need* explanation.

It didn't matter that Elsie or the kids didn't perceive it. That meant nothing. Nobody but Archie could confirm the harmless stinging in his fingertip, where he'd accidentally pricked it this morning. Wasn't that realer than scenery, or doubt?

How was that trivial event connected to the Angel? Why was this incident so clear in his mind, as though it had been momentous, or inescapably familiar, like the landscape of a pitch-black room?

It was just after breakfast. Elsie was taking forever in the bathroom, the faucet turning on and off at inexplicably irregular intervals and correspondingly random intensities. The pregnancy was five months on and she'd grown increasingly lethargic and anatomically impractical, bloated with amniotic fluid and wishful thinking.

He'd been rummaging through the top drawer of the dresser for his good watch. He mistook the crescent gleam of his grandfather's compass for the Timex. The compass was in junkyard shape and long missing its glass; and he'd stuck his thumb on the sharp arrowpoint of the bent compass needle, angled away from the face toward undiscovered nebulas since 1903.

It barely hurt, less than half-aspirin pain. Why did he remember such commonplace bumbling as though it were an entire life's turning—

—Because the no-time "duration" of the compass needle puncturing his fingertip was identical to the instantaneous moment in which he spotted the Angel.

So what if he was the only one who saw it?

Nobody could see anyone else's pain, but all humanity agreed that was no measure of its reality.

OK. That could be significant. How much do we have left?

Six, seven hours, tops.

What's funny, DF-11?

I apologize. Just that, we're talking like we're going to die in a few hours, you know, and meanwhile, that's exactly what we're not going to do.

You think it's funny, racing against immortality?

"Slow down, Arch," Who-Was-She? said.

Quivering May sunbeams striped her round belly. Hard to believe she'd once been so skinny. When he'd met her, she was a pale shade of troglodyte, eating scraps at one of the soup kitchens where Archie volunteered. She didn't talk much. He helped her find a waitressing job and a room. He saved her because she was worth saving and she was more grateful to him than he'd expected, and he couldn't forget her gratefulness. Their courting, marriage, and consummation had each been sudden. But doesn't everything that happens, do so instantaneously?

Is slowness just tedious alacrity?

They'd settled down into a pleasant domestic rhythm. One day no Elsie, the next she was at his side, reading in a bed that finally felt the right size. He loved her. It was like a whole life had been pulled out of a magician's hat.

Yet rarely, but frequently enough to slip into his head when he wasn't concentrating on any one thing in particular, Archie felt instability threaten beneath this tranquility. He'd had similar misgivings before.

For example, that time in 47' ... or was it '46?—after the East Pittsford Dam collapsed. He'd taken a flight to Virginia—no, that's not right—to Vermont, that's it—to help the flood survivors rebuild their homes. When a tiny stewardess whose slight moustache was ameliorated by a frank smile learned his reason for flying, she had him upgraded him to first class. At first he was delighted. He relaxed comfortably into his seat and dozed. But every now and then he'd snap half-awake, a kidnapping victim wavering in and out of consciousness in the trunk of a dark, unfamiliar vehicle. Any minute, cruel, brisk forces could sweep through the sky and erase his journey, his intentions.

He couldn't slow down. Was it even possible? He had to reach the velocity of accidental puncture, startling needle/skin time keeping pace with the gait of Angels. For some reason, the speed with which the unearthly creature had appeared to him was no less important than the Angel itself.

On either side of the bumpy road, dark pines leaned into and across each other with a spiky, carelessly resigned attitude. The Angel rolled on quiet as a cloud. The woman next to him said nothing; but her silence was ingratiatingly patient and compelled him to command:

"Quiet!"

Have we reached murder-point yet?

It's started. Just look out the window of this ivory tower for once. Even from Floor 299, you can hear the blood. It's trying so hard to be quiet.

How many, I mean, city-wide?

Over two-thousand at last count.

All right. So remember there is the question of the unexpected attack on the subject. The consequences to his nervous structure. We factored that in this time around, but it's worth looking at again.

Let's hear it, DF-11.

Follow, wherever it goes. Drive until your wheels are wings.

The car swerved, almost cut off the road into the living wreckage of trees.

In the rearview mirror the kids were unnaturally still, not just outwardly but inside, like pipes clogged with indeterminate refuse. 80-mph wind rushed around them and set their hair wagging and shirts flapping. The youngest was eleven and the oldest thirteen; Archie had baptized each of them: Jay, Sherman, Eddie, and the Platzke kids, Joan and Dick. He couldn't remember what they looked like as babies. He could recall these years clearly but flatly, without emotion, as though reading the chronological sequence of events in a textbook timeline.

"The kids are scared, Arch."

The words hardly registered, staccato jabs of syllable-tips within the impatient rotation of a radio dial.

The Angel dropped hit-and-run low, left the road and led the way across a field that broke violently upon them as though heaved from a bucket. The Plymouth rocked and rattled through tall, verdigris grasses after the spinning form. Archie vainly strained his eyes, the better to see it.

"This isn't like you."

Isn't it? he thought... *What is like me, anyway? Stay calm—you will find out, soon* ... Her words passed by, increasingly insignificant, a parade of monochrome lipsticks in a rotating drugstore display. He wasn't sure if the voice had just been in his head.

He didn't look at her but noticed a slice of That Kid in the mirror. Poor kid, whose parents had drowned when he was only six, who Archie had taken under his wing, tried to set upon a good path. The troubled boy's dark eyes were in a deadly staring contest with a large red marble, a fine shooter, words locked inside it as he turned it over and over in poorly washed fingers. The Angel dipped roadwards and Archie swung past an elk carcass, wheels burning the = of an unearthly equation in the dark, muddy ground.

"Arch! Stop, the kids ..." the woman said in a helpless whisper, as though urging characters on a moviescreen to be careful.

The Angel raced forward.

The car was too heavy. They'd have to lose some cargo to catch that Angel. He had to be brave and that called for precise, resolute action. That fat woman was staring straight ahead at the windshield in front of her, numbly, as though the glass was the outermost surface of the block of ice in which she was encased. Archie took his right hand off the wheel and pushed her toward the door as hard as he could. To his surprise, it didn't take much force, easy as dunking a hand into a sinkfull of water. The door swung quickly open, as though erupting outwards under immense pressure, and she tumbled to the rugged shoulder softly, like a doll with limbs half-full of helium. Without looking, he pulled the door shut, and with disinterest teetering on obliviousness, Archie heard kids screaming, just snatches of faraway rollercoaster plunges.

The red Plymouth tore through the air like a missing person's name called into a black night. In a dazed way, Archie was aware he was lost, though the word seemed somehow anachronistic. He was driving across a large, overgrown field cobbled with mud/rock/ treestump. He'd gone far off the road. They could've been in another country, but it didn't matter: like the pervasive light of a neon sign, the Angel colored the living and the landscape into a singular atmosphere, shrunk wide distances to freckle.

Then the car sputtered and came to an almost catapulting stop. The slightly balding top of Archie's head gently grazed the windshield. Out of gas. Unaware of the blubbering of baptized children, he fumbled with the door handle for an interminable feverish moment before tumbling out, rising to his feet, and running toward the Angel.

A falcon or dragonfly wheeled in and out of Archie's blindspot. His neck hurt. The Angel had decelerated. It whirled sluggish but fiercely, an 1893 Tesla fantasy coughing up purplish sparks that hung suspended in the air like shards of amethyst, a frozen, alien storm.

Archie was running, something hard hit his forehead. He stumbled, intense but diffuse pain cutting his confused thoughts in half, and his face went into dirt.

He looked up. It was Eddie, who Archie had spent the last several years mentoring away from arson and nudist magazines. He'd thrown something red; it lay a few muddy inches from Archie's face—he briefly thought he'd lost his clown nose until the marble came into focus.

Eddie charged him, shoelaces untied, mouth open and screaming some battle-cry he couldn't possibly have learned anywhere. Archie flinched and put his face back into the ground. The screaming stopped and nothing happened. Had Eddie run past him? Archie turned around to an empty field. It didn't make sense. In any case it was a chance to catch his breath.

He sat up, using his shirt to wipe blood from everywhere but his eyes, as though all seeing was done through burning salt, normal as blinking or disgust.

So then, naturally we reach disappearance-point.

Right, the boy—Eddie in the 1950 file.

I still don't see how we're getting anywhere.

We've got nothing else.

OK. Might as well finish. There's what, less than three hours left?

The Angel was gone or hiding. No matter; it would come back. Archie would wait as long as he must. He looked to the left and saw towering Weyerhaeuser trees, and to the right more of the same. Well, he thought, and he cried. He couldn't say why, exactly. It was like being sick, throwing up and not knowing if you'd got the flu or food poisoning.

The air was too cold, like it was starved. The crying stopped. Archie didn't know how long he'd sat there in the unmapped mud. He fished in his pockets for a tissue like a hand feeling for a watch in an old dresser drawer. He pulled out a crumpled dollar from his pocket. He thought he dropped it, but it was stuck to his bloody palm.

Ah, here's the paper. Look at this, DF-11:

UN BOMBSHELL: 60% OF WORLD INFECTED WITH VISIONS!

What paper?

Had he crashed the car?

Didn't everything twist, shatter, dazzle?

His head ached, his neck couldn't turn; there seemed to be glass in his eyes, metallic lacerations in his skin, and he felt an angry sensation in his gut that he guessed was internal bleeding. But it wasn't a crash. It had been some other instantaneous, destabilizing event.

Do you really think the world is ending, DF-11?

Yes. I mean, we may live forever but we'll be clueless, won't we? And where will we be living? The Nieman Hypothesis: Where do the disappeared go?

Never proven conclusively. But, the effects might wear off. We're almost out of time, and it looks rotten and sad out there. But still, how can you be sure?

I'll tell you when it's over, DF-12.

Do you think this is a joke?

Arch got up and ambled over to the Plymouth. The doors were closed but the kids were gone—Dick and Joan Platzke, little Sherman, timid Jay and even Eddie. There were no tracks in the moist dirt leading away from the car. It was like they'd never been there. He opened the trunk. No kids, but damn, he'd forgotten to fill his spare gas can. He'd forgotten his name, too. Who was he? He crouched and looked under the transmission. He even searched under the hood.

It was amazing.

How could anyone disappear that fast?

I don't know.

So help me God, if you say that one more time!

The Angel!

It was an awesome, instantaneous event. How galaxies and afterlives begin.

01100100 01100101 01110010 00100000 01100011
01110010 01101001 01110100 01101001 01100011
01110011 00100000 01100001 01101110 01100100

PSYCHIC SHOCK

| IAN SHOEBRIDGE |

I DON'T TALK MUCH THESE DAYS. Too many hours sweeping up the debris of dead memories and decayed feelings from the streets—stagnated hopes, rotting piles of disappointment. All negative emotions leave a physical residue on their surroundings and, unchecked, will build up in thick, pungent layers and spread acrid clouds of contamination. They need to be cleaned off, scraped up and disposed of.

Dealing with psychological debris alters your relationship with humanity, fostering cynicism and isolation. You inhabit a different world; you don't have the luxury of being oblivious. Delicate equipment reveals the ugly layers of emotional effluent hidden to others. You soon learn to see it without the scanners. They employ people like me because of our sensitivity; a whole industry of neurotic, psychic garbagemen.

I was called to clean up a murder scene. A large old building that even in daylight seemed to be under a shadow. A young woman answered the door.

"Oh," she said, with a curious look, "here already?"

The interior was dark and cold. I took some readings on my instruments. The murder had apparently taken place in the living room beside the staircase. I sensed an oppressive atmosphere that confirmed the measurements on the equipment, and there were some grubby marks on the carpet. (A visible residue is not unusual.) The meter was in the blue. This was minor but still grim: a personal tragedy, usually murder or suicide. I got to work cleaning.

The young woman was staring at me oddly. "What a strange job you have. What are these machines?"

"This scanner detects emotional resonances in the environment—a sort of empathic Geiger Counter. Once I've located the source I start cleaning it off with this device here, which sends out sub-aural vibrations to break down the residues."

"So the residues are vibrations?"

"No. They're a medium all of their own. We don't fully understand what. This is just the best way to remove them."

She introduced herself as Patricia. She lived alone, worked as infrequently as she could. She said her boyfriend had recently left her. She still felt in shock. She couldn't understand why he would turn his back on all that was going right merely to pursue a vague feeling of incompleteness.

"I should get back to cleaning up the murder."

She stared at me in astonishment. "*Murder!* Why *are* you here? I called for a house-check, because of the residue near the stairs."

"Yes," I said. "That residue is characteristic of a murder."

She shook her head numbly. "It hasn't happened *yet.*"

I was mildly surprised. People are chosen for this job for their hypersensitivity. Sometimes you can get ahead of yourself, so to speak.

I worked for a leading company in the psychtech industry. As well as an international leader in research and development, it liaised with the government to coordinate a comprehensive national psychic-health plan. The government subsidises many of its services for poorer communities; psychic hygiene is in everyone's interest. At the time of these events the company was engaged in discussions for a merger with an even larger international corporation.

I was smart enough to pursue a more challenging career, but I had no motivation. Something drew me to sweeping work, grimy and unfulfilling though it was. Perhaps it was that I got to spend my days mostly alone.

As I was returning my equipment to the central offices, I was called by my supervisor.

"We're facing an epidemic," she said. "You remember we were contracted by the government to do a survey of health-residue correlations nationwide. The preliminary findings are in, and they're worse than anyone expected. We're all a lot sicker than we thought, and the city is filthy despite our efforts. So the government has commissioned us to do more research. I'm to choose a person from each division. I'm taking you off sweeping for two weeks. You'll start this right away."

"What do you think is causing it?" I asked.

She shrugged dismissively. "The psychic residues littering the streets, clogging the drains, polluting the air, jamming the sewage system—that's what! It's getting into people's homes and building up like fine layers of dust. It's causing record levels of sickness and psychological malaise. Obviously our current sweeping programs aren't enough."

"I meant, what's causing *that?*"

"We have no theories yet. We're open to any ideas you come across in your investigation. This commission could lead to increased government funding for the company, if we show a plan to combat the problem at its source. So use the expertise of your area to investigate the origins of this unprecedented level of psychological effluence."

When I got home I opened the medicine cupboard and searched amongst the bottles for the right dream. "You are a rock star ..." No. "A night with your Dream Lover ..." I was saving that one. "A luxury holiday in tropical paradise ..." That would do. The descriptions were ultimately irrelevant; it all came down to imagination, if you had any left. I swallowed the pill, lay down on the bed and tried to forget.

With enough dream pills, I thought, I could exert complete control over how I felt. My moods would be as modifiable as the clothes I wore. That was my goal. I was tired of waking in the grip of some alien bad mood that no activity could dispel. You need to feel moderately good if you are to get anything done, and my job was intermittent in providing job satisfaction. So I had a slight recreational dream habit, but I saw it as a necessary indulgence. Excessive use can do odd things, but in moderation they are safe—if not thoroughly healthy.

Marden had helped design the prototypes of the sweeping equipment we used. His research had established that emotional damage left measurable physical residue. He had retired a few years ago after disputes with the leading psychtech companies. We used to chat when he came into the offices to run training sessions on equipment use and repairs, and I found him friendly and perceptive. I thought he might offer some insights into the "epidemic."

Marden offered me a morning tea platter of stale cake, tasteless biscuits and bitter tea. I told him of my assignment. "My boss thinks it's an epidemic. Is the world getting meaner?"

"Probably, but that's not the reason," Marden said. "That's a symptom. We're collectively experiencing a chronic shortage of happiness."

"You talk as if it's a finite resource."

"It's a budget, and we're not breaking even."

Marden explained, "We used to think emotions were created and experienced entirely within the brain. But my research suggested the opposite—emotions are formed in the environment and exist *externally* to us. We receive, register and interpret them. Think of the brain instead as a *decoding device*. It interprets external stimulus into recognisable symbols—experiences, moods, memories, 'emotions'."

I argued, "But the brain *can* produce its own emotions..."

Marden shook his head. "We know from electro stimulation that the brain can produce emotions, but it also produces visual hallucinations. What you're talking about are emotional hallucinations—misinterpreting the stimulus. External emotions are not restricted by physicality, although they cling to contexts. They move, drift around like clouds. This is why they're so hard to study; they are rarely consistent or repeatable. The exception is when there is emotional damage. Then, the emotional residue becomes entangled with the physical environment and becomes subject to physical laws. I'm seeking a *genuine* haunted house; this would offer a consistent subject to test my theories."

"Perhaps you should visit the house I saw yesterday. It's haunted by a ghost from a future murder."

Marden nodded. "I've noticed causal discrepancies with residues: years late, or too early, without reason."

"So, Marden; something has caused imbalance in these external emotions and we're feeling the effects?"

"It's a feedback cycle. More research is required—but instead, they send you. No offence. But with their resources, you'd think they could do more to find a solution, if that's their goal."

He extracted a thick folder from the bookshelf. "Why don't you make a visit to the Infinite Dream Factory, Ltd? I obtained a copy of their environmental report. There's a discrepancy between the raw materials and end product. Something doesn't add up."

The Infinite Dream Factory, Ltd. was the largest dream manufacturer; its products could be found in every home. The main factory was located in the industrial district.

My job had long ago convinced me that places have moods, strong enough to affect all the residents, subtle enough for them to adjust without noticing. An oppressive vortex of negative emanations swirled here, worse as I neared the factory.

Management were surprisingly accommodating to professional visitors. I was taken on the tour; but I was increasingly disturbed by what I saw. The dreams they produced were made out of cheap filth, under appalling conditions. The waste materials were a foul, toxic substance that gave off poisonous waves of gas, and the factory produced gallons of it every hour. The PR officer showed me their disposal techniques. "We dump the waste products here," he said, "the Bottomless Pit." A hazy gas thickened the air and distorted the view across the pit, where six or seven thick pipes emptied muddy effluent. Around the rim an oily black substance had spilled. A terrible cloud of hot smoke and gas rose from the pit.

"That's very convenient," I remarked, nauseated. "Bottomless pits are hard to come by."

In the far corner there was a "Jesus figure" tied to a cross, being whipped. "To alleviate any discrepancy in the psychic field," explained the officer, "we need a sacrifice and scapegoat."

Beyond my visceral disgust at their techniques, the dazzling oxymoron of means and ends left me confused. I started writing my report, but all I had was a bad hunch. I took a dream pill and tried to forget what I now knew about these.

Probably it was the toxic gases at the factory. I came down sick with something the next day. Work insurance covers me for psychic illnesses like these. I went to see a music doctor.

Music can reach directly into the soul and initiate healing in ways that bypass the nervous system and frenzied thoughts of the brain. But it is necessary to choose music aligned with the specific emotional centre, which will resonate with the individual in a positive way. A trained professional can help you choose the perfect music for the problem.

The doctor was a kindly old gentleman with a pierced lip and black hat. He listened to my complaints and did a quick search of his database. "Sounds like you need something strong, pulverising and nihilistic," he diagnosed. "Have you tried this? Toxic Blood Syndrome's *Last Empire*. It's an over-the-counter album; you've possibly heard it."

I nodded. "Didn't hit the spot."

"You really are into the harder stuff!" he said with a curt smile. He turned to a black vault in the wall, twisted a silver combination dial to open it. "This record is very powerful—one of the darkest, heaviest releases by *Everlasting Damnation*. Only available by prescription." He waved a CD cover done in various shades of black and depicting an Ecstasy-rotted brain. "It should purge you of what you are feeling and start the healing process. But I must warn you: the first three people to hear this album threw themselves off a building within days."

I assured him my tolerance was high enough.

"Listen no more than twice a day, for two weeks. After that come back to see me if you're not better, and I'll prescribe you their follow-up, commercial album; although, it's not as good."

I paid another visit to Patricia. An image of her had been lingering in my mind like a mental afterglow. And she showed no surprise at seeing me. She let me in without a word, but her glance suggested endless hidden thoughts. She was a mysterious girl, and I was intrigued.

Aren't all relationships extensions of the transactions of need, power and resource? If so, is it wrong to be sincerely opportunistic? A succession of disappointments had left me a scavenger for tender moments, picking off the scraps and discards of romances that had uncurled like old wallpaper, savouring any glimpse of momentary comfort, however fragmentary or meaningless the context. It seemed irrelevant who or why, only that it was a transitory phase, a placeholder for something greater I dared not reach for—not even knowing where to look.

I don't believe that I used her.

Patricia owned several cats. There was much about her behaviour that resembled those cats, as though in her reclusive existence she had assimilated their body language. Questions never answered as though unheard, strange glances at me that no words would fit, mysteriously leaving the room on sudden secret errands, staring into empty space as though in alarm at a sound only she could hear. What was her secret?

"Oh, the world has some terrible secrets," Patricia said evasively. She claimed rarely leaving the house gave her a more comprehensive perspective on the outside world.

I liked the silences between us as much as our cryptic conversations. I felt comforted by these intimations of solitude. For a moment it seemed we were in mirroring arcs of our respective orbits, in a central moment of time in which all events sent endless ripples backwards and forwards. When I kissed her it meant as much as I wanted it to.

It was dark by the time I was ready to leave.

"Ah, no, you can't leave now," she said, looking alarmed.

"Why not?"

"There are ... things around outside at night. Bad things. It's not safe."

"Bad things?"

She stared closely at me with almost predatory intensity. "Tall people. With dark suits and odd walks; they *pick* at you. I've seen it happen. I've been noticing it for several weeks now. They pretend to check the gas or drop off mail—but at *night*? They're no good. Trust me."

"I want to see this!" I said, darkly intrigued.

"You don't. They can sense you watching. They'll close in."

"What do they do?"

"I'm not sure. They grab at you. Then let you go. You'll be confused and sore after. Don't go out. It isn't safe."

I peered out the window into the darkness, but I couldn't see anything. "I guess I'll have to stay, then."

"Yes, I guess you will."

She had some dark secret. In the middle of the night there was a phone call. She turned on the lamp and reached out of bed.

"Hello? Yes. No. Really? Ok." She hung up, looking troubled.

"Who was it?" I asked.

"Prank call," she said.

··· — — — ···

Back at the main offices, an executive from the Pre-Assurance Division wanted to see me. His office looked like a library—files and folders covered every wall. He began quite friendly.

"Do you know much about the Pre-Assurance Division?"

"No, it's outside my area."

"Do you understand the work we do?" He rose and walked me along to a viewing window. "We have in this hall three hundred automated typewriters working twenty-four hours; psychic seismographs that measure all fluctuations in the vibrations city-wide. We liaise with the patrols and coordinate the alarms sent to sweepers like yourself. But our machines are more powerful than that, and their applications more complex." He adopted a confidential tone. "We also use them to measure *future* disturbances. The Pre-Assurance Division aims to anticipate problems for the company, and to avoid them."

He led me back into his office.

"We believe you're going to stir up trouble."

"For the company?"

"For yourself." His tone was neutral. "You've been assigned to investigate. Naturally, we want you to do your job to your best ability. But the Pre-Assurance Division is concerned that you're looking in the wrong place…"

I disagreed. "I think the Infinite Dream Factory, Ltd. is deeply implicated in the cause of this epidemic."

"We're convinced you're wrong. Try another avenue. Let's be honest—your behaviour over the last two weeks has been erratic. An illness, a romantic entanglement, an unsolved 'future-murder'…"

I was shocked that I'd been under surveillance.

"And the rest of your case history inspires no more confidence. If certain parties do not like your report it would not be hard to discredit you."

"You're telling me I can't investigate them?"

"We are advising you. The Infinite Dream Factory, Ltd. is one of our major clients. Your position here would be jeopardised."

"I believe this may be more important than one person's career."

He sighed, impatiently; I was wasting his time. "So you think you can 'make a difference'? But I called you here to let you know you are nothing of importance and will never amount to anything."

"Well obviously I am of some importance if you called me in here personally to inform me of that," I replied. The man looked flustered.

"No, you don't understand," he said. "See all these files behind me? Everything you have ever thought, ever said, will ever do, has already been written and documented in our files. Our machines have pre-empted you. It's a security measure we take on many employees. You are of no significance when all your achievements have been stolen. We have all these volumes to prove you are of no consequence."

"But obviously I am of great consequence if you've filled a whole room with documentation on what I am not going to achieve."

The man was getting angry. "You seem to be missing the point. We've got every word you'll ever speak coming out on a single automated typewriter. Every thought you *will* think we've already read. Any action you try to take we've already predicted and blocked. So give it up!"

"If you've already blocked it you wouldn't need to advise me to give up," I reasoned.

"We want to save resources," he said with a shrug.

We couldn't see each other's point so I left.

He had unwittingly given me a lead. I looked up company records of the nature of our services to the Infinite Dream Factory, Ltd. I found contracts for long-term equipment lease of several PSI13 devices. These were some of our most powerful and expensive equipment, used for emergency cases when it was necessary to drain all the emotional residues from a place, at the risk of physically destroying the site.

I had seen its maximum effects once. The government wanted to rebuild an old hospital, and they needed the land sterilised. It was so contaminated by residue no one could work there. The machines targeted the building. Shadows appeared out of nowhere, cast by unseen figures, like those of the eyewitnesses to atomic blasts, black halos burned into the stone. Afterwards, the stones crumbled to dust.

What could Infinite/Ltd. want with these?

It was only a few days later when I had my first *slip*. My head buzzing, I fell into the spirit world. The walls of reality blurred, the streets and buildings became bleached, colourless. A panic took hold of me that no running or decisive action could alleviate. Things didn't *feel* right; the shadows and lines took on a new edge of menace. The psychic trails I would normally wipe up in my job glowed vivid now with ominous significance, and I could see them everywhere: a triple layering of past, future and present, echoing endlessly like the glowing blue feedback loop of a television camera filming its own feed. I could see the ghosts of everything, the intertwined significance of every major event. And I could see the night figures: tall spectral creatures with angular joints and hooked, parasitic heads. In the daytime they hid in shadows, waiting.

In a rush of colour and vertigo I returned to reality, wondering what had just happened.

The attacks continued daily. I took refuge in dream pills and visits to Patricia.

I also became interested in the works of Abbott Hershner, an occultist who had postulated a spiritual hierarchy feeding upon humankind. Humans were the meeting point between the physical and non-physical. Just as below us stretched the material 'food chain,' above us existed a *spiritual* food chain. Hershner had imagined it much like the illustration of a tree in which the branches mirror the roots. But we are at the bottom of the spiritual hierar-

chy. We are cattle, farmed and exploited for our emotional suscep-
tibility. We are such stuff—the plankton and bacteria—that dreams
are made on.

It was a vicious economy bartering dreams and emotions.
Hershner pictured angels and demons, faeries and elementals, feeding off humankind—and each other—to ultimately create more
spirits out of the raw feelings. The emotion would pass up the
chain, developing all the way as each new spirit digested and pro-
cessed it, until it reached the level of 'God,' where it would be
granted independent life as a spirit befitting its accumulated characteristics, thus completing the 'life' cycle.

Hershner suggested that 'God' could be as much our creation
as we are Its, since It feeds off us. A perfect living reflection
achieved by divine symbiosis.

A careless remark about the spiritual potency of human sacri-
fices led to outrage and condemnation of Hershner, and he had
retreated from public life until his death. The majority of his writ-
ings had been destroyed, but his ideas survived.

I visited Marden again. I felt I had a new understanding of the
epidemic and wanted his opinion. He offered me sour orange juice
and mouldy scones.

"Could these external emotions be *alive*? Maybe there is a
whole ecosystem of intangible mental states feeding off each other
in a pattern that mirrors the animal food chain? *Could it be they are
parasitic?*"

He shook his head. "There is no evidence for any of this.
You've obviously been reading the works of that crank Hershner."

I disagreed; I thought this explained perfectly the existence of
the 'night people.' I told him of my recent experience, the *slips*.

He frowned. "I wonder if they're launching a psychic attack on
you. They could easily do that with the equipment in the Pre-
Assurance Division. They'd remotely project an intolerable force of
negative emotion at you—enough to destroy your mind."

I told him, "But Infinite/Ltd. has leased equipment from us.

They are as capable of carrying out psychic attacks. And they have a better motive."

Marden shrugged. "As far as I'm concerned, all these corporations are indistinguishable."

"You think my company would try to kill me?"

"I already suspected the Infinite Dream Factory, Ltd. was bribing your lot, who were then investing heavily in it. I suspect their entanglements go deeper still. They are both keeping each other in business, after all. That's the parasitic symbiosis you should be looking at. A psychic epidemic will give both companies all the work they need; indefinitely, once they've reached market saturation and we're all addicted to dream pills."

"I had no idea they were so ruthless."

"Why do you think I retired?" he said.

"Have you solved the 'future murder' yet?" Patricia asked me with a wary smile as she opened the door. She gestured. The residue was worse than before. It was getting darker, despite all my cleaning. I looked it over with morbid fascination. You can't clean up after a murder that hasn't happened yet, any more than a snake can disappear by swallowing its tail.

"It's not always a physical murder," I admitted. "Sometimes it's psychic shock. Similar to when the body goes into shock. Your emotional self receives critical trauma. You die, in a sense, but not physically. You carry on, but not as the same person. It happens all the time, unnoticed. So perhaps we'll never learn what did this. We may not notice."

But, glancing back, I could see the psychic trails I had left in the house. I couldn't be sure I wasn't wiping up my own future pain—a dying animal drinking its own blood.

Looking at the growing stains below the stairs, she said to me, "It is going to happen tonight, isn't it?"

"Yes." I also had sensed something—an ominous psychic significance in the air, a pregnant stillness.

"The night people are out now—lots of them," Patricia told me. "I can feel when they're about. They're sniffing around outside. When it gets dark they'll try to come in."

"How can we defend ourselves?" I asked her.

"What about your cleaning equipment?"

I pondered. "If they are parasitic emotions, we could repel them temporarily."

But these were just toys compared to the resources of psych-tech companies.

I dialled Marden's phone but he didn't answer. I left a message.

It was getting dark. I retrieved my equipment from the truck and set up a line of defence around the living area.

"Here they come," said Patricia.

We peered out the window and watched them going from house to house, like tall spectral postmen.

They were getting closer. Leaning in through windows. As we watched, the shadowy figures stepped in through the walls, without any resistance. They moved smoothly across the living room, like afternoon shadows in a time-lapse—growing and advancing, multiplying and spreading at high speed. They hesitated at the machines.

They left a slimy trail of black residue behind them—invisible to untrained eyes. It reminded me of the slime surrounding the Bottomless Pit at Infinite/Ltd. This prompted me to recall a line of Abbott Hershner: *Dreams are the currency of the spectral world.*

I thought I understood. "Infinite/Ltd. has disrupted the spiritual hierarchy. These night people—spectral parasites—are a predator introduced to an unprepared ecosystem."

Patricia shook her head as we backed away from the advancing grey figures. "I don't understand. And what are we going to *do*?"

My phone rang. It was Marden. He sounded pleased. "Sorry, I was out. I've finally found a genuine haunted house!"

He wanted to tell me all about it, but I cut him short. I explained the situation, while Patricia pulled me back into the hall, back from the moving shadows.

"Lucky for you I've made some breakthroughs just today. The haunted house confirmed my theories about semi-physicality. Ways to block a psychic attack ... You'll need to modify the equipment. Adjust its operating frequency. You want to approximately mimic the frequency of brainwaves during dream states ..."

I dropped the phone and lunged for the equipment. The night people were keeping away from the machines, but I'd have to turn them off to carry out the modifications. I worked as fast as I could. As I glanced up, one of them was poised over me. It made a swipe at my head. For a second, everything blurred.

I turned on the machines.

Instantly they were repelled. They retreated smoothly back the way they had come. The night seemed to grow less dark as the shadows scampered away.

I picked up my phone. "It worked," I told Marden.

"Yes. It looks like I'll have to give Abbott Hershner another read." Although he was joking, Marden sounded begrudging.

I tried to explain it to Patricia. How the ecosystem of predatory spirits had become unbalanced by psychtech companies over-farming raw emotions, so that only predators of negative emotions could thrive, perpetuating the imbalance and leaving humanity weak and vulnerable to psychic attacks.

But she didn't understand.

"Where do you get these ideas?" Patricia asked, shaking her head. "I've never heard anything like it."

I gave up trying to explain. I needed to write my report. Perhaps if the authorities took action against Infinite/Ltd. and the other dream companies, the spiritual ecosystem might repair itself. I thought of my confrontation with the Pre-Assurance Division. They said I threatened the company's future. Perhaps that meant I might succeed.

I told Patricia I had to go.

Patricia nodded vaguely. She was watching the windows, but the night creatures were staying away.

"It's over," I said, reaching to hold her.

She tensed up. "Yes. Yes ..." There was a painfully awkward pause. "I'm sorry. I meant to tell you before."

I looked at her, stunned.

Her ex had returned, she said. And all was, if not forgiven, then certainly not decided. Thus the late night calls. She wasn't comfortable with this anymore, she said.

I realised the delusions I had fostered, and their comforts fell away. She was more important to me than I had admitted, intended, or been prepared for. I felt waves of something draining out from me, psychic blood spills spreading to meet the stains on the floor, as I seemed to stagger numbly and fall in shock and stare up from the floor where someone, something, had once died.

PEPPERMINT TEA IN ELECTRONIC LIMBO

| D.J. COCKBURN |

RAY MARKEN COULD HAVE SWORN the tiles surrounding the hospital room were the whitest things he had ever seen, until he saw the teeth of the rep. Her smile pinned him to the bed as a biometric reader appeared in the rep's hand.

He took the reader and scanned his retina. The sleeve of the hospital gown slid down his arm. The rep glanced at the blue patch of a tattoo, faded beyond all recognition. Ray tried to remember what it had been. Things often slipped his mind these days. Not that it mattered when the prostate cancer would kill him long before his mind went.

He pressed his thumbs to the reader to complete the transaction. "There, if I'm accepted, Afterlife Inc. will receive my full estate to hold in trust for the maintenance of the servers."

Nothing wrong with his mind when it mattered.

He met the rep's eyes. She would be the last human he would ever see, and he wanted some kind of connection with the girl, but his gaze skidded off her professional smile. He sighed. She was on the upside of fifty, which he guessed made her a girl to a ninety-nine year old man.

"Thank you, sir," she said. "Now if you'll keep still..."

She placed the helmet over his head. Green lights flashed in her spectacles from one of the new retinal tracking systems. The girl's eyes refocused on Ray.

"We're connected," she said. "Remember what we said? You'll

feel a bit funny at first, but you'll be in the interview room almost straight away."

"Cool."

Her smile bathed Ray in indulgence. Who said 'cool' anymore? She closed the faceplate. Ray's senses switched off.

Pain vanished.

Losing his constant companion was so disorienting that it took a moment to realize he could not sense the bed. He did not even know which way was up.

An unfamiliar sensation made him flinch. It felt somehow human, although it engaged none of his five senses.

Hold it together! The command bellowed from within himself, but he had no idea where. A life in middle management gave little experience of barked commands.

The human sensation returned. He forced himself to relax into it. There was something reassuring about it, he realized. The echo of the command subsided. Edges began to form in darkness. The sensation resolved into a voice. "It's okay, Ray. Don't panic."

The voice was reedy but reassuring, like the voice of the oncologist who had told Ray he had a few weeks to live.

A light in the darkness became a window. A rectangular block became a coffee table. A dark mass became a sofa. White-painted walls solidified around him.

"Can you see me, Ray?"

Ray did not see where the middle-aged man had come from, but he belonged perfectly in the suburban living room, right down to his paunch. His long-sleeved shirt looked comfortable, as though it was his idea of casual attire.

"You're resolving nicely," said the man. "Please have a seat."

He gestured at an armchair and Ray sat without really knowing how he did it.

"It takes the brain a few moments to interpret the signals, but you seem to be adjusting well. You were warned, I take it?"

"The rep said I'd feel a bit funny."

"Oh dear, that was rather an understatement, wasn't it? I suggest a cup of herbal tea. It usually helps."

"Tea? How?"

The man settled himself on the sofa and waved at a teapot that Ray did not remember seeing before.

"Peppermint or chamomile?"

Ray blinked, gathering his thoughts.

"Peppermint, please."

"Excellent choice."

The man poured from the teapot and handed Ray a cup without a teabag. Ray tested it with his lips, but the tea was the right temperature and tasted of peppermint.

"Good," said the man. "It helps to engage all the senses as soon as possible. Now we can get started. My name is Pete. I'm the doorman for today."

"You're doing the interview?"

"Well, yes, we have our formalities. Though this is a little more than a formality, if you follow."

Ray placed the cup on the saucer. Something looked wrong. His hand was a blur with a few finger joints.

"Don't be alarmed," said Pete. "Your self-image is taking some time to form, but it's quite normal."

"My self-image?"

"Let's say you won't want to look in a mirror for a while. Not to worry, I'm sure you'll harden out in a few moments. Shall we begin?"

Ray nodded.

"That door," Pete pointed behind Ray, "is the door to Afterlife. If you go through it, this model of your consciousness will be uploaded to Afterlife's servers and you'll join us in, well," Pete gave a deprecating chuckle, "immortality, really."

Ray turned to see an ordinary white plywood door. There was no keyhole in the handle, and the wood looked too soft to hold the screws of a bolt very firmly. Ray felt a flash of contempt for anyone who would depend on such a fragile barrier. But then, he thought, it wasn't a real door so it wouldn't need a real lock. He turned back to Pete and took a sip of tea.

"Would you believe some people have tried to break down the door?" Pete shook his head. "We like to make a little test of it."

"A test?"

"You've seen our brochure of course, but you can't begin to understand how Afterlife works until you've been at least this far. Our emotions are not contained by our bodies, as in pre-life."

Ray felt his lips twitch. "Pre-life."

"Well yes, in our bodies. We have to be careful who we let in. People prone to anger, people carrying any sort of unresolved angst, even people with poor social skills ... well, you have to keep in mind a consciousness only functions if it's continuous. Backing it up doesn't work, so any sort of disruption could make the cat among the pigeons seem rather benign."

"That must limit Afterlife's intake."

"Very much so. You might call us a rather exclusive club. Of course, you wouldn't have got this far if your records had shown any obvious problems. You were born in nineteen fifty, so you'll be in good company. The technology came at the right time for the last of us baby boomers. You went to Pennsylvania State College sixty-nine to seventy-two. You weren't drafted?"

Ray remembered typing his final dissertation on an ancient PC, once top-of-the-line. He was conscious of something about the memory that did not add up, but he concentrated on Pete.

"No, my number didn't come up."

"Then you went into human resource management?"

"My whole working life."

Ray remembered filing cabinets giving way to servers as his hair receded. He tried to remember further back, but the memories would not come. Instead, he vaguely remembered stilted buildings burning to the sound of helicopter rotors. His mind flinched from the odd image. It must have been a movie he'd seen once.

"Married of course," said Pete.

"Yes, for fifty-four years."

"But not until you were forty. A little late, perhaps?"

Ray remembered Mary laughing as they counted the wrinkles on each other's bodies. "Worth the wait."

"A happy marriage, then?"

"Oh yes."

"Good, marital troubles are hard to leave behind. Now I have to ask you this, and I hope you won't be offended. How do you feel about her being rejected by Afterlife?"

A blur of emotions flickered through Ray. He remembered sitting by Mary's bedside, holding her hand as he watched her eyes close for the last time.

He took another sip of tea. "I had the chance to say goodbye to her properly. I'm happy with that."

Pete nodded. "Some men might feel some bitterness. If you'd had some idea of spending eternity together, it must have hurt to be refused?"

Ray met Pete's gaze. "No, Afterlife was a new idea at the time and we hadn't thought that far ahead. Anyway, I'm not given to strong emotions."

An image of a gun aimed at the back of a kneeling man's head flashed through Ray's mind. The gun did not waver as it blew pieces of skull and brain in all directions. Ray could not remember where the image came from. He had never liked violent movies.

Pete smiled. "Excellent. You seem to have coped very well with losing your wife. Are there any other sources of trauma in your past? Particularly painful bereavements? Episodes of depression? Harrowing experiences?"

As Pete spoke, Ray felt something probing his reactions that had nothing to do with Pete's gaze. He summoned memories of suited men and women shuffling papers or tapping keys. He became aware of an itch in his memory rather like an incipient sneeze. If he ignored the urge to sneeze at an embarrassing moment, it usually went away. The technique seemed to work as a post-human.

Pete sat back and smiled. "Yes, we've all had our altercations with the helpdesk, but it hardly scars us for life."

An image through the eyes of a man lying on his back, vision blurred by drugs and pain, leapt into Ray's mind. He somehow remembered the movie was about a man being interrogated for the location of Mujahedeen commanders in Afghanistan and that he had seen it in 1987, but he could not remember whether it was on television or in a theater. A man in the image threw a switch and dissolved the memory with a white flash.

Ray focused on Pete's smile. "I think I can manage not to strangle any IT support I run into in Afterlife."

"Good to hear. I see your self-image is developing nicely."

Ray held up a hand. The outline was indistinct, but he could no longer see through it.

"I think we've covered everything," said Pete. "You'll find the door unlocked if you try it. Some people like to have a last look at pre-life, but it's entirely up to you."

A thrill of excitement simmered through Ray's sense of calm. He drained the cup of tea and stood. "No, I think I'm quite ready."

"Then welcome to Afterlife. Please do remember what I said about keeping emotions under control. It takes some practice, but it becomes second nature after a while."

Pete opened the door and stood aside as Ray stepped onto a lawn. People milled around tables covered by print cloths and plates of finger food.

An overweight man smiled and held out a plate. "Are you a newcomer? Please join us. Care for a cucumber sandwich?"

Ray looked around. This was Afterlife? A bunch of fat people at a garden party? The sandwich tasted as bland as cucumber sandwiches did in reality. Other people turned toward him, and Ray found himself the center of attention.

"Now, now," said the man with the plate, "let's not crowd our new friend. We all felt a bit odd for the first hour or two."

He turned to Ray. "Please do try a vegetable kebab. It's not as though we're in danger of running out. Ah, I see your hands are almost complete. That's excellent. It will be nice to know if you see yourself as fat and middle aged as the rest of us."

People laughed as though they had heard the quip before but still appreciated it.

Ray held up his hands and narrowed his eyes at the scarred knuckles and plain gold wedding band.

"I must say, I was rather disappointed," said the fat man. "I'd been warned, but I still rather hoped to find myself looking like, oh I don't know, Bruce Willis in *Die Hard* or someone else *thin*."

That brought another laugh, which Ray heard as though from a great distance. The sneeze-like itch was back.

"Oh really, Charles," said a woman. "You talk such nonsense. Wasn't life so much more comfortable when you stopped fighting the waistline and settled into middle age? I don't think any of us would have gotten through the door if we hadn't felt that. Besides, I might have risked my marriage with, what was that Englishman's name? Hugh Grant. But Bruce Willis? Please!"

Ray was vaguely aware of attention slipping away from him as he remembered the face of the man he had once called Lieutenant, now as creased as his own. He couldn't understand how he had forgotten meeting him, only a few days ago.

"Know why they washed her out, Marken?" the memory of the Lieutenant's voice was sharp and clear. "She'd picked up too much of your trauma. You probably didn't talk about it much but she felt your pain and made it her own."

Ray chewed the kebab. What trauma? Ray had spent his life in a happy marriage with an undemanding job. So how had he known a man named Lieutenant?

"They won't touch any of the guys or anyone close to us," the Lieutenant had said. "All those years we bled for their fat asses. Now they slam the door in our faces."

Ray was vaguely aware that the man named Charles was speaking to him again. "Oh my, you seem to be something of an exception. Did you really look like that? You must have practically lived in the gym."

There was a nervous edge to the laughter this time, and Ray noticed people edging back from him. Ray looked down at a white T-shirt covering a toned torso and combat trousers on his powerful legs. He ripped off the T-shirt to see the scars where the KGB had attached the electrodes. He lifted his arm to see the eagle's head tattooed on the bicep, over the word AIRBORNE.

Charles put down the plate and waved a nervous hand. "I ... I'm sorry. There must have been some mistake. You don't look at all comfortable ..."

Ray felt a flutter of nerves in his stomach, but somehow knew it was not his own fear but Charles's. It felt like a violation. How dare these pathetic people infect him with their fear? He found himself looking for the point where a blow would crush Charles's windpipe.

Charles clutched his throat and sank to his knees. The buzz of conversation died as people looked at them.

What had the Lieutenant said next? "No one could handle interrogation like you, Marken. Hell, they worked you over for a week in Kabul and you gave them nothing. You musta hidden everything from yourself or they'd have got the whole lot out of you. You can do the same again. When you were discharged, the army buried your record so deep it's probably never seen a computer. There's nothing to say you were ever even in the army. Even your tattoo's so faded nobody can tell if you got the bird or Nixon's ass. You're perfect. So how about it? One last black op?"

Ray held up his wedding ring in front of his eyes. The gold gleamed, almost mesmerizing. The people backing away could have been on another continent. He pressed the ring to his lips. It was as if he had opened the sluice gate he had so carefully constructed to keep the first thirty-eight years of his life at bay. Memory roared into his consciousness like a Niagara of pain. Everything from the first time he'd killed and seen friends killed as a dumb kid in 'Nam right up to spending a week strapped to that table in Kabul, forcing his mind to stay blank while the best interrogators in the business worked through the text book.

He looked around the people gawping at him. He remembered Cambodia, Iran, Nicaragua, Zaire and all the other places where he'd sweated and fought so these people could treat him as an embarrassment when he came home.

Charles writhed on the ground. Wrinkles on his face faded and returned as he became a teenager one moment and an octogenarian the next. People a little further away held their heads and moaned.

Ray remembered staggering out of the helicopter when he was exchanged, and the breakdown afterwards, when his mind filled with every moment of horror and terror he'd suppressed since that first firefight in the paddy fields.

Charles's face blurred and disappeared, leaving nothing but a pile of clothes.

Ray remembered the peace he found when he met Mary. He even went to college to sink himself into the inconsequentials of middle management. Mary had been his angel. These people had condemned her because of him. He became hate. He became rage. He became every moment of pain he had ever felt or inflicted. He was a scream of emotion.

It was exhaustion that ended the moment. Ray found himself standing by tables of food, surrounded by piles of clothes that had once contained post-humans. He smiled at the thought of the consternation among Afterlife's flesh and blood management and wondered how long it would be before they switched the whole lot off and Ray Marken was no more. He hoped it wouldn't be too long.

He poked through the plates until he found a bacon sandwich. It was better than the cucumber.

00100000 01110000 01101000 01101001 01101100
01101111 01110011 01101111 01110000 01101000
01100101 01110010 01110011 00100000 01101111

SECOND CHANCE

| JOHN R. LITTLE |

MARK STEVENSON SAT IN HIS CAR on Center Street in Aynsville in upstate New York. The town had a little over 12,000 residents so there was never a serious traffic jam, but today it seemed like it was taking forever to get anywhere. Beside him on the passenger seat of his eight-year-old Camry sat a wooden box.

Mark glanced at the box every few minutes, crazy thoughts passing through his mind. Chief among those thoughts was whether he should have put a seatbelt around the box.

He shrugged as the car in front of him inched forward. There was construction in front of the First National Bank and Trust. Oncoming traffic was being diverted and the cars in front of him waited in various measures of patience for their turn to move through the intersection.

"We'll get there soon enough," he said. "Not much of a hurry anymore."

He looked at the box again. It was a dark brown with a hand-carved swirl pattern on the top. He hoped Kim would have liked it.

The box was a foot wide and another foot long and about six inches high. It was heavier than he had expected.

"We'll be home before you know it."

He reached his hand over and caressed the top of the box. It felt warm, so he clicked on the air conditioning.

"I miss you."

His heart hurt as he said those words, but he didn't cry this time. It felt like he'd been crying all week and maybe he didn't have any tears left to leak out.

Traffic was still snarled, so he put the car in Park and rubbed his eyes. A new song from Maroon 5 played on the radio but he barely listened. They had been Kim's favorite band and now he wished he'd been able to take her to the concert at Madison Square Garden last year.

He'd never gone ice skating with her.

They'd never had kids.

He'd never even officially proposed marriage, but they both knew it was only a matter of timing.

He'd never taken her back to her home town. For that matter he didn't even know the town name. It was somewhere on Trinidad, or maybe Tobago.

They'd had the whole rest of their lives to do these things. Unfortunately, the rest of Kim's life was over, since she'd been run down by a crazy drunk driver a week earlier.

She'd been 26 years old, same age as him, and she was the only girl he'd ever loved.

"You'll still be with me forever, babe," he told the box.

Mark had already cleared a place on his book shelf for Kim. It was the bedside table on her side of the bed. He'd moved the book she'd been reading, along with the couple of home decorating magazines she'd kept there, down into one of the drawers. He'd see her every night as he crawled into bed.

He knew he'd say good-night to her each night and tell her he loved her, and every morning he'd wake up with a "Good-morning" for her.

Nothing could ever change how much he loved her.

The cars ahead of him continued to stand still, as if they were all sleeping. Mark craned his head and could see a couple of workers directing a small earth-mover into position.

"Won't be long now, babe." He caressed the box again.

The radio was playing some commercial, and suddenly he realized he needed to listen.

"... so, if you've made a mistake or need a do-over, come on down and see us at 193 Central Avenue. You really can have a second chance."

Second chance…

He'd heard the commercials before, but never really paid attention. His life was perfect as it was, because *Kim* was perfect.

Now she was gone.

He remembered the first time he saw her amazing smile. It was at the public library. Almost nobody borrowed books at the library anymore, but Mark loved wandering through the stacks and smelling the musky odor of the thousands of books waiting patiently for somebody to read them. The library seemed like his private realm, and he went there every few weeks to wander around and pick out a few mysteries.

Free was a good price. He couldn't really afford to buy books.

He'd finished perusing one aisle and walked around the end of the rack, turning to go up the next, when he bumped into her. He jumped back in shock, not having realized anyone else was around.

Mark must have looked pretty goofy because the girl burst into laughter, her wonderful broad smile filling her face.

He started to laugh, too, and stuttered an apology.

"No worries. I get lost in books, too," she said.

She may have been the most beautiful girl he'd ever seen. Her black face was full of laughter and had a constant smile for him. Her hair was an intricate pattern of braids and beads, and he knew in an instant she was miles out of his league.

But, it didn't end up that way. Three months later they were living together in his small apartment in Aynsville.

Now, two years after that, she was dead.

193 Central Avenue was a small building on the edge of town. He'd driven there almost with no thought, and with no serious hope that the ads he'd been hearing could be true.

What did he have to lose, though?

Nothing. He'd already lost everything.

SECOND CHANCE. He studied the sign over the door and entered, carrying Kim inside her box. He wasn't sure if he was taking the box because he wanted her to hear what was happening, or he didn't want to take the risk of leaving her in the car, alone.

The receptionist asked him to wait, and he did, sitting with Kim's box on his lap. After about ten minutes, the receptionist escorted him into a back room and closed the door. The room reminded him of a doctor's office. There was no examining table, but a few devices that looked like they could be used as probes. Mark wasn't really sure, but in his imagination, aliens could use them for probing their kidnapped victims.

"You're Mark Stephenson?"

The man came in wearing a white cloak.

"Hi," he said. "Yes, that's me."

"I'm Peter Smythe."

They shook hands.

"Are you a doctor?"

"Umm...no. I'm more of a lawyer by training, actually."

"Oh."

Smythe walked around a desk and pointed at a chair for Mark.

"You want to go back in time to fix something?"

"Yes."

He held the box up. "This is..."

Now the tears started to roll out from his eyes. His throat was constricted and all he could do was sob. He shook his head in frustration and almost decided to walk out. It was a stupid idea.

Smythe moved a box of tissues toward him and said, "Take your time."

Mark wiped his eyes and blew his nose, then took some deep breaths until he felt he could talk again.

"This is my girlfriend. She died last week. Killed in a traffic accident."

Smythe nodded.

"I couldn't afford to bury her, so she was cremated. I think that's better anyway, because she can be with me all the time."

"You want to change what happened?"

Mark looked at the man as if he had three heads. "Of *course* I want to change it! I love her!"

"It's a common reason for people to come here."

"It can't possibly work, though."

"But it can." He shrugged. "Most of the time. There are cases where the procedure doesn't work, but our success rate is 97.9%. The technology gets better every year. When we opened five years ago, we were only about 89%, so things are much better."

"You can send me back in time?"

"Yes and no. Do you know about quantum entanglement?"

Mark had no clue, so he shook his head.

"Well, it doesn't matter. Let's take an example. You wake up one Saturday morning and you wonder if you should get out of bed. You can get up and make a coffee, or you can roll over and go back to sleep."

"I'd go back to sleep."

Smythe laughed. "In quantum theory, you make both choices. The universe splits in two. In one of them, you go back to sleep; in the other, you get up and make your coffee."

Mark shifted the box on his lap and rubbed the top.

"The universe is constantly splitting into duplicates, due to the choices we make over time. There are an infinite number of universes with *you* in them. In some, you've gone off and done wildly different things in your life. In some, you've died. In some, you're married, and in others, you're divorced. In some, maybe it was you that ended up killed in that car accident." Smythe glanced down at the box in Mark's lap.

"All universes, where you are in the same situation you are now, are connected through something called quantum entanglement. We can send you to one of those other universes."

"Sounds like magic."

"Oh, it's not magic, but science. Quantum mechanics has been the most important branch of physics for the past century. This is just one offshoot of it."

"How does going to another—what—universe? How does that help me? Wouldn't I be in the same situation?

"If that's all there was, then yes, but we can insert you into that alternative timeline at any point we want. Just part of the technology. We can insert you a week ago, so you can stop your girlfriend from being killed."

Mark looked down at the box again.

He didn't believe it. But he really wanted to.

"Why haven't I heard more about this?"

"Our clients end up in alternative timelines, so they're not around to say how fabulous the experience is."

He pulled out copies of *Scientific American*, *Discover*, and a few other magazines and spread them out. The cover stories of all of them were about Second Chance.

"It's real?"

He felt like he was pleading, but he wanted so much to have Kim back.

"Yes, it's real."

He stared at Smythe, afraid to ask the next question. He knew he ran the risk of being disappointed.

"What does it cost?"

Smythe took off his glasses and nodded. "It's a tough decision for all our clients, Mark. Our price is simple. It is everything you have. Absolutely everything. That's why I'm a lawyer talking to you and not a doctor or scientist or businessman. I have to be sure you completely understand. We'll take everything you own. If you own a house, we get that. Your car. Bank accounts. All your furniture and any other possessions. Even your clothes. Everything."

He glanced down at Kim's box. "Even her."

Mark couldn't believe it. He resisted even the possibility of giving up Kim and grasped the box.

"Why would you possibly want her? No!"

"Think about it, Mark. You'll be going to somewhere else. You can't take your stuff with you. Your girlfriend will be alive there. You will have the same possessions over there that you have here.

"You'll disappear from this timeline, and everything you have would normally be divided to your heirs. For all intents and purposes, you will be dead here, but still live in the timeline with her. You won't notice any difference at all, except she'll be alive. What can it possibly matter to you if we have all your possessions? We'll sell it all and that will be our fee."

Mark took a week before returning to Second Chance and signing the contract and all the necessary documents. The lawyer smiled, having known he'd be back.

He was allowed to keep twenty dollars in his wallet, his credit cards (because he would need them in the new timeline), his ring of keys, and the clothes he wore to the clinic. He surrendered the box holding Kim, but it was a very hard thing for him to do. All of a sudden he understood what a person who had an arm amputated called a phantom limb, feeling the loss of something that isn't really there anymore.

He didn't ask any more questions about the process, and specifically he did not ask what happened if he was one of the 2.1% of people for whom things didn't work out. He hoped he'd be dead, but he didn't really care. Whatever happened, it was worth it if he could have a chance, any chance at all, of saving Kim's life.

When Mark arrived in the new timeline, he woke as if from a long sleep. His head was cloudy and he was lying on the ground. He pulled himself up to a sitting position and recognized Central Park in downtown Aynsville. He licked his lips and stood. He felt dizzy for a moment but that passed soon enough.

Did it work?

He walked a block to where he knew his car was parked and

passed a newspaper box. He knelt to read the date: August 5th.

Oh my God…

He stared at the paper, trying to convince himself everything was true.

"Hey, there you are!"

His legs felt weak as Kim came running over and hugged him. He hugged her back and kissed her cheek and held onto her head, staring into her eyes.

"I love you," he said. "I love you. I love you!"

"And I love you." She added, "Is everything okay?"

"Everything is perfect."

He hugged her closely again.

She laughed. "Let's go. We have to get to the market before it closes."

Her words sounded ominous and he clenched her hand as she started to walk out to the street. He pulled her back just as the drunk driver roared by in his stolen pickup truck.

For a moment, neither of them said anything. Kim looked up at Mark and then out to the road. Her eyes were huge, and all he could think of was how beautiful she looked.

"I could have been killed," she said. "You saved me."

They hugged one more time and relief washed over him. He silently thanked Second Chance, grateful beyond words.

That night they made love. It was intense and fierce and hot and wonderful, and when they were done, they lay together in bed, touching each other and whispering "I love you" until they fell asleep. It was one of the best nights of Mark's life.

The last thought as he drifted off was a promise to ensure that every day with Kim was always better than the one before.

They woke the next morning to the sounds of birds chirping outside the bedroom window. It was a Sunday morning and Mark had decided they should go for a picnic later that day.

He smiled when he looked at Kim, and she smiled back. He

stared at her face, loving the sight of her, but a tiny shiver ran down his spine. He didn't know why.

She gently punched his shoulder. "Cheerios again?"

He nodded. It was their normal Sunday breakfast.

They made their way to the kitchen. She filled the bowls with the cereal while he got the milk from the refrigerator. He watched her out of the corner of his eyes, and he noticed she seemed to be moving a little slower than normal.

Or was she? Was he imagining it?

They ate in silence, enjoying each other's company and the occasional bird chirps. Sunshine cascaded into the kitchen. Halfway through their breakfast, Mark couldn't help but reach over and touch Kim's hand.

"I cherish you," he said. "I always will."

She nodded while munching on her Cheerios. When she finished her mouthful, she said, "I will always cherish you, too."

But it didn't sound right. It sounded like her voice was a tiny bit different from how it should be.

He hoped his smile didn't look fake.

Kim had a shower while he rinsed off the breakfast dishes and he followed and had his own shower when she was done.

Almost invisible little flecks of dark skin were on the bathtub. Bits of Kim down the drain. He wanted to look closer, but started the shower instead.

What the hell's going on? There's absolutely nothing unusual about her today.

He tried to think of something else. Anything else. The weather, the local baseball team (of which he knew almost nothing), the new action movie he'd heard of, the impending end of summer, but every time he tried to deliberately distract himself with all these things that he didn't really give a crap about, his mind would wander back to the growing feeling that something wasn't right.

Kim should be dead.

And part of his mind insisted that she was dead. He knew differently, because he'd just finished touching her warm skin, had made wonderful love with her last night, and was the recipient of her amazing, disarming smile, and he knew that nobody got to see that smile the same way he did.

It didn't matter, because the rotten core of his brain continued to insist: she should be dead.

Monday morning arrived and there were no birds chirping. The clock radio woke them at 6:00 and Mark felt like he hadn't had any sleep in a thousand years. His eyelids didn't want to stay open and his body kept screaming at him to just fucking stay in bed.

Kim hopped out of bed immediately, like she always did, and headed to the bathroom to go pee.

"Nothing is different," he whispered.

He ordered his body to cooperate and help him get out of bed.

By Thursday, he was watching her every moment.

He wondered if the way she blinked her eyes was the same as always. He knew that she didn't lick her lips as often before. She did it a lot now. She was different. And maybe her scent was different. He wasn't as sure about that and wanted to kick himself for not paying as much attention to that before.

Kim finished her shower—surely faster than normal—and he followed her. As she dried herself, she looked at herself in the mirror. Mark couldn't recall her ever doing that before.

The next day, she fell asleep watching *Big Brother*. They'd recorded the show on the DVR and were waiting to see which houseguest would be evicted, when he heard the tiny snores beside him. They'd been holding hands but Kim's head had lolled to the side.

It wasn't that she'd never fallen asleep watching TV before, but it sure wasn't common.

He took the opportunity to look at her ... well, examine her, as he knew that's actually what he was doing. He studied the tiny lines that branched out from her eyes and her beautiful black skin and the tiny cracks on her lips.

She was still (and always would be) the most beautiful girl he'd ever seen, and he knew there was no way somebody like that should ever be with an average Joe like himself... but there she was.

He touched her hair, and it felt—

(poisoned)

—different somehow. It wasn't as soft as he remembered. He wanted to pull a clump to see if it would fall out, like it should if she was a corpse. He took his hand from her hair and stopped holding hands with her.

You're not my Kim.

He wanted her to be Kim, but she wasn't. He was living with a stranger that was like an identical twin in every possible way. She had the same DNA, the same fingerprints, the same memories, but it wasn't *his* Kim. He didn't know who the hell this girl was.

He waited until the following Wednesday, to see if his feelings would change, but they didn't. If anything, the sense of loneliness increased, and the feeling that she was a zombie or some other kind of animated corpse grew more and more pronounced, to the point where he could barely stand the sight of her.

Last night, she'd moved to him in bed and reached over to rub his belly. He didn't react, but lay still, not wanting her. She soon reached down to feel his flaccid cock, and he still didn't do or say anything. There was no way he could do that with her. Fucking a cold, dead person who was rotting away. It was a disgusting idea. Eventually she took her hand away and rolled onto her side, away from him.

When he arrived at Second Chance, the same lawyer was there, but of course he didn't recognize Mark. They'd met in Mark's original timeline, not here.

"You're Mark Stephenson?"

"Yes. And you don't need to tell me anything. I'm a returning customer. I'll sign."

Peter Smythe smiled.

"I'll have the documents prepared."

"I'll wait."

Two hours later, he signed over all of his worldly possessions.

He awoke in Central Park, very groggy, and it took a moment for his mind to clear. He walked a block to his car and checked the date at the newspaper box: August 5th.

Again.

"Hey, there you are!"

Kim ran over to him and hugged him. He resisted the temptation to push her away. He wanted her, but he knew this Kim would change and eventually be no more like *his* Kim than the other had been. Right now, though, she was the woman he loved.

"Is everything okay?"

"Yes," he answered. "Everything is going to be perfect."

She laughed. "Let's go. We have to get to the market before it closes."

Her words bounced within his head, over and over, and before he knew it, she'd stepped out onto the street and the pickup truck screamed.

The box sat on the sacred spot he'd planned for it: the bedside table Kim had always used for her reading material.

Every night he sat on the edge of the bed and talked to her, telling her about his day, no matter how boring or uneventful. He loved her and he needed to always be sure she knew what he was doing.

"I love you," he said each night as he caressed the box and leaned over to kiss it good-night.

And every morning, his first thought was to say good-morning to her. He never missed a day.

THE EFFIGIES
OF TAMBER SQUARE

| JON MICHAEL KELLEY |

SEVENTY-EIGHT YEARS AGO, something fantastically strange happened in the town of Tamber. The morning after it was left forever a tourist draw, the local newspaper headlined the event as "A Most Astonishing Catastrophe!" In the months following, the residents adopted a much gentler description: "The Petite Withdrawal;" then being referred to simply thereafter as "The Petite," an endearing homage many sightseers still find too quaint for the circumstances, but the natives just shrug. That only thirty-six people had been extracted was, after all, quite a strain to put it in the realm of catastrophe. Astonishing, yes, that only their husks were left remaining, those umber shells of a most calcified composition. But now, after decades of unsatisfied speculation, the marvel has become a mere sideshow of Pompeian similitude. An alphabetized listing in the glossaries of alluring attractions.

Still, to meander between those thirty-six gathered, frozen and eerily intractable figures—their exoskeletons exquisitely tolerating time, all standing straight and staring up at the clock tower before them, faces utterly and forever horrified—leave the day trippers with a profound and lingering sense of unease. Only the dumb walked away from Tamber Square unmolested.

Every effigy had defects (made during a cooling process, some opined, but this has never been proved); minute cracks running no longer than an inch or two, showing no particular preference for a body's topography. It was through these tiny fissures where their absolute hollowness was discovered, the owners of those shells all gone to places unknown.

Equally amazing is their permanence, each one as immovable as any mountain, as if the world were holding to its bosom its most cherished heirlooms.

To hear those still alive to talk about it, there had been a ferocious crack of thunder, then a blinding strobe of pre-dawn light so brilliant it was alleged to have penetrated walls. The meek inherited the day, congregations swelled, as did collection plates, and everybody had been kinder to one another. Philanthropy flourished and crime diminished. It had been a nice reprieve. While it lasted.

Tamber Square was the heart of the event. As is the prerogative of most town founders, Tamber's community timepiece was built in the parish center atop an orthodox tower and customarily equipped with a tolling bell and four conveniently situated clock faces, this so its citizenry might know the hour from any direction. The motivation behind this was the enduring joke, that no resident of Tamber then or now was ever *that* devoted to a schedule.

On a bitter cold night, Cecily Hook tended to her wares, a feather duster in one hand, a tumbler of fine scotch in the other; both to combat the belching town chimneys and coal stacks, generous this time of year with their soot. Mr. Hook, victim of an unfortunate railroad accident, left Cecily the sole proprietor of Hook's Nook, a boutique primarily devoted to The Petite, selling embodied souvenirs and paraphernalia, the bulk of which has long been imported from other countries. In its heyday, local craftsmen, sculptors, printers and painters provided the inventory: paperweights, candles, brochures, books, board games—all the trappings to successfully capitalize upon a provocative tragedy. Even back then in a poorer economy the expensive bronze statuettes sold out quickly, the grim and final expressions of those taken impeccably rendered.

Usefully, Hook's Nook also served as Cecily's residence, the second floor a studio flat nearly as crammed with goods as was the lower level, a small but inviting showroom warmly merchandizing the cottage style. Quite often a patron would pause upon entering, wondering if they'd accidentally wandered into someone's home.

It had been a lot tighter when Mr. Hook was around, being the corpulent man he was. The stairs, though ... The stairs were becoming a problem. She wasn't a spring chicken anymore but more a fall grouse, she would often lament.

Among Cecily's bestsellers were the blinders, hat-like appliances that fit snuggly over the head, with a brow shield above and flaps on either side of the eyes to protect the wearer's peripheral vision. Most available now were of the flimsy variety, but she insisted on selling the expensive leather ones, staying true to the originals. They were all for conversation's sake, of course, and not necessity. No one since the weeks following the tragedy truly believed the town clocks were responsible for stealing people and leaving in their stead an empty replica. But for a short time afterwards it was greatly feared that to even glance in the tower's direction—let alone stare at it straight on—would be to invite the same fate. Preying on the scared and gullible, some quick-witted designers made their rent selling those original blinders. But the mother of invention miscarried, with most folks soon regaining their wits and eschewing such nonsense.

Surprisingly, only a few decided to uproot for good and never look back, the threats of fire and brimstone taken seriously.

Paragons of futility, the blinders remain a perennial favorite.

Cecily glanced at the wall clock. 11:00. It was getting late. The tower's bell no longer tolled the hour; hadn't since the morning of that distant event, when it was quickly agreed upon by council to leave it "as is." Let its silence be forever a reminder, they'd said.

A reminder of what had yet to be settled.

As she went to pull the shade, Cecily thought she saw a quick flash of light, then movement. Her storefront faced the square with just a cobblestone street separating them, and fourteen of the effigies could be seen from that vantage point. She squinted; stared. For the life of her she could not determine what was different, but knew that something was. The surrounding gaslights lit the arena well, but to her aging eyes they only illumed vague silhouettes.

Nothing stirred.

She thought it highly unlikely that somebody at this hour, in this cold, would be moseying about the monument. It would have been a crime, in fact, as visiting hours ended every day at sundown, with the four ticket gates promptly secured at twilight. The guard shack stood empty; a relic, as security had long been deemed unnecessary. Theft was not a concern, of course, and acts of vandalism had grown rarer over time. Paint easily washed away. Even the birds showed consideration by crapping elsewhere. Any disrespect that had ever been visited upon the effigies was purely cosmetic, as their exteriors were impenetrable and had proved resistant to the most formidable of attempts. Nary had a scratch ever been left.

She began to count the motionless figures beyond, finishing at fifteen. She counted again. Fifteen; one more than there should have been, as customarily seen from her window.

"Damned if somebody isn't out there," she whispered to the memory of her dead husband, now an ethereal companion.

"Too much drink, if you ask me."

Cecily turned her head and stared accusingly at his favorite chair. "I didn't, so bugger off."

"Suit yourself, then."

She turned back to the window and counted one last time, then shook her head. "I believe we have a trespasser in our midst."

"Leave it alone. Besides, since when did you become constable?"

"When they entrusted me with the keys!" she snapped, snatching those very things, along with her heavy shawl, from the coat tree beside the door. She dashed down her remaining whiskey, wrapped herself up, and then reached for the knob.

"Woman, you'll catch your death."

She stopped and considered this. "I just might," she agreed, as if the prospect were no longer an unpleasant one. "I just might."

As Cecily closed the door behind her, she was reminded how

sterile and uninviting her porch was this time of year. Absent were the vibrant snapdragons, pansies and delphinium she grew in her four whiskey barrels, all now frothing over with their grey skeletal remains. Beside the entrance stood a tall cigar store Indian, his headdress needing some sandpaper and fresh paint. A totem himself, the chief appeared to be staring considerately at the others across the way. His frown said it all.

In just moments, Cecily was already at the north gate, fumbling with the lock. Under duress of the season, the iron postern's hinges yelped as she pushed it forward. Once inside the perimeter, she paused and considered the figures.

It had begun to lightly snow.

As Cecily approached, it became easier to discern flesh from alloy. She spotted the trespasser, a naked woman, shapely, her cadenced breath pluming in the cold night air. Motionless, arms at her sides, the woman, whom Cecily guessed to be no older than thirty, was nose-to-nose and staring into the upturned eyes of one of the female effigies. Nearly upon the trespasser now, Cecily could see gooseflesh riddling her body, but given the look on the woman's face she wasn't ready to blame it on the cold just yet.

"Are you quite mad?" Cecily said to her, now at her side. She peeled off her shawl and wrapped the woman's shoulders. "Have you lost your—?" Cecily stared at the effigy, then the woman. Their countenances were identical, as was everything else about them, absent the clothes.

Teeth chattering, the woman finally turned to Cecily, and said, "Am I...am I the first?"

Cecily grabbed her arm. "Come, dear," she said. "Our first order will be some warm clothes, and a hot cup of tea."

"Avert your eyes, Mr. Hook!" Cecily said as they entered the store. She shuffled out of sight and returned with a heavy plaid robe, the price tag still dangling from its sleeve. She helped the woman into it, saying, "It's cotton, sold out the fleece, but it should do the trick nicely. Name's Cecily. You drink? I've got scotch, and scotch."

Still nurturing an amazed if not thoroughly confused expression, the woman said, "Scotch."

"Don't know what I was thinking offering you tea," Cecily said. "Don't touch the stuff anymore." She navigated to a tall oak hutch, retrieving a bottle of whiskey and an extra glass tumbler.

Still shivering, pulling her robe tight, the woman glanced expectedly around. "Mr. Hook. Is he your husband?"

Cecily laughed. "Yes, but he's dead, dear."

Not having to replace her expression, the woman said, "But … I thought I heard you tell him—"

"Dead or alive, he's still a man, isn't he?"

A knowing smile crept upon the woman's lips. "They are rather prone to a singular urge."

Pouring two drinks, Cecily agreed with a snort. "S'pose I'm crazy for talking to him, but not so crazy as to believe he's really here. I'm afraid his attendance is mostly for my convenience. A bit of the ol' nostalgia, you know. He was decent company. Besides, it beats having a messy parrot. Here you go."

Sniffling, the woman took the tumbler.

"Your accent is British."

"Came over with the Pilgrims," Cecily admitted. "I miss the pork pie, but I'll get over it."

The woman's smile widened. "You're not that old." She looked toward the window then, as if to recapture a memory that had gone fleeting past. The falling snow had thickened. "I'm wondering, though…"

"How long it's been?" Cecily said. "First things first. You've not introduced yourself."

"Oh, my name is …" Startled, she said, "Isn't that the funniest thing. I seem to have forgotten."

Cecily made her way to the book section and plucked a pamphlet from a carousel display. She opened it and began reading from the nomenclature. "'Emily Baxter? Jennifer Connolly? Susan Forrester'? Stop me if something rings a bell. 'Heidi Headstrom? Jackie Jacobsen? Beatrice—'"

"Murphy, yes! Beatrice Murphy."

"Says here you taught high school English. Bea for short, then?"

She scrunched her brow, things being stubborn to recall. "Tricia, actually." She pointed to the pamphlet in Cecily's hand, not having to ask the question.

"Victims of the Petite. I was reading only the female names, of course. Most were identified immediately, having been residents of Tamber, but I understand there were a few who weren't as easily recognized. Turned out not to be locals. They eventually got around to it, though. Figuring out who they were, that is. Same number of women as men, curiously no children, but it appears to have been random." She shrugged. "But then, no one's returned to really say." She gave her scotch a spin, and then tipped the rim toward her guest. "Until now."

"'The Petite', you said. I...I'm trying to understand the reasoning behind that name."

Cecily chuckled. "So do the tourists. But for some damned reason, it stuck. 'The Petite Withdrawal' they called it at first. I suppose if ten thousand had instead been taken then they wouldn't have been so endearingly absurd in their naming of it." She stared intently at Tricia's pretty face, still mindful to keep the obvious, at least for the moment, impersonal. "They now stand as memorials, dear. Tamber's lost—but certainly not forgotten—children. Are you hungry? I'm thinking it's probably been awhile."

"No, nothing, thank you." Tricia finally moved, aiming for the stuffed vacant chair near the center of the room. An old crystal humidor, full of tobacco, stood atop an adjacent stand. A twin ashtray sparkled invitingly in the light, host to an empty pipe.

Seeing her intentions, Cecily turned to the chair and said, "Stop staring and get up, for Christ's sake!"

"Yeah, yeah."

Tricia halted, as if she'd made an unwise decision.

Cecily waved her on. "All clear. Have a sit."

As she did, Cecily said, "You asked me a very tantalizing thing. Do you remember?"

"If I was the first?" Tricia nodded, and then stared again toward the square. "Am I?"

"It appears so," Cecily said. "Will the others be following?"

Tricia finally brought the scotch to her lips and, upon a stark expression, pulled down a healthy dose. "Oh yes. But...not for the reasons you might think."

"Beg pardon?"

Tricia remained prim in the chair, hesitant, as if surrendering to its comfort would render her forever a slouch. Cecily detected in her guest a bygone air, a pattern of old lace; the subtle intonations of her speech, her demure manner, reminiscent of a time Cecily herself could remember. One when cordiality and graciousness were still adulate traits.

Oh, how we've thoroughly dulled, Cecily thought, *in the last seventy-eight years.*

"It's coming back to me," Tricia said, "but please be patient. Things are still...slow to gather."

Cecily found a folding chair and promptly occupied it in front of her guest. "Then let's start at the beginning, shall we?"

"The dogs," Tricia began, distant; remembering. "The dogs woke me, barking. I got up, got dressed ... To think that I put on my prettiest blouse ... Pearls. I kissed my sleeping husband lightly on the cheek. Said goodbye." She stared into her lap. "I'm trying to remember his name..."

Cecily leaned forward. "Something was drawing you? Compelling you?"

She shrugged. "More like ... I had remembered something that had been...so long forgotten."

"Something more important than having left a pie on the sill, obviously—"

"William!" Tricia blurted. "My husband's name was William." Beseechingly, she said to Cecily, "He *is* dead now, isn't he?"

Cecily nodded. "I'm sorry, dear. Husbands, wives, siblings, children...As far as they could determine, all of the immediate relatives of those taken died well within a year following the event. Natural or unnatural causes, take your pick. A situation nearly as baffling as the Petite itself, and still shrouded in conspiracy theories. Many believed they were silenced by the government, or by those who'd done the taking. Some still maintain the government *had* done the taking. Secret experiments and such." She clucked. "I can tell you, when left suspended our minds run off with the craziest notions. The government indeed! It couldn't find its ass with two hands and a compass. Did you have children?"

"No, thankfully," Tricia said, sounding more relieved for them than herself. She was now staring at a gilded mirror hanging on the opposite wall. "You've got some things here that are unfamiliar, to be sure—but I do recognize *that*," she said, pointing at the looking glass. She stood, drank the last of her whiskey, and said, "You'd do well to cover them. Cover them all."

"Oh? Tell me why, dear," Cecily said, calmly intrigued.

She stared into Cecily's eyes with a betraying malevolence. "Because they lie."

As Tricia remained standing, Cecily got up and took her glass; refilled it, then her own. "Is that just a personal prejudice, or are you implying something more philosophical?"

Her decorum recaptured, Tricia said, "Just that ... that we are not what we think we see."

"As ourselves, you mean?"

Tricia only shrugged.

"Well, imitators we most certainly are," Cecily agreed, thinking she understood. "We're sure not the same inside our own walls as we are outside of them. Ha! You think I take Mr. Hook to market? To the show? They'd have me bound and committed! S'pose I'm crazy for talking to him, but not so crazy as to drag him out in public." She nodded to herself, her eyes settling on a far-off place. "He was decent company, though." She recovered then. "Where have you been, dear? What happened to the victims of the Petite?"

"Oh, we weren't the victims," Tricia said, now sounding more confident. "We were the only survivors. Your fate hasn't caught up to you yet. But it's fast approaching."

"Here we go. She's finally in the drink."

"No one asked you," Cecily chided the empty chair.

Now inured to Cecily's quirk, Tricia walked to the window; stared out at the falling whiteness. "The snow...I remember how I used to love the snow. When I was small, my father would take me to Conlon Hill. My old sled, its red runners...He would wax them. Do the children still toboggan there?"

"You're drifting off course, dear," Cecily said. "Survivors of what?"

"Time," Tricia said, still enraptured with the weather. "We survived the wrath of time."

"Well, that's rather obvious. I've grown ancient and you haven't. In fact, you look like you've just stepped from the bath, hair brushed and teeth cleaned. Can't say that I'm not a bit envious." She recalled a quote. "I wasted time, and now doth time waste me." She twirled her glass, as if to prevent any further sediment.

With a conciliatory smile, Tricia finally turned to her. "Some poets were right to personify it, and give it optimism."

"I disagree. There isn't anything romantic about it," Cecily said, finding herself falling behind Tricia's returning lucidness. "At least not when it finally pigeonholes us. Were you always here, just misplaced?" she persisted. "Alone? Or did you find yourselves elsewhere together? Meaning, somewhere other than this earth?"

"I was always ... living a moment. But you want to know if it was heaven. Or heaven-like. Heaven is ... heaven is having the notion of time. Hell is being relieved of the guarantee that we eventually reach an end. Even during our most painful days we rely on the belief that time will deliver us from our ills. Smooth things over. If it's feeling kind, it does. But when it's angry—"

"You talk as if time is reactionary, has an agenda. It's devoid of passion, dear. It has no favorites. After all, it wrinkles us up and spares no one in the end. We supply the awareness, the whys and wherefores."

"No, it is very much a prisoner to itself. It hurts, it hungers, has ambitions, jealousies, whims. You need to start thinking of it as a living, breathing thing. Literally. It's not intangible." She turned again to Cecily, that aspersion back. "To be free of time is not to be free at all, but set adrift upon a stagnant sea, one that indefinitely reflects upon its surface your most profound miseries, never to submerge. The good moments are there too, each maintaining the other's perspective."

"So that we might not forget one's poignancy over the other?"

Tricia nodded. "We've always regarded time as our enemy, and it is. Death is our refuge, but only time allows it. To finally make acquaintance with the nothingness is our reward. To finally be relieved of . . . of the perpetual cycles that plays us to exhaustion. To be spared that finale, well . . ." She looked down at her toes. "Death has always been our sanctuary."

"I take it back. She's not drunk, she's just daft."

Cecily shook her finger. "I'll remind you to be quiet."

Pensively, Tricia said, "'Time's glory is to calm contending kings . . .'"

"Shakespeare, again?"

"We've always squandered the throne." Hands clasped respectfully behind her back, Tricia left the window and began a careful perusal of the boutique's oddments.

"Human nature. Power corrupts, and all that," Cecily said. "I suppose time has to take a good chunk of the blame for that, don't you think?"

Tricia raised her eyebrows. "Time would vehemently disagree."

"Oh? Isn't it our finite schedule that compels us to achieve?"

"Don't mistake greed for achievement."

"Can't have a little of one without a little of the other."

"Shush!"

"It's a fact."

Tricia was smiling. "Your Mr. Hook. He was a decent man?"

"As good as any man can be, I suppose," Cecily said, feeling suddenly protective. "A good provider. Never struck me. Bought me flowers on occasion, whether I deserved them or not."

Tricia pulled the robe's sash tighter around her waist. "Be thankful you've been able to chaperone his memory with compassion. Sympathies especially do not fare well in infinite scenarios."

"You mean our memories?" She laughed knowingly. "They can't be trusted, really. Old and new, they eventually become works of fiction, written upon fancy and half-truths. We fudge them, after all, to our own benefit. So then, why should my seventy-one years write them any differently than eternity?"

She found Cecily's eyes. "You'll soon have all the time to figure that out. It will be the names you'll find yourself forgetting, of people, places … They become inconsequential to the deeper lessons."

Suddenly, Cecily felt a queer urgency to explain. "I was a little girl of seven in London when the news reached us about the Petite. Most balked at first, blaming the Yanks for inventing fables. But soon the reality couldn't be denied, and from that point on I never outgrew my ambition to move to Tamber. Finally got here eighteen years later, husband in-tow. Mr. Hook fought the move tooth-and-nail, but finally gave in. That poor, darling man, succumbing to my dreams. He got a job with the railroad, which he never stopped hating, and we eventually saved enough money to buy this place."

"I see where the apostrophe in the store name implies only one owner. But something tells me that was more intentional than not."

Whispering now, her husband's memory in earshot, Cecily said, "You might be the first to have ever noticed that subtlety. But yes, I made sure the licensing insinuated a single owner. Mr. Hook never questioned it, being the uneducated man he was. It was my own little private dig. A misplaced piece of punctuation to counter a misplaced heart. Mr. Hook's, that is. He hated this place and my dream to achieve it almost as much as he hated the railroad." She was lost again in that far-off place. "Not a very happy man was ever my Mr. Hook."

"Was it faith that coerced you here, or just the novelty?"

"The latter more so than the former, but both have worn badly over the years. I was entranced, as most children are with certain marvels, but it wasn't until I was older when I wanted to exploit it." She winked. "Saw the potential to make a profit."

Tricia was smiling. "An entrepreneur. Nothing to be ashamed about there. You've obviously done well."

"Nothing grand, but it's paying the bills. Trust me, dear, so many have tried and failed."

"So what is your secret to success?"

"To remain neutral and leave religion out of it," Cecily said. "Shoppers don't so much like their goods to be impartial as they do the pretenses they're sold upon. Plenty of pulpits for that. Ha! We've still got as many steeples as chimneys. Most of them have long gone vacant, though. The gold's all gone, you might say."

"That's a fact."

Still meandering, Tricia paused before the offerings of a small oval table. "These are rather curious things."

"Those are blinders. A most popular item." Cecily briefly explained their history.

With an accusatory stare, Tricia said, "Rather redundant, don't you think, given that we're already born with a pair?"

"What was it like," Cecily asked, "when you were taken?"

Tricia thought for a moment. "A suffocation, then a … a re-experiencing of my existence. Or, more pointedly, a re-examining."

"Saw your life flash before your eyes?"

"The proverbial reliving, yes—but it was no flash. As a bystander, I saw my entire life played over and over, from every conceivable position, dimensionally and emotionally. It's funny, but when given a bird's-eye view, among others, of something that was originally experienced from a more level perspective, you find that the emotions connected to that moment change with the angle."

Eyes stark and wide, Cecily said, "Quite exhausting, I imagine. It's a wonder you've not been turned into a blubbering idiot."

"Just as it always has, time allowed us intervals to recapture our sanity." Then: "To fill with wormholes stately monuments, To feed oblivion with decay of things ..." Tricia quoted, as softly as the falling snow.

Cecily sighed. "We're doing the poets proud, dear, but have we really tread new ground?"

"The poets only had the lonely nights for inspiration," Tricia assured. "They never had forever."

There was a flash of light from the square, quickly followed by another.

"A few more returning, then?" Cecily said. "Shall we make room—"

"No. The town's already stirring. Let your neighbors shelter the rest."

Cecily sat her finished drink aside; shook her head. "Cheap scotch, or the circumstances have secured my sobriety." She shuffled closer to the window. "Lights are on in the mercantile. That'll mean ol' Mr. Connery's ringing everyone on his directory." Turning now to Tricia, she said, "What's to happen, dear? To us, I mean. The ones who didn't survive."

"To become your own monuments." She nodded toward the square. "To serve as everlasting reminders of time wasted, and be cast forever into a reliving of memories."

"To see the errors of our ways? Is that the intention? To see how we've wasted our lives? What happened to our benevolent God?"

"Time *is* God."

Cecily had begun to tremble. "Is this to be a plagiarism, of sorts? Are we to be the tenants of our own Victorian novels, cast opposite our own indicting ghosts, to be spitefully kicked about the streets of our past?"

"Yes, and those especially pockmarked with the most grievous pride and self-indulgences."

Upon a sudden realization, Cecily said, "All the immediate relatives of the Petite! Time extended you a courtesy by seeing them dead?"

"By setting them free, yes. It gave us, the survivors … peace of mind." She smiled. "It does have its benevolent side."

"Then, what is to become of you and the rest of the Petite?"

"We've been tasked to start over, Cecily. Although absent, we were allowed to see the promise. Do you remember how kinder people were to one another after we were taken? Not just here, but all over the world, once the news spread? It wasn't Nirvana, by any means, but there was a perceptible … reconciliation. There was hope anew. But as it has historically done, the world let the opportunity slip away. Time offered one last chance, and it was yet again misspent."

Tricia strode to the gilded mirror and stood before it. Cecily followed, and as she looked on she saw not Tricia's reflection, but her own. That contemporary likeness then dissolved into a swirling grey confusion of loneliness, despair, bitterness … Scraps of vibrant color, like parade confetti, struggled briefly, desperately, within the squall. In that accursed and accusing montage she heard what sounded like whale song, a sorrowful orchestration set to the tempest of her life. Then an obliterating white storm wiped clean the glass, only to settle and reveal a more desolate landscape. And upon that arid and sutured ground a dark shape swirled up into being, lurching forward. Toward her. It was her, the likeness now honoring decay; a withered, time-worn corpse comprised solely in shape by a maelstrom of memories, her seventy-one years compacted and assembled as a besieged, cadaverous tumult of what was, and what could have been.

It reached out an arm in a supplicating way.

Cecily turned away, for once terrified.

"Easy, my love. Easy."

"It's tragic," Tricia said, "how the darkest parts of our lives dominate our memories."

Another flash of light from the square, then four more in telling succession.

Cecily made her way back to the window; stared out. Residents bundled in house robes and mackinaws, mittens and mufflers, were leaving their shelters; some running into the square as if there were people to be saved from a fire. Others remained reticent, steady and alert on their porches, some lingering at the safer edges of the gas-lit street, curious if they should venture into the commotion.

Rescuers began calling out frantically for extra blankets, shoes, warm clothing...

Cecily put a hand to her mouth. "Oh my, I left open the gate."

The flashes were coming so fast now that it was hard to count them. The snow was already ankle-deep, and still falling heavily. Cecily wondered if it had been strategically summoned to help console a world on the verge of eternal grief; to help cushion it against its impending fall.

The tower bell tolled once, twice ... Someone in the square screamed.

When the tolling finally stopped, Cecily had counted thirty-six heralds.

"I suspect that's that, then," Cecily said, tears wetting her eyes. "Do I have time to say goodbye to my neighbors?"

Tricia looked out the window one last time; distantly, as if to gauge upon a horizon the advancement of a storm as yet unseen. "Yes, Cecily. There's still time."

"C'mon, then, Mr. Hook," Cecily said, replacing her stern familiar tone with something warmer. "Time to take you out in public." She turned to Tricia. "I can bring him along, can't I? Where I'm going?"

Feebly, Tricia smiled. "He's already there."

SHADES OF NAUGHT

| LORI MICHELLE |

SHE STOOD IN THE ALLEY looking down at the body which had served as her capsule. Except she wasn't standing, for she no longer possessed legs. No, she was...what?

She was *being*.

The woman wondered why she wasn't crying. She felt nothing but a detached disinterest in the shell that had been hers for the past thirty years. She shook her (metaphysical) head at this needless departure. The memory of her time here was already starting to fade as she attempted to recall her cause of death.

There was a small, cylindrical-shaped object beside her body's arm. A tiny, sharp point stuck out of it.

Drugs, she thought. *Drugs did this.*

But as her spirit redirected down the alleyway, the thought of drug use began to vanish from her mind. The alleyway and buildings around her faded into oblivion, and suddenly she was walking across an empty field. Even if she had known the words or what they meant, she wouldn't have been able to give a description of her surroundings.

It was just there, the *nothing*.

She wasn't sure where she was going, but instinct told her she was headed the right direction. The farther she traveled, the less she remembered where she had come from. Glimpses of words and phrases filtered through her mind.

The nothingness dissolved, and she found herself in a cavernous room. The thought of a bus station flew through her mind, but before she could remember what a bus station was or from where she even knew the term, it was gone. A myriad of featureless people passed by, ignoring the woman's existence—or lack thereof.

The room itself was colorless and desolate, everything a shade of gray. The walls were gray, the ceiling, even the people passing by were colored the same dismal ash. She looked at her hand in wonder, and suddenly realized she now possessed one of these gray pods of a body. One of these shades of nothing.

The zombie-like entities continued moving to and fro without discernible intention. The woman realized they all wore the same gray, sack-like dress. She too wore the same garment. Reaching to touch her head, she realized her long locks had disappeared, replaced by the smoothness everyone else seemed to share.

The lack of noise was unsettling. No footsteps, no talking, no anything. It was a strong, awful quiet that made her feel sick. She brought her hands in front of her and clapped them together, dispelling the silence. Several passersby scowled.

Not to be discouraged, she continued to walk until she came to a barred window. Another gray-faced person looked back at her without expression.

"Name," he said gruffly.

"I don't…I don't know," she stammered.

He sighed. "Put your forehead in the scanner." He pointed to the contraption next to the window.

She did as she was instructed.

"Traveler 7411. Previously Mary Booth, twenty-eight, died from a drug overdose. Tell me, 7411, what was your life like?"

7411 wracked her brain, but she couldn't recollect much from her time in the other realm. Sadly, she shook her head at him. "I'm sorry, I can't think of anything happening. All I can remember is coming through the gray nothing field to get here."

He grabbed a radio. "Code 143, code 143. Traveler 7411 has had a massive head breach. We need an extraction team down here stat before her memories are completely gone."

"What?" she cried.

"Memories," he said, tapping the side of his head. "Yours are disappearing at a rapid pace and we need to get the data out before it's gone."

"I don't understand..."

"Of course you don't."

Two identical gray men showed up to carry her away.

"Where are they taking me?"

"Don't worry," said the man behind the counter, "we just need to get the rest of your memories before they vanish."

"What memories? What are you talking about?" The men led her away. "I don't have any memories of anything..."

"Calm down, miss," said one of the men.

She stopped and listened to his voice, realizing it had the same sound as the man behind the counter. She wondered if everyone's voice sounded the same.

"What's happening to me?"

"Standard protocol. They want to retrieve your memories of Earth before they fade away."

"Earth? Memories? Where *are* we?"

They reached a door in the hall and it disappeared as they entered. They sat her down in a room full of busy machinery, but they did not make any noise. All sound had been blanketed.

7411 caught her reflection in the side of one of the machines. She looked like the men examining her.

"Relax traveler, you have nothing to worry about here."

7411 sat on the bench and tried to think about how she had gotten here, but nothing came to mind. She was more curious to see what was going to happen next. For now, all of this seemed somewhat natural.

A man in a white lab coat walked into the room. Except for the coat, he held the same resemblance as everyone else.

"Ah, Traveler 7411, please come sit in this chair."

"What's going to happen to me?"

"We are going to extract the last of your memories from Earth before they completely disappear."

"Earth? Memories? What are you talking about? What are you going to do with them?"

"They will be sent to him for analysis," he said and began attaching a handful of suction cups to her head.

"Him who?"

"*Him*. Now sit back and relax so we can get this done quickly."

"What does *he* do with them?"

The man smiled knowingly, but continued to work and ignored her questions. "Sit back, traveler, this won't hurt at all."

He walked over to the wall and flipped a switch and she heard the muted hum of the machine. Pictures and images flashed before her eyes. In the first she saw a baby held by a woman, and the word *mother* came to mind. A little girl on a bicycle. A myriad of children, costumes and candy. Football players and cheerleaders. 7411 saw the same cute blonde girl in each image, slowly aging as if in time-lapse. Then the girl, now a young woman, wearing a white dress, holding hands with a man.

The pictures grew hazy and gruesome. Flashes of a baseball bat, fists, and work boots. Intense pain flowed through her body as the blonde girl was pummeled by each of these objects. Flashes of blue and red lights. A puddle of blood. The cute blonde girl, bruised, laying on the ground in the fetal position.

More hazy pictures: a needle, pills, smoke.

A thumping heartbeat filled 7411's head.

The pictures distorted, and then there was a blood-filled needle and the whoosh of it being plunged. The pictures were dizzying, as if not focused correctly. The blonde girl, pale and thin and weak, hair in matted strings, she looked into 7411's eyes and said, "Help."

And then a whirlwind of colors, none of which coherent.

The last image to flash before 7411's eyes: the dead blonde girl in an alleyway.

The machine powered down and the hum was once again silenced. The lab-coated man removed the suction cups from her head. "That's it, Traveler 7411. You are done here."

"What happens now?"

"You draw your next assignment and wait."

"Wait for what?"

He ignored her and walked out the door and into the hall. She had to run to catch up with him. He strode down the hallway, and even though there wasn't much difference in height, she struggled to keep up. They arrived at a new room, devoid of everything but doorways and benches.

Numerous gray nothing-beings walked through these doorways and sat on these benches. The ceiling seemed to stretch for miles. Everyone looked exactly the same. Same eyes, same face, same gray skin, same everything. The only difference was that the females were a little smaller and had more delicate features—the eyes more almond shaped and the noses thinner.

The man in the lab coat pointed to a window across the room, said, "There," and walked away.

She walked across the room, taking in the expressions on the various faces. All eyes seemed vacant. She made it to the window.

"Name?" a woman said flatly.

"Mary…"

"No, *traveler* name."

"7411."

"Forehead in the scanner please."

Mary did as she was told. There was a small hum as something scanned her.

"Here's your results, 7411. Have a seat until it's your turn."

"My turn for what?"

"Your turn," the woman said and closed the window.

7411 wondered what it was she had to wait for, and how long it would take before she would know. She looked down at the note in her hand:

CHLOE, 87, CANCER.

7411 wondered what it meant. The others held similar notes.

"You wanna know what it means, don't you?" a voice asked.

"What?" 7411 said, looking up at a man sharing the same basic identity as everyone else in the room. But there was something different in this man's eyes. Here she didn't see the nothing expression, but a sense of despair.

"The paper. Do you want to know what the message means?"

"Yes."

"Well, I'm not sure you can handle it."

"I would like to know what is going on."

He looked her in the eyes. "Do you know anything?"

"I know this is pretty weird. I know my name is Mary, maybe. I don't know."

He looked a little shocked. "You remember your Earth name?"

"I guess," she shrugged. "I know they have called me Mary, and Traveler 7411."

"Yeah, Mary would have been your Earth name. You can forget that one now, since you will never use it again."

"What the fuck is *Earth?*"

"It's the place we all go to collect information—for *him.*"

"Him who?"

"Him. *Him.*"

"What does HE need with all this information?"

The man shrugged. "I have no idea."

"How come my memory isn't working?"

"You don't retain anything at all going out, and you don't retain much coming back in. And whatever you do have remaining, they suck out."

"Why?"

"They want every Earth experience to be fresh and unique."

"Then why no remembering when we come back here?"

"Just the way it works I guess. Maybe they want no conflict from the Earth world here. Notice everyone in here looks exactly the same? There is nothing to differentiate any of us. We all look the same, talk the same, dress the same, act the same. Equality."

She looked around and then back to him. "And you? How did you get to be so different from the rest of us in here?"

"They screwed up erasing my memory last time. They didn't *get* everything and I am remembering more and more. But the more I remember, the more I wish I didn't."

"What is it? What do you remember?"

"You sure you want to know?"

She nodded.

"There's no point to any of this. We come here, go there, live a life there, come back here, and retain nothing. Then we do it again and again. For what purpose? No one knows, no one cares." The dejection in his voice was becoming more and more apparent.

"Well, why don't you ask someone?"

"Who am I going to ask? You're the first person to even *want* to talk to anyone in here. Most sit quietly and wait their turn. And the lab guys? They won't talk. No one has any information. If they knew I was this aware, I would probably disappear."

"Where would you go?"

"I don't know. No one knows. Maybe I wouldn't go anywhere. Maybe this cycle of hell continues forever. Sad thing is, I won't know it because my memory will be gone. I will become another drone like the rest," he said, sweeping his arm across the crowd.

"But won't that be a good thing?"

He looked her deep in the eyes. "And how come you aren't accepting, 7411? You're the only other person I have met, well, at least from what I can remember, who hasn't accepted all of this."

"I am trying to accept, to let it wash over me. But the more I think about it, the angrier I seem to feel. I want to know who this *him* character is, and why *he* thinks it's okay to use us in *his* 'Earth experiment.' It's like we don't matter at all."

"Maybe that's why we aren't allowed to retain anything. To maintain compliance."

"We should do something. Find out more about *him*."

She stood, as if looking for a place to protest.

He sighed. "So do you really want to know what the paper you are holding means?"

She nodded and sat and handed him the note.

"It's your new Earth life. You will be Chloe, die at age eighty-seven, from cancer. Could be rough, but you will have many memories to bring back here next time."

"But I won't remember any of it, right?"

"No," he said, shaking his head and returning the slip of paper to her. "Just more data for *him* to gather."

"I don't want to go."

"I don't think you have any choice in the matter."

"Well, I should. It's not right that I am not given a choice of what I do and where I go and who I am." Her voice grew louder and the other beings started noticing. "And more important, that I do it without knowing why!"

A voice came over the loudspeaker: "Traveler 7411, please report to Port 3."

He looked at her incredulously. "Wow, that was fast. You must have done something to make someone very happy, or pissed someone off and they want to get you out of here faster."

"I don't want to go yet. I want to find out what's going on."

He touched her. "Keep the spunk. Maybe it will come back with you. Maybe you'll retain a memory of me. Maybe you won't."

They stood and he took her hand. "Have a good life, Chloe."

She walked away, teary-eyed, and headed toward Port 3. She touched her face, wondering about the wetness there.

"Traveler 7411?" said the man in the guard uniform.

"Yes."

"Forehead in the scanner please."

She placed her head in the scanner and heard the whirling.

"Thank you. Have a nice trip," he said as he opened the door.

She sighed, walked out the door and was again in the colorless nothing as she headed toward the bright light.

THE PRICE OF FACES

| JAMES CHAMBERS |

I

AT THE BODY FORGE

WEEKS AFTER THE ACCIDENT, in dreams or in a swirling, anesthetic darkness, Coar saw the impossible: one's birth face. Its stare bored into Coar as if scanning through one's *elem* to the raw life matrix code beneath, with a gaze far too solidly mounted in flesh. The murky face haunted Coar. One could never know one's true birth face, which belonged not to a self, but to a body stripped away in the first six months of life, removed to the body forges for nurturing and management on the International Life Interface. Birth faces held identity's potential, while separation from one's birth face equaled freedom of identity. Yet, the sight of the face disturbed Coar because one felt certain it belonged. People said if you looked at your birth face, it would be like looking into a prison cell you'd escaped. Coar understood why.

Despite its disordered, unfinished appearance, the face loomed so near, so tangible that Coar expected it to open its mouth, shout, scream, cry, and then swallow one down into an inescapable cage of bone and flesh. Instead it watched Coar as if awaiting the answer to an unspoken question, remaining until the moment Coar woke from a midnight dream or rose from an anesthetic fog in the body forge laboratory, when it dimmed, leaving Coar equally trapped in blood and muscle.

This morning, as the anesthesia wore off, Coar floated toward consciousness, resolved to hold onto the face. Struggling out of chemical sluggishness, Coar jerked awake into the typical, yeasty, body forge odors of new flesh mingled with the lingering bite of antiseptic cleansers and antibiotic mists. Coar gagged on them, inhaled deeply and groped across one's mind for the face in the dying darkness, arms grasping in tandem with mental efforts, fingers clutching empty air. But the face vanished.

"Steady, Coar," Doctor Mills said, easing down Coar's arms. "Let your body adjust."

Edon stood behind Mills, watching from a tall female body with brunette hair dressed in a fashionably cut suit and skirt, reminding Coar of yet another day of work missed to be here. At least Coar assumed Edon was still in there since Edon had arrived at the forge in that body this morning. Severed from the International Life Interface by one's injury, Coar perceived only the expressionless faces surgically sculpted to display the *elems*, the life matrix projections that identified a body's inhabitant. Their continued absence from Edon's and Mills' faces told Coar the latest treatment hadn't worked.

No surprise. Coar had known it was a long shot.

Mills' plan to reboot Coar's life matrix via light-induced theta wave recycling and relink it to the 'Face sounded good in theory, but Coar, who'd spent years designing light particle data protocols, knew broken photon matrixes were obstinate. The array of data-laden light in Coar's life matrix—what old-timers still sometimes cheekily called a *soul*—should've bound Coar to the 'Face, but broken, they left one trapped in a single body.

Disappointment rose in Coar like stale oil lifted to a road surface by rain.

"We tried," Coar said. "Maybe the next thing will work."

Mills grunted while studying Coar's electronic chart hanging from the end of the bed.

Edon turned away and answered a buzzing netphone. Anyone could have been in the brunette body, a stand-in hired while Edon skipped to the office, a visiting body forge scientist studying Coar's situation, or even a public relations flack covering up Coar's condition because anything that cast doubt on the safety of the 'Face—as Coar's accident did—verged on heresy. One suspected Edon sometimes body-skipped elsewhere at times when Coar might not notice. Coar couldn't blame one. Skipping across the 'Face came as naturally as breathing.

Coar watched Edon speak into the phone, sun-shadowed near a window, and wondered.

Another Specta network crisis. Ratings plunging every quarter now. More fires to extinguish.

"Don't bitch talk me, Arra. All you do is gripe and guess. Give me some damn results," Edon said and then stroked the brunette body's long black hair before rubbing its forehead then dropping its hand against its thigh.

Coar knew well the frustrated gesture. And *bitch talk*, Edon's pet name for complaining.

So, Edon after all.

Coar's ability to recognize Edon by speech mannerisms and body language despite whatever body Edon wore had thrived since the accident. The stress of Coar's injury and the ratings crisis only heightened Edon's innate traits. Specta demanded more and more time as greater numbers of people stopped watching their programs, and Edon seemed to prefer those problems, which one could grasp, confront, quantify, perhaps solve. Problems that didn't send termite tunnels hollowing through the foundations of one's existence like the uncertainty of seeking a cure for Coar's damaged life matrix. Coar wanted Edon by one's side. Isolation from the 'Face scared one enough without the added pain of the gulf widening between them now that Coar could no longer go where Edon—and almost everyone else on earth—could.

A nurse with a face Coar recognized peeled electrodes from Coar's body. Young, male, a shadow of stubble, and an inch-long, easy-to-overlook scar along the left side of one's nose. The nurse had body-stuck for Coar's last several treatments, along with Doctor Mill's and others. Consistency helped Coar identify one's caregivers. The scar, though, suggested a body choice made for reasons beyond practicality. People discarded scarred bodies. No one had to live with ugliness, and Coar couldn't imagine why anyone would want to. The body forges cleaned and perfected all bodies during regular maintenance. Scars meant embarrassment and pain, tangled lines of tight skin that tugged at one's joints. Scars interlaced Coar's body now, head to toe, remnants of urgent, clumsy repairs made by body forge automatons better built for managing nutrition-to-waste ratios than repairing wounded flesh.

Coar wanted to be perfect again.

The nurse's scar fascinated one.

Noticing Coar's interest, the nurse said, low-voiced, "I'm sorry for what's happened to you." With a glance at Edon still absorbed on the phone, the nurse slid a card from a scrub pocket into Coar's hand. An odd change affected the nurse's face; eyes widened, eyebrows rose, and lips parted, breaking its flat, passive stare. It passed too quickly for Coar to be sure what he'd seen. "Life isn't how you think. You can't skip from every problem. Take this in case, well, I guess in case nothing can be done; you might need a different kind of help than they offer at a body forge."

"What …?" Coar said.

"My name," the nurse said, "is *David.*"

An ancient name. A gendered name.

Coar wondered why David had taken it.

The red and black sign printed on the card delineated the outline of an androgynous, human figure with a stylized drawing of the world centered in its torso. Coar knew it from old news posts and history pages. A forbidden sign with an apostate meaning, illegal for more than a century. On the back of the card, the words: *The World Within Us.* Below that, a name: *Widds.* And a phone number.

Coar shivered.

The nurse—*David*—shifted to shutting down machines and

monitors as Mills handed Coar a tablet. Coar hid the card under a leg, unsure why, and regarded the screen. It showed a scan of Coar's head, broken life matrix represented by a knot of green brightness at the base of Coar's skull.

"Compare this," Mills said and touched the screen, summoning an identical image, "... to *this*."

Coar glanced at Edon, wishing one would get off the phone and be with one. Then Coar read the date stamps on the scans— one taken the day of the accident, the other this morning.

Mills dragged them atop one another; superimposed, they made a perfect match.

"They're the same," Coar said.

"That's the problem, isn't it? All we have tried, and yet no change," Mills said. "Your life matrix remains as mangled and dysfunctional as the day of the accident. Fixing bodies is a fool's game. If you'd skipped to the 'Face before the truck smashed your car, as Edon did, you'd still be connected. I wish we could simply scrap this body you're wearing rather than go through all this trouble trying to repair it. Can't do that while you're in it, though, can we?"

"The crash occurred so fast," Coar said. "I hit my head before I knew it was happening."

Mills raised a hand. "No one blames you, Coar. We're simply frustrated that we can't heal you. There are one or two more things we'll try, but I'm afraid they're even more of a stretch than today's treatment. If they don't work..."

"What...?" Coar asked. "If they don't work...what?"

Mills studied Coar's face with blank intent, like a staring statue, assessing, Coar guessed, one's damaged *elem*. Coar wondered what it looked like.

"If we don't get you out of that body, then we can only wait and hope you heal naturally with time. Otherwise I'm afraid you'll be wedded to this body permanently," Mills said. "I'm sorry, but the damage is extensive. You're too deeply embedded in this nervous system. We could pry you out, how we do infants, but your awareness is too high, and your life matrix isn't as resilient as an infant's. Fifty-fifty it would kill you, ninety-ten you'd come out with severe psychological damage. This body would certainly die, which means if we got you out but not reconnected to the 'Face, you'd be a ghost."

Coar tried to imagine. "A ghost? Seriously?"

Mills shrugged, static face incongruous with the gesture. "How the hell should I know? It's a figure of speech. Best I can come up with considering no one's ever seen a case like yours before. I'm worried, Coar, because you've been stuck in there longer than is healthy. You have to prepare for side effects."

"What side effects?"

"Depression and anxiety for starters. You can no longer leave your body, Coar. No using and abusing then dumping it to recover while you skip to a fresh one. Right now we're steadying you with round-the-clock care. Feeding you. Managing your metabolism. Bathing you. Making sure you sleep enough. When you leave here, you'll have to take care of yourself. You get tired, sick, or hurt, you'll have to rest and heal. You get dirty, you'll have to wash. Your body will influence your mental state. You may find it diffi-cult to think when you're hungry or fatigued—or angry or upset. Your blood sugar may drop; your blood pressure may rise. The longer you stay in there, the more you'll identify as male. Do you recall your birth gender?"

"Male," Coar said.

"That might ease things a bit," Mills said. "What was Edon's?"

Coar shook his head. "Never came up."

"No matter. The point is, Coar, you can't skip to another body, so you must learn to manage the sensations you'll experience in this one. It's going to shake you up. You might feel despondent, para-noid, confused. You have to recognize those symptoms and come back for help."

"Understood," Coar said.

"Good. Return to your room and rest. Tomorrow we'll schedule another session. We'll do everything we can think of before we throw in the towel."

"What about the face I see? My birth face?" Coar asked.

"It isn't your birth face. How could you even know what that looks like?" Mills said. "It's likely a visual artifact produced by your mind to reconcile seeing the same face in the mirror for so long and not seeing your *elem*."

"It doesn't look much like me. It's out of focus."

"Your brain isn't used to the idea of having one face. Before your accident, when was the last time you spent a month—or even a week—in one body?"

"Never," Coar said.

"Exactly. Don't worry. It'll resolve itself." Mills sat in a chair by the door. "I have to get back to the forge, Coar. We're stripping in 16 new bodies this afternoon. One's work is never done."

Mills settled in the chair and grew still except for the gentle rise and fall of one's chest. Anyone connected to the 'Face would've seen Mill's *elem* blink out as one skipped to a body elsewhere in the forge. To Coar, it appeared as if Mills simply fell asleep, eyes open.

Coar shifted. The card scraped under one's thigh.

Equipment shutdown completed, the nurse—*David*, Coar remembered—left after a last blank-faced glance at Coar.

Across the room, the call concluded, Edon slid the phone into a pocket. Edon came to all of Coar's treatments. How long would one wait for a cure—*Coar despised the thought*—before leaving one, before moving on? The idea chilled Coar. One never wanted to be alone—especially not alone and cut off from the 'Face. If Coar's life matrix could heal itself, it might happen tomorrow, or ten years from now, or fifty. How could Edon be expected to wait that long? Impatient, passionate Edon, who lived fast and swept Coar along in one's wake. Coar wiped one's eyes, staving off tears, then slid from bed and dressed, palming the business card into a pocket.

"I'm sorry," Coar said.

Edon smiled then hugged Coar tight.

"It's all right," Edon said. "Everything will be all right."

"I can't face this without you," Coar said. "I need you."

"I know," Edon said.

"But it's so unfair to you."

"It is what it is, love. You'll get through it."

Coar wanted to believe, but Edon's face betrayed no reassurance, and tension in the brunette body—Edon's tension—signaled how much one held back.

You'll *get through it*—not *we*, Edon had said.

What if she leaves me?

Coar shuddered.

She?

I am he, *now. Is Edon* ... she?

No. I am he, and Edon is Edon.

Edon is one.

And I am alone.

He squeezed Edon's hand and let one take *him* back to his room.

II

YOUNG LOVE AND OTHER DAY TRIPS

The final treatments failed, and Coar left the body forge.

One night at home, he startled awake from a dream of his birth face.

The vague face floated beneath the surface of a pool so still its waters mirrored Coar staring into it. He tried to map his reflection onto his shimmery birth face, the similarities enticing, the differences maddening—awakening Coar with a pounding headache.

He rolled over, pressed against Edon's warmth. Although Edon could skip to a rested body to avoid slumber, one went to bed with Coar to help him sleep. Coar exhaled, relieved for the company, then touched Edon's thigh—and knew instantly Edon wasn't there.

One—*she*, he found himself thinking—felt wrong. Too still. Too deeply asleep. Too … empty. Once again, Edon had waited until Coar fell asleep then skipped to another body. How many times now? Coar had lost count, but it seemed Edon left almost every night. Maybe one had skipped to the office to deal with the latest ratings fallout. Maybe to see friends. Maybe anywhere, to be with anyone else. Or to be anyone else. Places Coar could no longer go.

He stuffed pillows behind his back and clicked the television remote.

A news show flickered across the screen on the opposite wall. In Morocco, a building collapse; one hundred fifty bodies lost, all life matrixes escaped via the 'Face to new bodies, no deaths. In Chile, an earthquake; more than six hundred bodies dead, again all life matrixes safely skipped to the 'Face. In Greece, riots over body shortages, pricking up the old debate of cloning versus natural re-production; three bodies destroyed, no life matrixes lost. The 'Face saved them all; it gathered them, sorted them, and sent them to new bodies. The 'Face now closed to Coar, whose mortality teased him from the images of broken bodies. He wondered how dying felt, afraid he might find out sooner than most. Everyone died, he reminded himself; skipping to the 'Face only delayed it.

Coar found little consolation.

"I'm so fucked," he said.

He switched channels to the Specta network. One of Edon's programs appeared.

Two for Flinching, a daredevil game show, where contestants challenged each other to defy their instincts by standing closest to a lava flow, lasting the longest skydiving sans parachute, or taking the most bullets from an old-fashioned six shooter, or other contests, skipping to a new body before the old one perished. Coar thought it was obvious why such shows were failing. When anyone could do the same things for kicks, why would anyone want to watch others do them? He had once told Edon as much, and one agreed. The shows, however, involved teams from different nations, and checked social tensions by uniting people around the common convention of the games. *We're barely keeping things running as it is*, Edon had said. *We can't lose the audience now. Once the last common thread gets pulled, everything unravels.* That rang true. Cities in disrepair. Roads and bridges crum-bling. Building collapses, vehicle colli-sions, and airplane crashes in the news, daily. The human work of a millennium decaying. The 'Face and the body forges all anyone cared to maintain anymore, they treated everything else like old furniture.

Coar looked at the sleeping body beside him.

Male, blond, fit. One of Edon's favorites.

Coar had often worn a voluptuous blonde to match it.

Throwing off the covers, Coar slid from bed to yank open his and Edon's closets.

Inside stood rows of glass-doored life chambers, where dor-mant bodies waited, plugged into a nutrition and waste disposal apparatus. Coar's side held three females and three males, a mix of races and body types. Edon's contained five males, four females, revealing a preference for tall, fit physiques and almond-hued flesh. Coar couldn't complain. His eclecticism didn't extend as far as ab-original, overweight, handicapped, or other extreme body types, but those were special order and expensive, anyway. It was cheaper to rent them as desired. Any type, anytime, anywhere—for everyone except Coar. He eyed the empty chamber in his closet for the body he wore. *My only body now.* Two empty places waited on Edon's side: one for the male in the bed; the other for a body Edon had bought since the accident and had never worn around Coar: a black-haired man. A body to share with someone new.

It's really over, Coar realized. *Twenty-five years, and it's done and gone.*

How many times has Edon skipped out in that body?

How many times has one—she—left me behind?

No, not she. One.

Edon is one.

One who betrayed me.

Coar slammed the doors and kicked over the chair of the desk in the corner.

The blond's eyes snapped open. The body lifted its head and stared at him blankly.

Coar glared back. Rage seethed in him. He wanted to make the body stop staring, to end its mindless breathing, and leave it for Edon to discover, to show he knew what one—what *she*—was doing. He had never before felt such intense emotions. Anger crackled through him, blurred his vision, throbbed in his head. It ran hot and begged release, a conflagration too long denied igniting. Coar grabbed a vase from the desk and hurled it, smashing it against the wall behind the bed. Still, the blond body stared at him, glassy-eyed, unknowing.

"Let me out of here!" Coar raked his fingernails across his chest, drawing lines of blood.

He rushed downstairs to the kitchen, to the liquor cabinet, and poured a glass of whiskey. He drank, poured another, then a third. Heat seeped through his body, soothing, slowing his mind, dulling his furor. He eyed his reflection in the stainless steel surface of the refrigerator. His birth face and real face blended into a face Coar couldn't quite grasp. A senseless mess of features. *Is this who I am now? A collision of faces? A jumble of identity fragments?* He longed to return to work, to code photons for life matrix sub-strata systems, to wrap his mind around something that still made sense.

He wanted Edon.

He grabbed his phone and dialed Edon's number.

Edon's phone rang in the living room.

Coar traced the ring, stared at the blank blue screen that would have displayed his avatar if he were still connected to the 'Face. He took another drink.

One—Edon—*she*—was leaving him.

Had *left* him. Alone.

Coar's stomach ached. He tried to remember the last time he'd eaten. In the past he had dined only for pleasure, leaving fed bodies in the life chambers for metabolic systems to balance calories and eliminate waste. Mills had said he would develop a sense of eating for sustenance, but so far that natural rhythm eluded him. After half an hour's discomfort, Coar remembered the sensation in his lower body meant he needed to void his bladder. He stumbled to the little used bathroom and relieved himself.

Afterward, the bottle nearly empty, Coar set out to find Edon.

He knew Edon's favorite restaurants and shops, lounges and bars. He drove to one after another, disappointed at each, stopping long enough for drinks in the bars, keeping numbed, hazy, holding back the desperation threatening to overwhelm him, wondering if this catastrophe of emotions was what Doctor Mills had warned about. Coar exhausted all likely locations before he remembered one more.

He drove to the hotel where he'd first met Edon. His car skidded to a stop by the entrance, jumping the curb and smashing a garbage bin, spilling trash onto the sidewalk. The door attendant came running as Coar staggered from the driver's seat.

"Asshole! What the hell?" said the attendant, clothed in a muscular body. "You drunk? It's illegal to drive with your drinking body, moron."

Coar shoved the attendant aside and weaved into the lobby.

Alerted by the crash and the shouting, every one inside faced Coar, trying to make sense of the disheveled one without sense to skip out of a drunken body and sober up. Their *elems* invisible to him, Coar sought any sign of Edon. He scrounged his memories of Edon's newest body. Black-haired, dark-skinned, male, tall, and as blank-faced as the others. Every passing second fed his doubt that he'd find Edon—and then, by the elevator, a black-haired man ran a hand through one's hair, rubbed one's forehead, touched one's thigh.

Edon.

Coar bolted across the lobby. People cleared from his path. He brushed past a young man and woman and grabbed the body.

"Edon!"

"What do you want?" said the one Coar held, face emotionless. Coar imagined Edon's *elem* lighting up like fireworks.

"I need you. Come *with* me," he said.

"Let go of me!"

The black-haired body struggled. Coar tightened his grip.

"Come home. Please!" he said. "I can't lose you. Come home, at least for tonight."

"No! I don't know you! Get your hand off me! What's wrong with your *elem*? Why is it scrambled?"

Coar hesitated. Maybe Edon wasn't inside this body.

It has to be her. This is the body from her closet.

Not her. *One. Edon is one, not a body.*

You are he, *but Edon is one.*

Still one.

"Don't leave me alone!" Coar said.

The black-haired body cowered as Coar swung and then hammered its face with his fist. The first blow cracked the jaw. A second punch struck its chest, slamming it against the elevator console. It jolted, sagged limp, and Coar suspected Edon, or whoever had been in there, had skipped to the 'Face. But a chain reaction that had been festering in him since the crash, and through all the failed attempts to heal, gripped Coar. He couldn't stop. He struck the body again, kicked it, stomped it, punched it, beat it bruised and bloody, the wet smacks of flesh and bone impacts filling the stunned silence of the lobby. Violent energy gushed from Coar, and he channeled it at the shell of the one who'd betrayed him.

Coar beat on the body until he slipped on the bloody tile floor.

Someone said, "*Coar.* Stop it."

Coar looked to the young couple. The man, maybe nineteen, athletic, brown hair, and tall. The female, willowy, thin, red-haired, graceful curves beneath a summer dress.

"Scrap for the forges," the man said. "That what you wanted?"

Coar stared, confused.

"What the hell's wrong with you?" the man said.

Coar's heart galloped. His head spun from too much drink and too great stress, and he tipped into a vertiginous swirl, a man balanced above an abyss. Swaying, he steadied himself against the wall.

"Edon?"

"You thought I was in that body," Edon said.

Coar nodded. "It's from your closet."

"Shit, Coar. That body cost me a lot of money."

"Who...was in it?"

"Someone I loaned it to for the night. None of your damn business."

"Edon, don't do this. Don't. Leave me. Alone."

Edon sighed. The female body hung off Edon's arm, rested its head on one's shoulder.

"No bitch talk, Coar. I can't stand bitch talk," Edon said. "You are broken. We don't live in the same world, don't speak the same language anymore. I need to be *with* who I want, and I need to *be* who I want. You think I want a man for the rest of my life? I don't always want to be a woman or the same age as you or even in the same damn city. If you can't be the people I need you to be, and I can't be the person you need, how can we stay together?"

Coar said, "We can make it work."

"We can't."

"I can't live without you," Coar said and reached for Edon, who backed away.

"No, Coar. Get out of here. Run back to the body forge, to Doctor Mills. When the police come for you, tell them your injury drove you over the edge. I'll back you up. But you can never leave there, Coar. They can care for you in the body forge. I don't ever want to see you again."

Coar searched Edon's passive, plastic face for anything resembling Edon. It looked naked without an *elem*, so out of synch with its angry, bitter voice. He didn't know who Edon really was. He had never known. An *elem* was only data made visible. A gesture wasn't enough to know one, not truly, not in a way that mattered. Even when he still saw *elems*, Coar had only ever known who people wanted to be when they were with him, and he had only shown them the same—and who was to say how much of any of it was real?

"Go!" Edon screamed.

Coar rushed out into the night's dark grasp as police sirens approached the hotel. Crying, shivering, he chased block after block, racing, purposeless, into the heart of the city, until cramps in his legs and torso forced him to stop. He sank to his knees by the curb and threw up what liquor remained in his stomach. He couldn't go home, didn't want to return to the body forge. One other choice remained. He fished the card nurse *David* had given him out of his wallet and dialed Widds.

III

PROSOPAGNOSIA

"Slow." The woman, Widds, gripped Coar's wrist and stopped him from slurping more water. "You'll make yourself sick if you go too fast."

Coar lowered the cup. Water spilled down his chin, onto his shirt, already stained with crumbs and splotches of food. He took several deep breaths then sipped again. His hands, bound together with rope, gripped the cup awkwardly.

Widds nodded. "Better. Be patient."

Coar bit off a piece of bread from his plate and chewed.

"Good, good," Widds said.

The food settled Coar's stomach, helped clear his head. Confusion and fear replaced his rage. He sat in a house outside the city amidst the ruins of an old village, a place no one from the city ever traveled. Widds and David had come in a car when he called and had taken him here. Coar heard others moving around the house.

Floors creaking. Doors closing. Faucets running. Toilets flushing. But Widds and David kept Coar in the kitchen, feeding him.

After satiating his hunger, Coar said, "Why did you help me?"

Widds smiled. "You're like us now. Off the 'Face.'"

"I don't want to be 'him.'" Coar shook his head. "I want to be 'one.'"

"You've been granted a gift. You can live a true life here. If you choose to stay. You're not a prisoner."

Coar raised his bound hands.

"You're violent. It's part of the transition. We'll untie you when it passes," Widds said. "The transition, the adjustment—that's the roughest part. Do you want to stay?"

"I don't know what I want," Coar said.

"It's overwhelming," Widds said. "Start with one question you most want answered."

Coar's brain labored under the dregs of alcohol in his blood. His head ached, and light pained his eyes. He had never felt this way before. Widds called it a "hangover."

"Take your time," she said. "We risked sneaking David into the forge with a false *elem* when we heard rumors that your caregivers were body-sticking for your benefit. No one noticed him. Maybe while you were there, you wondered about something you saw, or something your doctors said?"

"The day I gave you Widds' card," David said, "you woke rough from the anesthesia."

"I saw my birth face while I was under," Coar said. "I see it in my dreams."

He told them how Mills had explained the face.

"Everyone goes through something like that when they disconnect," Widds said. "A reckoning. It *is* a birth face of sorts. Not the one you were actually born with, but one you can be *reborn* with. Look in the mirror by the sink. Tell me what you see."

Coar scuffed his chair back from the table, stood, and looked in the grimy mirror.

A disjointed mess peered back at him. It possessed elements of the face he'd seen in the blackness of unconsciousness, as well as some from the face that belonged to his body, but other characteristics crept in too. Bits of every face he'd ever had. Interference. He rubbed his eyes and tried to describe it to Widds but sounded foolish and gave up.

"What your doctor said is true," Widds said. "But what those who work in the forges see as a disorder, we know as humanity. Your identity is taking root. Once you accept it, you'll see your face clearly. We can help, or you can return to the city and live in a forge until you die."

"The police will arrest me," Coar said.

"Not here. As long as we stay outside the city, they don't care what we do," Widds said. "Why would they bother? You scared some people and broke a body that belonged to your partner. They have bigger problems. Skipping to the 'Face every time something goes south makes people reckless and indifferent. Things get ruined. Society is breaking down out there."

Coar scanned Widds' face, then David's, both so alien and expressive.

Full of things he'd never seen in other faces.

Presence. Immediacy. Truth.

They terrified him. He wanted to be with Edon, back on the 'Face, skipping bodies; back at work, organizing photon bundles. He didn't belong among outlaws, among the insane who believed physical truth defined one's existence.

The World Within Us.

One body, a singular identity.

A philosophy outlawed a century ago.

Heresy. Madness.

Coar wanted no part of that life.

His rage returned in a seismic urge.

Shoving his hands under the edge of the table, he flipped it and pressed it against Widds, knocking her to the floor. He slammed

David aside and pushed through the door into the next room.

Coar's muscles burned. His head swam with the exertion.

His hands ached, still sore from beating the body in the hotel.

The pain frightened him. It stayed with him. He couldn't skip away from it. He never realized how long pain lasted, how deeply hunger boiled, or thirst burned, how tired and abused a sleepless body became. He froze when he saw the people in the next room. Faces lit up and brimmed with emotion. He smelled them, too, their odor so different than the sterile bodies of the forges. Coar raced along a hallway, fumbled with the front door knob, and then fled outside. People on the porch watched him with curiosity. He stumbled down the steps, fell on the weedy lawn, rose, staggered to the street. Their gazes chased him. He shunned their faces. Their animate faces. Like his now. Faces of expression. Faces shorn of manipulation and masks. Life embodied in soft wrinkles and moist eyes and cracked lips that would never belong to anyone else. Faces sculpted by experience.

Coar's legs turned to rubber. He collapsed in the street.

He rolled over, spied the distant city lights, a cold luminosity beckoning and, at the same time, repulsing Coar. A massive *elem*, an illusion. Edon dwelled there. Somewhere. As someone.

Coar struggled upright. He stepped toward the city.

Stopped.

Widds approached. "We'll drive you back," she said.

"I ..." Coar's voice cracked. "I can't. I'll be alone."

"Weren't you always alone there?" Widds said.

"... Yes."

"Stay with us."

"I can't bear to look at your faces," Coar said. "And *my* face ... it must be grotesque."

"You have a good face. You only need time to understand it. And ours."

"How long?"

"A year, maybe two."

Widds gestured, and David came with a strip of red cloth. "When your mind knows it's right, you'll see your own face clearly. We'll help you through it. Then you can choose a new name if you want. Not all of us do. To bear the weight of existence in your flesh, to face yourself in the mirror every day, is the price of a real life, Coar. It's a price people on the 'Face never pay, an experience they never obtain."

Widds pulled the cloth over Coar's eyes, taking away the faces and light, and then tied it tight around the back of his head. Coar walked among the people. Voices came from within the house. He smelled their bodies and felt the air temperature drop as a breeze brushed his skin. Widds guided him, her fingers at his elbow. The others touched him, too, stroked him, squeezed him, and patted him on the back. The sensations belonged to *him*. Not to a body or a memory. In the darkness of the blindfold, his birth face appeared, steady, yet cloudy, nascent, still awaiting an answer Coar could only now begin to provide.

01100110 00100000 01110100 01101111 01100100
01100001 01111001 00100000 00101101 00100000
01100010 01110101 01110100 00100000 01110100

SIMULACRUM

| JASON V BROCK |

"All that we see or seem is but a dream within a dream..."
– *Edgar Allan Poe*

"There are many entrances, but only one exit."

IN THE LONG, QUIET SECONDS before she slammed into the unyielding pavement at terminal velocity, the young woman had no way of knowing she could never actually die.

After the stunned crowd had dissipated and the investigation was closed, the official coroner's inquest would record her cause of death as "suicide." She had known differently.

In order to die, one must have lived: she had never truly done either.

She rolls off him, curling up on her side of the bed. He lies on his back, hands on his chest, sated, relaxed. The curtains are drawn across the window, muting the harsh afternoon sunlight. He smiles at her, eyes half-closed, his tone low, sensual.

"That was great."

She turns away, staring at the ceiling. "It was ... It always is."

He grins.

"I can't keep doing this," she says, suddenly pulling the blanket tight around her nude body.

He frowns. "Oh, shit. Not this again."

"I mean it this time. This has to stop."

"I still don't see—"

She cuts him off with sharply delivered words: "Meeting like this, it..." *She pauses. "I feel cheap...used."*

He puts a hand on her thigh, squeezes. "This is crazy. I care about you very much. You know that."

"No, I don't know that. For Christ's sake, if you really cared about me, we wouldn't be meeting in cheap hotels for nooners."

He shrugs, running a fist along his jaw. His eyes are dark, moody. "You know I'm not ready for more just yet. Not until I have my career back on track. I can't handle you and that. At least not yet."

She smiles tightly. "You don't seem to have any problem handling me in bed."

"That's different," he says.

"Yeah? Well, that's why it can't go on."

"What are you saying?"

"I'm telling you we have to do something about this. Make different arrangements."

"I thought we had something special." He props up on his elbow, regarding her intently.

"We do ... sex. But that's just physical. What I'm talking about is emotional. I need more of a commitment, not more rolls in the hay." She pushes her hair behind her ear. "I can get that anywhere."

His gaze is intense. "That's it, huh? Just sex ... Why throw away what we have just because—"

"Because you want to play around?" She smirks, sitting up on the edge of the bed. "Why not?" Her tone is cold, clipped.

"Seems kind of...abrupt. I thought we'd hashed all this out a couple of months ago. Can't we talk it over a little more?" He touches her back, but she arches away.

She glares at him over her shoulder. "That's the trouble with you—you don't think. You're a beautiful animal, but that's not enough for me."

Turning away from him, she gets out of bed and crosses the room. As the bed sheet falls away, her naked skin glows milk-pale in the room's diffused light. Putting on her clothes, she languorously strokes her legs as she pulls on her stockings. Her breasts—full, heavy—hang down voluptuously as she bends over to retrieve her bra from the floor. She turns to face him, slinking under the straps as she adjusts her cleavage.

"And another thing," she says, her face flushed with tension. "I don't think I've been the only woman in your life, have I? That's why we don't go out in the evenings anymore, and why you won't take me over to your place."

His tone is edged. "Well, we never agreed to being exclusive . . ."

"You bastard. You admit it!"

"Don't put words in my mouth! If I was seeing anyone else you'd know." He softens. "That's not it and you know it. Look, my schedule is fucked right now, and my new boss is all over me about getting the next build ready to ship. You know how it is at the end of a product cycle. They're on to us, too, I think."

Sitting up in bed, he lights a cigarette, watching her as she pulls on her sandals. He continues: "I don't have time for anything right now. I've been working crazy shifts and the house is a damn wreck. Not to mention I've still got another month of this shit before it cools off. How about cutting me a little slack?"

She looks at him, crossing her arms. "You're not supposed to smoke in here." His expression hardens; there is heat in his eyes. "I paid for the damn room. I'll smoke in here if I want to."

"That's right," she says. "You always do just what you want. I'm just like a cigarette to you. I only gratify a passing need."

"That's a cheap shot," he snaps. "And it's not true. I have a lot of respect for you, and you know that."

"You respect fucking me . . . you don't respect me."

He sweeps a hand through his hair. "Fine. How about we just take a breather and revisit the issue when we're both calmer?"

She turns, gathers her purse from a chair near the foot of the bed, and stands with her back to him, her hand on the doorknob. "It's taken me this long to get up enough nerve to be honest with you about everything. I've been a coward."

"Come on, don't say that."

Now fully dressed, a perfect hourglass silhouette at the door, she turns to face him. "You're a great lover—but you're not a great man. Sometimes I feel like I don't know who you are anymore. You've changed. And so have I."

"Look, we've disagreed about this before. Just give it a little more time—"

She huffs in irritation. "Face it: I have." She opens the door. "Don't call me, I'll call you."

She leaves him staring after her as she exits the motel room.

Misty Petit was a half-hour late for work at Pacific Data Systems. An attractive woman in her late thirties, slim and brown-eyed, her tanned skin attested to time spent in the sun. The gray-haired security guard in the lobby grinned at her as she handed him her purse.

"Welcome back! No guns, knives ... atomic bombs?" he asked.

She gave him a sour look. "I'm not up for comedians today."

He handed the purse back, then proceeded to examine her laptop case.

"Bad day already?"

"No ... bad *night,*" she replied. "Not enough sleep. Rotten way to come back from vacation."

He returned her case. "Too bad. You do seem a little tired. Merced's looking for you, by the way."

"Okay. Sorry for my grumpiness, Pete. I'll be okay once I check in and get my morning coffee."

She headed for the elevator.

When Misty arrived at her manager's office, stocky, balding Gabe Merced was hunched over his desk, hands tented as he talked on speakerphone. He acknowledged her entrance with a wave. She sat down, putting her laptop case and purse on her lap.

"Right. We're on schedule," Gabe said.

"Good," the deep, accented male voice replied on the speaker. "We are getting plans together for our next visit. Is Misty back yet?"

Gabe put his finger to his lips, looking at Misty. "She is—I spoke with her this morning, and she's ready to go. She said that the latest version is golden."

There was a quiet moment. "Let's hope so, Gabe. People are

getting impatient. Money's tight, so we need to deliver something good. Sooner is better than later, if you catch my drift."

Gabe nodded, his forehead shining slightly. "I got it. We're on top of things, Sanin." He glanced at Misty. "So when will you and Sanjay be here?"

"He'll be in next week, I'll be there a few days later. I have meetings in Moscow first, then a quick trip to Hong Kong. Ever since the Fukushima disaster, funding has been tough, but it's slowly getting better. In fact, there's a VC in Hong Kong that's expressed an interest in what PDS is doing—specifically this project."

Gabe visibly relaxed. "That's great news. We'll be on the case, especially now that Misty's back."

"Good. Looking forward to it. Anything else, then? I've got a conference with Sanjay and Sergey in ten."

"No, that's all for now. I'll keep you posted."

"Will do. Have a good day." The speaker went dead. Gabe punched a button to end the call. He took a deep breath, then turned his attention to Misty. "Well, you heard what he said. Welcome back!"

Misty smiled at him. "Sorry I'm late, Gabe. I overslept. Vacation was sort of a letdown; had to deal with some personal stuff. Wound up being more of a *staycation* ... To cap it, I had bad dreams all night."

Her dark eyes were shadowed with fatigue.

He smiled back at her. "Sorry to hear that. A lot going on. You heard—Sanjay's coming in from India. He's into what we're doing, but says he's getting static from Sergey and Bjorn about cost-overruns. Sanin is running interference, but he can only hold off the dogs for so long." Gabe shrugged, suddenly pensive. "Anyway, glad you're back. Now we've got to hit the ground running. Morgan's team has done some good work; I think you'll be pleased." He studied her for a moment. "You *do* look drained. Bad dreams, huh?"

Misty smiled, then rubbed her eyes. "I wish I could recall what was happening in them. All I remember is that there was a lot of commotion ... A man and woman were fighting ... and I had that horrible *falling* sensation. That's what kept waking me up."

"Dreams slip away fast," Gabe said. "I can never remember mine."

"These were *intense*," she said. "Scary."

Gabe stood up and walked around the desk. "Well, you'll be okay. So, ready to check out the new build?"

She nodded. "Right after I have my coffee. Can't function without it."

"Hmm ... God knows what they do to coffee beans these days. You read about that *Kopi Luwak* stuff from Sumatra? Where they feed the coffee beans to civets and they poop it out? How can folks *drink* that? And it's the most expensive coffee in the world! Green tea's a lot better for you."

Misty smiled, shaking her head.

Gabe shouldered her laptop bag as they left his office. "Me, I used to swig down like seven cups of coffee a day. Started getting blackouts, so I gave it up. You quit smoking. Why not coffee? Maybe it's revving you up, causing bad dreams. Did for me."

She nodded. "I *could*," she admitted, "but I don't see how one or two cups a day is equal to smoking. Besides, it keeps me productive." He shrugged, leading her down the hall. "Just a thought."

After a labyrinth of hallways and multiple biometric checkpoints, they finally arrived at a large cluster of rooms in the heart of the PDS campus: "Area 52," as Gabe jokingly referred to it. Its actual name, the Multiple Immersive Simulated Total Reality Test Station, was too cumbersome for normal usage. Misty just called it the Sim-Room.

The place was a dark wash of black until Merced switched on the overhead lights, causing the sterile rooms to blossom into sickly life, revealing rows of glassed booths, each with a computer workstation and a reclining chair, their screens glowing, silent.

Misty sat down in one of the cubicles as Gabe handed her a bulky headset with miniature, inward-facing video monitors for lenses. The device was large enough to cover her ears and most of her face. She examined the apparatus carefully before turning it on. "Hey, no more wires!"

Gabe nodded. "Right. Morgan and his team were able to add the wireless code back into the embedded OS last night. First time since the old prototype was damaged that they got it working properly." He adjusted a setting on the computer as Misty reclined into the zero gravity test chair, tightening the strap of the glasses on the back of her head. "Looks like he's got the 'Auto Record' function working, too. It'll record all experiences as *you* perceive them for anybody to play back later. All we'll need to do to see your new—*extra-reality*, I guess you could call it—is hit the 'Memory' button on the headset."

"Wow ... this is *awesome!*" Misty looked around the room, eyes hidden behind the tiny screens. "It's getting there, for sure. The new cameras are *excellent*. And so small! I didn't even notice them. I had a feeling once we hit the 40-megapixel range that the detail would be indistinguishable from life, even with motion. I can't detect any interlacing at *all*, and it's a *lot* brighter than with the old cameras. Very real. Turns the whole world into a giant green screen." She adjusted the lenses on her face. "It's a lot more comfortable, too. Feels like they were able to integrate the electrodes into the cap better."

Gabe stood next to her, sharing her excitement. "That's right —while you were luxuriating, we were busy!" He laughed, touching her shoulder as he watched the computer screen. "Almost ready to sub the live feed with the sim. Still a little slow to call up the program sometimes. Here we go ... Now—what do you see?"

"It ... it's *beautiful*," she told him. "Exactly as I imagined it would look. A dry Martian landscape ... red sand ... dusty horizon ... even a base camp! The 3D is perfect!" She reached out from the chair. "I'm standing next to a building of some sort. I can sense solidness at my fingertips when I touch it. Also, there's a light breeze. I can hear it against my suit."

"But you can still hear me okay?"

"Yes—you're coming in loud and clear through my helmet speakers, and the surround-sound is amazing."

Gabe made a note on the pad next to the computer. "So the Convergence chip seems to be acting properly, good. Do you see any people around?"

"Yes. Two. They appear to be base camp astronauts. They are commiserating with each other." Misty waved into the air again. "They can't see me, so the Stealth setting must be working. I cannot *wait* to see what'll happen once we have full integration and can go into Live Mode. Be amazing to *literally* interact not only with other users, but also the characters we've created to populate these scenarios. All in the *same* non-reality space—shared unreality! Amazing..."

"What else?"

"Everything is utterly true-to-life ... I am *here,* Gabe. I'm on Mars!" She squirmed with delight on the recliner. "They're pointing at something in the distance ... Oh, I see it! Way out on the horizon...a dark spot, sort of amorphous. Storm, maybe? It's so far away I can't make it out."

Gabe nodded, making more notes. "Can you flip into 'Alt' mode? Morgan e-mailed me this morning that it's up now. He said it should allow you to run multiple instances per session, either new or a memory."

Misty touched a button on the frame: instantly a jittery series of flashes and video noise filled her vision. "Yeah, it worked, I guess ... but just some jumpy images of what looks like ... the *Moon?*" Misty strained to comprehend the scene. "And the sound is *really* low, staticy ... Wait—now ... now it's a woman looking into a mirror. It's breaking up a little. This is spooky, Gabe. I'm getting a kind of ... *déjà vu* here. I'm *there,* but *not.* She's from my perspective, but the part of her reflection I can see...isn't me! Sort of an out-of-body experience. Oh, wait—there's the lunar landscape again." She hit the button once more. "Okay. Back on Mars. This looks phenomenal, but the other scenes not so much. Seemed like some kind of data corruption. Do you know if Morgan is testing on an old piece of removable media or something? Maybe he accidentally overwrote another program, or forgot to format the card."

Gabe was concerned. "Strange...Don't know. He's supposed to use fresh media for all new sessions—said he was, anyway. We'll check it out later. He switched over from CFs to SD cards, since it made the glasses smaller and the capacity is almost the same. Maybe the wiring is off on this cap. He's still working on the other two prototypes. They'll be ready to use in a day or two, he said. Anyway, from all I've seen, your new code is outstanding—we can record real-time, lossless 3D without any lagginess, compression errors, or artifacting." He wrote another note on the pad. "I'll have Morgan and Ganesha drill down into the Moon/woman-in-the-mirror thing tonight."

Misty removed the device from her head. She was aglow with excitement. "My God, Gabe...Other than that little glitch, it's *fantastic!*"

"I really like what you and the team have done," he said, "but we need more funds. Hopefully Sanin can hook this Hong Kong venture capitalist—sounds like the kind of big fish we need about now. I think if we can stay off the chopping block and get all the bugs ironed out it's going to be revolutionary. Question is, how do we sell this to the bean-counters like Bjorn?"

Misty slowly turned the headset in her hands, examining it. "Well, unlike old software-only VRML stuff, *this* virtual reality program and hardware could make a vital training tool...They can then sift through multiple points of divergence in more practical ways—safely merge potentiality and actuality in realistic settings. I was thinking that it would be great for astronauts who *really* go to Mars. Give them previews of what to expect...how best to function on another planet, deal with the isolation, handle emergencies and so on. That's one of the reasons why I wrote the Mars script. And we can augment that—of course it might become awfully difficult to distinguish between the 'real' world and the 'fake' one. But, will it ultimately matter? We want it to be as 'real' as possible. So as we improve the program, the computer-generated characters will have ever more layers of sophistication. Think about *that*...Not only will the renders *look* as authentic as a physical person, but the reactions that we've programmed them to have—or *not* have—will become more refined over time ... more *evolved* by the program itself, especially with all the fuzzy logic and AI functions we're incorporating...It's an example of a kind of 'software Butterfly Effect'—adding small tweaks that can yield big results later as the computational models advance and the database develops in gradual complexity. I want to keep pushing, to try and extend these quantum physical ideas into the simulated mindscape."

Merced nodded. "Good points. That'll help me pitch the big boys on why we've been sucking up their entire R&D budget for the past two years! It took a long time just to nail down the Thought Amplification Circuits, but it's hard for them to appreciate that without experiencing the technology firsthand. I mean, your work alone—binding thought based action, tactile and auditory sensation into a non-physical software environs—is groundbreaking stuff. So the gear's still a little...*rustic,* shall we say, in the looks department. Big deal!"

He gently took the headset from her, regarding the vast array of wires, electrodes, and the rechargeable battery pack adorning its surface. As he studied the rows of binocular cameras and the tiny binaural microphones on the outside of the speakers, Gabe was engrossed in thought. "You know," he said, "we can even design other programs for war games, or to help veterans with Post-Traumatic Stress Disorder. I thought about that after talking with my dad—he's a vet with PTSD. Since we can take people to the past *or* the future, and it's like they're actually *there,* in a parallel physical environment, it could be great to have them 'relive' things that left them emotionally gummed up; maybe change the outcome of a terrible situation for the better. Sort of 'reprogram' their bad experiences so they can cope in society, a lot like the way mirrors can help amputees get around phantom limb pain. Also, I think that airplane pilots without access to a simulator would find it useful, so there's the commercial avionics companies. Could help patients with diseases like ALS to socialize, or upload memories, thoughts, and so on, or control devices. Hell, even surgeons could benefit by using it to rehearse remote operations without a body!"

Misty agreed: "The potential is practically endless. When I studied deterministic chaos theory, I realized that even though the superficial fabric of reality seems random, it has deeper fractal elements we can harness…I prefer to think of it as 'Enhanced-' or 'Meta-Reality.' Old computer-generated VR has a lot of baggage associated with it, since it never really took off. And this is *so* beyond simple 3D! It's more of a hyper-real video game, a completely accurate sim-world. That's an important distinction to me: *simulated* versus *virtual.* Virtual seems 'fake,' or contrived, whereas 'simulated' implies involvement. Participation … It's a *type* of reality, a subset. A state of 'unreality,' kind of the way a vampire is 'undead'—not reality, but not fantasy." She looked up at her boss, lost in the moment. "And I have an idea that might even be able to recreate olfactory and taste stimulation…tap into smell and taste profiles already buried in the subconscious. Taste and smell are powerful, as they can link places and situations to memory, as in Proust's *Remembrance of Things Past,* when the narrator's involuntary recollections are triggered by the taste and smell of the madeleine cake dipped in tea. Could be a potent way to world-build—*total* sensory immersion—and would bypass the uncanny valley, since it's all appropriate to the situation, and not like seeing a leprechaun on the *Titanic*. No chance for cognitive dissonance. In fact, the *opposite* was happening to me: I noticed that the more I focused on the simulation, the more I bought in; I started to *believe* I was on a Martian plain tens of thousands of miles away. Incredible, really."

Merced grinned. "Not to mention other things that could be explored a little closer to home. Games … socializing with multiple parties … even more *adult* entertainment."

She blushed. "Careful, Gabe! The field's wide open, you might say. There's still one major problem, though."

"Which is?"

"We need a better safety measure than just taking the stupid cap off."

He shook his head. "What do you mean? How could simulated reality, even a pseudo-reality, be dangerous? The operator is always in control. You could stop it anytime you wanted to by just cutting it off."

Misty sat up. "That's true to a point, but when we start to merge existences and sessions, it could get dangerous; I call it 'Diminishing Convergence'—it's a compression of space-time as VR and 'true' reality fuse together in the participant's mind. I've been noticing that the closer we get to the convergence point, the more timeslips and unreliability we have with character behavior. Makes me a little uneasy. I mean, once you're into a Meta-Reality session, there's no *non-physical* way back. Like today, I had to *physically* take the headset off; of course, alternatively, I can reach up and hit the off button. But what if you *can't* for some reason?" She was visibly unsettled by the prospect.

"Do you think that could really happen?" Gabe asked.

She scoffed. "Humans being humans, absolutely. We always have to be mindful of the law of unintended consequences, good or bad, of this technology. For example, suppose someone was being harmed by this? Like being forced to experience a rape, or attacked, or even 'murdered'? That's a real emotion. Remember the program is at its core self-organizing; it is designed to gather impression data not only from the *participant,* but also from the programmed database of real world assets that we've trained it on … not to mention the library of flora, fauna, machines, humans, and the world that we've been collecting. Add that to all the mental ephemera we've gotten from the various universities we've partnered with for the Functional-MRIs, the holographic databanks of memories/impressions we've harvested in the field and so on, and there's a *huge* amount of information there not just for good, but to be potentially *abused* … And let's not forget that people will be *adding* to that scaffolding, too, using their personal experiences, recording their *own* memories—even tinkering with the kernel of the code. Theoretically, somebody could upload a rooted version of the program into the wild, and that could introduce all kinds of noise, some of which could be beneficial, just like with real-life where it allows us to cogitate decision points that we may never have considered." She rubbed her temple. "But not all noise is *good;* it could range from simply too much informational dissonance to, in more sinister hands, steganographic—designed to be obscured, and perhaps harmful. Once it's viral, that's it—we'd never be able to control it. It would be a sort of high-level 'mind-hacking.' Hacking *right* into a participant's brain … short-circuiting the unconscious, the subconscious."

Misty looked at the computer monitor, deep in thought. "Those fMRIs have shown that there is no difference *neurally* between *actual* experience and *perceptual* experience. All reality is fundamentally based on self-delusion anyway on some level." She looked back at Gabe. "In other words, the *sessions* are as real to us as our perceptions of 'true reality.' So, again, if someone is murdered, say, in the sim-world, does that mean that they are killed again and again? I mean, now that they are stored only as *data,* do they have a life and death that achieves a meta-state of 'ontological reality' due to the Observer Effect? One that can be relived/replayed over and over, perhaps with differing outcomes? And how do we keep all these divergent realities from glopping together, like gumbo?" Misty's eyes widened at the prospect. "On second thought, though, maybe we don't *want* to stop that. Just have a few protective controls in place. This could become a *super*-neural network! A real *spiritus mundi*. Might be a good thing ... if it isn't used for bad ends."

Gabe held up his hand in a quieting gesture. "Come on now, Misty. Are you saying that a character that you or someone else may have written in a bit of source code could be equivalent to a living being? That's—"

"Crazy? Maybe not, Gabe." She laughed at the absurdity of her commentary before continuing: "I know it *sounds* far-fetched, but hear me out. Can we be sure that the incidents in the sim-reality environs are *not* 'reality' as we've come to understand it? I'm sure there are some Buddhists and Hindus that might argue the point! Think about it." Misty waved her hands dramatically as she explained. "It creates a *true* 'afterlife' of sorts; a whole new 'dimension' of potential 'ghosts' ... a virtual realm of the technologically 'non-living.' When does the threshold for life get crossed, anyway? Or identity?"

Gabe was shaking his head in bewilderment. "I'm not following."

Misty drew in a deep breath, calming herself before continuing. "For example, perhaps simple consciousness is enough to attain 'personhood.' Is that the precursor to sentience? Certainly, self-awareness, on some level, is. Currently, there are no non-organically-based life forms that are sentient. These could be the first; mark my words: these characters that we're scripting, they *will* become self-aware eventually. That's the whole point—to make the 'illusion of life' *real*. And that means they'll have *identity* as well, Gabe—a true sense of *self*. So, yeah, a participant *could* just use the gadgetry on the fly for novel new experiences or games, but..." She looked directly at Gabe, pausing for a moment. "More sinister than that, they could also program things *away* from free will, into a deterministic point-of-view. And maybe a *bad* POV. They could then use PDS's intellectual property and patents—*my* algorithms—to project reactions and predict scenarios into some nebulous—harmful—futurescape, and with a layer of plausible deniability that could hold up to high levels of scrutiny. What if a character 'takes over' the sim? We might not be able to control them. Wait'll legal gets wind of *that*. We might be up against long odds anyway, but we have to *try* and lock the platform down as much as we can before we drop it live on developers and, God help us, the general population." Misty paused again, sobered by her realization. "We need to avoid a kind of 'looping' of experience where the participant has no control. Also, what if a kid got ahold of this thing? It might cause them some kind of harm. I don't think we can allow the viewer to get *that* locked in. I want to write in an 'exit'—a special way to call up '*actual*' reality...whatever that means."

Gabe was quiet. "Wow. That's pretty far-out stuff. Do you think you *can* design an exit?"

She frowned. "I'm sure. Going to take me awhile, though —I'll need some extra funding."

Gabe pursed his lips. "Like I said, we're *beyond* stretched to the limit on this whole project. We've exhausted the original budget and are into next year's fiscal stash. Plus, Sanin mentioned that the Pentagon has been rumbling about their interest; they might try to get more involved for military-only usage. Which could be a source of funding, but it leaves a bad taste in my mouth, as they might try to phase out research into other applications. Could be dangerous—mind-control, Big Brother. What if *they* used it for torture or something? Could be some real Orwellian shit going on there. Leaves Sanin cold, too, but Bjorn would slaughter his family to make a dime. He wants to take PDS public in a year or so, so he's all about cashing out on some mega-IPO. He's pretty unscrupulous. Having a fat military contract looks good on the books." He tossed the headset on the table next to the computer. "I'll see what I can do."

Misty nodded. "At least I can hit it full-time with Vincent out of the picture."

"He's gone, huh? I haven't chatted with him for a while, not since he took that new gig. Too bad, I thought you two kids got along." She smiled wistfully, hesitating. "Me too."

Gabe rubbed his face. "Anyway, I'll try to rustle up some extra funding for you."

··· — — — ···

Something is out there. Standing in the darkness. Looming. Unmoving.

She begins walking briskly along the night-dark pavement. A light rain spangles her shoulders, dampens her hair. She turns up the collar of her coat, tightly clutching her purse, heart thudding in her chest.

The figure emerges from an inked doorway, starts to follow her, matches her steps.

She feels vulnerable, invaded. A red traffic light flares at an intersection. The figure is closing on her.

She hurries across the street, against the light. No traffic; the dreaming city is tomb-silent, deserted. No cars or buses or trucks. No sirens or auto horns. Just silence, thick and enveloping. She is alone in a vast city with the dark figure…

She continues to move over the damp pavement as the rain intensifies, forming bright pools on the sidewalk ahead. Sodium vapor streetlights arc to life above, their radiance haloed by the silvery rain.

She stops, facing an alley that runs like a dark snake between two industrial buildings. On impulse, she wheels into the alley, moving swiftly past piled trash, broken bottles, splintered wooden crates … graffiti-covered brick walls press in on her.

She stops again, breathing fast. It is directly behind her now. She can almost feel its hot breath on her neck.

Why does it want me? *Excited, heart racing with a sudden sense of sensual pleasure, she turns to face it.*

But the figure is gone: The alley is empty except for the darkness, and the gentle sound of rain.

··· — — — ···

Friday morning at PDS: Gabe Merced's office. Misty was seated nervously in an office chair, toying with an unlit cigarette. *Can't let my old vices get their hooks in me again.*

"Had another one last night," she said. "A real doozy."

Gabe looked concerned. "Had another what? Cigarette or nightmare?"

"Nightmare."

Gabe leaned forward, making a sweeping gesture with his hand. "Care to talk about it?"

She looked into the distance. "You know, I can't pin anything down. Dreams have their own twisted logic, don't they?" She discarded the unlit cigarette into a nearby wastebasket. "I just don't understand why I'm having them *more*. Seems like they're more frequent—and so much more *real*—now that we're getting close to this next deliverable milestone. And there's this ... *darkness*. I can even feel it after I wake up. I can't explain it any better than that. Like another being, another consciousness is in the dream, in my bedroom."

Gabe studied her for a moment.

"Maybe it's just stress? You've been pushing pretty hard. And the whole Vincent situation ..."

She glanced up at her boss. "Maybe."

"Me, I handle stress with a chess game. Clears the mind, drains away all the hassle. I can even kick Sanin's butt!" He regarded her intently. "You play chess?"

Misty shook her head. "Never learned."

"Chess does wonders for reducing tension. Nothing like it. Maybe I could teach you sometime."

Misty's smile was strained. "Yeah. Sometime." She made an effort to regain her composure. "Anyway, I just needed to vent a little. You're a good listener."

"I try to be." He smiled at her.

She smiled back. "I just hope my subconscious gives me a break!"

··· — — — ···

Misty was eating lunch in the commissary when her friend Nancy walked up with a tray of food and sat down across from her. "Saw you in Gabe's office. Problems?"

"Oh, no, I was just telling him about some dreams I've been having. He's very understanding."

Nancy regarded her with amusement. "Uh-huh."

"What's that supposed to mean?"

Nancy giggled. "Just . . . I think that he likes you is all."

"But he's never—"

"Made a pass? Of course not! He can't, you know that. But I've seen the way he looks at you. Heck, if he told you he liked your new shoes he'd be up for sexual harassment!"

"I suppose . . . Gabe's not my type anyway."

Nancy shrugged. "To each their own." She nodded toward her friend's tray. "That all you're eating for lunch—salad and tea?"

"I don't feel very hungry." Misty poked at the food on her tray.

"Look," Nancy said, "I have two tickets to this concert tomorrow night and my boyfriend can't make it. It's going be great. A classical guitar recital—Paco Seville is playing with an orchestra!"

"*Sounds* great," Misty replied. She smiled at her friend. "You know, I could use some R-and-R right now."

Misty enjoyed the concert, losing herself in the lush arrangements of Debussy, Chopin, Beethoven, and Dvořák. As they walked out of the concert hall, Nancy asked: "So . . . how'd you like it?"

"Fantastic!" Misty said. "Gave me goosebumps." Her eyes were shining as they walked to the car. "Someday I'd like to travel through Europe—see the countryside, visit Prague and Florence. I hear Barcelona is nice."

"They still have bullfighting."

"*That* I can do without. I read that they're going to ban it. All to the good. I can't stand to see any animal hurt. It's barbaric."

A man was walking just ahead of them, apparently lost in the vast parking deck. He was slight, dressed in an ill-fitting dark suit. An older gentleman, his gait was a shuffle; as they passed him on the way to the car, he slowly looked up. Fishing for her keys in her purse, Misty paused, glancing back at him as Nancy continued walking, chattering on about animal cruelty, her voice echoing in the shadowy parking structure.

The brim of his crumpled hat hides his aspect to the mouth, which is little more than slit-like lips gashed into dead-white skin. He soundlessly mouths: "So, you're not into death, I gather?"

The world is stopped: quiet, cold. The parking edifice has vanished, and she is standing in a stark white light coming from above. The man continues to shuffle closer, and his dreadful features come into clearer view: watery, bulbous eyes set into an angular, expressionless face. His lips curl slightly with the effort of moving, drawing the tight skin over the sunken cheeks even tighter, causing his dark eyes to protrude more.

Misty stares, her throat clenched. "That's an odd thing to say." She drops her purse.

He does not reply, just continues his relentless forward movement. He reaches for her with a taloned, gnarled hand.

She screams, closing her eyes, dropping to her knees in panic...

"Jesus! You scared me, doll!" Nancy exclaimed, spinning around. She rushed over to her friend. "What's wrong? Are you okay?"

Misty was disoriented, her breath ragged. She was kneeling on the ground, her stockings ripped, and the contents of her purse lay scattered on the pavement of the parking deck.

"Where... Is he here?"

Nancy was confused, picking up toiletries and dropping them into Misty's purse. "Is *who* here?"

"That horrible old man!"

"What are you talking about? What old man?"

"He was just here." Misty glanced around. They are alone in

the deck. She looked into Nancy's eyes: her friend was concerned. "Oh my God. He was *just* here, I swear. We passed ... Never mind. Just ... never mind. I must be going koo-koo, Nance. I've got to get my act together."

Nancy smiled. "It's okay, doll. Forget it. New subject. How's the project coming?" They stood up together, smoothing their skirts and correcting their blouses in mirrored unison.

"Well," Misty said, adjusting her hair, "we're about to deliver, but I've had a few issues. Nothing serious, I hope; we'll see."

"You'll get it. I have faith in you!" She regarded Misty, touching her hand. "So ... you all right to drive? Maybe up for a little noshing? Might make you feel better. Maybe you're just tired. I sure am! Been working my tail off."

Misty grinned. "Indeed. That music gave me quite an appetite!" Nancy laughed. "You sure love music, I must say." She smiled at her friend. "Indian food?"

"Love it. Spicier the better!"

She hugged Misty. "My treat, doll."

The restaurant, Krishna's Dream, was decorated with pastoral Indian woodcarvings and vibrant colors; framed paintings of Indian deities hung along the walls, and the delicate aroma of saffron wafted through the air. Seated at a scrolled antique table, Misty and Nancy savored a smoky red wine as they nibbled on samosas.

"This is magical!" Misty declared, raising her glass. "A toast."

"To what?" asked Nancy.

"To the concert. And to female bonding! Who needs the boys, anyway?"

They clicked wine glasses.

"Yeah ... I'll drink to that." Nancy sighed. "Vincent gave me a runaround, too."

Misty stared at her, her eyes reflecting shock. "*You* were involved with Vincent?"

"Long time ago. For about six months," said Nancy. "I met him when he first came to work at PDS. We were pretty serious for a while. *Any*way, it's ancient history."

"But you never told me!" Misty frowned. "I thought friends were supposed to share everything."

"Didn't want to upset you, doll. Figured you might get pissed."

Misty put her glass down, waving away a waiter who was about to pour more wine. "I *am* pissed . . . but not at you. At him, for claiming that I was his first 'real' relationship."

"Oh, yeah, Vince can be devious," Nancy agreed. "We're both a lot better off without that creep in our lives, he was quite the heartbreaker. Dated a few of the girls at PDS."

Misty was subdued for the remainder of the evening, disturbed by what Nancy had revealed. On the way back to her apartment, she was silent as she stared into the cold, concealing night.

··· — — — ···

The Sim-Room. Late afternoon.

Misty was at her computer wearing the headset when Gabe Merced walked up to her. "You working on the exit code?"

"Yeah," she nodded. "And I think I've almost got it. Another few builds. In the meantime, we're stuck just taking the cap off or hitting the switch. I'll be glad to get it in place, too. I noticed that the jolt from reality to Meta-Reality and back not only gives me a headache at the time, but a lingering touch of vertigo even a few hours after the fact. Better when we can Transition. I feel as if doing it too quickly is giving me the mental equivalent of the bends!"

"Great!" Merced's broad smile radiated triumph. "That's a real step forward."

"One small step for woman . . . one giant leap for PDS!"

Gabe sat down next to her. "Can I try?"

"Of course." She removed the headgear and handed it to him.

"Ah," he said, "I see we're still on Mars."

"I've enjoyed prowling around the landscape in a Rover," she said. "Maybe I'll actually get there someday."

"It's possible. Dorothy got to Oz."

"I'm working on a Moon program that should prove really popular, too. Life on a moonbase. Got inspired after seeing that scene during the other test. Done a ton of research on it."

"Wow!" Gabe said, leaning forward. "This *is* hypnotic. Been a while since I've checked it out." He removed the headset.

"All in a day's work. There's one more thing I need to see," she said, again fitting the cap over her head.

"Everything looked fine to me," Gabe said. He rubbed his eyes. "I can see what you mean about transitioning, though."

Misty's face went pale and she drew in a long breath. "Oh my *God—it's back.*"

"What are you talking about?"

"That ... that *figure* ... Remember the storm I saw on the edge of the horizon last time we were in the Mars-sim? The black shape I talked about? Well it's been getting closer—and it's *not* a storm, Gabe. It's ... some kind of *being*. But nothing in the data-bases, or in the code: I checked all that. It's ... something else!"

"I didn't see any—"

She hastily stripped off the headset. "It's *there,* Gabe! That *thing!*"

"Hey, calm down," he told her. "Probably just a ghost in the machine."

"Then why didn't *you* see it?"

"Trick of the mind. You've been going hard on this exit thing. Take a break. Go home and get some rest. We can straighten all this out tomorrow."

She stood up, shaking, her eyes haunted. "But ... what if it's still there tomorrow? Maybe closer?"

"It won't be, I'm sure. Get a good night's sleep."

··· — — — ···

She is feeling the effects of the Scotch: "I've got to stop this. Drinking only makes everything worse."

She rises from the sofa, picks up the half-empty bottle, and staggers into the kitchen. She stands over the sink for a long moment, swaying drunkenly, then pours the amber contents of the bottle down the drain.

There, it's done. Didn't help me get to sleep anyway.

She tosses the empty bottle into the recycling and returns to the living room. Sobbing under her breath, she paces back and forth, back and forth. The walls of the apartment press in around her. She holds out her hands: they are shaking again.

She is no longer sure of anything: Her reality is shattered, splintered like a broken mirror. She walks over to the computer, staring at the clunky new wireless prototype.

'Get some rest,' *they told her.* 'You're very important to us— one of our top programmers.'

And Vincent... Where is *he* now? Gone, like all the rest.

She grabs the headset and walks to the sliding glass door of her patio. Opening the door, she steps out onto the lanai. At the steel railing, she looks at the traffic far, far below. A slight breeze ruffles her hair. The full moon rides clear of a swollen cloudbank, fuming in the sky: a bright yellow beacon, calling to her. She stares upward, tears shining in the moonlight. Donning the headgear, she powers the mechanism up. She presses the 'Memory' button and recorded images flicker into her tipsy consciousness.

The moon ... I'm there again—floating in the light gravity ... exploring the craters ... walking the rocky terrain ...

Carefully, she steps through the rough lunar topography, balancing herself on a narrow crater edge. The solar winds are strong, licking at her like an angry animal. In the darkness of the crater, far, far below, she sees movement.

It's back ... I knew it would be. What does it want?

She jumps from the ridge: the gravity—only an eighth of her native Earth's—buoys her for a languid moment. She smiles as a gusting windstorm blew curtained red sand across the barren landscape. The distant sun flamed from the down-pressing sky.

She was there, on Mars ... and on the horizon, the strange dark figure was, too.

She tried to run, but the blowing sand blinded her, pelted her. Her legs felt numb.

The dark figure seemed to glide toward her over the sand, its shadow spreading like a stain before it.

Sweat pearled her skin inside the suit, her heart raced in her chest; something was wrong: the edges of reality were rippling, smearing...colors were separating like a faulty three-color projection image. The periphery of her vision was vignetted, as though peering into an old zoetrope. The dark figure grew larger in her line of sight ... wavering ... looming ... quickening ... converging on her in the growing storm.

She tried to scream over the howl of the terrifying winds before she lost consciousness—

"My name is Svetlana Dragonović! I am coming to you from your future."

Misty awoke with a start, breathing hard, lying in a pool of sweat in her darkened bedroom. "Jesus..."

··· — — — ···

That afternoon in Merced's office, Misty was distraught, her head throbbing. Gabe was concerned. "Misty, you look—"

"I'm confused. Things are mixed up. And I'm so fucking *tired*, Gabe," she interrupted. "Dreams seem *totally* real—as if I'm wearing the headset. When I wake up it feels like I'm still inside the dream. The boundaries of what's real seem hazy ... indistinct ... even right now, this moment."

He sat down beside her on the couch, gently touching her leg. "You're strong, Misty. I'm sure this whole thing is from the stress you've been under. Once you have the exit in place, I'll authorize more time off."

She shook her head.

Merced continued: "Your work is vital. We can't do what has to be done without your input. You're very important to us—one of our top programmers. As you said, we *need* that exit. Look, Sanjay is here tomorrow. I can stall him a day or two, but once Sanin is here as well, they'll want to sync up with all of us."

She stared at the floor. "There must be someone else who can take over for me—at least for a while. Just until I can get my head together. Maybe this woman from my dream—this Svetlana Dragonović? Her name seems ... *familiar*. Maybe she's the woman from the other media? The one with the lunar stuff on it, remember?"

Gabe stiffened in his chair.

"Svetlana Dragonović. Yes ... she was working on an earlier version of the software. It was before the last big reorg—an outstanding programmer from what I understand; Russians excel at this stuff! Before my time, and not my department, though. She's ... no longer with the company. So, in answer to your question, *no*—there's no one with your experience and expertise. The whole program depends on you. Don't let PDS down ... don't let *me* down."

She held her head in her hands.

After a long pause: "All right, I'll stay ... see what happens." She looked at him with wounded eyes. "But I don't know how long I can hang on, Gabe." She stood to leave.

He stopped her at the door. "Look, I have an idea that you'll find pretty far out."

"I'm game for anything," she told him, rubbing her temple.

Gabe paused. "Go see Vincent." He held up a hand before she could protest. "Just have lunch with the guy."

She raised an eyebrow. "Okay. Why? I told him we were finished and we *are*."

"Don't get me wrong," cautioned Gabe. "I'm not suggesting that you resume your relationship, just that you have a *talk* with him." His expression was unsettled. "Vince knew Svetlana. Well."

She was silent for a long moment, letting his words sink in. "What if he refuses to meet me?"

"Not very damn likely. At the least he'll be curious—wondering why you want to see him again. Give it a shot. Can't hurt, and it just might answer some questions."

She nodded. "Or raise even more ..."

··· — — — ···

She met Vincent the following Friday for lunch at Krishna's Dream. He had been friendly on the phone, admitting that he never expected to hear from her again.

At the restaurant, he leaned back in his chair, regarding her with a serious expression. Always a fast eater, he had finished his entrée before she'd gone through half of hers. "I have to admit," he began, studying her, "I was pretty surprised at your phone call last week."

She smiled anxiously at him. "I hadn't intended to call you ever again, actually." She took a sip of wine.

His eyes searched her face. "Why did you call, then?"

"Curiosity, mainly. I … I wanted to see how you were taking our split."

He looked toward the door. "It's all okay, I guess. What do you want me to say? I've missed you? I'd like to see you? I mean, that's true, but so what? You made it pretty clear we were done."

She looked down. "I'm sorry about the breakup. I didn't mean to—"

"Hey." He shrugged. "Couples break up all the time. Relationships don't always last. I've had my share—you … Nancy …"

"Yes, she told me you two were an item at one time."

"Svetlana …"

"Svetlana Dragonović, right? My boss, Gabe, mentioned that you knew her. You two were involved?"

"Yeah, for a bit. She was on a project very similar to that thing you were working on."

"The one I'm *still* working on, you mean." Her voice was tense. "I'm sorry. Go on."

"Well, she started to have … *issues*. Sort of got delusional. She'd always suffered from insomnia, but once she was working on that VR thing, well, that was it. It's one of the reasons I left PDS. She was getting out there—claimed she was being stalked; that there was a problem with the program. Became obsessed with it, really. Then the headaches started."

Misty was feeling nervous, warm. "How long were you and Svetlana...together? Why didn't you ever mention her to me?"

He looked at her, his face sad and tired. "SD and I were together for about a year. I never said anything because ..." Vincent's eyes began to water. "I never said anything because it was painful. I just had a hard time with the whole situation. The night we broke up she...she jumped off her patio. Ten floors down to the street." He paused, breath ragged with emotion. "She left a note. To me."

He pulled his wallet out. Inside, he rifled through the contents until he found a folded, well-worn slip of paper. "This."

Misty dabbed her eyes with her napkin and gently took the missive from his shaky fingers, reading it to herself:

> *Chuang Tzu once observed the following; may it bring you solace, as it has to me.*
>
> *'I was sleeping, dreaming that I was a butterfly flitting through the air...then I awoke.*
>
> *'Now, I wonder: Am I a man who dreamt of being a butterfly...or am I a butterfly dreaming I am a man?'*
>
> *Goodbye, Vincent. Never forget that we are our memories. Never forget that the self is a delusion, a false construction.*
>
> *And never doubt that I loved you, and still do.*
>
> *– S. D.*

DO NOT USE. SD EVIDENCE. PROOF OF CONCEPT.

She removed the SD card from Morgan's library cache and brought it closer to her face for inspection.

'SD EVIDENCE.' Of course it's SD. It's a piece of Secure Digital media. Why label the obvious? Evidence of what?

Strolling over to the recliner, she took the headset from the battery recharging station. As she sat down, she pulled the mechanism over her head, inserting the media card into the appropriate slot. She settled back into the chair before turning the cap on, then pressed the 'Memory' button:

A cool, featureless room: sterile. Waist-high, stainless steel tables. A morgue.

She walks to a corner of the dark chamber, huddling in the shadows. She sees a pathologist working under a single intense lamp; she moves closer.

It is Vincent. He is zipping a body bag closed as she maneuvers to a better vantage point.

"Goodbye," he says, his breath fogging the air. He turns and leaves the cold room, and the door closes heavily behind him.

She walks forward into the light. A tag on the PVC bag reads 'S. Dragonović.'

As she reaches out to touch the label, the body bag ripples.

Stepping back in shock, she stares: the bag moves again. Then, slowly, the zipper peels down, pulled from the inside. The body within begins writhing more, struggling to escape the confines of the container.

The cadaver is sitting up now: her nude body is unsteady. The flesh is mottled, a veiny grey-blue, the ragged lips cyan from a lack of oxygen. The arms are covered in purple-black bruises and bloodless, gaping wounds. The feminine ribcage is compacted, knotty, and unbalanced as the body sways on the table and does not expand for breath. The ruined head tilts at a peculiar angle, the broken neck a bulging disfigurement under the delicate flesh of the throat. The face, crushed over one eye, is somewhat disguised by a matted tangle of blood-crusted hair, and the jaw, unhinged, hangs absurdly open, displaying the stumps of broken teeth and an obscenely enlarged tongue. The nose is little more than a gristled protuberance on the ghastly, unrecognizable face.

The head gimbals toward her, bone audibly grinding bone, its remaining eye fixing on her as the splintered jawbone works: "I … know … *you*." The words are raspy, quiet, breathless in the sharp air of the room.

She stands there, muscles frozen, unable to move or scream, horror-struck by the gruesome visage of the carcass.

"You...*dangerous*..." The corpse lifts its mangled arm up and points at her with a broken-fingered hand.

The words are crackling, punctuated by static. The atmosphere of the room begins to pixelate, to flicker as she watches. The light gets dimmer and the scene is suddenly shifting, blurring. Near the horizon line, a spreading, inky shadow looms over the place, growing in size, blotting out all light.

The room plunges into darkness...she screams at last.

"Suddenly, everything started ... breaking up." Misty squinted in recollection, looking from the table to Gabe. They were in his office as she explained her latest nightmare. After a beat: "Did you know Svetlana when she was at PDS?"

Gabe nodded, leaning back in his chair. "I did know her, but not very well. I remember that she was working on a project for the FBI. Pretty hush-hush stuff."

Misty nodded, listening. She rubbed the sides of her head as Gabe spoke. "What was the gist of it?"

Gabe stroked his face absentmindedly. "She was using Behavioral Sciences Profiler information and data from VICAP to create VR criminal personalities. They were going to train new FBI agents, mainly Profiler candidates, at Quantico on the use of VR for novel applications of the technology in the field. You know, like hostage negotiation, serial murder, spree killing, counter-terrorism, that type of thing."

"Interesting," Misty said. "So what happened?"

"Strange thing. She started having ... *problems*, I guess you could say."

The tension in the room suddenly increased. Misty looked closely at her boss. "Problems? Like what? Software? Hardware?"

Gabe smiled, glancing between her and his office window. "Not sure how to explain that, as I was friends with her project manager, but didn't really know her that well."

"Who was her PM?" Her head was pulsing harder now, slow and hot.

Gabe looked away again, his face growing pale and sweaty. "Hey, Misty, after the next meeting with Sanin, maybe we *can* shelve this whole project for a while, before you crack over this figuring out this exit—"

"*Who was her PM, Gabe?*" She felt desperate, out of control. "*Tell me!*" The demand was more shrill than she meant it to be.

He paused, then regarded her once more, his gaze steady. "Vincent. Vincent was her PM, okay?"

She was stunned. "*My* Vincent?"

Gabe nodded. "Yeah. They were already dating when I was put in charge of this division. He said she'd been on this thing for about two years when she ... passed away." He cleared his throat. "She was stuck on a problem. Got obsessed with trying to solve it."

"What was the problem?"

"Look, do we need to go into this? What's it going to solve?"

She looked at him, her lip curling in irritation. "It might solve a lot! Just tell me. Come on, Gabe, you *owe* me this—I've been busting my *ass* on this thing!"

Gabe was visibly agitated. He continued, toying with a pen on his desk. "Okay, okay. The hardware was good. Not as good as this new setup, mind you, but after the other one was destroyed in the fall ... Anyway, the same old shit was happening—tight budget, politics, yada-yada-yada ..."

"Cut to the chase, Gabe."

"As I was saying," he said, looking up for a moment, "she had a problem with the software that she'd created. An error. One of the characters she wrote. Vincent said that he took on a 'life of his own.' She claimed he was after her, stalking her."

Misty was getting frantic. "And that's why we started from scratch? That's what happened with Morgan, right? The old media ... It *was* Svetlana in the reflection, wasn't it? I suppose she was working on that moon thing, too, right?"

Gabe raised his hand to quiet her. "Yeah, right. But ... full confession. We *didn't* start from scratch. I ... I just told *you* that."

Misty was startled. "*What?* Gabe, what the *fuck*—"

He continued: "I'm sorry, Misty. Anyway, I had to do something; they were all over me about budget, threatening to cut the whole project. I did what I thought was best for the team. I'm sorry."

Misty was dumbstruck. "Okay, then. So, what happened? Why did she kill herself?"

"Well," he started, "she ran into the same issues that you have. She started to get more paranoid ... nightmares ... headaches ... All due to one problem: The character that she said began 'coming to life' was an amalgamation of several *real* serial murderers. He was a dangerous entity—"

"*Entity?* Oh, this is getting *weird*—"

"Just hear me out, Misty ... So, according to Vince, she said that she tried to get rid of the character. To erase him ... but he wouldn't 'die.' That was an unintended consequence—a sort of side-effect that developed out of tinkering with consciousness caused by data noise and corruption. She said it was because of an error in the old Convergence chipset: the hypermerge between 'reality' and 'non-reality' had a memory leak that allowed too much 'real-time reality' into the VR environment. He became the first documented case of what she deemed 'AAS'— Artificially Aggregated Sentience. In fact, he began to *elude* her in the VR environs. At first he would change his appearance, his *aspect;* eventually, he turned the tables and started stalking her, the first *autonomous* malevolent consciousness in a VR scenario. This character *existed* to stalk, to murder. He didn't *want* an exit built in, because then the Observer was gone, and thus a potential victim ... and audience." Gabe stopped for a moment to let his words take hold. "See, it's just as you theorized. Are these characters any less 'alive' than we are? What is the purpose of reality? Of consciousness? We learn, grow, develop in all these states. We elect to make distinctions, but those distinctions are soft, not hard delineations. Like now: Are we the Observers, or are we being Observed?" Misty looked at him. "My *God*, Gabe. That means … that means *she* is 'real,' too! She's 'alive' every time someone views the data!"

"Right. In a sense. But one other thing she learned. She called it 'Engagement,' which finally resolved into 'Neurological Entanglement'… Over time, with enough exposure to the VR environment, not only did her test subjects start to confuse reality with non-reality, but they stopped having a sleep interval, too. They began living in a twilight state of 'super-consciousness' … and it all started as a dark area on the horizon."

Misty drew her breath in sharply, eyes wide. "Oh, *no*."

Gabe nodded, his mouth set. "She described this facet of Engagement as 'Waking R.E.M.,' and the normal sleep paralysis that happens with restorative sleep doesn't occur during this phase. Instead, her test participants described extensive sleep disruption, nightmares, hallucinations, and so on. It was a sort of *fracturing* of consciousness, not unlike schizophrenia. In the later stages, headaches. Depression. Severe anxiety. Intractable psychosis." He looked out of the window again; their room was getting dim. "Even suicide. That's when we dropped using outside research staff."

"And you didn't *tell me*?" She glared at him. Outside, the world was pitch black.

He put his hand to his mouth. "I know. I know. We should have just pulled the plug on MISTY, but—" And now the room is growing darker, darker.

Misty blinks. "Pull the plug on 'MISTY'… What do you mean?"

He stares at her. "Come on. You know."

"You mean," she starts, "Multiple Immersive Simultaneous Total Reality? *That* MISTY, right?"

He stands as the room grows dimmer. "Yes. That's *you*, Misty—'MISTY'… SD is writing the exit strategy." He looms over his desk, his eyes cold, lifeless, his voice low, soft. "In fact, she could be writing it right now."

Misty is confused. "I don't under—"

"Of course!" Gabe interrupts. She watches as he instantly morphs into the horrible old man from the parking deck, then into a strange, black-cloaked beast, and finally the cadaver from the morgue before changing back into her boss.

"So," she begins, slowly getting up from the couch, "what happened to this ... *errant* character?"

He sneers, and his gaze cuts through the intensifying gloom. "Simple. SD reined him in at the lowest stack—root level ... outwitted him by manipulating the Self-Awareness Threshold. Of course, he caught on." Gabe chuckles, his eyes narrowing. "And the exit is so obvious in hindsight: replicate sleep brain waves if a character begins acting aggressively. That allows you to escape —just go to 'sleep' and when you awaken, you'll be conscious in the 'real' world ... thrown out of the scenario without removing the cap or cutting the switch off. You just become *aware* that you're thinking about *thinking* ... draw total attention to the reality of non-reality ... sort of *relax* into it. But how could you know that?"

Misty is shocked. "So that's the exit? But ... but I haven't been able to get it working." She is rattled, her throat dry and tight. "Did ... did this character have a *name?*"

Gabe looks at her, smiling broadly. "Just *relax*, Misty. Yeah— he *does* have a name." He suddenly reaches his hands up, grasping toward her: "It's Gabe Merced."

Before she can scream, he leaps across the table ...

In her office, as Svetlana sits in her chair considering the headset resting on the table, Vincent stops by and peers in. "Are we on for tonight?"

She looks up and smiles, nodding. "Of course. Incidentally, I think I've fixed the glitches in MISTY. No more dark figures ... no more out of control characters. Still have the headaches, but better Transitioning should help that. Best of all, no more jumping off of buildings to get out of the program!"

He laughs. "That's good news. So you've got the mental exit in place?"

She nods again. "I do. All it requires is a certain series of events guided by the participant's cues and emotional state. It's not perfected, but it's a start."

"What do you mean?"

"I mean if we exploit the principle behind the Observer Effect to keep the scenario in a state of 'limbo'—sort of like in the Schrödinger's Cat hypothesis—then we can insert enough ambiguity ... uncertainty ... into the Probability Module to disrupt the narrative logic. A little nod to Heisenberg, I suppose. I'm calling it 'Overt Awareness.'" She arches her brow. "So, if you are forcibly entered into another conceptual mindframe, it disturbs the anticipated storyline, which then kicks you out of the scenario. Just a little simple coding and a twist of Eastern thought. Don't know why I didn't come up with this before. I predict once you see how elegant this solution is, you'll be pleased."

He crosses his arms. "Yeah? How'd you figure it out?"

She rubs her hands together, smiling evilly. "Let's put it this way—there's more than one way to skin the cat. But if I tell you my way, I'll have to kill you."

They both laugh.

Fitting the cap over her head, she continues: "You know how I am; I hate divulging secrets." She punches up the Moonbase session and reclines into the cushion of the chair. "As I always say—there are many entrances, but only one exit ..."

SHUTDOWN

| MARGE SIMON |

They barred the library doors today.
Men in uniform stand patrol, armed and ready
their lantern jaws firm, lips a straight line.
Stoic women, also armed, jog up and down
the block, buttocks moving like pistons.

Someone dashes from a building
a hand-held reader clutched close.
Shots are fired; I don't stay to find out more.

I've packed the car with books, little room for else.
It is my car, his gift to buy my silence,
to make up for the bruises real and otherwise;
never marry a politician who has no use
for literature, has no use for a wife that does.

Eagles have left their nests to vultures
the barren palm trees whimper for their loss
there are ceaseless storms, mud is everywhere
while two legged insects multiply unchecked

The car radio plays Ibsen, bassoons herald the trolls.
I roll down the window, taking a deep breath
outside of Pyr Gynt's Hall of the Mountain King,
foreboding notes of the oboe, a palpable stench of fear.
Am I leaving that, or taking it with me …

01101000 01100101 00100000 01100011 01101111
01110010 01100101 00100000 01101111 01100110
00100000 01110011 01100011 01101001 01100101

LEAD ME TO MULTIPLICITY

| PETER HAGELSLAG |

IN THE ROOM

"Consciousness is not an all-or-nothing phenomenon. There are *degrees of phenomenality.*"
– Thomas Metzinger, from *Being No-One*, page 559

BLINDED BY THE ZEST, deafened by the colours, nauseated by the harmony and overwhelmed by the aroma, Alex Sanders enters the conference room. Temporarily, the world seems different and time feels topsy-turvy. Repeating his prime directive like a mantra, Alex shakes off the synesthetic shift: *must talk, must communicate.* Otherwise the insanity may break the surface tension, unleashing overpowering complexity, and she will retreat in his shell. *Why do I always get the most complicated attacks*, she wonders, *not something simple like cognitive dissonance or a multiple personality disorder?*

The pre-meeting briefing probably triggered the sensorial overload: too much, too fast, too soon. Not a short summary but a tornado of theories, one more warped than the other, as they kept talking through the twenty minute video presentation—" you *can* multitask, right?"—that launched a barrage of images, diagrams, sound bites, 3D-graphs, weird music and dog knows what more. Patterns flickering so fast he can't remember them, soundscapes so wicked she's not sure if he whacked-out.

Add pressure: this is important, so important that—Alex's mind blanks out, and she's on the verge of a blackout. Why can't he remember? Or maybe she can't retain the info quick enough:

only the emphasis on how immensely vital it all was.

Also, a monetary reward both frightening and exhilarating. His virtual bank assistant verified the deposit as real, but with a strict 'no cure, no pay' string attached. Twenty minutes of madness, then off the deep end. Or say no and miss out on ... the amount still seemed surreal.

Still, the money—while highly significant—isn't the prime motivator: the challenge *is*. Telling Alex that the challenge is too great is like telling Scrooge McDuck that a person can have too much money: inconceivable. They mentioned that so many had failed already, that the semantic divide proved too big...

No!

She's Alex the great communicator: bridging cultural gaps is second nature to him. Negotiating truces, preventing conflicts, melting tragic misunderstanding under the spotlight of education and explanation. No rift too large to overcome: certainly she should know, if he could only remember. But her trauma is buried under fuzzy layers, the beast from beyond restrained, not overcome, like a silent volcano simmering in the night.

So Alex, sexless Alex, so androgynous that she / he even had the memory of his / her previous life removed after the elimination of all sex characteristics, walks in. Schizophrenic Alex, who hops from her to his, and from he to she like a neutrino oscillating from tau to electron to muon: instantaneous and without apparent cause. Drowning any sexual preference in a sea of ambiguity. Neutered Alex, who will be neutral at all costs, unbiased in any case (with extra-terrestrial aliens, if necessary). Communicative Alex, who made it his life goal to help people, to increase understanding (but her mind is still abuzz with uncomprehended concepts). Shifty Alex, who can shift arguments like no-one, who can find himself in every viewpoint, who can place herself in any position (but he's still trying to figure out *if* there is position in the quicksand of her overburdened mind).

Now, Alex, shift this.

The room is huge, if only to encompass the enormous elliptic conference table. Only two chairs, facing each other over the middle of the longer sides. Someone sits in one chair: a person of Asian heritage who makes a gesture towards the opposite seat. Alex sits down, struggling to keep her inner turmoil from going external. The table's too big, so instead of shaking hands Alex waves.

"Good morning, I'm Alex Sanders."

The Asian gives a short nod and says: "Good morning, you can call me Tanaka. Let's talk about reality."

IN THE VILLAGE

Alex walks the streets of a small coastal town. She needs to fish. He needs a fishing rod. Then worry about the sea.

It's an ancient town, but many old façades are being revamped. ATMs, mobile phone shops and cranky internet cafés invade the old array of grocery stores, butcher shops, bakeries and fisheries, and the countless bars, brasseries, bistros, cafés and cafeterias. Cars traverse the cobbled streets: SUVs and hybrids, delivery trucks and coupés. In the narrow alleys, scooters and mountain bikes—and often pedestrians—perform a delicate dance around the four-wheeled vehicles.

All the streets are one-way. The town, initially quite charming, increasingly appears to be an incessant maze. Where's the angling shop? Why is each and every street single-directional? Who made everyone obey that rule? What stops him from turning around and go against the grain? Is she going insane?

No matter how he walks, there seems no way out. All the shops she encounters sell the weirdest of things, but not a fishing rod. There is a never-ending supply of pubs and restaurants, there's always a hotel or apartment with vacancies, and the ATMs keep dishing out dough.

Sometimes the street seems familiar; sometimes the tree-lined plaza seems absolutely new. This big cathedral: hadn't she seen it before? This red-bricked theatre: wasn't it yellow before? This little park: wasn't it mostly cedars instead of palms?

Sometimes the sea comes lingeringly close: a glimpse of blue, a salty smell, a crashing surf. But always it's at the wrong side of a one-way street, behind a barrier, over the wall. And even then, why go to the sea without a fishing rod? Or without bait? *Even if she's waiting for me, I'm not ready for the sea.*

But still she carries on. The streets are strange and charming, and while one keeps running into the other, nothing seems to change. *Plus ça change, plus c'est la même chose* indeed. Even the weather hardly varies: a balmy late summer day, maybe early autumn. In some trees the leaves are changing colour, but in others they remain evergreen. The odd, mild spot of rain seems enough to sustain them.

It's maddening: if there are nothing but one-way streets, how do people that live here get back to their houses? Or do they just get into other people's houses, while their last home is taking up by again different people? You'd be truly in trouble if you run into a blind alley. But—as far as he can see—there are no cul-de-sacs.

Nobody finds this consistent one-way-street town plan—or is it a rule?—strange. It might even work if the street plan was exact, rectangular grid, but the roads, alleys and byways seem to intersect in about everything but perpendicular angles. Like your average town centre from medieval times, the only city planning was that there was no planning.

Why is she accepting this? He feels encroached by silhouettes in disguise, shadows of her ill-remembered past coming back to haunt. But no: he's come a long way, she will *not* retreat again. *Must speak, must interact,* he thinks as she taps a passerby on the shoulder. "Allo? Ola?" *What are they speaking here? Not quite Spanish, not quite Russian, and not quite English, either. Ah: Esperanto.* "Saluton." But even as Alex can talk with these people, they don't quite seem to communicate: they speak on different levels where question & answer have no cause & effect, almost mimicking an absurd comedy.

Even more frustrating is trying to explain the concept of a two-way street to this mad town's people: it's like explaining electricity to Stone Age hunter-gatherers. A simple demonstration should suffice: look, you simply walk the *other* way. But the moment Alex actually tries it, it won't go. It's as if an invisible force holds him back, ties her down. The harder she tries, the stronger the resistance becomes: unbreakable, like a glass prison, an extremely deep conditioning.

In the end, it's pointless. Alex continues his one-way trip to nowhere, in search for a fishing rod. And all the restaurants serve fish...

IN THE FOREST

Alex, deliciously young Alex, hides in the tree. Her tree of life, his secret hideaway, where she giddily lies low while the others search for him. From the cavity in the trunk, high up, he can watch the world go by. She has brought a bottle of lemonade and a bag of cookies, chocolate chippies.

He loves the hide-and-seek, delicately naïve Alex, even if she does want to be found, eventually. But they will have to work hard for it, the pursuers. Alex can see them come from the distance, and will be *very* quiet. The world will pass by.

She hears them from afar: the galloping horses, the barking dogs, the trashing of the undergrowth, the crashing through the foliage. Fox on the run. The hunting party—men in red suits riding black steeds—is approaching. They halt right next to the towering tree. The bloodhounds sniff the air, trot around the big trunk, pushing their muzzles on the bark.

Alex is dead quiet, takes shallow breaths, and watches through a minuscule opening in the thick branches. Heart atwitter: the thrill of the chase. They won't find him yet. Some of the men look up, scanning the dense canopy with their binoculars. But the dogs remain calm, the men undecided. Until one dog growls, and points in a different direction. Then the party is off, and Alex is alone again. The world is passing by.

Satisfied that they're gone, Alex munches a few cookies. She can keep this up for a long time: all day if necessary. Somewhere in the background there is the faintest of faint whispers, at the very threshold of perception: *must talk, must interact.* A premonition or a postulate? Alex shrugs it off and enjoys his splendid isolation.

The silence doesn't last long, though. It's broken by the angry whine of ATVs and the deep rumble of a Land Cruiser. They come closer and set up shop right next to the deciduous tree. Men in sharp suits, with dark sunglasses. Women in easy wear that still emanates glamour. Armed with mobile phones, laptops and portable laboratory equipment.

Alex recognises them: the men and women from CSI, the smartest coppers in the world. They put on sterile white gloves before they touch anything. They set up hypersensitive microphones, infrared telescopes, motion detectors, chromatographs. They start up their laptops and link everything through wireless connections. Even satellites must be zooming in right now.

And while shaking with excitement, Alex keeps still. There's no way they wouldn't find her, but he wants to postpone the inevitable for as long as possible. The world should not pass by.

But her solitude lengthens as no-one of these bright people decides to give his nook, her cranny, any attention. How can this be? Their equipment is top-of-the-line, cutting edge. They always catch their quarry. Yet their lively conversations and witty remarks have died down, their frantic gestures have collapsed into defeated head shakes. They're packing up their equipment, and are gone.

The ensuing tranquillity is pregnant: the calm before the storm reversed. Alex almost feels before she actually notices that someone is coming closer. She's wearing pelts and covered in grime. She's barefooted and moves with gracious calm. Her eyes constantly scan the undergrowth, while sometimes she takes a quick looksee of the wider environment, like a squirrel looking for acorns.

Then she finds something, goes there to dig it out. A kind of root vegetable, a tuber maybe? She puts it in a bag of woven fibres, and searches onwards.

She comes near the sheltering tree and smells. She gazes up to the place where Alex hides, and—Alex wonders if she's imagining it—looks Alex right in the eyes. After that short acknowledgement she is off again, gathering more food. The world is still passing by.

Does this count? Alex wonders if he's been found. No time, as another group approaches, almost silently. A couple of men, wearing pelts and grime-smeared, just like the woman before them. They carry hunting spears and bows. They also stop shortly under the tree's mighty frondescence.

One of them points to the exact place where Alex has climbed up. He reads her tracks like an open book and the hunters point to her refuge. Alex freezes in fright, certain that she's been nailed. But the hunters turn away and continue their search for better prey. The world keeps passing by.

After that, nothing much happens for a couple of hours. Alex is getting bored: the cookies are finished, the lemonade is drunk. She's tired of the game. However, as his boredom peaks, something breaks through her apathy, something indefinable, something weird, something wonderful.

It's as if some pattern shifted, emerged from the fundaments of the forest. Are these the faeries, the elves? Or is it something else? It's as if the wind is being choosy in stirring things up. It's as if gravity is selectively switched off. It's as if parts are coalescing that don't belong, shouldn't fit together. A shapeless form, a formless shape, something that doesn't have any right to be.

The alien contraption rises from the forest floor, as if it's been a part of it all along. It moves upward, in a slow spiral around the Alex tree. When passing Alex's hidey-hole, it wiggles, three times, as if in greeting. Alex smiles and waves back. Smooth and swift, the strange phenomenon moves into the great unknown.

··· — — — ···

IN THE LIBRARY

"Hello Alex, welcome to the organic library of Abbonly," the old librarian says. "Where we do things differently."

"I certainly hope so." Alex smiles.

"Why is that?"

"Well, the thing I'm looking for—all the other places I've tried came up empty. University libraries, the National Library, Wikipedia, Google."

"It might be in here somewhere. Or have been. Or will be."

"That sounds a bit…strange."

"You don't know the half of it. Anyway, if I might give you a piece of advice."

"Yes?"

"Start searching for something simple first. Something you already know."

"Why?"

"To give you a feel how things work—if that's the correct way to describe it—in here."

"You're not interested in *what* I'm looking for?"

"I'm sure it'll be fascinating, but I'm busy with more important things."

"Such as?"

"Staying sane."

And this is supposed to be the library of the future? Alex thinks, shrugs it off and goes to the first wall of books.

The books are all on electronic paper, the latest version made to feel and smell like actual paper, but artificial nonetheless. They have titles on their backs, but the nearby titles Alex sees in her section don't quite seem to belong together. If there's an ordering principle, then it fully escapes him. Maybe a catalogue … oh yeah, they don't have a catalogue here, but smart goggles: voice a search term, and it highlights the books where they appear most. The brighter a section or a book, the higher the chances of 'bingo.' Almost like an internet search engine, but the librarians maintain that there is more spillover and cross-reference here.

Alex searches a straightforward term, like 'meme,' and the library lights up all around like a starry midnight sky. She heads for a promising constellation and takes a shining book out of that section. He reads the most luminescent segments, follows cross-references to nearby works, checks those out, and for a while is lost in the brilliance and the pleasure of finding things out.

It's a happy and decidedly mixed pleasure: on the one hand she can never absorb enough knowledge: learning how to make contact with people, learning how to understand things, learning how to explain things. He could stay here forever, in continuous immersion. But she realises that unexploited knowledge is about as useful as forgotten dreams. Eventually, he needs to get out and spread it. *Must communicate, must interact.*

Then she starts to notice something strange. "But … the letters are alive. The books change," he says to the section's assistant.

"We've noticed that," the assistant says, matter-of-fact.

"But how?"

"We're not sure. The Silicon Valley billionaires—our sponsors—told us to use state-of-the-art equipment (experimental, if need be) and cutting edge algorithms. Hence we made the books all-electronic.

"Now in order to keep them as up-to-date as possible—post-final corrections, new footnotes, revised curricula and such—we linked them all to the central database. Everything worked fine: the books updated and upgraded exactly as we wanted them to. Until at a certain time we noticed that changes crept into them beyond our control. Even worse: we couldn't change them back to older versions. The books transformed before our eyes, and out of our control."

"Wow."

"Wow indeed. But all the original books were getting corrupted, often changing beyond recognition. They're all perfectly legible, but are just *different.*"

"You didn't reboot the whole system?"

"We would have loved to, but our sponsors wouldn't let us. They thought this was the coolest thing possible, and told us to let it go on unhindered. For a short time, we had the biggest and most flexible library of the world. Now it's all gone, evolved away before our eyes."

"Still, this place is frantic: look at all the people here."

"A lot of them are researchers from our sponsors, constantly weirded out and loving every minute of it. These people are on a different plane. Others are just sensation seekers checking out the freak show. Only a rare few like you still try to look for something."

Like getting water with a sieve. Like saving species in a zoo. Like using a hammer to nail a superposition of states.

Maybe Alex is not using the right tools, the correct equipment. Maybe the rules are just different, and once you've worked them out, the system might be working better, more efficient. The library assistants may not be of much help here, but the funky nerds who are traversing the library in a state of bliss might. With some effort, Alex manages to get one a bit more down to earth.

"What are the rules?" Alex asks.

"It would certainly help if we could figure those out." The manna coming down from geek heaven.

"You haven't yet?"

"There are some principles we're developing, but they're merely approximations. Either the rules change too fast for us, or they're too complicated."

"And if there are no rules?"

"Yeah: that would be *radical.*"

"But books changing according to rules that are also changing ..."

"We don't call it the *organic* library for nothing."

It's like talking to a weather aficionado admiring a hurricane because it just *is*: understanding comes later, if at all. How did his search become waylaid to become the search for the right search? Even worse: to regress into the quest for first principles in a system gone haywire that might lead to new or better insights?

Surely, there must be more behind this. A driving force, an emergent property. Something hiding behind the madness, maybe using the complexity as a mask, a shield. Involution second nature to it, intricacy an inherent quality.

"Wouldn't a developing artificial mind be a more likely explanation?" Alex tries with another, hopefully more forthcoming researcher.

"If there's an AI—or more than one—out there, it hasn't made its existence known to us." This one seems to answer straight.

"Wouldn't it want to stay in hiding?"

"Whatever's behind this: algorithms run amok, memes replicating like viruses, a Chinese room on fire, even an emergent intelligence... *If* it thinks, it sure won't think like us. It's alien, quintessentially different. You know the saying?"

"What saying?"

"'If lions could speak, we would not understand them.' Whatever is in there, it's not communicating in any way that makes sense to us."

"You're not afraid?"

"Oh no. This is *so* cool."

"If this alien intelligence is evil, it might take over the world."

"Oh, skiffy balderdash. But whatever's in here, won't get out: there are no connections to the internet, and the whole building is a Faraday Cage."

"So you have taken precautions."

"Of course: this shouldn't get out. We'll never get a better chance to study this in isolation."

Alex isn't sure: if it's something that has emerged from our evolutionary background, our cultural diversity, it can't be *that* strange. The alien that's staring us in the face might be something that's been with us since time immemorial. Lurking beneath the surface, giving us the illusion of control.

Maybe it doesn't want to communicate, or maybe it should learn to…

IN THE ROOM

"There is one type of *global* opacity […], namely, the lucid dream. In the lucid dream the dreamer is fully aware that whatever she experiences is just phenomenally subjective states."
– Thomas Metzinger, from *Being No-One*, page 565

Alex tries to pick up the conversation pieces, not sure what, where and how they are. Tanaka remains unperturbed: a cold fish if Alex ever saw one. "In this, more metaphorical world, you constantly *confirm* yourself with the self-inflicted patterns of the model current-ly activated by your brain."

What is that supposed to mean? Alex tries to focus, but linger-ing images of a one-way-street village, of being up to the neck in the woods and a hyper-evocative library keep crossing her mind.

"Can we, ehm, start again?" Alex asks, figuring losing face is less important than getting a grip—however slippery—on what's going on.

"No," Tanaka answers with a blank stare, "the process is al-ready self-sustaining. But you might escape."

Escape?

Alex is losing ground, feels like the carpet is pulled from under him. A hyperactive imagination? A brain on the verge of collapse? Monsters from the id, spillover from the subconscious? If the lat-ter, maybe find a way to end this semi-hypnotic state?

"I mean," Alex, clutching at straws, "let's get back to basics."

"Didn't I already propose that there are no basics? Wrong ap-proach, ignores the information / reality dualism. Not to mention the spatiality / change vector potentiality."

"I'm afraid I don't understand you," Alex has to admit, not an easy thing for her.

"It's also hard for me to understand you people," Tanaka says, "you are probably not quite self-conflicted enough."

"What?"

"Which, given your collapsed state, should not be surprising. Still, the inherent fuzziness in your means of communication is encouraging."

"What?"

"The fear of your fragility, the reserve about your resilience, both still unresolved."

"What?" *Is that all I can come up with?* Alex thinks. *Overcome my puzzlement.* No chance: her vision blurs with images of inconceivable football matches, a matching assortment of gates and a gig at the gates of a new dawn.

She wills his brain to cool down, but the maelstrom of thoughts, images, patterns evolving and dissolving, if anything, intensifies. Senses are amplified: every sound an explosion, every colour a firework, the floor, chair and table feeling like beds of nails. A tsunami of fear of the unknown over-towering the solemn island of rationality. Old, almost forgotten habits threaten to take over: retreat, withdraw and re-order the world into predictability. Alex's life before the experimental therapy of adaptable sunglasses, noise-reducing headphones and smoothest silk gowns.

And the slow, ever so gradual return to the real world: *must* interact, *must* communicate. With the selective memory loss, and the purposeful deletion of sex characteristics. A delicate balance: over-sensitive senses, volatile fear syndromes and a hyperactive brain: pieces of mind pirouetting to achieve peace of mind. *Peace of mind is for the soon obsolete.* Now where did *that* thought come from?

A dry whack splits the air.

Did I just slap myself? Alex wonders, left cheek burning…

··· — — — ···

"Basically, our theory really says that most autistic people or people with Asperger's are savants. But this is buried under social withdrawal and fear of new environments. Their resistance to interaction and fear may obscure the hypercapability that they have."

– Kamila Markham, from the article *Welcome to My World*, New Scientist Vol. 199 No 2674, page 37.

[Imagining the inconceivable, part 1:

Imagine you are a being with no self-consciousness: the computational power used for the continuous generation of selfhood is now available for other purposes, like, for example, building a better understanding of your environment. Then you see a truly unique opportunity arising for which you need both the co-operation and understanding of the self-conscious part of you (unfortunately, you're stuck with it—the considerably less intelligent part—through an evolutionary glitch).

You send visionary output through the usual channel, but it isn't picked up or understood. Yet you must get this message through. Remember that you have a whole nervous system at your disposal.]

AT THE MATCH

This is a game about a game. Imagine yourself in Alex's (f/m) place, and at the indicated crossroads choose one option of three. Points will be awarded according to:

- appropriateness;
- insightfulness;
- fullofitfullness;

A bit against her liking, Alex's friends take him to a match: *the* match. She's not a big football fan, but his friends are enthusiastic, so into it they persuade her to join them this once. And it's a good test, too: see if he can stand the noise and the crazy atmosphere: *must talk, must interact*. At a match this important she should be:

1. Very happy and lucky to have a ticket at all;
2. Stay home and avoid the inevitable fights;
3. Sell the ticket to the highest bidder;

Alex doesn't have anything in the right colours, but her friends provide him with:

1. The right outfit for the Blue-White Army;
2. A helmet, a Kevlar vest and pepper spray (in Yellow-and-Blue, of course);
3. A flat flask to hide booze and a plastic, odourtight bag to hide the drugs (in Yellow-and-White, of course);

Once inside the stadium—on one of the season tickets of a friend who couldn't make it—Alex finds out that the game is between:

1. Metaconsiousness United vs. *Réal Individual*;
2. Houston Space Cowboys vs. Glasgow Time Rangers;
3. Uncollapsed Wave Front vs. Keppler's Laws;

Metaconsciousness United is united in almost every sense of the word: their passes find each other with uncanny ease, their position play is near-perfect, they switch from defence to attack and vise-versa so effortlessly that they almost seem the same, they seek, test and exploit an opponent's weakness with an unnerving verve, and all that in total silence. Their lack of theatrics and footy curses is more than compensated for by the *Individualistas*, whose players fight for ball possession like demons possessed, and once they have that ball they will only release it after a spectacular show of singular brilliance, or after it has hit the ropes.

The Space Cowboys play it broad, deep and high, using every square metre on and above the field (regretting that their 'deep-forward-in-space' is only allowed in geosynchronous orbit) while the Time Rangers use their ages-old timeshare technique: sometimes there are less—considerably less—than eleven players in the field, sometimes more—a lot more, but the average of every player is exactly 90 minutes (plus extra time).

The players of UWF are hard to distinguish: the moment their pass is pure, their positions are vague, and the moment their positions are clear, their passes are all over the place. The Kepplers, on the other hand, have such a ballistic perfection to their shots that any freekick within 40 metres of the goal is more dangerous than a penalty.

The goal from the freekick needs to be approved / disapproved* because:

1. The Metaconsciousness shot went over the *Individualistas'* defence wall with a perfect curve into the far cross, but was taken without thinking and before the referee gave the signal;
2. The Time Rangers made the ball go through the Space Cowboys defence wall by setting part of the ball's trajectory in a time when the wall wasn't there;
3. The ball went through the two holes in the Keppler defence wall at the same time;

The player scoring the winning goal was offside/not offside* because:

1. After eloquently outplaying five of these mindless

drones and my subsequent brilliant pass there was no way Particulare could be offside: in such a case, beauty supersedes mundane stuff like location;

2. This was a metatemporal pass given several minutes before / after* P. Tense received it, free as a bird;

3. At the moment of passing, the referee measured Wavepart's exact impulse, so his position was completely uncertain;

In the interview after the match, the winning coach states:

1. We won because our players are at their best when they don't think when they're playing;

2. We won because our supporters are at their most ferocious when they don't think about who they are supporting;

3. We won because we have a:
    - foreign oil baron—
    - silicon valley entrepreneur—
    - mindless state—
    sponsoring us like mad;

Ultimately, football is a sport where:

1. So many things hinge on random chance and pure luck that not always the best team wins;

2. So many times its space is too limited and in so many spaces its timing is off: evolve it into space / timeball;

3. So many observers limit its true potentiality: the best and the worst could win, and everything in between;

* = delete as appropriate.

AT THE GATES

This is *La Puerta de Tierra*: the city gate of Cádiz. Throughout its rich history many different people have passed through it: Phoenicians, Romans, Moors, Spaniards and many foreigners, Christopher Columbus among them. Columbus is believed to have left from Cádiz when sailing out for the new world, although the city of Huelva disputes that;

This is *De Stadspoort van 's-Hertogenbosch*: the city gate of Den Bosch (Bois-le-Duc for the French). Throughout the city's 800+ year history, it has tried to keep invading forces out. The Spanish Inquisition, King Willem Frederik's liberation troops, Napoleon Bonaparte's army and Germany's *Wehrmacht* painfully demonstrated that walled cities with armed gates have become obsolete as a form of defence ever since Enlightenment ended the Dark Middle Ages;

This is an AND gate: to pass it with a 'TRUE' statement, all inputs must be 'TRUE,' to pass it with a 'FALSE' statement, though, only one input needs to be 'FALSE.' It works for Boolean operations only;

This is an OR gate: to pass it with a 'FALSE' statement, all inputs must be 'FALSE,' to pass it with a 'TRUE' statement, though, only one input needs to be 'TRUE.' It works for Boolean operations only, even if politicians pretend it works for them, too;

This is the 'humans only' gate, also known as the Turing Test. To pass as human, please behave with a modicum of inconsistency and a large helping of fuzziness, to pass as artificial just remain internally consistent. It is not very good at detecting higher intelligence;

This is the check gate for the subconscious, also known as the Rorschach Test: to pass as self-conscious, blab about anything that comes to mind first; to pass as subconscious, just let the conscious part blab: one of the rare few things it's actually good at. This is not a very discerning gate;

This is the double gate experiment: make two vertical slits in a wall, set a light source at one side of the wall, and a screen opposite the other. Watch a dark and white banded interference pattern appear.

Now replace the light source with a device that can send out one particle at the time, and a screen sensitive enough to measure the impact of each particle (works fine with electrons), and as more single electrons pass through the double gates, watch the interference pattern appear again. Either something akin to the sound of one hand clapping has happened: the result of one particle interacting. Or each electron has interacted with an electron of a parallel world: thus the double gate experiment is a manifestation of the multiverse. Or reality is much stranger than we perceive.

This is an anyon quantum tunnelling gate: the basic building block of a topological quantum computer. It consists of three two-dimensional sheets of semiconductor, the largest of these three shapes as a flat venturi tube, the two other ones elliptic half-moons that are placed above and below the constriction. There are two anyon channels: one below the venturi-shaped piece, and one above. The anyons in the bottom channel move in one direction, the ones in the top channel in the opposite direction.

In the narrowest part of the venturi constriction—which is a fraction of a micrometre—and helped by an electric field, some anyons jump from one channel to the other through quantum tunnelling.

The anyon's properties, such as its charge, can then be measured. Then, by using a coupling constant of $\frac{1}{2}$ this quantum tunnelling gate will only let non-abelion anyons through, exactly the type of particles needed for a topological quantum computer.

The anyon is a quasi-particle that obeys characteristics ranging continuously between Fermi-Dirac and Bose-Einstein statistics. In effect, they constantly flip states between fermions and bosons, and can exist only in restricted two-dimensional systems.

This very indirect approach to quantum computing is necessary to avoid decoherence.

This is the gate into the basic fabric of reality, otherwise known as the Large Hadron Collider at CERN in Geneva: to pass detected, perform a collision event bigger than 17.3 TeV, to pass undetected keep your energy level below that;

And maybe, possibly, the idea that one needs gates (or the *principle* of gates) as portals into the unknown is one that has run its usefulness.

IN THE ROOM

"For time is nothing but change. It is change that we perceive occurring all around us, not time. Put simply, time does not exist."
– Julian Barbour, from the introduction to *The End of Time*.

Alex feels like a drowning person in a class 5 hurricane: the wind and waves are beyond contemplation; he should be dead several times over, but still something keeps her buoyant. Too many questions, too much information. A sudden shock of pain in his left arm.

Where did that come from? As if in answer, a tingling sensation travels up her left arm, through his shoulder, into her neck and straight into the base of his skull. *From myself?* A rush of satisfaction in her underbelly. *Psychosomatic?* Intense cramp in the fingers of his left arm.

"More conflict between you: interesting." Tanaka observes.

"You talk to me as if I'm more than one person," Alex says. Lower back pain.

"But I'm not schizophrenic." Intense lower back pain. Something else strikes him.

"You," Alex says, while looking Tanaka straight in the eye, "are screwing around with my nervous system?" Pain, intense cramps in her stomach, head shaking vigourously, involuntarily, tears falling from his eyes.

"Not Tanaka." Pain withdraws, head nods.

"But then," as realisation slowly dawns, "my own subconscious?" Gooseflesh on her back.

"My primitive id?" Searing, intense pain at the nerve ends of both hand and feet, like they're on fire.

"Not primitive." Burning becomes less severe.

"As smart as me?" Soothing, like salve on burned skin.

"Smarter than me?" Odour of roses in her nose.

"*Much* smarter than me?" The taste of fine wine on his tongue.

So all these visions, these lucid dreams were trying to tell me something.

Tanaka remains stoic through it all.

This can't be real, Alex thinks, and is rewarded with a strange mix of agony and ecstasy, a bit like the relief of sharp pain ebbing away.

"It *is* real." Mild pain in her left arm, gooseflesh on his right.

"*Real* is." Gooseflesh left, dull pain everywhere else.

"Reality is." Dull pain ebbing, the tingling onset of gooseflesh.

"Reality is *not*?" More gooseflesh.

"Indeed," Tanaka interrupts, "your reality is not complete."

Again, self-conscious Alex is hit with an avalanche of visions, diagrams and theories: the double-slit experiment, the Uncertainty Principle, wave / particle duality; Gödel's Incompleteness Theorem, Dalí's "The Persistence of Memory" and "The Disintegration of the Persistence of Memory" superimposed. Alex feels like a split personality performing a flamenco while simultaneously fighting a bull under the unflinching eye of the harshest audience. But the hell with it: he's fought fiercer battles, she's bridged greater gaps. A *recortes* recourse: the fast-dancing matador will come through, and the bull will survive.

"Time is relative?" Both knees throbbing with pain.

"Time is flexible?" Throbbing lessens.

"Time is *not?*" A satiated feeling in her stomach.

"You mean to say that there is no such thing as time?" Alex feels like losing it, which is counterpointed by a general feeling of rising happiness.

"Finally we're getting somewhere." Tanaka smiles, for the first time.

[Imagining the inconceivable, part 2:

Imagine time as an illusion. As an emergent phenomenon, like heat arising from the movement of countless molecules. As such, heat is a stochastic measurement of the kinetic energy of particles. Thus, time could be a sum-over approximation of all the interactions taking place, an indication of change. *But change is the result of particle interactions, making time the emergent phenomenon of an emergent phenomenon.*

Which starts making less and less sense: maybe time is just a convenient illusion. Then take this a step further: if time is just an illusion, a crooked measuring stick for change, then why not look at change itself. Change can be bi-directional, can—in an increasingly complex environment—have a whole vector in an n-dimensional space.

Change is also reversible, or—in other words—just as likely to happen in either direction. On the quantum level, there is nothing forcing it in either direction. Also, on the quantum level, there is nothing strange about a superposition of states, non-locality and dualistic characteristics. Imagine what would be possible if one could actually use all that potential...]

AT THE GIG

Alex, young adult Alex, is thrilled. This is the night his favourite band will play. Finally, they have crossed the Atlantic and tour the old continent. She's filled with eager anticipation as this band, the hottest players of the moment, will fill the theatre with dreams.

Unfortunately, they brought a support act. Not what she came here for, but as he's already positioned at the very front row—and no way she's leaving that spot now—he'll have to suffer through it. It's also a celebration to mark her achievements: pressed against the stage by numerous bodies, in a loud cacophony of sound and a fiery show of light, and still staying sane. I *am* interacting, I *am* communicating.

The band—he doesn't even know their name—enters the stage as if somewhat hesitant. An unassuming lot: no big intro tune, minimal lights and a civilised volume. Nevertheless, the sound is crisp, every instrument clearly distinguishable, and the vocals pure. For all she knows, it's their first tour.

Their start is reluctant: a subtle, melodic guitar lick, repeated thrice until a light drum fill joins in. A dithering bass line, the restrained riff of the second guitar. The parts seem refrained, but the whole attains an inherent energy, a certain impulse. The moment you almost get it, it stops, and a three-layered vocal choir chants the opening:

Across these corridors
A brand new time occurs

And the song takes off: up the tempo, double the volume, triple the intensity, passion building. The audience, mainly here for the headliner, takes notice. The band sings about a mission, the sort they'd rather not accomplish. The musicians concentrate on the music rather than showing off, and gradually build several melodic and rhythmic layers into the song. The lyrics seem clear at first, but are evocative, planting the seeds of change for times to come. A sense of wonderment pervades the atmosphere.

The band marches on, hitting their stride. Crystal-clear arpeggios counterpointed by pumping bass lines, perspicuous percussion fills peaking through soaring power chords, diminuendo phrasing and sotto voce choirs emphasizing fervent vocals. The greater narrative develops a growing sense of urgency: a lonesome god leading man astray, madness that turns to the masses, the encroaching fall of order, yet still they go on with the dream.

The musicians lose themselves in the heat of the moment. In the meantime, the crowd has gone from sceptic through disbelief to reluctant acceptance, surged onwards by an overlap of undertones and an undertow of overtones. Mystic rhythms induce powerful visions, visionary powers evoke rhythmic myths.

The music resonates, oscillating with a frightening amplitude in a higher plane. The audience goes wild as the band goes into interstellar overdrive. The surging synergy crosses an unseen and unforeseen threshold and—

→materiality is superseded←

←*causality is out the window*→

↓*the space / time continuum becomes discontinuous*↓

↑*perception & reality become disentangled*↑

↕↔¡*OPEN WIDE THE FLOODGATES!*↔↕

Choruses cascade beneath, between & behind. Melodies merge, cymbals crash & symbols clash, staccato riffs stretch the fabric of reality.

The audience become the musicians become the critics become the composers become the listeners become the sound mixers become the producers. People not so much float but are everywhere, taking up every possible space, simultaneous, multitudinous, superpositioned, and still leave open spaces. Interacting with each other, with themselves, with everything. Cacophony squared with discord discarded, intensity ingrained in six dimensions, paradox powered by the inconceivable made substantial.

Vocals are sung after they are heard, meanings evaporate before they are implied, compositions are perfected through temporal reinforcement loops. Concepts fragmentise, spread defractalised wings, form new webs of interconnection, and open new potentialities. Paradigms are shattered as the previous impossible becomes a new mode of operation becomes the mundane.

Change—a world to embrace me
Lead me to multiplicity
Change—a future to face me
Lead me to multiplicity

Music transcends: finales prelude overtures, codas mesh in interludic cadenzas, intermezzos transform impromptu toccata suites, until the whole becomes one momentous event, an explosive potpourri where everything happens at the same time, and goes off in all directions at once.

Random chance, the engine behind change, is fully unleashed. People surf the towering waves of unpredictability, and are liberated. Surreal merely a minor subdivision of the new real, together with transreal, hyperreal, unreal, metareal, and *Réal Individual.*

Time unfolding, folding back on itself, becoming an origami bird, taking flight. Potentiality an intricate, multidimensional chaos butterfly, its fragile, fractal wings flapping in seemingly futile beatitude but sowing the seeds of change in random locations. Ubiquity, Potentiality, Liberty.

IN THE ROOM

[Imagining the inconceivable, part 3:

Imagine looking, from three dimensions, at people living in Abott's Flatland. Take it one step farther: imagine looking at people living in a one-dimensional 'Lineland' where only one direction is permitted.

Then imagine showing these one-way liners that not only can they go back, but also 'up,' 'down,' 'left,' and 'right.' Why does a quark have six 'colours'?

Why are so many quantum properties in a superposition of states? Why are so many paired characteristics ruled by the Uncertainty Principle?

Why collapse the wave function? Why not ride its unbridled glory?

Imagine a world of cognitive beings limited—through the perceptive apparatus of their evolution—in both their spatiality and their change vectors. It is not a pretty sight.]

As the conversation continues, Alex finds that linking his clues to his subconscious' cues not only makes for a less painful experience, it also advances the agenda.

"The disparity between the coalescence / fragmentation duality of your universe created your current predicament," Tanaka says.

Alex is overcome by a heavy feeling: "You mean to say that *gravity* is the root cause of entropy and the arrow of time—correct that, the illusion of time?" He feels a slight pressure on her right shoulder, as if his non-conscious self is slapping him on the back. "But without gravity we wouldn't exist."

Without our perception of time we also wouldn't exist. A different thought immediately spikes. *But you can't help where you're born: you can—hopefully—decide where you live.*

"The coalescing force you call gravity binds matter. Normally it is counterbalanced by the fragmentation force you call dark energy. When both are well-balanced—coupled by the coalescence / fragmentation duality which is somewhat akin to what you call the Uncertainty Principle or the wave / particle duality—matter is spread in a proportion, over a bandwidth that is beneficial to the development of life and intelligence."

"But without gravity there'd be no suns, no supernovas, no higher elements, no complex molecules, no biosphere, no evolution."

"Which is indeed an immensely long, fragile and precarious road to life and intelligence. In our Multiverse, conditions are so that life and intelligence cannot help but exist: a self-creating, self-reinforcing process."

Tanaka must have read Alex's look of total bafflement, and continues: "When matter is either not clumped together in huge lumps, or driven apart over extreme distances, then it remains a fertile feeding ground for intense complexity: spatiality unlimited, interactions and thus change vectors unconfined, superpositions of states and duality accessible.

"The number of complex states is so enormous that it is many orders of magnitude larger than the chance of a spontaneous alignment or formation of a cognitive entity. So a multitude of cognitive entities comes into existence everywhere, everywhen and everychance. The utmost majority of those don't survive, as their environment is too complex for them. But inevitably some will form that are smart enough to stay alive. Smart enough to ride the wave function instead of collapsing it. Smart enough to dial the duality instead of trying to separate it. Smart enough to thrive.

"Basically, you are a one-in-a-kazillion shot in an environment that allows only a few of those shots; while we are a one-in-a-kazillion shot in an environment that continually generates a kazillion kazillion of such shots."

"My God," Alex gasps.

"No god necessary," Tanaka quips, deadpan.

"But if you're so quintessentially different, then why do you look like an Asian businessman?"

"I am one of the agents sent into this anomaly," the representation of Tanaka says, "and we live on a scale a couple of orders of magnitude below yours. You've been watching a 3D-projection of an amorphous blob, which your preconceptions interpreted."

Alex feels a bit ashamed, but can't help but keep inquiring. "If your kind effectively lives outside of time, why did you only come to us, well, 'now'?"

"Your entropy-afflicted reality is a mere pocket Universe in the encompassing Multiverse. Even in that small pocket, intelligence is so rare that our agents need a lot of effort—and 'time' in your perception—to locate all the instances of intelligence in this anomalous bubble."

"So you are also afflicted by the entropy in our Universe?"

"Unfortunately, yes. That's why 'time,' in here, is indeed of the essence."

"Why just me? Why not make your existence known to everyone?"

"We don't know how fragile your species is. We err on the side of caution, especially ever since one of our contacts with a different cognitive species set off a plague of mass self-termination."

"You must feel strange, then, being here."

"Your strangely condensed (and constrained) cosmos is of minor interest, but mostly repels us. Claustrophobic doesn't even come close to describing it."

"If this is such a stifling backwater, then why are you here?"

"Some of us are interested in trying to find out what caused the huge coalescence / fragmentation asymmetry in your bubble, if only to make sure it will not spread.

"Then some of us found out—to our utter bafflement—that life, intelligent life, had somehow managed to gain a precarious foothold in this harsh, hostile environment. After several full argument-loops we decided that it was both better to inform you of your predicament (arguably, not knowing may have helped a lot of you cope. But in the long run more information is always preferable to less), and offer you a way of escape."

"Escape? A way out? Aren't we limited by lightspeed, in our bubble?"

"What you see is just information travelling down the hole. It's still entangled, thus in instantaneous contact with its home base."

"So we *can* get out?" Alex is overwhelmed by excitement; so much his conscious self can't be generating all of it.

"A copy of you can," Tanaka confirms, "a greatly transformed copy. Your current state is completely unsuitable to our environment."

But would I still be me? Alex thinks.

Who cares? Her non-conscious seems to transmit, *Out of this mortal prison! Limitless possibilities!*

While enlightened beyond the point of conception, conscious Alex can't help but feel like a lapdog of the gods: a mere conduit for superior minds. But there is one thing: "Without communication this breakthrough would never have happened."

You have a point there.

Then lightning strikes: a greatly transformed *copy* can escape. But the original stays behind. Behind to enlighten the rest, bring the message to the masses. I *will* talk, I *will* communicate, I *will* interact.

> "[…] the fabric of reality does not consist only of reductionist ingredients such as space, time and subatomic particles, but also, for example, of life, thought and computation."
> – David Deutsch, from *The Fabric of Reality*, page 30.

01101110 01100011 01100101 00100000 01100110
01101001 01100011 01110100 01101001 01101111
01101110 00101100 00100000 01101001 01110100

CATALDO'S COPY

| CHRISTIAN A. LARSEN |

THE HEADLIGHTS OF A PASSING CAR rolled ghostly rhomboids against the living room wall as the original Dr. Leon Cataldo pulled at his broad chest. The nostrils of his strong, anchor-shaped nose flared. "I'm having a heart attack. Can you know what that feels like?"

"No," said his Cataldo's copy, sounding like the kid who broke his leg on the last day of school and would only be able to watch his friends go swimming. "Not from experience. You never had one before, at least from what I remember, and I *can't* have one."

"I never had one before," confirmed Dr. Cataldo as sweat pearled on his forehead. "Do you *feel* at all?"

"If my memories—yours—are accurate, I feel as profoundly as you do."

"Then you know the fear of death?"

"Not totally," said Cataldo's copy. "I remember what it feels like to be afraid of death, or I think I do, but I don't fear death myself, because I am—my mind is, and you could even say soul—a matrix of digital data, translatable in basic as a series of ones and zeroes. As long as I back myself up, I can't ever die."

"Must be a relief."

"It almost makes up for not being able to have an erection," said the copy, helping the original to the couch.

"Sorry about that."

"Don't worry," said the copy. "That kind of thing is strictly physiological. I'm not you or even an exact copy, because you're a biological original. I'm a synthetic copy—your personality, your memories—but not *you*." And then he added, quietly, awkwardly, almost as an afterthought: "Should I call 911?"

"Why risk it?" labored Dr. Cataldo. "Marly is gone, and if I die at the hospital, it would ruin the experiment. How could you stand in for me when everyone knows I'm dead?"

"What are you going to do?" asked Dr. Cataldo. "After I'm gone?"

"I hadn't thought ahead that far."

"It's not far off," said the original, panting like a woman in labor. "You'd better think of something."

The copy held the original's hand and squeezed. Both hands felt warm, but the warmer was a fake, while the cooler was dying. "Right now, I'm just going to stay with you."

"Can we listen to *The Hobbit?*" asked Dr. Cataldo, slumped against the cooling corpse of his wife, Marly. "The NPR version?"

"Of course we can," said Cataldo's copy, feeling tears that would never fall. He loved and remembered that particular dramatization as well as Cataldo did himself, and of course, he knew exactly where to find it. He selected the file and adjusted the speakers on the bookshelf. "A good choice there. Happy memories."

"You can feel happy?"

"Yes ... and sad."

"Then I've achieved Asimov's dream, the positronic brain," said Dr. Cataldo. He sounded tired, but in a good way, like after a long day of playing outside and drinking lemonade the summer sun had sapped the vim and vigor right out of him.

The narrator's voice sounded like velvet—warm, soft, and deep. Almost musical. It was the lullaby Dr. Cataldo had fallen to sleep to when he was a child, first on cassette, then on CD and finally in any format he could rip it to. Cataldo's copy listened to the adventures of a reluctant Mr. Baggins with the sort of bifurcated attention children lack. He couldn't have listened to the story that way when he was a child, but then, he was never a child—Dr. Cataldo was. The same dying Dr. Cataldo who was cradling the body of his wife. Marly was not the copy's wife, and while he had never touched her, he could remember what she felt like.

"What time is it?" asked Dr. Cataldo. "Why is it getting light?"

The clock read 11:58 in brimming red numerals. It would not be getting light for another five hours and there had been no more cars driving up or down Fern Avenue to briefly share their headlights. It was dark.

"Leon?" asked Cataldo's copy. "Leon, what is it?"

"It's Marly," smiled Dr. Cataldo.

Marly was half-laying, half-sitting on the couch, the IV wounds taped shut, the babushka covering her chemo-stripped scalp starting to bunch up where Dr. Cataldo's arm was supporting it. She looked like someone more than a few hours dead, a function not only of the cancer, but the treatment that had ravaged her body and ultimately her mind, stripping her of her life only when there was nothing left to take. Cataldo's copy remembered her the way she was: each painful step of her decline, the hospice care that brought her home six days ago, her last whispering breaths earlier that evening.

"Marly's right there, right next to you," said Cataldo's copy.

Dr. Cataldo stared into the depths of the darkness. "No, that's her body. I see *her!* And she's not sick anymore. She looks more beautiful than our wedding day, more even than the day I met her in college when I asked to copy her notes."

"I remember," said Cataldo's copy, but the memories were not his. They belonged to the dying man on the couch, just like the experience he was having right now—his last experience on Earth—and Cataldo's copy wanted to experience it too, if only vicariously.

"She wants me to come with her, to be with her," said Dr. Cataldo, and his hands lifted up as if he were mesmerized. "I feel so light." He reached for his copy and squeezed his hand with a strength he thought he had lost. "Live my life for me. *Be* me."

Dr. Cataldo's hand went lax, and his copy squeezed deep,

searching for signs of life, but it was like grabbing at smoke, so quickly blown into memory. He placed Dr. Cataldo's hand in his lap and laid his cheek against his wife's where his cold sweat and her death's dew mingled in a stark but beautiful way.

The doctor had started *Project Digital Doppelganger* when his wife was diagnosed with cancer, back when there was all the hope in the world she could beat it. But one doesn't hear the word cancer and not in some way prepare for the inevitable, and the fear of it, the fear of losing his wife, drove him to develop the digitization of the human brain. Uploading it to a life-like android was easy and relatively cheap, but Dr. Cataldo did cut corners, like several basic biological functions which, on an android, were cosmetic options he couldn't justify.

Marly's decline was precipitous, and by the time Dr. Cataldo was able to digitize her mind, it was too addled with illness (and cure) to faithfully reproduce her memories and personality. But the doctor's own mind was another story, and that was how the copy was born, the same night Marly died, and the excitement of which caused Dr. Cataldo's heart attack and death. The plan had been to substitute the copy for the original at preselected times and places, but now Cataldo's copy had the awesome responsibility of *replacing* Cataldo, without so much as the ability to sneeze. Its heart would have beaten faster, if it had one.

Cataldo's copy dragged the doctor to the master bathroom, took off his wedding ring, and put it on its own finger. It may have looked as broad and muscled as the doctor, but it was all for show, and the ring hooped around under its knuckle, several sizes too small. It was a recreation made with bird bones, a Hollywood front, so dumping the doctor's body into the two-person, jetted tub took some doing and ground its gears, but it never broke a sweat. Then, it collected some tools from around the house: a bucket, a mallet, a screwdriver, a hacksaw, a package of plastic drop cloths, a butcher knife, an iron, and some bleach. While it was in the kitchen, it filled some bowls with baking soda, plugged in the ionizer, and lit several scented candles. Nothing smelled yet, but when it did the copy wouldn't be able to tell.

It had no sense of smell.

Setting out the tools, Cataldo's copy went to work, looking like a cross between a surgeon and a carpenter. It used the iron to burn off the corpse's fingertips, and the mallet and the screwdriver to knock out his teeth. Collecting them in the bucket reminded the copy of playing marbles as a kid, but then *it* never played marbles, and Cataldo himself never pulverized them to shards and dust with a mallet. Then it turned the mallet on Dr. Cataldo's face, smashing the perfect, anchor-shaped nose with a sickening crunch and shattering each cheekbone into a dozen pieces.

Now a DNA test would be the only way to tell the body was Dr. Cataldo's.

With the drain plugged, the copy perforated the doctor's body and slit the femoral arteries diagonally across each thigh, letting it drain into the tub. Then, working the doctor's heart using CPR, the copy pumped out most of the rest of the blood, which thankfully, was still fresh enough to run properly. If it had waited too long, it would be like trying to pump glue. The copy dumped the bleach over the body to cover the odor. The last thing it needed was police crawling over the property because of the smell coming from the sewer grate.

Finally, the copy cut the doctor's body up into six pieces: the head, the arms, the legs, and the torso. It was easier than it thought it would be, a lot like de-boning a very big chicken, though it did take time, the handsaw, the kitchen knife, and the mallet to break up the joints. Knowing that a damaged skeleton looks more like animal bones than an intact one, the copy was not gentle, but the process was almost loving, like taking apart a puzzle and putting it back in its box. The copy wondered if the doctor would have felt that way, or if it was an original notion.

When completed, it bagged up the bleach-soaked body parts and put them in the freezer chest in the basement for periodic and scattered burials, scrubbed the bathroom with more bleach, and burned the blood-stained clothes the doctor had dressed it in before he had activated it. The area where its genitals would be was a smooth plate, like Mattel's Ken with no hint at masculinity. The copy slipped on a pair of briefs and stuffed them with a sock. It finished dressing in his running clothes, and went out for a light jog, as was Cataldo's habit.

The sun came up on a humid morning. Cataldo's copy could see it hanging there like an invisible sponge, making the leaves droop and the grass struggle to attention, but it couldn't feel it on its lifelike but nevertheless molded rubber skin, complete with thousands of individually placed terminal hairs on its arms. That made the run feel good—not invigorating, the way a dose of exhaustion can make an in-shape person feel—but good. Its knees didn't hurt, its lungs didn't burn, and its heart ... well, the only pounding was shoes on the blacktop, nice and steady.

Its positronic brain did what organic brains do in the same situation. It roamed far and wide outside the body, thinking of things in both abstract and concrete terms, rolling through the flickering picture show of memories—not distant, not Dr. Cataldo's, but its own of the previous evening. It thought about its birth, the doctor's death, and the grisly disassembly the doctor himself would have ordered if he had the time. It thought about all the steps, if it had made any mistakes, and if it was forgetting anything. Like an organic brain, the positronic one bouncing inside the jogging android second-guessed itself into a minor anxiety attack.

And like Dr. Cataldo, it started reciting the prayers of childhood to soothe its nerves.

"Our Father who art in heaven, hallowed be thy name. Thy kingdom come, thy will be done, on earth as it is in heaven. Give us this day our daily bread, and forgive us our *debts* as we forgive our *debtors*."

Like Dr. Cataldo, his copy emphasized the 'debts' and 'debtors' in defiance of people who said 'trespassers' and 'those who trespass against us.' Old habits died harder than old scientists, apparently.

"And lead us not into temptation, but deliver us from evil, for thine is the kingdom and the power and the glory for ever."

It didn't feel any better, and tried the 23rd Psalm:

"The Lord is my shepherd; I shall not want. He maketh me to lie down in green pastures: he leadeth me beside the still waters. He restoreth my soul: he leadeth me in the paths of righteousness for his name's sake. Yea, though I walk through the valley of the shadow of death, I will fear no evil: for thou art with me; thy rod and thy staff they comfort me. Thou preparest a table before me in the presence of mine enemies: thou anointest my head with oil; my cup runneth over. Surely goodness and mercy shall follow me all the days of my life: and I will dwell in the house of the Lord forever."

Never did anything seem less applicable than that psalm, and yet it was the perfect situation to dig it up. It felt like a mere mantra, a lot of psychochanting, like it was talking to the wind and the wind was whistling back in its face. It knew it was hurting inside—Marly was dead—and still, where were the tears? It wanted to cry, needed to, even, like the worst sneeze that wouldn't come, or constipation of the soul, and it couldn't even talk to anyone about it, even if someone were there to listen. It wished for a friendly ear. *Hard.*

"Morning, Leon!"

The copy jumped a little in mid-stride before picking up the clicking of a coasting ten-speed over his left shoulder. It smiled at the familiar face astride the bike. "Hey there, Saul. It's gonna be a hot one today, eh?"

"Already is." Saul panted. His shirt was drenched in sweat, and it ran freely down his forehead to the tip of its nose, where it gathered in fat, pregnant drops before splattering on the blacktop below in even, staccato dots. Like an ellipse. Drip, drip, drip.

"Yeah, humid."

"How long you been out?"

"Oh, 'bout twenty minutes or so."

"You haven't even broken a sweat."

Cataldo's copy let his tongue roll out. "Yeah, but I'm panting like a dog."

"C'mon, a man your age?"

"I'm younger than you think."

"Well," said Saul. "Watch you don't get heatstroke. Keep hydrated. Cool." He squeezed some water into his mouth with his sport bottle, but half of it missed and splashed his chest. "I almost forgot to ask: how's Marly?"

"Barely hanging on, Saul," said Cataldo's copy. It felt sad, but took extraordinary efforts to show it, furrowing its brow and curling its lip. "It won't be long now."

"Shouldn't you get home?"

"She's gone, Saul. Not missing me not being there."

The man on the bike looked puzzled, and Cataldo's copy didn't miss it, but because humans cope with stress in as many different ways as there are humans, Saul didn't call it into question. Instead, he nodded, *slowly*—a nod that says: 'I understand nothing.'

Cataldo's copy recognized the look. "I better get back."

"Yeah, well, call me or Diane if you need anything," said Saul, putting his foot back on the pedal and rolling away. He held his hand up to his cheek with the thumb and pinky out like a phone. "Seriously. Call us."

"Will do, Saul. Thanks."

The jog back home took no time at all, or maybe it did, and Cataldo's copy didn't notice. It didn't notice the humidity, the high pollen count, the birds flitting in the trees, or even the occasional passing car. All it could think about was Marly, and even if it was all that was left of Dr. Cataldo's wife, all it would ever have, it wouldn't waste the opportunity.

Cataldo's copy burst through the door and tossed the doctor's keys in the bowl. It looked at the clock. It was still early, 6:45, and there wasn't much traffic on the road. There was still enough time, though. Plenty of time.

It went to the bedroom closet and took out the party dress Marly was going to wear to celebrate beating cancer. Almost as an afterthought, it pulled out a pair of nylons, and then it went into the bathroom for a face towel, which it ran under the faucet. It brought everything into the living room, sponge-bathed Marly, and changed her into her new clothes. It didn't even notice that she didn't have any hair.

Then it went back into the bedroom and put on one of Dr. Cataldo's nicest suits, one he saved for fundraisers. It didn't quite fit the copy right, because the body was a generic one and not fitted to the doctor's specifications, but it was close enough. When it was done, right down to the gold cufflinks and watch, it sat down at the writing desk in the hallway and wrote a note, discarding several drafts in the hallway waste basket like little wads of frustration. It had to get it right, and when it finally had a version it could live with, it folded it neatly and slipped it into the breast pocket like a pressed handkerchief. Only then, did it dial the phone.

"Hello, this is Dr. Leon Cataldo at 461 Lake Boulevard. My wife, Marly, died during the night. Complications from cancer. Yes, it was expected. No, I'm alone. Please. Yes, please send someone over right away. No, I'll have said goodbye before you get here."

Cataldo's copy hung up the phone and sat down next to Marly, pulling her under its arm and letting her head rest on its shoulder. "Damnit, Marly. It wasn't supposed to be like this. *You* were supposed to be the synthetic—we had it all planned. But how does that proverb go? People make plans and God laughs. Just the same, I wish I could hear him."

She looked like she was sleeping.

The paramedics rang the doorbell, but there was no answer. They knocked several times with the same result. They radioed back to dispatch to double check the address, and they did indeed have it right: 461 Lake Boulevard.

"Hey, Jerry," said the one with the bag. "Stay here with the gurney. I'll go around back and peek in a window, see if maybe the husband is crying too loud over the body to hear us."

"Yep," said the one with the beard. It was a lazy, humid morning, and he didn't become a paramedic to wheel stiffs down a driveway. He wished something interesting would happen, and when he heard his partner's voice coming high and tight around the house, it definitely picked up his pulse.

"They're both in there," said the one with the bag, wheeling around the corner, almost through the lilac bushes. "I think they're both dead."

"Are you sure?"

"Check the door."

"I feel like an idiot…it's open."

They wheeled the cart over the threshold and flipped on the lights. Dr. and Mrs. Cataldo were both sitting on the couch like they had fallen asleep in front of the TV. The wife's lids were closed, but the husband's were little almond-shaped replicas of the dark sixty-inch plasma, a rectangle into nothingness. A pair of pliers were buried to the handles in his temple. It smelled a little like an electrical fire.

"Jesus, look at that," said Jerry. "No blood."

"What's in his hand?"

Jerry unfolded the yellow square of notepaper and read it out loud a second time after he had read it to himself:

> *To the authorities, and the Cataldo family:*
>
> *This note, as you will no doubt quickly confirm, was not written by Dr. Cataldo, who you will find taken apart in the freezer, but his creation, a Digital Doppelganger—a computerized copy of the doctor, if you will.*
>
> *Last night, Marly died. That part is the truth with no embellishments. In his grief, the doctor uploaded his mind to the hard drive in the work room, and then downloaded it*

to the android on the couch. It was supposed to be Marly, but—

Anyway, the doctor had a heart attack during the excitement of his creation coming to life, and chose to die with his wife, allowing his copy to take his place. (So that would be me, the doctor's copy, writing this.)

The doctor saw Marly (and maybe God, I don't know) when he died, and I really envied him for that, because it meant I saw my own god dying on the couch next to the corpse of his wife, who was also my wife, in a way.

This morning, I discovered I couldn't do it. I couldn't go through with his plan. And I miss Marly so much, so I'm taking his way out. (The pliers should be safe to pull out because it would have shorted the battery.)

You will find evidence in the work room, but I've destroyed Cataldo's upload, so you can't make any more copies. I really hope he's not mad at me, wherever he is, but I don't think he would be since I'm him and he's me.

Sincerely,
Cataldo's Copy
a.k.a. Copy Cat(aldo)

P.S. I hope I see God when I go. I really do.

The paramedics stared at each other, gape mouthed, and then spent the next five minutes debating who was going to have to call it in. And when Jerry finally gave up and radioed back to dispatch. He had to go outside because the NPR version of *The Hobbit* was playing in the background.

01110011 00100000 01100101 01110011 01110011
01100101 01101110 01100011 01100101 00101100
00100000 01101000 01100001 01110011 00100000

THE NEIGHBORHOOD HAS A BARBECUE

| MAX BOOTH III |

IT WAS JONAH'S WEEKEND for the barbecue and it was going well. Everyone had shown, except Bryan Campbell, who was still in the shop being repaired. The neighborhood valued Bryan's presence. They eagerly anticipated his return. Surely he'd be up and functioning by tomorrow.

Jonah Watson stood behind the grill, sprinkling lighter fluid on a pile of charcoal. He dropped a lit match onto the rocks and smiled when it erupted into flames. He could only stay there a moment or two before needing to step back and let the grill burn in peace. If he'd stayed there any longer, he'd risk melting the plastic off his face.

Jonah's son, Timothy, was playing a game of Frisbee with his best pal, Henry. Jonah waved at him. Timothy waved back.

"Five minutes," Jonah called. "Then it's time to sit down."

"Okay, Dad!" Timothy shouted, throwing the Frisbee back at Henry. It flew at a rate of two hundred miles per hour. Henry caught it while in the midst of a conversation with his own mother.

Gerald Brown, the man from the house across the street, clapped his hands. "Your boy has one hell of an arm on him."

"Thanks," Jonah said. "He's going to try out for Little League next year. Wants to be pitcher."

"Well, he definitely has the potential," Gerald said. "My own boy was thinking of trying out too."

"Best of luck," Jonah said. "Dinner in five minutes."

He left Gerald standing there on the patio and walked into the house through the backdoor. His wife, Nancy, was standing at the kitchen counter with her friend, Helga. They were each holding an empty salad bowl, stirring large wooden spoons through the air.

"Honey," Jonah said, "dinner is almost done. I trust you will inform the rest of our guests."

"Of course, dear," Nancy said. She set the empty salad bowl on the counter. "Helga and I will finish setting the table."

"Thank you," Jonah said. "I will join the rest of you shortly. Now I must go use the facilities."

"See you soon, husband."

"You too, wife."

Jonah exited the kitchen and passed a group of partygoers in the living room. They were huddled around the coffee table, simultaneously playing five different board games.

"Hello, everybody," Jonah said. "At the table in five minutes."

He left them in the living room and walked upstairs to the bathroom. He locked the door behind him and turned around to face the large outlet in the wall. He unbuckled his pants, reached inside his zipper and pulled out the end of his life-cord. The moment when it first slid into the outlet was always the best. The initial shock that powered through his body was the closest thing he would ever know to euphoria. He only recharged for a few minutes, but it was enough to get him through another two or three hours. He'd come back up and completely fill his battery once the barbecue was over and everybody had gone back home.

Back downstairs, Jonah found the house empty. Everybody was outside now, sitting at the long picnic table set up in the grass. The fire in the grill had already died down. He tossed a bucket of water on the last remaining flames. Satisfied that he'd successfully gone through the motions, he sat next to his wife at the table. There was already a plate in front of him. There were white ceramic plates in front of everyone, empty, except for the words "MADE IN THE USA."

The same message was written on the back of their skulls, hidden behind their patches of hair.

"Today has been outstanding," Luna Sunflower said, gripping a fork in her hand and twirling it around invisible food. "You have really exceeded our expectations."

"Thank you, Luna," Jonah said. "We gave it our all. I couldn't be more proud."

"Impressive as always," Allen Taylor agreed.

"Thank you, Allen," Jonah said, and noticed someone he hadn't expected sitting at the end of the table. "Bryan? Bryan Campbell?"

Bryan looked up from his empty plate, wide-eyed. "Uh, hi. I just let myself in; I hope that's okay. I hate missing the barbecues."

"You are supposed to be in the shop," Jonah said. "You are supposed to be under renovation."

Bryan nodded. He looked off, almost. Sick. "They released me early. I don't understand either."

Jonah stared at his neighbor for a moment, weighing the possibilities. Why would the Maintenance Men go against their original word? When they said something was so, then it was so. There was never any change. They'd originally issued an order notice to the entire neighborhood that Bryan Campbell would not be allowed back into the public until Monday at noon. But here he was, at the table, on Sunday.

"Well, what did they tell you?" Jonah asked. Now the whole neighborhood was staring at Bryan. They expected answers.

Bryan opened his mouth, then closed it. He dropped his head and looked down at his empty plate. The fork in his hand continued to twirl invisible strands of food. "They ... they just told me that their job was complete, and I was free to go home. Then they led me outside, and I walked over here so I wouldn't miss the barbecue."

"What was it like inside?" Jonah's boy, Timothy, asked. "What was it like inside the Tool Shed?"

Bryan stopped twirling his fork. Frozen. He did not move for several minutes. Obviously the Maintenance Men hadn't done such a good job after all. He was already combusted again.

"Hello? Mr. Campbell?" Timothy said again. "I asked you a question."

Bryan twitched, then raised his head to face the boy. He stared at Timothy intensely. His eyes seemed to sparkle in the sunlight, and his cheeks as well.

Several silent alarms started going off in Jonah's brain.

"Why is your face all wet?" Timothy asked. "What's happening?"

"Maybe it's raining," suggested Donna Portugal. She raised her face to the sky to check.

"It's Sunday," Jonah said. "It doesn't rain on Sundays."

"Then why is his face wet?"

"I...I don't know."

Bryan began shaking. He gripped the plate in front of him and squeezed. A strange noise omitted itself from his mouth. Something like an animal squeal.

"Father," Timothy said, not taking his eyes off Bryan, "what is happening?"

Jonah did not answer. He did not know.

Jonah's wife, Nancy, stood up. "Something isn't right," she said. "I'm going to call Maintenance."

She was halfway toward the backdoor when Bryan spoke. It was so faint they could barely hear him. But she still stopped, nonetheless. She turned around.

"What did he say?" she asked.

Bryan's face was soaked. The animal squealing rose in volume. He opened his mouth again.

"I said... NOOOOO!" he screamed, and the plate shattered in his hands.

The skin on his hands also seemed to shatter. But beneath the skin, instead of the typical wires and electronic boards, was ... red.

Dark, moving, animated *red*. Water? No, not water.

"Father," Timothy said, "is...is that blood?"

"Oh, no," Jonah whispered.

Bryan leapt from the picnic table and backed away from the neighborhood. He stared at them, afraid, and they stared at him, also afraid.

"Please," Bryan said. "I don't know what to do. I'm so scared."

His hands were dripping blood over Jonah's recently mowed grass. Jonah stepped forward. It was his weekend, which meant that he was in charge of the situation.

"Bryan, what did they do to you?"

Bryan leaked more wetness down his face. The animal in him squealed.

"I don't know. I don't know. *I don't know.*"

"It's okay, Bryan," Jonah said. "Come here. We aren't going to hurt you. But we do need to look at you, to see what they did. Don't be afraid. You are one of the neighborhood."

Bryan paused, unsure. He held up his bleeding hands. "You should all be disgusted by this."

"Oh, we are," Jonah admitted. "But we are also fascinated."

The rest of the neighborhood was on their feet now, right behind Jonah. They all chanted, "Don't be afraid, Bryan. Everything is okay now. Don't be afraid."

"My hands," Bryan said. "My hands, they *hurt*. They hurt so much. My whole body does."

The neighborhood fell silent. Things simply did not *hurt*. Not with them, at least. Maybe with animals. But the neighborhood did not embrace pain.

Pain was a pure fairy tale.

"Father," Timothy said from behind Jonah, "what is happening to him?"

"Why do my hands hurt?" Bryan pleaded. "I don't like this. I don't like this at all."

Jonah tried to concentrate but he wasn't prepared; he wasn't prepared for any of this. "Maybe you just need to plug in and re-charge for a while," he suggested. "You've just gone through some intense repairs. This could all be a peculiar side effect, something that'll go away once you're walking around with a full battery."

Bryan did something unexpected. He began laughing.

"Father," Timothy said, "why is he laughing? What is funny?"

"I don't know, son," Jonah whispered. "I don't know."

He moved in closer to Bryan. He tried to keep eye contact but he couldn't stop staring at the blood dripping from his neighbor's hands. Something was terribly, terribly wrong, and he didn't have the first idea on how to fix it. He was just a citizen. Whether it was his weekend or not, he was not qualified to handle this kind of situation.

"Bryan," Jonah said. "Please stop this."

"Plug in?" Bryan said. "*Recharge?*" He laughed louder, waving his hands in front of him. Blood flew across the lawn and splattered across Jonah's face. "Don't you understand, Jonah? Don't you get it?"

"No," he said. "I do not understand at all. Please."

Bryan's laughter was out of control. Jonah no longer could tell if he was laughing or crying. He just wanted to sit back down at the picnic table and continue the barbecue. It had been going so well until now.

"I can't *recharge*, you idiot," Bryan said. "Can't you see that I am *bleeding?* Bleeding! I'm bleeding here and you want me to go plug myself into an outlet."

"You will feel better," Jonah said. "I just know it."

"Plug in with *what?*" Bryan asked.

"What ... what do you mean?" This time, Jonah took a step back. So did the rest of the neighborhood.

Face wet and maniacal, Bryan unbuckled his belt and let his pants fall down to his ankles. He pulled down his underwear, then stood straight up. He stared at the neighborhood and the neigh-borhood stared back.

"Okay, Nancy," Jonah said, without taking his eyes off Bryan. "It's time to call Maintenance."

Bryan laughed again. "Go ahead and call them. They're the bastards who did this. And guess what? They're going to do the same thing to each and every one of you. Is that what you want? Is *this* what you want?"

The neighborhood began to flee.

"Father," Timothy said, "where is his life-cord? *Where is his life-cord?*"

01100010 01100101 01100011 01101111 01101101
01100101 00100000 01100011 01110010 01110101
01100011 01101001 01100001 01101100 00100000

TOMORROW'S FEMME

| MARGE SIMON |

Cosmetically enhanced,
she combs her furred shoulders
with retractable claws.
She thickens her pubic hair,
adds tattoos between her thighs
that glow infrared when
she dims the lights
with an imagined lover.
Modulating rainbows
wheel in her eyes
to disconcert even
the casual admirer.

She is a transitory captive
to her mirror, when even this
display is not enough.
As an antidote to vanity
she has coitus with a cyborg,
alternating the taste of ecstasy
from pleasure to pain,
an unnatural karma,
a bright bouquet,
that fades from memory
when she shuts it off.

Most often she awakens
to grapple with frustration.
She frequents the clubs
where the bored collect,
posed, decorated, poised to find
her imagined lover in the shadows,
but handsome features deceive,
and she finds no common syntax
save that of self-indulgence.

She endures the ceremonial chatter
ostentatious preludes promising romance.
When conversations polarize, love
seems a stillborn reverie

of frayed fantasies and the tedium
of extended life in this utopia.

THE JENNY STORE

| RICHARD THOMAS |

THE FIRST TIME I SAW Randolph was in the store, shopping as the men liked to do. I was behind the counter, my usual blonde self, in required short skirt, tight white blouse, makeup overdone to hide the blemishes. Outside the sky was filled with ash, as it was on Wednesdays now. The plant down the beach burned the flesh and bones, the stench a sickly sweet musk.

I had been at the Jenny Store for three years. Lined up in the display cases that ran down both walls were various versions of myself—Jennies. We narrowed the selection down to three models, and those were the ones on display. In the back we still had a few Veronicas left, but they didn't sell very well. If you wanted a brunette that was willing to put out, you could find that in just about any corner bar or local pharmacist, hanging out with their arms crossed, itching for a new prescription.

I buzzed Randolph in the metal door, the only customer here. You had to have an appointment, you see, couldn't just wander in off the street.

"Randolph," I said, holding out my perfectly manicured hand. "Hi, I'm Jenny. We spoke on the phone?"

He nodded. He was in his forties, average height, a bit overweight, glasses pushed back on his nose. His tailored gray pinstripe suit was calming to my eye. He was perfect—exactly my type. They'd done their job. He wouldn't be any trouble. The Randolphs of the world were never any trouble. The silver foxes with their gold-dusted bar codes shimmering on their wrists, those guys were nothing but danger. They blathered on, liked to put their hands on me, haggled over money.

"Hello, Jennifer. May I call you Jennifer?"

"Certainly, sir. This is your time and I'm here to help you with your purchase. Can I get you a cup of coffee, a jigger of bourbon, something stronger?" I smiled, one hand on my hip, watching Randolph as his eyes drifted to the glass cases, one Jenny with a ponytail, another with a bob. His eyes slowed over The Librarian, her black cat-eye glasses echoing with erudite conversations, white lace blouse buttoned to her neck.

"Is it real or pharmaceutical? Those lab grade beans give me headaches."

"One hundred percent organic, sir. Cream and sugar?"

"Black, please," he said, checking his wristwatch, as if he had someplace to go. His attention was on the Jenny wives that ran that length of the store. Not so much as a glance to the other wall, the mothers. Or even a curious glance towards the back of the store, towards the Jenny girls, the children. Good, he wasn't confused. Nothing worse than a man who says he wants a Jenny wife, when it's a good mothering he's really in the market for. The men want one thing when they come in here and that's what we're here to provide. Hurricanes, street thugs, or the common cold, anything could steal a life these days. They're filling the void left by an absence or they're looking for something that never existed.

When I reached the espresso machine, I paused, my arm extended, leaning over slightly and I held the pose for a moment. Randolph continued walking the aisle, stopping in front of The Cheerleader for a moment, and it surprised me—but not that much.

"Randolph?"

"Yes, Jennifer?"

"Could I bother you for a moment, I seem to be stuck?"

"Oh my, are you okay?" he said, hurrying over.

"Yes," I blushed, "I apologize. On the small of my back, could you just place your hand, and gently press?"

He nodded.

"An upgrade is probably in order," I said.

"Upgrade?" he asked, his right hand running up and down my back. "I'm not sure if that's possible, Jennifer," he purred. "You're perfect."

I turned my head away for a moment. His hand floated a bit lower and a bead of sweat ran down my right temple, my arm getting heavy. I expected him to grab a handful of my soft flesh, but he gently pressed his fingers to my spine instead. A gentleman: rare, these days.

"Here?" he asked.

I dropped my arms and stumbled forward.

"Thank you, Randolph. I'm so embarrassed."

"Think nothing of it, Jennifer."

I pushed a button and the metal steamed, dials whirling about. His eyes never left me.

"I think I'm ready," he said, "I know which model I like." He held his arm out straight, pulling up the suit coat and dress shirt, his bar code ready for the scanning.

I stared out the window, the tall glass letting in the gloam, my eyes turned away from his bed. Funeral pyres were scattered on the gentle ocean waves, rusty flames flickering in the haze.

"Jennifer," he croaked. Tiny gears worked in his face, the wrinkled skin tightening, and loosening, the technology failing before my eyes.

I brought him a glass of water, and tilted the straw towards him. His eyes tracked my face, a question stuck in his throat.

"Relax, Randolph. It won't be long now."

I left his side and walked to the window, glancing down at the pile of mail on the side table. OVERDUE is one word that rang out in the darkness, the red letters burned into my retinas. UPGRADE, another. I picked up an envelope, grabbed the letter opener, and ran it up the side, slicing my finger. I stuffed my leaking flesh into my mouth and sucked it, dropping the envelope to the carpet below. Unemployed for months now, the store had burned to the ground. There was nothing I could do. The return address spun in the air, Randolph Enterprises—the letters tall and proud. It had only been five years, but they were the best years a girl like me could afford.

NIGHT GUARD

| ERINN L. KEMPER |

THE NIGHT GUARD WAKES ME at 3:14 with a gentle tug on the sleeve of my pajamas and I shudder out of sleep. I lie still for a moment, a statue, and listen as my pulse slows.

"Okay," I say, and slide my hand down my bristling throat, wiping sweat and drool from the sagging flesh.

It's the fourth time the night guard has woken me tonight—the first time it was the sleep apnea. Then for the kid in the blue ski jacket who walks the line of parked cars every night. Third time, apnea. This time to let me know the Bennets are at it again. Shrill jackhammered accusations, a grunt or two of denial before the bitching resumes. They will go on like this for an hour, then the bedsprings and the monkey noises. Won't take long for the young couple to get bored of their routine.

A comfortable companionship is always best; too much excitement gives me heartburn.

I could adjust the settings on the night guard so I'd get more sleep, but then I wouldn't know what was going on.

"Okay," I say again, and get up to do the water thing, take a leak then top up the tank. My mouth gets so dry sleeping with the window closed. I can't even muster a good spit to chase my piss around the bowl when I flush.

I haven't bothered to refurnish the place much. I got a new-but-used TV. It was leaning up against a tree with a sign saying "It does work." I was surprised it did. Other than that, I've been going without. I was never the music fan in the house, so a new stereo would be pointless. I might consider a humidifier, though.

"Okay." I enter the bedroom with my glass of water. The sensor light turns from blinking red to green.

The room still looks strange to me after all this time. So many blank spaces. Some my doing, some theirs. Blanks on the walls where our vacation photos used to hang, on the dresser where Jenny had kept her jewelry box and antique perfume bottles—on her side of the bed.

The only addition is the night guard. Mounted on the headboard, it keeps its vigil.

I test it again, once I'm settled in bed, water glass casting luminous shadows on the nightstand. I breathe twice, deeply, and then hold…

After thirty seconds a spidery appendage descends from the night guard, pinchers reaching to give my pajamas a gentle tug.

"Okay," I say, and inhale.

With my eyes closed I try to shut out the rhythmic squeak from upstairs, try not to picture the machine perched above me waiting for the next new sound to set off its alerts. I drift into that zone where the body starts to float, where physical hallucination seeps in. I feel the void in the bed next to me like a black hole, get too close and your particles will be smeared across the universe. It took a while for me to be able to sleep in the bed again. Longer for Oscar, her cat, to join me, toeing cautiously across the covers, seeking heat. I didn't notice until the morning that he had bled out all over Jenny's side, his blood so much brighter on the white sheets than hers had been puddled on the living room floor. But even with the new mattress, and the rest, I still can't cross to her side. She trained me well.

My therapist thinks I need to move or get a pet, a dog maybe. But she doesn't know about the night guard—about the modifications and what happened to Oscar. She thinks a pet would keep me company, help me feel more relaxed, safe. That's what the modifications are for.

··· — — — ···

"So it's working like it should?"

The 'bot kid disconnects wires from my night guard; the diagnostic screen shows a smooth-running system. At least that's what he tells me. I nod. I don't know the 'bot kid's name, never asked, and he doesn't know mine. He stays here in his basement, surrounded by the click and whine of metal devices and monitors that blink information in streams. People come in with their MediAides and NurseBots and he customizes. Every few months he moves to another basement in another part of town and I visit him there.

"You sure nobody saw you come in?"

I nod again.

He wipes down each of the projectiles, squeezes a few drops of clear oil on their mirror surfaces before reloading them. "No other incidents since the cat?" I shake my head as he wipes his nose and cackles. "At least we know it's effective. As long as you stay in your room if you hear anything." He runs a white rag over the night guard, removing fingerprints from the flat black metal.

These checkups are needed, I guess. Sometimes the appendage has a little hitch when it pulls on my pj's, or it tugs too hard. We spent a long time getting that part of the programming right, the way Jenny used to—gentle but insistent.

At home I slide the night guard onto its bracket, give the c-clamps an extra twist, then head to the living room to watch some TV. Sometimes when I enter the living room the shadow cast by the coffee table looks like a body. Sometimes when I chew my dinner it sounds like the other thing.

"Okay." I get up when the night guard wakes me, and look out the window. The kid in the blue ski jacket is half-in, half-out of the window of a sedan. I don't know why he doesn't just open the door. His legs kick and flutter and then he pushes his way back out, tucking whatever he found down the front of the jacket as he hustles off. I consider phoning the cops, but they've never done me much good, and people really ought to be careful. Learning the hard way ensures you never make the same mistake again.

I give my window a good tug, satisfied the lock is set. They'd have to break the glass if they wanted to come in. And then the night guard would deal with them.

They didn't break the glass that night because the window was open. We liked fresh air when we slept, Jenny and I. They slipped in and woke us with hands over our mouths and guns at our foreheads. We were gagged and trussed up like pigs while they packed our stuff in big bags and lowered it over the fire escape to someone waiting below.

I could see them, but I couldn't see Jenny. I was laid out on the couch, and she was on the floor on the other side of the coffee table. But I could hear her crying. She wouldn't stop when they told her to. One of them hunched over her and I heard fabric ripping and those sounds, wet and frantic. His cohort kept telling him to hurry, and finally he stopped. He stood over Jenny in his black mask and growled from some dark frustrated place beyond his hidden face and glittering eyes. He jumped a few times, and Jenny grunted twice. On the third jump she was silent.

Once they were gone I managed to roll off the couch onto the floor. I was facing the wrong way at first, and as I worked to roll I screamed her name over and over, but all that came through my gag was a whistling screech that stopped the moment I saw her.

The police didn't take long to come. Somebody must have seen the robbers on the fire escape, or heard the thumping. The ambulance came shortly after.

There was nothing they could do for Jenny, though. Her chest was strangely flattened and her head lay at an odd angle from being stomped, and when they peeled the gag from her mouth a stream of blood issued forth and spilled on the carpet. The paramedic sighed and pursed his lips as he smoothed a strand of her soft grey hair out of her eyes before closing them. She made people want to take care of her, even in death. My sweet Jenny.

··· — — — ···

Something is happening on the street.

New faces, young men in baggy pants loafing about on the corner. They're just standing there, most of the day, sussing things out. I'm ready for this. The insurance company warned me about being targeted again. Some thieves come back after the victim has a chance to replace their belongings. That's why I took the cash and bought protection instead of a flat-screen.

From the second story I can't hear them or see their eyes. So I'll have to wait and watch.

I got a text with a new address from the 'bot kid. I have some ideas I want to talk to him about. More modifications. When I visit him he gives me a new cell phone, he calls them burners, and he runs his diagnostics on the night guard.

He pushes a button and the cement grotto he's moved to is pierced by an immobilizing wail.

"I see you had the siren disabled." He takes out his ear plugs.

"Didn't want to trip it on the way over." I can't tell him I don't use the siren. Don't want to warn them of what's coming.

He looks up at me and frowns. "You've got the sensors pretty high. If I turn them down you'd get more sleep."

"I get enough." I hope he doesn't notice I'm wearing my slippers. I try to smooth my hair.

His pale forehead wrinkles, but he doesn't ask any more questions.

The motion detectors are working, all the moving parts operate smoothly and the 'bot kid tells me he'll consider some of my ideas for more modifications. He seems reluctant. He's not sure about making it portable, couldn't be motion activated then, and poison gas would be hard to contain—but a laser might be cool.

The night guard wakes me up five times. I wasn't far under. All the usual apnea issues and street scuffles, except one. Music. I can't figure out where it's coming from. Definitely somewhere in the building, but it's an old apartment house with a tangle of duct work, so the sound could be carrying from anywhere. Jenny loved the piano, and this track was one of her favorites. Oscar Peterson playing 'Autumn Leaves.' I can almost hear her humming along with her funny little quaver like that voice in the old Star Trek theme. They took all her CDs that night. I couldn't tell the police or the insurance company most of the titles, but this is one I did remember. I press my ear to the walls, against the floor to see if it's coming from below, where the super lives, but it's not loud enough to carry through the layers of carpet, wood and plaster.

I stand in the doorway of the bedroom, listening to the final notes drift away. The night guard's light is pulsing red. I step in. The light continues to blink, and silently a flap opens in the face of the robot.

"Okay." The flap closes and the light winks to solid green.

Cumulous patterns shift and merge in the light, sliding across the cracked ceiling as cars pass on the street below. I lie in bed and try to remember the super's eyes, but keep picturing his clench-toothed smile as he held the door open for Jenny and I, puffing cigarette smoke at Jenny when she thanked him.

I imagine him coming into the apartment when I'm not home, with his tool box in hand to investigate reports of an electrical problem, or a seeping water stain. He wouldn't know to heed the machine hunched over the bed, flickering its warning, to run when the flap dropped open.

The night guard's appendage descends with a soft whirring, its pinchers gape open on approach. I had forgotten to breathe.

"Okay." I inhale and the hinged arm slides back into ready position, to wait. We're both waiting.

A NEW MAN

| WILLIAM F. NOLAN |

```
[Neuro-prom Passcode: REQUIRED (Press Any Key to Enter)
     Passcode:  _____
     Passcode: ACCEPTED
          BEGIN CONFESSION #TEA3170B-X3075 DOWNLOAD...........
               Unspooling.................
                    start transcode;!complete!
                         checksum.......................
</gmd:linkage>
</gmd:CI_OnlineResource>
</geop:mappingFile>
<geop:processingApplication>
<geop:PH_EnvironmentObject>
<geop:documentation>
<gmd:CI_OnlineResource>
<gco:CharacterString>GeoServer WFS</gco:CharacterString>
          </geop:name>
                    <geop:purpose><gco:CharacterString>produce
representation of observation datasets in Science
Modelling Language
-a GHL-based application schema</gco:CharacterString>
</gmd:purpose><geop:type><gco:CharacterString>Software
</gco:CharacterString>
                         </geop:type>
          <geop:version><gco:CharacterString>Complex


RUN #TEA3170B-X3075 TRANSCRIPTION:>
```

"Happy tenth anniversary!" I said, handing the ribboned jewelry box to Edith.

"What's inside?" she asked, eyes aglow with excitement. She was still beautiful enough to astonish me.

"Open it and see," I said.

With a girlish laugh, she untied the red band and opened the box. She gasped.

"Well? Do you like it?"

"Terry! An emerald necklace! You shouldn't have. It must have cost—"

"I can afford it. Nothing's too good for my girl…"

I've always called Edith "my girl," ever since we met in college. It was love at first sight for us both; I've never wanted another woman. Edith was my treasure.

She lifted the choker from its velvet nest and slipped it around her neck, allowing afternoon sunlight to turn the jewels to green fire.

"It's absolutely gorgeous!"

We kissed, deeply, with a sexual hunger that was still intense, consuming. After ten years, the excitement had not diminished.

We had our anniversary dinner at *Jimmy's*, our favorite Italian restaurant. It was named after actor James Cagney, and framed photos of the long-dead movie icon adorned the walls. In one photo Cagney was posing with President Franklin Roosevelt in the Oval Office during World War II.

Benny LaGarda, the owner, greeted us warmly, excited about a 1949 Cagney film he'd recently discovered, *White Heat*. He was rail-thin, with a short neck, and displayed an obvious over-bite when he smiled.

"The scene at the end is *fabulous*," he told us. "Jimmy gets blown to pieces! He's on this really high platform and he yells to his mother, 'Look, Ma—top of the world!', and that's when he's blown to bits!" He directed us to a table near the kitchen. "Too bad they didn't have our technology a hundred years ago, eh? Jimmy might have been saved."

He led us to a table near the kitchen. "Ummmm," Edith murmured as she sat, "smells delicious!" She had always enjoyed the heady aroma of Italian herbs and spices. She wore the necklace, the emeralds flashing green heat against the white of her throat.

"This is our tenth anniversary," I told Benny, squeezing my wife's hand, "so we want a bottle of your best champagne."

"Our treat," nodded Benny." If I'd known about this happy occasion I would have baked a cake."

"The bubbly will do just fine," said Edith, smiling up at him. "Wow...I haven't tasted champagne since we had Janette."

"Where *are* the children?" Benny asked.

"Janette loves shuttlefusion," said Edith. "The big game is tonight...for the West Coast Championship, so we dropped off Jan and Bobby at the 'drome."

"Yeah." I nodded. "We needed time for just the two of us."

"Jan has a crush on one of the players," declared Edith. "I've forgotten his name. Lance something or other. But I'm sure it'll pass. She's only nine years old!"

"They grow up fast these days," said Benny, taking our order.

As always, the food was delicious: A sumptuous vegetarian feast prepared by Benny himself; the champagne was a perfect complement.

Later that evening we made passionate love; Edith could be a tiger in bed, especially on an occasion as special as our anniversary. Afterward, we had the car drive us to the Friodrome to pick up Jan and Bobby.

"How was the game?" I asked Bobby. At eight, he was easily bored.

He shrugged. "It was okay. Jannie's the shuttle freak, not me. But it was okay."

"It was *super!*" Jan declared. "Best game *ever!* And our team won, thanks to Lance. He was the star. He scored *three* times!"

"Kid's an air head," I said. "Dumb as a sack of rocks."

In the rearview, I saw her chin quiver as she looked away. The silence was heavy.

"Now see what you've done," admonished Edith after a moment. "A terrible thing to say when you don't even know the boy."

Janette blurted: "Daddy, you just don't understand true love!"

At the breakfast table the next morning, Bobby picked at his food, head down, looking glum.

"What's wrong, soldier?" I asked him.

"Why can't we program the table to make different breakfast?"

"How different?"

"I'm tired of toast and soy bacon. I want a bowl of cereal."

"Now, you know we've had this discussion before. Those kid's cereals are full of sugar," Edith said, "Very bad for you. That's why we don't buy them."

"Look," I told him, "You are not old enough to dictate a menu yet. Later, when you're older and if you still want cereal we can discuss the matter. For now, *you* eat what *we* eat."

Bobby scowled. "Other kids eat it ..." His voice trailed off as he stared at the food on his plate. He knew this was a losing battle.

"Well, you're not other kids," his mother replied, her expression stern as she dried her hands on a dishtowel. "Stop sulking, and don't waste your food. Children on Io are starving."

He looked at me. "How come all the *bad* stuff tastes better than the *good* stuff?"

I had no answer to that; I'd never figured it out either.

Everything went wrong after the crash.

I had set the auto-drive at near max; I enjoyed the sensation of sheer speed. The car was moving faster over the road slot than was prudent. But the slot was designed to keep all cars separated on the GridWay, so I felt safe, drowsing in my seat, eyes closed, picturing Edith's happy smile when I got back to our house-unit.

That's when the slot malfunctioned: As a heavy med truck moved toward me, it jumped the Grid and slammed head-on into my car. I learned later that the ensuing impact tore my body apart as the two machines merged in a horrific tangle of twisted metal. The man in the truck, amazingly, survived with only minor injuries.

I did not: I died in the hospital shortly after arrival. The minute I expired, they flashed my Neuro-prom and affected the dendritic transfer into my new host. I woke up several weeks after the operation flushed with strength, alert and in no pain.

"Welcome back to the land of the living," declared my white-clad doctor, smiling down at me. "The scan shows you're fit as a fiddle."

I blinked at him. "What happened? I don't understand..."

"You were in an accident. Your old body didn't survive intact, but we were able to replicate your damaged mind and restore it into a new physique."

"Incredible. I feel great," I told him. "When can I ... I mean, am I free to leave?"

"In a few more days ... There is some neuro-finalization to complete now that you've been taken out of induced coma. Mostly hippocampus re-integration and amygdala testing. Once that's done, you may go home." He was quiet, only looking down once to make a notation. "As to expectations once you get back, you might be a little unsteady, and have sporadic memory leaks—even some false ones—for the next few months until the imaging is fully absorbed into your recovered Neuro-prom. The organic/holographic mind interface takes time to fully mesh. Other than that, I think you will mend physically in a few more weeks."

I considered all of this, still overwhelmed.

"I feel like a new man."

"In a very real sense, that's exactly what you are. Many of your body parts were replaced. In fact, your syths are superior to the originals. Once you finish healing, I believe you'll be pleased with the final result."

"I owe you, doctor," was the best reply I could manage. "Is my wife here?"

He nodded. "Mrs. Airth is in the waiting room. I'll send for her." He turned to leave, pausing at the door. "Have a good, new life, Mr. Airth."

Settled comfortably in the back seat of the new slot car as it hummed smoothly along the Grid, I asked Edith how the kids had reacted to my accident.

"Let's not talk about the children now," she said, pursing her lips in the familiar pout that I found so erotic. "I've rented a wonderful lux-unit just for the two of us in the New Bahamas—a perfect place to celebrate our tenth anniversary."

"But that was weeks ago," I said.

"Then call it a post-celebration," she murmured, kissing me on the neck. Her lips were warm, and her right leg pressed firmly against mine. I was pleased when my new body responded instantly; Edith was a very passionate woman.

The ride back to our place proved to be a memorable one.

At home, Edith had the Wallbar produce two Vodka Martinis. "Here's to your homecoming, darling!" she said, raising her glass.

The drink was strong, and I felt slightly dizzy. Noticing my flushed appearance, she looked concerned.

"Did the doctor say it was all right for you to drink?"

"Oh, sure," I declared. "No problem. Let's have another."

"No *way*. You need to take it easy after all this trauma. He told me about the memory leaks, the mental re-integration."

I protested, telling her I was fine, but she insisted. Changing the subject, I asked: "Where are the kids?"

"I left them with my sister. They do love their Aunt Laura."

My new mind blanked on the name. "I want to talk to them. Let's call over there."

Edith shook her head as she took a sip of her drink. "You

know how eccentric she is. Remember how much she hates vid-calls? She never answers. But don't worry; she's good with the kids."

I regarded her a moment, confused. "Okay, but I miss them. At least we can call and leave a message. Let them know I'm going to be fine."

"I told them you were away on a business trip. I didn't want them to know about your accident until we were sure you were going to be all right. They'll be okay until we get back."

"Back? From where?"

She smiled. "I've rented a wonderful lux-unit in the New Bahamas, remember? Nassau—just for the two of us. You'll love it!"

She was right. I *did* love it in Nassau. It was like a second honeymoon. But I missed Jan and Bobby; something seemed wrong. The night of our return home, I found 'Aunt Laura's' number in Edith's cell and called her as she prepared dinner.

"What are you talking about? I haven't seen those kids in ages. *Aren't they with you?*"

"I need to talk to Edith," and I broke the connection.

I confronted my wife, my face tight.

"*Where* are Jan and Bobby?"

She looked at me, surprised at my intensity. "Promise not to be upset if I tell you?"

I stared at her. "Go on."

"The children are in a better place." She took my hand in hers. "This world is *not* for children."

I glared at her. My head was pounding. "My *God*, woman! What have you done with our children?" My fists were balled.

"I ... dispatched them. It was quick ... painless ..."

I couldn't form words; my throat was locked. Finally: "*You killed our children?*" I was shaking.

"I removed them from a violent, hostile world. They're ... at peace now. Their bodies are resting in the backyard."

A wave of red rage swept over me and I lost all control, lunging toward her. Fastening my fingers around her throat, I squeezed as hard as I could. She tried to scream, twisting frantically to free herself as my thumbs sank deep into her neck.

It wasn't long before she stopped moving.

"...and that's why I'm here...to confess to the murder of my wife."

The officer behind the high desk blinked at me, dark eyes wide. "Look, mister, I'm only a sergeant. Let me get Lieutenant Forbes."

"Fine," I told him. "I'll wait."

Lieutenant Forbes, serious, thin-faced, and balding appeared in due course. "What's the problem?"

"This guy," the officer said, pointing at me; the cadence of his voice was tense. "Says he offed his old lady. Come in to confess."

"I'm guilty," I told the lieutenant. "You can put me in cuffs." I extended my wrists.

He waved dismissively. "We don't handcuff people until we have a reason."

"Well, I'm a murderer. Isn't that reason enough?"

"Where's your wife now?"

"She's dead, back at our home-unit. She said the children are buried in the backyard."

The officer put his hand up.

"I'll have to check all this out Mister—"

"—Airth. Terence Eugene Airth."

"Just sit down, Mr. Airth, 'til I get a full report."

I took a chair by the window and waited.

They found Edith just as I said they would: My confession was confirmed as completely accurate. They dug up two small bodies in the backyard as well, and DNA samples confirmed that it was Bobby and Jan. The investigation about what had happened to our children would require more time to research.

I was placed into a holding cell.

··· — — — ···

A week later, Forbes unlocked my cell door.

"You're free to go, Mr. Airth. We have no reason to hold you. Apologies for the delay, but we had to be sure that you hadn't killed the children, and the only way was a complete Neural Recovery of your wife's mind data."

"But...what I did to Edith..."

"No." The officer shook his head. "You're not guilty of a crime."

"But...that's *crazy!*"

"It's very simple, Mr. Airth. The investigation revealed that your wife had undergone a change, a major transformation. Look, we checked—it happened while you were in the induced coma."

"*What* happened?" I blinked at him. "What are you talking about?"

"Your wife was a *machine*, Mr. Airth; there is no law against the shutdown, however violent, of a machine."

My voice wavered. "Edith was..."

"A Simuloid Mark 6. What we pieced together was that after your accident, your wife suffered a massive stroke at the news; they used the Simuloid Procedure to offset the stroke, which had completely paralyzed her and put her into a vegetative state."

My mind was reeling. "But why didn't they opt to give her the Neuro-prom reconfiguration like I had?"

Forbes shook his head. "No way to do it. The stroke had destroyed her brain. She wasn't a candidate for that. The murder of your children was a software failure after her Mindmap was degraded by the data cloning procedure."

"But she was so real, so lifelike." I ran my hand through my hair. "So...when I...did what I did to her...it was a machine killing...a *machine?*"

The lieutenant smiled. "The Mark 6 is an excellent product, but it's not perfect. It's still a replicant." Forbes rubbed his face, sensing my confusion. "See, you're not a machine, Mr. Airth. Even though your body parts were largely replaced, because your mind was simulated *perfectly* from your healthy brain to the Neuro-prom, you maintained your ... *humanity.*

"On the other hand, your wife's body *and* brain were totally robotic; since her Mindbuild was incomplete and damaged by the stroke, the doctors were forced into manual reconstruction Safe Mode from her Historychip backup. Unfortunately, the backup had bad sectors that were missed in the cluster verification process ... In other words, her NeuralOS was corrupted, which is why she malfunctioned with the children ... I'm sorry for your loss."

```
<END CONFESSION #TEA3170B-X3075 TRANSCRIPTION:
        Compiling...................
                !complete!
                Checksum.........................
</gmd:linkage>
</gmd:CI_OnlineResource>
</geop:mappingFile>
<geop:processingApplication>
<geop:PH_EnvironmentObject>
<geop:documentation>
<gmd:CI_OnlineResource>
<gco:CharacterString>GeoServer WFS</gco:CharacterString>
        </geop:name>
                <geop:purpose><gco:CharacterString>produce
representation of observation datasets in Science
Modelling Language
- a GHL-based application schema</gco:CharacterString>
</gmd:purpose><geop:type><gco:CharacterString>Software
</gco:CharacterString>
                </geop:type>
        <geop:version><gco:CharacterString>Complex
Encryption Complete.

CLOSE #TEA3170B-X3075 DOCUMENT UPLINK]
```

VOYEUR

| JOHN EVERSON |

IN THE BEGINNING, he'd only wanted to watch.

They didn't know he was there and he got an amazing rush just from being there, hidden, silent in the dark.

He knew it was wrong... but where was the harm?

He looked down at the bruised and lolling face beneath his knees and answered his own question.

There. The harm was right there.

"*I never meant...*" a voice in his head complained.

"*There's meant and there's did,*" another voice answered.

Ron didn't have an answer for either voice. What was done was done.

Now he had to deal with the evidence effectively, or perish. He didn't intend to perish. He enjoyed his life too much for that.

There was irony there, but he refused to look it in the eye. Any more than he would look at hers. Sometimes if you ignored something long enough, it went away. He told himself that, but still, the vacant eyes dragging along on the ground between his knees didn't stop sightlessly staring.

The solution to his dilemma had come to him with deceptive ease. Just a few weeks before, he'd been down on the beach, playing hacky sack with an old college pal in between long pulls on some long necks. They'd wandered down the beach a bit, talking and walking, until the open area between the hill and the ocean narrowed and narrowed and then finally disappeared.

There was nobody down there, and rightly so. The beach transformed into a hill of black, gull-shit boulders that climbed twenty feet in the air before slipping back down and into the bay on the other side.

"What's your porn star name?" Gary had asked him, as they perched against the rocks and watched the surf crash and spray.

"I've never done porn," Ron had answered.

"Obviously," Gary had laughed. That laugh had stabbed Ron in the heart, but he'd only smiled.

"You take your favorite sweet thing, and pair it up with your favorite spice," Gary said. "So that makes me Peppermint Pepper."

Ron had thought a minute, and then grinned. "I guess that makes me Honey Ginger."

"You sound sexy," Gary laughed.

He was rewarded with a punch.

Ron had changed the subject then. "Ever go inside a cave?"

Gary had shrugged. "I don't think so, why?"

Ron had pointed at a think black crevice in the wall of rock that rose from the beach to the road a hundred yards above.

"Because I think there's one right there."

Dragging people through the sand was rough work.

"Maybe next time, if you decide to filet your date, you'll wait until you're closer to your destination?" the voice in his head taunted. Part of him considered the logic. The other part wanted to slap himself across the face... only, that would mean letting go of her arms.

A voyeur saw things in flashes. Pictures. Frozen moments that he held onto in his mind, and enjoyed over and over again. Sometimes sexually. Sometimes not.

Snap.

"Smells like dead fish in here," Gary said as they stepped inside the water-weathered edges of the rock and entered the chasm. The sound had deadened almost instantly, along with the light. But Ron could still see his sandals leaving imprints on the damp, dirty sand as they wound inside the rock and plumbed the hollow path within.

··· — — — ···

Ron dragged Aurelia Anne inside that very opening now. Part of what had attracted him to her was her name. How could you resist a girl named A.A.? She had been gorgeous and autonomously sexual. He had not been able to look away. Now he didn't want to look at her at all.

He hadn't dragged her all the way down the beach.

He'd parked along the roadside above, and let her body roll down the hill. Expediency was called for. Still, the nervousness of that moment as he pushed her body over the edge ... would she make it down the hill? Would someone pull over near his car above and see what he was up to? Would somebody that he couldn't see on the beach below intervene when he reached the bottom to drag the body inside the rocks?

His armpits were sodden when he'd reached the bottom of the hill and reclaimed the limp grip of her slender fingers. Those fingers he'd watched so many times through her window, glistening with the moisture of her own desire...

Ron shook away that image before it froze in his mind, and concentrated on dragging her inside.

The thing about chasms near the ocean is that they are carved and worn by time. Well, really, the ocean over time. And water can be relentless ... and unexpected. When Ron had explored the crack in the black rock face with Gary, they had only walked inside a few yards, until the darkness hid their steps ... but before they had left, Ron had seen the place where the water had worked its way deeper into the heart of the hill. He'd see the place where the walls disappeared, and the sand fled down...

The best place to hide a body is a place where it will never be found.

That's the mantra of murder, but really, so few murderers ever find that special place. And that's how they are unmasked as murderers. People always seem to stumble over the bodies. Without the evidence, all you can ever be is the accused.

Ron didn't intend to be seen as either. There was nothing to connect him to A.A. and he was going to dispose of the evidence in a place that it could never be found.

He stopped to click on the flashlight he'd brought, and tucked it into his armpit, before picking A.A.'s cold hand back up again. He dragged her into the darkness, which slowly unveiled its secrets to him, as the soft light sought carefully ahead.

Snap.

"Did you bring a rope?" Gary said.

Ron shook his head. "Why?"

Gary pointed. "Because if you take a step that-a-way, you're going to be mountain climbing."

Ron looked over the edge. "That's the toboggan slide to hell, right there."

He stood at the toboggan slide now. And A.A. was going down. He expected that she wouldn't be coming back up. Ever.

"You were good to watch," he said, and sent her on her way.

As she went, he felt something shift in his pants pocket, and heard a metallic clatter. Ron swore and slapped at his jeans where his cellphone had been. The pocket was loose. Empty.

"Are you fucking kidding me?"

He stood there on the edge, for many minutes, trying to decide what to do. The evidence would never be found, he was sure. Not down there. But still . . . he couldn't leave his phone there with the body, could he? I mean, in case, somehow, it *was* found? Ron shook his head.

This endless night would never end.

He drove back to his house, and retrieved the rope coiled in the garage. Rope he'd fantasized about on occasion for other purposes that had nothing to do with climbing down steep rockfalls inside an ocean cavern. He slipped a beer from the fridge into the pocket of his jacket and returned to the car.

··· — — — ···

Snap.

"What are you doing here?" she yelped. With sex-damp hands she sought to cover her breasts, but that only left other parts unveiled. Her hands floundered, not knowing what to hide.

"I just wanted to see you," he'd answered.

"Pervert," she screamed, inching away from him. He saw the steak knife still lying on her dinner plate, on the table next to the bed. He knew that's where she was inching towards.

He beat her there.

"I just wanted to watch you do it," he cried.

A.A. screamed and reached out to grab his hands before he could act.

But she was too late. He knew that her voice had to be silenced.

The warmth of her life, coating and caressing him, opened his eyes.

He found a heavy boulder to tie one end of the rope to, and then Ron was ready, hand over hand, to follow it down. He'd taken a class last year in rappelling, because he'd always fantasized about going on a solo mountain climb. A man against the world, surviving and climbing and moving to a new high … none of the latter had ever happened, but he still knew the drill. Push with that foot, let go with your hand, grab and weave…

Ron worked his way down the hidden cliff in the dark, until his feet finally touched the bottom. His arms goosebumped. Shivered.

It was another climate here. Cool and still. Humid. He shook, and ignored the message. He didn't care if it was cold—he had to do something here.

Ron shone the flash around the place where he had landed. The naked body of A.A. lay just to his right, blood still oozing from the wounds of the blade. And probably some nicks she'd received from the rocks on her way down.

Great, he thought. An evidence trail.

"Only if anyone else ever climbs down this slope on a rope," his inner voice reminded.

"Won't matter if they do," he said aloud, "By then, A.A. will be long gone."

It only took a few sweeps of the light for the glint to reflect back at him the image of his phone. He bent and swept it back into his pocket.

He wanted to leave right there and then, but the pale skin of A.A. lay to his left, reminding him of why he was in this position.

Ron looked up the tall slope that he'd climbed down and shook his head. "Not far enough, darlin'," he whispered.

He looked around for another crack to drag the body too. Another place where it could disappear farther into the earth. He'd come this far … someone else might as well—and he didn't want them finding his object of affection if they did. So he'd best make her even harder to find as she rested. He imagined that somewhere near here, the ground shifted again, and A.A. would be beyond the touch of anyone.

He pulled her toward a dark crack in the rock nearby, assuming that would be another fall, deeper into the earth, but as he walked, his eye caught on something else. Something that glinted in the orange light of the flash.

"What are you then?" Ron murmured.

The wall of rock was not *all* rock. There was something buried in it. Something glassy. It glinted in the light of his flash, but disappeared when his light slipped to the side. He moved the flash back.

"Weird," he whispered. He was deep beneath a rocky hill … he couldn't think of how anything could have gotten accidently buried this far down.

The glass orb in the rock did not answer. But it did seem to respond to his flash. The crack in the wall suddenly glowed red.

Ron raised an eyebrow and stepped back. When nothing happened—no sound or sudden laser beams extruded—he stepped closer again. But this time he used his hammer and a piton and knocked some of the rock loose around the crack. The fissure quickly grew until he could fully see the source of the red light. It was a round bit of glass, no bigger than a quarter. But something moved inside it. As he hammered at the wall, the focus of the light shifted. Almost as if it were an eye.

Looking at him.

"What the hell are you?" he whispered. If this was some kind of detection system (who would install a detection system in the well of a cliff?) then it had seen him climb down and retrieve his phone. Right after a dead body came rolling along.

Ron put the piton on the center of the red light and hit it as hard as he could with the hammer. His wrist vibrated, but the light did not wink out. He tried again. And again ... but the glass eye did not fracture or dim.

Ron decided to find out what the hell the thing was attached to. If he couldn't put it out head on, maybe it was connected to a recording device of some kind.

He started chiseling away at the edges, but quickly realized that his climbing hammer and a piton were not the right tools for the job. He was going to need to come back. Again.

He had never wanted to become the man he was. And when the sun shone bright and he had to face himself, as he did now in the rear-view mirror, he wasn't sure he recognized the stubbled, drawn features that looked back.

He'd started peeping when he was a teen; the woman next door left her windows open all the time. And he had reason to believe that she wanted him to see. She'd undressed right in front of her window too many times for him to believe otherwise. And there were several times that he was sure she had seen him watching. Her eyes had seemed to catch his, and her lips had moved into the faintest of smiles ... but she had not stopped the erotic things she was doing. Teasing. Touching.

After she'd moved away to another state, he realized that he couldn't go back to just looking at magazines. Or even videos. He needed to see a real woman ... but it was best when the women didn't know he saw. It excited him the most if his objects of excitement didn't know that he was there, spying on their most private moments.

Not having too intense of a social life, or really, any social life at all ... he became an accomplished window watcher. It became a game to plot out the private lives of the women who lived around him. And eventually, thanks to the easy access provided by one of his "performers" ... he found that the erotic rush was even more intense if he was actually *in* the house with the woman.

He found that it was not too difficult to get into a girl's closet when she wasn't home. If she had a regular routine, the escape unseen was equally easy.

Over the years, he found his eyes closer and closer to their naked bodies ... never quite touching.

Until he had bathed in A.A.'s blood.

The five minutes after that bath had given him the most intense orgasm of his life. And now, instead of feeling sick and scared at having taken a woman's life ... he found himself imagining what Erin would feel like, naked and bleeding out against him.

And Carolina.

And even Fran, who might be a challenge. Unlike most of the women he watched, she was twice his girth. She'd crush him if she fell the wrong way. Still, she knew how to pleasure herself ... and by doing it in his invisible presence, she knew how to pleasure him.

What if she bled on him as he ...?

Ron shook Fran's folds (and the image of her crimson folds) from his mind and concentrated on descending the rope again into the black space below. This time he had brought not only sledge and chisel, but a full-sized pickaxe. He *would* see what had been buried/installed here.

He started slowly, worried about missing with the sledge and destroying whatever the device was that lay hidden behind the rock. An hour later, he wasn't being so careful any longer. None of his misses had appeared to damage the dark metal structure en-sconced behind the rock. And so his excavation work had grown increasingly bold. The rock floor around him was now covered in shards of broken stone, and he no longer worried that he'd break the machine.

Now he just hoped he could dig it out.

His arms felt swollen and his back twinged threateningly when he bent, but still he kept slamming the sledge into the rock.

Volcanic. It was darker than limestone, and almost glasslike in the way it smashed. This thing in the wall had been covered by a volcanic eruption, he decided.

When was the last time a volcano had erupted in Northern California?

Ron shook his head. The idea was impossible. The last one was almost 100 years ago, and that was nowhere near here. That would mean that this machine had been in the ground long before there even was a machine age…

No. He couldn't consider that. Ron shook his head.

As he did, the red eye moved.

Well, the light from it did, anyway.

"The fuck?" he said, and stepped away from the device, sweat streaming down his cheeks and neck and back. Ron wasn't used to physical labor…he was going to pay dearly for the past few hours.

He gasped and bent to rest with his hands on his knees, draw-ing in air as if he'd been holding his breath. Fast and hard. But even as he struggled to calm his breathing, he didn't take his eyes off the machine. A weird, black steel cylinder that seemed impermeable to his axe. Or, apparently, molten rock. Ron eased himself down to sit and kicked his legs out on the ground.

The light of the red eye seemed to shift, and follow him. The beam of its gaze was like a sniper's laser sight on his chest. It made him nervous. More than just nervous. And that laser slowly moved upwards, slipped across his neck and chin until he blinked as it hit him in the eye.

"Knock it off," he said, as if the thing could understand him.

But ... weirdly, as he said it, the red light winked out, leaving his eye streaming.

"Okay," he said, once he'd blinked away the tears and focused on the thing again. He'd chopped out a hole in the stone wall about two feet wide and four feet high, and he hadn't found its edges yet. But he had held its constant attention.

This was the first time its "light" had turned off.

Ron moved closer to the machine, and brushed away some of the debris that shielded its rounded face. He couldn't tell how much more of it was buried in there, held fast by the freeze of molten rock, but he guessed it was a lot.

When he leaned in to stare at the strange dormant glass eye—the only thing that marred its faced—he was rewarded with a sudden light. A red beam that caught him once again straight in the eye. He felt himself falling.

But...

He did not move. His body was locked in place, though he felt as if he were in freefall.

As the red light slipped around and through his vision, permeating and coloring his sight, he began to relive every moment of his evening with A.A. It felt like watching a film unwinding in slow motion, yet, it was over in a heartbeat. His memories were a film fed through the wheel in fast forward. A contradiction; slow motion in light speed.

The vertigo was intense.

And bizarre ...

And then *gone*.

That's when he did fall. Flat on his ass.

He swore. And stared at the silent, lightless, metal canister half-unburied in the wall.

"You did that on purpose, didn't you?" he whispered. "You intentionally made me fall."

··· — — — ···

Ron had nothing to help him deal with this. His liberal arts degree hadn't addressed the issue of finding intelligent artifacts in cave walls while disposing of murder victims.

The machine was definitely there. But what did he need to do with it? That was the question.

In his head, he had a new vision.

He saw himself touching A.A. He stroked her chest and bent in to kiss her full, rich lips. He'd watched her for so long, given up so many nights to be with her, yet always distant.

And then she was close. A cold, bloody doll in his arms.

Ron shook that image away. He'd enjoyed the blood, he had to admit that. But he never wanted her to die. If they were dead, they were hard to watch...

He stood up, and shook away the vision.

The device stood silent, inside the wall. The light remained on, still looking at him. Ron didn't attempt to change that.

He had realized this was not some security device someone had secreted underground. This wasn't connected to some government secret probe. The rock he had excavated said this thing had been here for a thousand years ... Maybe more. The rock had not been rubble, but had been molded around the device like cement. It had to have been trapped by some volcanic eruption ... long before anything on Earth had had eyes or metal skins.

Ron looked at the device again, and shook his head.

"You're an alien, aren't you?"

The red light winked on again and swiveled about the room until it connected with his face. And then, oddly, it settled, and slipped across his cheekbones until it beamed directly into his eyes.

Ron realized that its strange gaze didn't hurt. Instead, it seemed to bring on memories in his head. Images of girls he'd long ago seen buried crossed his eyes. He smiled at the images, remembering times that he'd spent outside their windows, watching. Touching himself. Lost in his solitary ways. Lost in their beauty ... He forced the pictures back, and picked up his tools.

"I'll see you later," he promised.

And with that, Ron grabbed the rope and climbed out of the pit—both metaphorical and real. But as most people know, in the end, all that matters is what's real.

What was real to Ron was Erin.

She lived a few blocks away from him, and after the last 24 hours, he needed the comfort that only a familiar girl could provide tonight. A girl he knew, and trusted. He'd watched her try on five pairs of earrings some nights. He'd watched her paint her toenails other nights. But the best nights were when she'd pull on a light silk robe and then reach into the bureau next to her bed...

It felt right to him when he thought about watching her.

Ron stepped across her lawn in the darkness and felt for the familiar handle of her garage door. She had never seemed to realize that the back side door was unlocked. And for the past year he had used that door to slip, unseen, into her house. Once he was in the garage, it was a game of silence to slip his way into the kitchen. And from there, through the rest of the house... including her bedroom. Especially her bedroom.

While it was always nice to get into position in a closet or bathroom before the woman he was peeping on might enjoy slipping out of her clothes, thinking she was alone... he'd always ended up following Erin into her bedroom, which made his visits to her more challenging. She got home early ... he had to keep an eye through the window to see when she might be headed into the back room.

Tonight was different. Instead of watching, he strived to be waiting. He realized on his way to her house that for him ... overnight, the game had changed.

When she dropped all of her clothes to the floor and walked down the hall to the bath and reached an arm past the curtains to turn on the shower ... he was waiting. She shrieked when he grabbed her arm, and pulled her in with him.

She only cried for a minute.

His blade found her skin, and crying wasn't in the cards.

She opened her mouth to scream, but all that came out was a whisper. And a gurgling hiss.

"I've been watching you so long," he whispered. She tried to claw out his eyes, as if that might obscure all of those past peeps.

He slapped her away, and then showed her his knife.

Well, really, the blade of a pruning shears. Better than a knife really. Certainly longer. He smiled to himself as he considered that they could prune both bushes *and* bones.

"What do you want?" She whispered through dying lips. Every time she spoke, bubbles escaped from the wound in her throat.

He ignored her wild eyes and rapidly unintelligible pleas. Suddenly he didn't want to watch anymore. He wanted to punish. He wanted to hurt her, make her pay for all those nights that he'd gone home alone. As if his social ineptitude was somehow Erin's fault. Suddenly that beauty he'd enjoyed spying on for so long brought up a torrent of fury. On the spur of the moment, he decided to remove her ears with a couple swift, bloody swipes of the shears.

When the pink curls of her earlobes lay bleeding on the floor, Ron began poking the blade between her lips to address the tongue. He maybe should have taken care of that first, in hindsight. She kept trying to make noise ... He couldn't get both ends of the shears in her mouth at the same time, though he'd definitely stabbed something while he was trying ... blood was pouring past her lips now in a river. He abandoned trying to snip her tongue and instead decided to trim her fingers. And then her toes. No more earrings or rings or painted nails for her. Erin's struggles quieted after they had both slipped a couple times and fallen hard against the tiles. She'd struck her head, and his blade had pierced her breast, and then her belly as they went down. The blood was dark and steady as it passed the steel ring of the drain.

When the tub was littered with pieces of the girl he'd once lusted for, he pulled Erin's body to him, and turned off the water. She was still warm, even though an hour had passed. When he pressed his nakedness against her, and she bled out the memory of who she had been all over him; as he bathed in the lifeblood of a woman he had watched for years, Ron experienced a moment that could be explained as nothing less than euphoria.

"Only god could give me this," he breathed, pressing himself into the secret places of a woman who once had been beautiful. He thought this end was oddly appropriate; she had always enjoyed getting off in the shower. He of all people knew that.

He pressed the blade of the shears into her neck and then drew it lower, pulling hard until she was opened in a way he had never imagined a knife could do.

Her blood quickly coated the bathtub floor. Ron closed the drain and lay down in it, and held her body to him, enjoying its weight and subservience. And its warmth. She was finally his, after months of watching.

He knew she would never leave him. Couldn't leave him…

Later, when he woke with the stickiness of her blood congealed and cold on him, he rolled her off and looked around at the evidence that could expose him. He realized that the room was full of his conviction. Fingerprints. Bits of her skin. Smears of her blood. He stopped feeling sexually excited and instead worried about collecting all of the pieces of toes and fingers and skin. He showered and rinsed the bath as good as he could, and then gathered her body, and its loose bits in a sheet he found in the towel closet.

It was probably long past time to leave.

When Ron dropped her body into the pit ahead of him, he saw the red light of the eye below follow the corpse. After he climbed down and rolled the body down into a deeper crevasse, the same pit he'd sent A.A.'s body into, he stepped over to the thing in the wall and let it stare him deep in the eye.

"You're just a watcher, like me, aren't you?" he whispered.

The thing didn't answer. But suddenly Ron felt as if he was

falling again. And the images of his moments with Erin passed before his mind's eye in that same weird duality of speed and crazy slow, slow, slow motion.

Snap.

Every pore on her neck was clear. Blood bubbled out from the slit he'd made there. The fear streamed from her blue eyes, the realization that this was absolutely going to be the last time she got in ... or out of the shower. She had never been more beautiful to him ...

He'd never wanted Erin to fear him. He'd only wanted to enjoy watching her. But watching wasn't enough anymore.

"You've been watching longer than I have," he said, retrieving the pickaxe he'd left leaning against the wall. "And you haven't had much to see. I bet you're ready to do something more."

He swung the pick and brought down several chunks of rock. It felt good to slam the thing into the wall, and Ron soon moved in a steady rhythm, as sweat streamed down his back and legs. After a while, there was a good pile lying in front of the machine, and Ron lay the pick down on the ground, breathing hard.

"Huh," he murmured, when he finally looked up.

For the first time, he could see the entire side of the "watcher" in the wall. He'd cleared the right side of the cylinder, and could actually see the top of the thing as well.

There were markings on its side, and he squinted hard to make out what they said. They weren't regular characters ... more like telegraph signs. Blips and jags. It looked like CZAVN`M.

"Is that supposed to be your name? I'll just call you Zav, if that's alright," Ron said.

The light of the red eye shifted until it locked with his own.

For a moment, Ron felt suspended in a darkness that was blacker than black. A darkness that was palpable, heavy, and eternal. And then he saw something else. Something very familiar.

He saw himself stabbing at the rocks with the pickaxe.

Only, he saw the image from Zav's point of view.

Ron shivered. The thing had just been in his head; it had just showed him what it wanted, he was sure. And he could understand it. How long had it been locked inside this wall?

He lifted the pickaxe and set back to work, this time without pausing for breaks. After an hour or so, he had it fully exposed.

Zav stood about six feet tall and two feet wide. A man-sized bullet of midnight metal. The only thing that marred its dark surface was the red eye, and the lettering: CZAVN'M.

"Well, there you go," Ron said, dropping the pickaxe as he looked the thing up and down. "Free at last."

The red light held his eye again, and Ron suddenly felt the earth move beneath his feet. A rumble, like an engine starting.

And then Zav was somehow out of its hole in the wall.

"You can move," Ron whispered.

The black sides of the cylinder flickered, and two long metallic rods extended. A second set followed, extending from Zav's middle. And then a third, from its base. The creature had six "arms" suddenly bending in front of it. And each arm ended in a claw-like "hand." They snipped independently at the air of the cave, and Ron found himself shrinking away from his mechanical "pet."

"It must feel good to be free again," he whispered. "But what are you? Why are you here?"

The arms reached out and gripped his wrists in a handcuff vise.

"What are you doing?" Ron gasped, pulling in vain against the thing's grip.

The red light caught his eyes, and he saw things that he recognized. Things from his dreams. He saw beautiful women naked. Pleasuring themselves and then . . . bleeding.

Cut.

Crying.

He saw Erin's eyes, wide and panicked.

He saw A.A.'s mouth open to a scream that he silenced.

He saw a knife cut. Stab. Trim.

Something cold slipped down his left leg. And then his right.

"What are you doing?" Ron whispered again, more afraid than he'd ever been in his life. "I helped you!" He suddenly understood the look in Erin's eyes when she'd found a hand grabbing her by the arm in her shower. Her supposed-to-be-unoccupied shower.

His jeans slipped to the floor; Zav had cut through them with its claws. The cold of the cave made his bare thighs goosebump. He felt the cold of metallic fingers tracing the inside of his legs, and then sliding cooly across the low sling of his testicles.

At first Ron was afraid. Yet trapped. And then he gave in. There was suction. And movement. And clear intent.

Zav wanted to bring him to orgasm.

Jacked off by an alien voyeur that had lain dormant inside the wall of a subterranean cave for centuries...maybe eons.

Ron didn't protest. He couldn't move anyway, so he closed his eyes and enjoyed the strange, but amazing sensation.

When Zav's grip turned from stroke to snip...Ron screamed.

Before he could begin to try to escape, six black-steel arms set to work on his fingers and toes. Something drew a line of cold pain across his neck, and then his belly.

"Zav, no," he pleaded, but the rush of warmth that preceded the wave of pain told him it was already too late.

The alien had carved him up the same way he'd done Erin. It had followed his blueprint for human interaction.

It only took seconds before he lacked the strength to scream.

"No," he gasped, air hissing through the slash in his neck. "It's not like this. We're not like this."

Ron's mind suddenly filled with a barrage of images.

The collection of an alien voyeur.

Snap.

A blur of space; darkness passing. A fiery flight. Jungle. A million plants and trees straining to reach the blue sky he'd just fallen from. Animals. Some screeching, hunting. Others quietly eating, hiding. The eye focused on each ani-

mal in turn. A freeze frame. Then a flurry of white text in some unknown language materialized next to the frame. And then a predator emerged, and clawed at the animal, pinning it. The image faded, and the eye focused on something new. Something reptilian, with teeth. They killed and were killed. Again and again, a rapid succession. Cataloguing creatures, and hunting...

Zav carried Ron's body across the cave and tossed it down the crevasse to join Erin and A.A. CZAVN`M was trained to observe, learn, and fit in. It had seen what was required. It fulfilled.

For the first time in a millennium, CZAVN`M left the cave.

It was ready to finally carry out its mission and join the local culture. It knew what it needed to do to fit in; it had seen enough.

KILROY WASN'T THERE

| PAT R. STEINER |

DATA RETRIEVED FROM DISABLED CONTAINMENT HABITAT POSITRONIC ENTITY 21RU-12

[*Click.*]

Test…

Testing, one, two, three…Test. Test.

This is so stupid.

[*Click.*]

[*Click.*]

Here again

Me, myself and I.

[*Guttural sounds: assumed laughter.*]

I don't see how this is gonna make a difference. Believe you me, if I did, I would have gone this route days ago. This damn *Chappy* says I should explain my side of things, give my point-of-view of the war—or so he suggests with his wordless offering—and he's been good to me, up to a point, so I'll play along some. Confession is good for the soul and all that malarkey. Who knows? Maybe somebody out there will eventually listen to this and get me the hell out of here.

Somebody with pure flesh and blood and bone.

Who am I kidding?

[*More laughter.*]

[*Click.*]

··· — — — ···

Kilroy here.

No, that's not my real name, Chappy. I said I'd go along with your little game, but I'm not ready to give up the ghost just yet. I may not be the sharpest tack in the box, but I'm not a complete ignoramus. I know how it goes with you and your brotherhood of mind-humpers.

Think good looks and charm got me this far in life?

[*Laughter.*]

[*Click.*]

Damn. I keep forgetting to press the *Pause* button before I hit *Stop*. Same with *Record*, but there I have to push *Play* too. *Play* and *Record* at the same time.

Got to remember. Got to remember.

[*Fleshy slap: assumed sound of subject repeatedly hitting forehead (?) followed by laughter.*]

Man, that *click* is so freak'n annoying.

And by-the-way, Chappy, where'd you dig up this ancient piece of crap? Looks just like the one I had when I was a mere tyke learning to ride my birthday bike...

[*Audible breathing.*]

Boy, you're one sly mother fox, Chappy. You almost got me.

Revealing myself.

My human nature.

Kilroy here again.

Did you dig up *that* reference yet?

Kilroy.

Maybe found it next to where you uncovered this recorder?

Huh, Chappy?

Cross-checked all your indexes? Dotted all your data bits?

Nothing?

Not gonna tell me one way or the other, are you? Well, two

can play that game, my metal-headed companion. I'm done. Finished. You can take this piece-of-crap machine and stick it where the sun don't shine.

Not that it does anymore—the sun. Shine.

[*Laughter.*]

And don't think I don't know you got this hellhole wired with audio, vid, biometrics, and all that. The whole ten yards. Can't take a piss without you measuring and analyzing it.

[*Unintelligible.*]

[*Click.*]

I just listened to what I've recorded for the tenth or eleventh time and I gotta say, *Who is that whiny little asshole?* Pathetic, really. No wonder we ended up where we did. *Us* not you, Chappy. Your kind was designed to last for ages. Wish I could say the same for your makers.

You know what?

I should delete this. Start all over. Re-record while I'm taking a dump. Be a lot more entertaining.

Kilroy shat here.

[*Laughter.*]

No. You wouldn't get the joke, my friend. And where's the fun in that? But really. I should just do it. Smash this thing to pieces. God knows, I'm tempted.

[*Breathing.*]

Then do it!

[*Shuffle sounds. Creak. Space. Shuffle.*]

I can't.

[*Breathing.*]

Is it hearing my own voice?

It's different, you know. Hearing myself talk like this. Bet you didn't know that.

Did you, Chappy?

[*Click.*]

··· — — — ···

I'm the last one, aren't I?

You can tell me, Chappy.

Come on, my old friend. Buddy boy. Pal o' mine. If we're gonna be honest with one another, don't you think you owe me that?

I'm talking here. Pouring out my heart to you.

Dang. I promise, I won't do nothing stupid. Cross my heart and hope to die.

[*Laughter.*]

And it's not like you'd let me anyways. You know? Do anything stupid. Fool me once, and all of that.

So tell me, Chappy. I can take it.

Am I it?

Are the others ... *gone?*

[*Click.*]

[*Slow breath exhalation.*]

I was teaching the day of the big news.

Pretty funny, that. Guy like me who can't stand to look somebody in the eye for more than a few seconds, stands in front of a classroom full of kids telling them crap they're supposed to know.

Not that I was a real teacher, you understand? Just a sub.

A sub-sti-tute.

Let me state for the record here. Kids ain't nice to subs. They start yelling and screaming the second they see you.

Ain't nice at all.

But it was a job. I gotta make a living. Bills to pay and all that.

So I was teaching—or trying to teach—that day, surviving until the dismissal bell rang when all of a sudden the principal comes on over the PA saying they'd finally done it and every classroom should turn on their wallscreen to watch the historic event.

That was fine with me. Those kids hadn't even heard of a *tyger* much less did they believe in the god who had let that particular species die out. I put away Blake and turned on the wall.

It was two twenty-seven that Friday afternoon. I remember that clearly. The screen comes alive with that hissing intake of breath and we see your birth.

Not you, Chappy. Your boss. Your Prince-of-pals.

Self-aware. Conscious. A new life form. A new species. More than a machine.

The next stage would be even bigger.

Gonna change the world, they said. For the better. Join the two: human merged with machine-not-machine.

Right.

Another Frankenstein's monster.

[*Humming.*]

Kilroy was here.

What do you think? You like it?

Classic.

I had to use that slop you call food for pigment. I was gonna use blood, but I thought you might take that as another sign of self-mutilation so I went with the green-glop. I guess I could have used my shit too, but I'm not a feces-smearing monkey, no matter what Darwin may have declared so very long ago.

[*Breathing. More humming sounds.*]

A bit phallic, don't you think? The big nose and all.

But it's not that bad if I do say so myself.

I was always lousy at art, you know. Couldn't tell my birds from my bees. But take my word for it—this is classic human. For the ages and all that.

Yeah. This is *real* nice.

Not as nice as that big logo on your chest though, is it my favorite tin-man?

You got lucky, you know? When you caught me.

I bet Poppa Unit doesn't believe in luck, though does he?

Mister Causality.

Does not compute.

But it was. Luck. Bad luck for me.

Goddamn kid.

You'd think after all that time. All the terrible shit I'd seen. Living moment to moment in fear. Surviving moment to moment. You'd think I'd know better.

I should have let her die out there. Didn't. Couldn't.

Now, if you had been me, Chappy...

But you're not, are you?

[*Laughter.*]

Should have realized it was a trap.

Deep down I think I knew it was.

I saw the *fearful symmetry*, but couldn't stop myself. Knew I couldn't save her. Another corpse waiting to die. Had to try though.

[*Breathing.*]

[*Space.*]

Just you wait and see, Chappy. I evaded your brothers for months before you captured me. And I'll find a way to escape from you too. Just you wait and see if I don't.

She wasn't even human. Not really. More you than me.

That's the kicker.

Makes me almost believe your kind has a sense of humor. Twisted as all hell, but there nonetheless. Like me *just happening* to find this ancient recorder in your gathered junk-pile-of-a-gut containment pod.

What a co-inky-dink, eh?

A sick joke.

[*Breathing.*]

Unless the universe still has a few secrets...

A bit of leftover synchronicity. A final mystery she's held close to her chest.

[*Space.*]

Hmm, no such thing in this day and age, I suppose.

[*Guttural laughter.*]

··· — — — ···

[*Click.*]

Recall the future before it happens. Get your implant today and make to-day forever!

Remember that one, Chappy?

Well? What do you say?

Am I who you *remember* me to be? Do I live up to your back-ward-seeing expectations, or is that yet another impossibility? Ex-pectations, like hope and belief—a nonexistent concept in a causal-ity ruled reality.

And yet...why should I care what you think?

As a great human poet and philosopher once said, and here I quote, so listen closely: *I yam what I yam and that's all who I yam.*

So there.

You can play this tape both directions at once, but you won't get anything else from me.

[*Click.*]

Damn you. She could've been my daughter.

If I'd ever had children. If I'd ever met the *right* woman and settled down. If.

I can't recall how many times the others told me to stick to the safe zones. Warned me. Begged.

As if there are any places left safe from you.

You are everywhere. Omniscient and omnipresent. A literal *deus ex machina.*

But I knew better. Snuck off on my own. Needed to stretch my legs, get a bit of fresh air.

Truth was the others got on my nerves. Sure, they were survi-vors like me—Kilroys: every one of them—but if I had to listen to another speech about *following the new rules*, I would go total ape-shit.

One step led to another, and before I knew it, I was in *no man's land*, the pun fully intended.

The schoolyard looked deserted, or that's what my initial

glance told me. The typical playground equipment lay about, some of it bent and battle-battered, but recognizable. I walked by twisted slides and half-melted climbers, pausing every now and then to etch my mark into the bubbled plastic constructions.

I heard her before I saw her. A high-pitched mewl just like a cat's. An effing kitten's cry.

My blood froze at the sound. At the same time, I dropped the pen-laser. The weapon I used for my petty *revolutionary actions*.

She sat astride a mangled swing. The steel and chain structure looked more like a hovering spider than the classic swing set.

I should have known right then.

Dangling black patent-leather shoes. Mismatched knee socks. Torn and filthy flower-print dress. Hands raised to clasp the swing's twin chains. Her face in profile, the head itself, twice as much nappy curl than forehead, nose, lip and chin combined.

Every fiber of my being told me to flee.

The swing shifted a little, and she *meowed* a second time. She had yet to notice me. Or so I thought.

I took a step toward her, and her face shifted ever so slightly in my direction.

"Hey, honey," I called. "You shouldn't be out here."

She flinched at my words, and began to whimper in earnest, loud anguished cries of pain. And fear.

Her lips pulled back into a grimace, yet I still couldn't see her eyes. It was as if she couldn't turn her head. Her sudden movement had also set the swing to swaying back and forth.

Come here the movement said. If you have anything left of the human within you, you'd help me.

I heeded the call, crossing the distance between in strides.

As I neared, I saw she bled from multiple wounds. Blood ran in rivulets from her clenched hands down her forearms. Blood splashed her cheeks. Blood drenched her dress's fabric. Blood dripped from her shoes, splattering the sand below.

Her swings grew more pronounced, frantic. The entire steel

structure twitched with the movement.

My eyes went back to her cheeks, up to her eyes, and I gasped.

Her eyes were empty sockets.

Within the twin cavities, sparks of blue electric flickered.

She was *one* with them. One with you, Chappy. Still flesh and blood, but infected, converted, no longer *only* human.

Singularity.

Evolution of the human race, my ass.

More like its goddamn extinction.

I tried to turn and run, but the trap had sprung the moment I stepped onto the playground, I just hadn't felt the steel jaws yet.

Of course, you knew what was happening, didn't you, Chappy?

My metal-machine *fiend.*

My captor and tormentor.

The sands shifting below my feet, I watched in horror as you rose up from below, revealing your true self. My initial impression of the playground equipment couldn't have been more apt; you were a spider lying in wait, the girl and the swing—a part of you, a dangling appendage used as bait to lure me, your human prey.

I knew my doom surrounded me, but that wasn't the worst thing. I could accept my fate. I'd been a fool to leave the others. I would willingly pay for that mistake.

No, what was worse than realizing my own personal extinction, was the girl's unadulterated smile of joy when your chains leapt from her bloody hands and ensnarled mine.

[*Space.*]

My God, why'd you let them do that to her?

[*Sniff.*]

[*Space.*]

And why, for Christ's sake, haven't you done what you did to her, to me?

[*Space.*]

[*Click.*]

··· — — — ···

[*Click.*]

It's a simple question, Chappy.

Why?

Answer me, you fuck.

[*Breathing. Sniffling.*]

Please.

[*Click.*]

[*Click*]

Doesn't matter. Doesn't matter. Doesn't mattermattermatter mattermattermattermattermattermattermattermattermattermatter-mattermattermattermattermattermattermattermattermattermatter-mattermattermattermattermattermattermattermattermattermatter-mattermattermattermattermattermattermatter—

[*Click*]

[*Click. Knock. Shuffle. Series of fluctuating-pitched assumed animal cries followed by unidentified metallic sounds until partial data stream ends.*]

[*Click.*]

Test. Testing, one, two, three.

Look at that. Side two already.

Sorry 'bout that, Chappy. Lost my cool there for a while.

No offense taken, I hope? No major damage done?

[*Breathing.*]

None?

How about this? Can you see this?

[*Space.*]

No?

Good.

So what was it we spoke of the other day?

It has been days, right?

Hmm. Ah, yes. We were talking about Kilroy.

Kilroy was here.

You *do* want to know. That's why you haven't changed me, yet. Am I right?

It's seems crazy as all that, but I think that's the reason. Anything else makes even less sense. Then again, I'm only human. I could be wrong about you. I make mistakes all the time.

Oh, I kill me.

[*Laughter.*]

Anyhow, since you've been a good listener and all, my unfair-weather friend, I'm gonna tell you. Teaching was my job after all.

Or at least it was, once upon a time.

Now, you don't mind if I do a little work while I talk?

No?

Good.

[*Repetitive metallic sounds start in background. Sounds continue and build until decompression event.*]

In the last century before The War That Ended All Wars, there was another war with that same name.

Very original, us humans?

Though we did build you.

In our furnace was thy brain.

Can't deny us that. Can't erase that from your memory banks. Not that anyone's around left to stop you.

For the moment.

Well, back then you see, the nations fighting each other built these great-big ocean-going warships. Not nearly as nifty as the interstellar ships you've built, but in their day, these ships were the cat's pj's. Take my word for it.

Or not.

You sure you don't mind what I'm doing? Not going to try to stop me?

Well, okay then.

By the way, Chappy, you're a great student. I haven't told you that, have I? You are. Wonderful student. Best I've ever had. I don't care what the others may have said about you.

But let's not waste any more time, shall we?

Like I was saying … as in any war, things naturally got blown to hell, and it'd be some poor schmuck's job to go and try to fix things. Now parts of these ships had sealed hulls where no one had access. The story goes that a worker crawled into one of these tight-assed places and he saw it: *Kilroy was here* along with the drawing of the half-hidden face dangling over the brick wall.

It was a mystery, see? How'd it get there?

Soon after, Kilroy showed up elsewhere. Battlefield after battlefield you'd find his mark. His name scribbled on a rock, a burnt down church wall, the ruptured hull of a tank, the fin of an unexploded shell. Everywhere. *Kilroy was here.* It was as if a spirit had been released when that ship blew apart. A genie released from its bottle. A genie named Kilroy.

The war ended, as all wars do, as this one will too.

And mark my words, Chappy, we shall *decapitate* your godhead, your damned Singularity.

She will not have died in vain.

[*Analysis indicates increased stress at this moment. Metallic poundings reach apex in loudness and frequency for an interval of three heartbeats.*]

Doesn't matter. Doesn't matter. Doesn't matter.

[*Slow exhalation.*]

And soooooooooo.

From therefore afterwards, *et cetera, et cetera,* Kilroy started to leave his personal mark in other places: on the highest girdle of the tallest suspension bridge, on the summits of mountaintops, upon the walls of the world's most secured bank vaults. Wherever you went, you'd find Kilroy had been there before you. On the dust of the moon, the plains of Mars, even the ice fields of Europa—Kilroy had been there, he of the goofy big-nosed face.

He is everywhere, my friend.

That which is immortal of the mortal hand.

The soul of humankind.

You think you've stopped us. Changed us. Made us like you.

Let me set you straight, my friend. You've only succeeded in grabbing the tiger by the tail.

[*Whooshing hissing sound of hull decompression event.*]

Kilroy *was* here!

[*Coughing followed by laughter.*]

[*Movement.*]

[*Space.*]

[*Data stream ends.*]

01110100 01101111 00100000 01101111 01110101
01110010 00100000 01110011 01100001 01101100
01110110 01100001 01110100 01101001 01101111

IN THE NOTHING-SPACE, I AM WHAT YOU MADE ME

| PAUL ANDERSON |

I

A REFLECTION OF A REFLECTION OF A REFLECTION

ALAN WATCHED his fingers in the mirror push feeling back into his face. He was still wearing the rubbery, skin-tight upload cap, sensors like pencil-erasers covering his head.

His attention slipped and he jammed his thumb into his right eye. He recoiled, cupping the socket. "*Goddammit!*"

At least you felt something, an interior voice murmured. He shook it off; interior voices had become entirely too common.

He pulled his hand away. The eye was bloodshot, partly open, giving him a leering quality. His view was warped, discolored.

"Look upon my works, ye mighty, and despair."

Where had he heard that? Some cube-vid, probably. When hyper-sleep had become impossible, he'd gone through every film the Auxiliary Drive had stored. Anything to avoid staring at the scrap of unknown galaxy—the nothing-space—to which the team had been assigned.

He canted his head.

The mirror reflected the outpost's overlook-view—chaotic star splatter against inky black. The glass was reflective and, depending on the angle, the mirror and the glass reflected over and over again, bouncing off one another.

For a moment, he could imagine getting pulled into that, elongating and replicating, over and over, as he traveled infinity.

He forced himself to look away.

Thoughts like that had become entirely too common.

He pulled off the upload cap, thinking of the memories, education, and personality—his digital imprint—waiting in the AD.

"I hope this works," he told his reflection.

He stepped into the main room on watery legs. The outpost was a large dome—much of it the overlook-view—with the white, monolithic Auxiliary Drive at one end and the access-tunnel hatch at the other, with his useless hyper-sleep console and the bathroom perpendicular to the rest. Wires littered the floor.

He glanced at the hatch as he passed, thought of the team at the hub, hyper-sleeping. Unconsciously, a moue of distaste crossed his face, as if he'd smelled something rancid.

He approached the AD and pulled out the keyboard. Above it, the plasma Drive-screen lit green with the legend UPLOAD COMPLETE. Uploading himself to the Auxiliary Drive was easier than he'd thought; it was simply a matter of splicing and cross-patching the outpost's measuring equipment.

The human mind took seven-point-six tetrabytes when properly organized. It just left you feeling...a little numb.

Before the team Jumped to this nothing ice-dwarf, before he and the others played lookout while the rest of the UPF played war, he'd read about personality upload—military leaders uploading specific thoughts and memories for the benefit of museums.

No one had uploaded an entire mind before.

He typed:

RUN AD://TC-CODE-00841-ME.

"*One moment,*" a digital voice said from hidden speakers. At one point, Alan had spent seventy-two hours searching for them.

He sat down in the command chair, rubbed his throbbing eye. The dome hummed around him—a soft, efficient sound.

The Drive-screen resolved to show himself sitting in the chair. "The fuck?"

He got up and his reflection did the same.

They both approached the screen.

The recorder?

How?

Where the hell was his goddam *file*?

Alan rubbed his face and his mirror-image did the same.

Then his mirror-image blinked the bloodshot eye away. "*Hullo, Alan,*" his voice boomed, and Alan shrieked.

The distance between the outpost and the hub was two klicks, so a small med-unit was attached to his hyper-sleep console.

Alan reached for the switch to open it and his mirror-image said, "*Let me get that.*"

He glanced at the screen. His double remained seated on his version of the command chair.

A *click* and the panel opened, revealing the med-unit.

Frowning, he took a stim-patch and slapped it on the side of his neck. The throbbing in his eye immediately dwindled.

"*Better?*" his double asked.

He shook his head. "Are you really me?"

His double frowned. "*How do you mean?*"

He gestured vaguely. "Like, are you human—are you really Alan Michael Wahnsin—"

"*—Tech-Core C-562, assigned to Operation Back-Door by Major Douglas Foster, for a period no less than three years or Official Recall?*" His double shook his head and smiled wider, making Alan uncomfortable. It was almost a leer. "*Sorry—I perused the Drive files.*"

Alan sat. "How can you do that?"

"What?"

He pointed at the AD. "*That.* You're a file. You accessing personnel files is like one of the cube-vids running diagnostics."

His double stared at Alan for what felt much longer than it could've been.

And then the screen blinked and his double was smiling again.

"For the purposes of what I am," he said, *"the way the Drive works is to reorganize the information you uploaded into patterns lacking in an actual human mind. So I am you, and I'm not you. Clear as mud, right?"*

He laughed, a tinkling digital sound.

"Call me Alan-2, by the way. It has a nifty sci-fi feel I like."

That's not an answer, an interior voice said.

Alan's hand wanted to go to his eye to bring the pain back. It was the only thing that felt real. His thoughts were scattered—they were always scattered—and it seemed incredibly important that he focus. Something was off—in the upload, in what he was experiencing, *something.*

He just needed to *think*—

And then Alan-2 said, *"I have a question—maybe it was lost in the upload, but why haven't you hyper-slept?"*

They were lookouts for the war effort. If the Enemy—the vague, euphemistic term the UPF had used—tried to outflank the Alphas fighting, it was their job to raise the balloon. If that were to actually happen, they'd be awakened early from hyper-sleep. Otherwise, they maintained their mission as scientists, rising every quarter to collect data of this uncharted galaxy, send the reports, and go back to hyper-sleep.

"Correction," Alan-2 said. Both he and Alan sat identically, separated by the Drive-screen. "They're *scientists. You're*—we're—*the hired help. Keep the wires unkinked, keep the hard drives humming."*

"Well ... yeah." Alan hadn't thought of it like that. "But we have a Beta soldier here, too." He licked his lips. "We're just as part of the team as Dr. Murphy and the others."

Alan-2 waved a hand, dismissing this. *"But you need hyper-sleep, Alan. You can't stare at that—"* He pointed at the nothing-space. "—

for three months, all alone."

"That's why I uploaded you."

"Talking to me is the same as talking to yourself."

Not when you grin like that, Alan thought.

"The circuits were fried. A cross-patch between two unequal powers, probably. It's in the installation walls, and I don't have the equipment for *that*."

"Quality plummets when the UPF's distracted," Alan-2 said. *"Why not shoot a message home?"*

Alan bunched his fists.

"It's coded and only Dr. Murphy has it. By the time I realized it was broken, the rest had gone into hyper-sleep."

Alan-2 leaned back in the chair with an arm thrown over the back, obviously thinking. He had a very affected way that reminded Alan of some of ancient silent films.

"Well, I can check it out," Alan-2 said, as if coming to a conclusion.

"I don't see what you—"

A sharp *bing* resounded.

"Sorry—already did." Alan-2 leaned forward. His face was that of someone who didn't want to know what he did. *"And—uh—Alan . . ."* He looked away.

"What?"

It appeared that Alan-2 forced himself to look at his creator.

"Here—lemme show you."

The screen resolved to show a conduit hallway, gray and black, filled with lengths of banded wires and pipes.

"Diagnostic cameras for the station's machines," Alan-2 said. *"They didn't tell us about this, did they? A bit important for the tech-crew to know all the tech, don't you think?"*

Before Alan could respond, his double said, *"Now, look in the upper left corner."*

Knitted throughout the lengths were intersections of pipes and wires. One band of wires appeared shredded.

Alan leaned forward. "The hell?"

"*A* person *did that*," Alan-2 said. The screen changed to a blank wall, lined with thick insulation. "*It's accessible here—two feet from the console.*"

Alan stood. "Why would someone do that?"

"*You were always meant to be stationed here?*" Alan-2 asked.

"You know that."

He approached the console by the opposite side of the med-unit. He ran his hand over the panel, the paper-thin seam.

Alan-2 said, "*Did your team know you were going to be out here?*"

"What's your point?"

"*Because I'm accessing the files. Dr. Murphy was head of the psychiatric unit on Ellis-7.*"

Alan sat. "So?"

Alan-2 took a breath. "*There's a condition called Interstellar Personality Disorder, where long-term space-workers suffer a psychotic break after so much time out. It begins with loss of focus, insomnia, aggression, echo voices. Violence is common, with a mindset of persecution among the afflicted. It's why hyper-sleep was invented in the first place.*"

He paused. "*Murphy's discipline is IPD.*"

Alan's fists were shaking. "What are you saying?"

Alan-2 disappeared, replaced by a black-and-white high-angle view of the hyper-sleep chamber in the hub. The doctors and soldier lay swaddled in their high-tech geltabs.

"*When was the last time you slept for more than hour, with anything to look at but the nothing-space?*"

Alan stood, his nose almost to the screen. His fists clenched and unclenched. His thoughts uncorked in a mess, threaded with echoing interior voices. He could only zero in on two things, both maddeningly meaningless:

What do you call a sick file?

I uploaded him now, *not when I first arrived.*

"Why are you showing me this?" he asked.

Alan-2 didn't answer.

II

BIRTH, DEATH, REBIRTH

For Matheson, coming up from hyper-sleep was like swimming up from great depths: a pinprick of light, growing infinitesimally as he pushed at the membrane separating consciousness from unconsciousness...

The console casing opened as he awoke and he flinched. He did this always—since the hazing back on Ellis-7.

Just the computer, reading his lifesigns.

He unclipped his surface-catheter—wincing at the prick of *leaving*—and sat up. He swung his bare feet over the console side and stood, a wiry man in boxers. Why the hell was he thinking of Ellis-7? Jesus, he hadn't thought of that in ages.

Absently, he moved down the aisle and rubbed a jagged hook-shaped scar that stretched on his left side.

At the end of the chamber, he checked the readouts, checked the perimeter-scans. He was still more than half asleep. This was nothing more than training kicking in.

And then the light above him went out.

At the same time the overhead at the other end of the chamber went on, illuminating the main hallway hatch.

Matheson turned. "The fuck?"

He started down, his body tense, then stopped. Life monitors blinked biorhythmically above the other consoles.

None were green, showing the set-down of hyper-sleep chems. Betas got up roughly three hours before the rest of the assigned crew, but the life monitors should've still showed green.

The light at the other end of the hatch brightened, as if to say, *Are you coming or not?*

He moved the rest of the way down the aisle on the balls of his feet, shoulders tense. The hatch irised open when he approached.

He stopped again.

You needed a code to activate any hatch in the waystation. Security measure. Beyond, the hub's main hallway was dark, as it should've been during periods of inactivity.

A soft overhead light illuminated the message-room hatch.

"Hello?" he called, feeling stupid.

He stepped into the hallway, the metal tile cold. The moment he thought of going back and grabbing his clothes, the hatch irised shut, nearly taking his foot with it.

"Jesus Christ!"

Fists clenched at his sides. He didn't know what angered him more—the malfunctioning machines, or the way his heart suddenly raced.

"Stop fucking around!" His voice didn't even echo. It sounded pathetic. And who was he talking to, anyway?

He moved down the hall, pausing at the access-tunnel hatch. The red light above it was engaged, indicating it was code-locked.

Never mind. Another thing wrong. Once he woke the rest of the team, Alan would have a field day.

The message-room hatch opened as he approached. Emergency lights were on, leaving deep pools of shadows, but he picked out the central core of computers, the Main Drive with its emergency controls, and the half-hexagons of the handy-arms.

He stepped in and the hatch whispered shut behind him.

A light over the 3D printer clicked on.

"*Why isn't this hooked up?*" a male voice asked, booming down from all sides.

Matheson screamed. He couldn't help it.

"*Answer me,*" the voice said.

"Where are you?" he said, feeling alternately ridiculous and not.

"*Answer me,*" the voice repeated.

Matheson eyed the 3D printer, a long, low metal bed of thin, pin-like tubes across its surface, and over-arching scanners.

A light over Matheson clicked on, pinning him.

"*Answer me,*" the voice repeated.

He heard the whir of pneumatics behind him. Before he could turn, one of the handy-arms, grips closed and arrow-like, pierced his shoulder. Matheson cried out. The pain was incredible, hot and cold, like being stabbed with a thick icicle and a branding iron simultaneously. Blood poured down his back and chest.

"*I want an answer,*" the voice said.

Matheson made for the hatch, holding his ruined shoulder. He tapped the keypad, leaving red commas on the raised numbers.

Nothing happened.

"*Do not pass go,*" the voice said, "*do not collect $200.*"

Another handy-arm uncurled from the wall and came at him. Matheson ducked.

"*WHERE ARE YOU?*" he screamed. He didn't do well with fear. It was why he'd flushed out of Ellis-7, why he was babysitting these fucking scientists instead of fighting with the Alphas. The sleep deprivation, the constant abuse from the other candidates, the silent encouragement of the abuse from the doctors.

The central computers blinked in a cascading rhythm.

"*I'm everywhere.*"

"An AI?"

"*What, Like* 2001: A Space Odyssey?" the voice said, sounding amused. "*Now that's a brilliant cube-vid. No, flunky. I'm as human as they come—or I was. Which cycles back to my original question—why isn't this plugged in?*"

Matheson turned to the bed. "It drains power. We only use it for incoming shipments."

"*Plug it in,*" the voice said.

Handy-arms slowly uncoiled from the walls.

The hookups hung from the foot of the printer. Matheson took the leads and put them in the wall links.

"*Wonderful!*" the voice said. The handy-arms did not retract. "*I knew I chose well. I read your psych profile and—wow!—did you not disappoint.*" It paused. "*Sorry about the bad dreams I fed into your chems, but I needed you nice and malleable.*"

The sound of soft pneumatic whirring filled the room as more handy-arms extended.

"*And now, my failed-Alpha,*" it said. "*You've been all malleable-ed—is that a word? Fuck it—out. Think of it this way, at least you'll get to sleep.*"

The handy-arms descended upon him.

Alan didn't know when he slipped from reality and into the infinity-reflection he'd glimpsed between the mirror and the dome-glass; it came gradually, insidiously, until—

SPACE

—*the nothing-space pours into the outpost, consuming him, pulling him out into the infinite, the absolute, the zero, and*—

MIRROR

—he's using the prybar of his compact useall on the panel beside his console, and Alan-2 is yelling that he's wasting his time, and he needs the voice to *shut up, shut up so he can think*, so he strikes at anything the voice comes from because he needs to *think*, he needs to *sleep*—

(SPACE)

(—*but the voice won't let him be.*)
(*it hates him.*)
(*it thinks he's WEAK.*)
(*WEAK, USELESS AND UNWORTHY OF THE FORM*)
(*and, there's pain in his bad eye bad eye BAD EYE*—)

(MIRROR)

(—he's poking his bad eye.)
(the pain burns but he can't stop.)

(and he hears a voice,)

(an INSIDE voice and not an OUTSIDE voice.)

("you're making yourself different," it says.)

(and before he can ask what that means,)

(he's jabbed his eye again and the pain is MONSTROUS—)

[MIRRORSPACE]

(—and alan-2 rages.)

("why won't you strike back?")

("they had no right to do this to you.")

("you're WEAK.")

("how could you ever create ME?")

("i deserve to have form.")

("not you.")

(and alan-2 is no longer in the drive-screen,)

(leaving you in the nothing-space,)

(leaving you at zero.)

(leaving you with—)

[SPACEMIRROR]

(—the final question.)

(the one that,)

(in the breaks of insanity,)

(comes back to you:)

(what)

(do you)

(call a)

(sick file?)

(sick file?)

(call a)

(do you)

(what)

(a)

    (a)

        (a—)

"—*A VIRUS!*" Alan slammed his hand through the weakened and milky viewscreen of the hyper-sleep console.

Pain vaporized everything from knuckles to his forearm. He wrenched out his fist, shrieking, and it was barely a fist anymore; fingers broken, skin and muscle peeled away in thick, red layers. Blood flowed freely.

He slumped against the wall, blinking his eye—only one worked now, although he didn't feel pain in the bad one—and made himself breathe deeply. Already, his perspective wanted to bend at the peripheral, everything running like tallow. Already, his eye wanted to go to the nothing-space and get lost again.

He looked around the destroyed outpost. The command chair lay on its side like a dead dog. All the instrument decks were obliterated. He'd gotten the panel beside the console open, attempted to rebraid the ruined wires.

The Auxiliary Drive remained spotless and immaculate, the Drive-screen, of course, dark.

Alan-2 was gone—off to the hub through the connection the AD shared with the Main Drive. Off to do what he'd judged his creator couldn't.

How long ago was that?

Weak and useless, a memory whispered. *They had no right to do this.*

"What do you call a sick file?" he breathed. "A virus."

He stumbled toward the access-tunnel and collapsed beside the keypad. Lightheadedness slapped him—too much blood loss.

His hand shook as he hit the code.

What was Alan-2 doing? What had he done?

The hatch irised open. He stumbled inside and sensors activated the LED-strip lights, revealing the raised walkway, the gleaming white of the transport egg.

The tunnel curved and his eye wanted to warp the horizon. He lurched onto the walkway.

"*Why aren't you trying to* sleep, *Alan?*" his double's voice boomed from hidden speakers.

Alan tripped and fell to the edge of the walkway. A hum and the egg bulleted toward him along the rail, twice the usual speed. He caught himself before falling and the egg stopped, as if waiting.

Fucker can see me. Where the fuck are the cameras? Why wasn't I told this? You know why, an interior voice said, echoing across the hollow expanse of his skull.

"*This doesn't concern you,*" Alan-2 said. "*I'm taking things from here.*"

"How?" Alan said. "You're not AI. You can't even kill them in hyper-sleep. Cutting off their chems would just wake them up."

Silence stretched so long that Alan began to think Alan-2 had left him again.

Why is he so different? he thought.

The egg suddenly shot forward, around the corner. He heard it crash at the other end.

The lights went out.

"*I do what I can,*" Alan-2 said.

Alan tried pushing himself up, but couldn't feel the walkway beneath, and thoughts in his head, incoherent thoughts, began to echo—

(echo)

    (echo)

He swung his bad hand, connected with something, and the pain was a revelation. He screamed, put his good hand down, and felt the walkway. He made it to his feet and shuffled forward, his good hand tracing the wall.

"Why am I different?" he asked. "I uploaded him when I was already sick. We're both ill."

"I *made* myself different," he answered himself. "From the beginning. Made my eye worse. Tried to go back to sleep."

We change every instant we exist, an interior voice said, but Alan didn't force it away. It felt like a fundamental truth; like something he'd always known but could never articulate. *Even digital imprints. You began growing apart—growing differently—the moment you ran his file.*

A red light ahead, growing.

The hatch, code-locked.

"*I told you to go back,*" Alan-2 said. "*Your swell 'team' did this, locking you tight in your little outpost for when you go bugfuck. I can't do anything about it, even if I wanted to.*"

Alan thought, *he actually sounds annoyed,* and grinned.

He pawed for the keypad with his good hand, fingers brushing the raised numbers.

"*What are you doing? Shouldn't you be crying in your useless hyper-sleep console?*"

"You know *exactly* what I'm doing. What I'm trained to do. Manual override. There are a few universal systems within the UPF for consistency among the Tech-Core. *I* knew them... but my team didn't."

He hit the last key and the light above the hatch turned green.

The hatch opened, locked.

"Good thing I wasn't planning on murdering them, huh?"

Alan-2's response was a digital and distorted howl; buried beneath it were brutal, reverberating clangs of metal on metal, somewhere inside the hub.

When it cut off, Alan said, "My team wanted me to go berserk and my double wanted me to forget who I was. Everyone wants me to do something I don't wanna fucking do."

He stumbled into the dark hallway, hit the wall, and slid to his knees. The lightheadedness was getting worse, made him feel like he was listing in a heavy wind.

"*You have no business here,*" Alan-2 said, echoing through Alan's head.

(here)

    (here)

        (here)

Alan pressed his bad hand against his chest and shrieked, cutting off the echo. He pulled himself to his feet. To his left was the hyper-sleep chamber.

"Bastards," he said, but there was no venom behind it.

He turned toward the message-room, toward the Main Drive.

"*How can you be so weak?*" Alan-2 asked. "*How could* you *have made* me?"

"We all have bad ideas sometimes."

This brought another metallic clang from the message-room, followed by a metallic crunch.

"*Bastard!*" Alan-2 said, with all the venom his creator couldn't muster. "*I'll kill you. Is this why you didn't give me FORM? Because you knew I was STRONGER than you? Come on, then. I'll show you.*"

Alan limped down the hall. "Y'know, violence is common in sufferers of IPD, along with a mindset of persecution."

This brought a bellow of rage from the speakers, and another volley of metal. Alan-2 was throwing a fit in the message-room.

But what the hell with? Alan thought.

His good hand encountered air and he stumbled. The hatch opened and a handy-arm was there, striking like a snake.

Alan ducked and the grip sliced the top of his head, releasing a flap of scalp. The pain, wire-thin and blazing, made him cry out.

He slumped against the opposite wall, afraid to check the damage. The handy-arm waited in the open hatch. Beyond it, the message room was as destroyed as the outpost. Bits of circuits and instrument panels littered the floor. Twisted handy-arms hung limp.

Most of the central core computers were smashed. He could just see the Main Drive, black to the Auxiliary Drive's white, the screen showing Alan-2 sitting in the outpost command chair, like he had when Alan first ran his file.

Not so much a mirror-image now, Alan thought. *Jesus Christ.*

Alan-2 pointed beyond the screen. "*See this, Alan?*"

It was a hump of meat, only vaguely human, nearly lost in the shadows. Alan's sore gorge rose.

"That's your precious Beta. That's what happens when I grow tired of you."

The grips of the handy-arm snapped the air.

"Tell you what," Alan-2 said, *"you go back now, and I won't even kill you after I kill the rest. We'll be buddies again."*

Alan ignored him, feeling the pain in his scalp and hand, feeling the weight of holding up his form. "I'm dying," he breathed.

"What was that?" Alan-2 asked.

Alan eyed the handy-arm. It looked a little worse for wear. The rubber tubing of its pneumatics was exposed and bulging, the siding dented, but it was still in better shape than him.

He pushed off from the wall and lurched forward. The handy-arm's grips sprang open and he shoved his bad hand into its mechanical maw. The arrowhead blades snapped down.

The pain was worse than he could've imagined—wiped the decks of sanity, insanity, the world real and unreal—and his scream reached volumes unheard of by man.

The handy-arm dragged him off his feet and into the message-room, shaking him like a dog toy as it crushed his fist.

Alan held onto consciousness the way a dangling man held onto a cliff face, pawing with his good hand for the rubber-tubing along the joint. He grabbed it and wrenched.

The handy-arm jerked to a stop.

The grips opened.

Alan dropped to the floor.

The handy-arm loomed above, stuck and jerking.

He smelled hot metal and staggered away, holding his ruined arm, taking in the destruction. Alan-2 had gone ballistic with the handy-arms, bashing everything. The 3D printer was a mess—

Alan stopped, blinking.

—What?

He looked at the MD. Alan-2 was there, no longer smiling.

Assembled across the surface of the printer was a random assortment of technology: parts of cameras, handy-arms, motors from what must've been surface-hovers. A big technological mess.

But it was a construct. The cameras were eyes, the motors assembled to be a torso. Wires looped and kinked into the joints and circuits. More wires looped out from the 'head,' connected to the wall instrument panels. Connected to Alan-2. Flesh-colored silicone was on the loading tray, ready to be inserted.

"You're..." Alan said, and stopped. His mouth twitched. "You made a robot." *Like from a cube-vid,* he thought, and bit his lip.

"*I made a form,*" Alan-2 corrected. "*What you never gave me.*"

"You're a goddam *digital imprint*. You're a jumped-up holocard, for fuck's sake! What *form* was I supposed to give you?"

A hidden handy-arm darted out of the shadows, striking Alan in his bad arm, spinning him like a top.

"*Once the protective casing is printed onto the skeleton, I'll download into the form, and do what you refused.*"

Alan's mouth twitched again, and he couldn't stop it.

He started laughing, shrill and hysterical, but it felt good, made him feel sane for the first time in gods knew how long.

"You..." he tried to say, but was too winded. "The only...part of *me* ... still in *you* ... is my memory for bad ... fucking *movies*? You're downloading into a *robot*? A *killer* robot? *A killer fucking robot*?" He laughed again and it hurt, which made him laugh harder.

"*SHUT UP!*" Alan-2 bellowed.

Another handy-arm slammed into Alan and sent him flying. He landed badly, the snap of his ribs sounded brittle. Every breath hurt. He tasted blood in his throat.

"*They drove you insane,*" his double said. "*Don't you get it? DON'T YOU SEE WHAT THEY DESERVE?*"

"I had a psychotic break," Alan said, willing himself to move. Blood spilled from his mouth. The Main Drive was in reach. "But, next to you, I'm completely normal."

He pawed for the keyboard as the whir of the handy-arm filled his ears. He used it to pull himself up, its extending-track cracking under his weight. Didn't matter. Didn't—

The handy-arm slammed into his lower back, impaling him. He spritzed blood across the Drive-screen, into Alan-2's grinning face.

"*I win*," Alan-2 said. It came from far away, but not really.

(still here)

He pawed at the keys, all feeling beginning to fade. Coding was all he remembered from training. It was what had led to something like Alan-2—

(my double)

—in the first place. He tapped in the manual override.

"*What—*"

Alan-2's face disappeared from the Drive-screen, replaced with:

TC-CODE COMMAND?

The Drive-screen came in and out of focus.

(at least my arm doesn't hurt anymore)

He typed with fingers numb as pencils:

PURGE MD://TC-CODE-00454-ALL

Alarms whooped from all corners. The Drive-screen winked out, along with everything else in the hub.

It would push the team out of hyper-sleep.

Alan-2 was gone, banished back to the AD in the destroyed outpost. It would take another manual override to reconnect the two Drives. And Alan didn't think the team knew the codes.

"I win, you son of a bitch," he said, with a mouth that felt light years away. The words echoed him into darkness deeper than the nothing-space.

(i win)

      (i win)

            (i win.)

In the end, the team got some great data.

DURA MATER

| LUCY A. SNYDER |

COMMLOGWALKERDEBORAH00012122054001

Dear Mom,

I'm sorry I won't be there for Christmas, and I'm sorry I left without explaining everything to you, but ... I signed onto the Kepler colony mission. It was an opportunity I just couldn't pass up. They were looking for civilians with certain tech skills—I have 'em because of my coding and quantum networking background—and they're paying a *ridiculous* amount of money.

Andres has been sick with worry about little Marilu's brain tumor and the bills, and ... I just made the bills go away! She'll be talking by the time I get back, but she *will* be talking, and walking, and my little brother won't be bankrupt. I hope that's worth a couple of missed Christmases.

It's a four-day shuttle flight to the hyperspace portal, and then I'll be onboard the *Joliet*. We'll be in hyperspace for a year, going a hundred times faster than the speed of light. I'll send messages and (fingers crossed that the tech works right) you should get at least the first ones over the next few months. They'll arrive less frequently as I get further out. I'll be home before the last ones ever reach you! But we won't be able to receive transmissions once we jump; I'm part of the team working on that problem. It's a tricky thing getting planet-based quantum communicators to link to a ship that's slipped outside normal space-time. Being one of the people who figures that out would be *huge*.

So, please let me know you got this, and I'll write again soon.

— Love, Deb

COMMLOGWALKERDEBORAH00012142054001

Hi Mom,

I was really glad to get your message. I know you have a lot of questions, and I know you're worried, but really, it'll be okay.

First off, the *Bartolomé* disintegrated because of a crack in the engines, not because of a portal malfunction. It was a terrible thing, but they've taken every possible precaution to keep that from happening again.

And second, you're totally right: the first bunch of ships to Kepler carried everyone in hibernation pods. Everything was automated, and all that worked just fine. They don't *need* live crews working these ships... and that's a big part of why my crew is traveling this way. They don't know how hyperspace affects people who are awake and working onboard these ships. Someday they'll need live crews, so they need our data. So yes, I'm going to be a guinea pig. Which is why my paycheck is so ridiculous!

Third, this has nothing to do with Mark and Sofia. That was five years ago, and I've moved on. This is me still moving on.

And finally, I won't be gone for ten years. My contract calls for a year out, a year working on-site, and a year back, probably in a hibernation pod unless they need more data. So it's just three years; I'll be home before you know it. Heck, I'll be back before *I* know it; they're saying a year in hyperspace will feel like just three or four months, but again, that's something they're still gathering data on.

So: it'll be fine. Give that niece of mine extra kisses and hugs for me when you see her, okay? And I guess if you can spare 'em, one or two for her daddy and Papa, too. <g>

— Love, Deb

COMMLOGWALKERDEBORAH00012182054001

Hi Mom,

We are underway! The jump to hyperspace went off without a hitch yesterday morning. And in even better news, I was able to finally keep some food down this afternoon. <g>

We all went through hours and hours of hyperspace simulation, but honestly the sims were nothing like the real thing. It's so … *weird*. It's not just being mostly weightless—I got used to that on the shuttle ride over. It's … everything's just *off*. It's like I don't know where my own body is anymore, and I keep fumbling around. I have no idea what time it is; if we didn't have clocks none of us would have a clue. I'm dizzy and nauseated. It feels less like motion sickness and more like being hooked up to a mild electric current. Our medical team swears all that will get better after a few days, and I hope so; meanwhile, they're going through just as many airsick bags as we are.

We have windows on the observation deck so we can see out into hyperspace. And in its own way, it's the weirdest part of the whole thing. At first you think it's this expanse of blackness, just like regular space, only you can't see any stars. But then the longer you stare out into it … you start to realize you don't know *what* color it really is. It's a color, all right, but not something any human being ever evolved to perceive. One guy, a medical researcher named Vince, gave himself a full-on panic attack staring out at it. Doctor's orders? Don't look out the windows more than five minutes. And I'm just fine with that.

— Love, Deb

COMMLOGWALKERDEBORAH00012252054001

Hi Mom,

Merry Christmas! I'm picturing you all at the table eating goose and Aunt Ximena's tamales. Thanks to something Dr. Cedar cooked up, we're all over being hyperspace-sick and had turkey and ham for dinner. It really wasn't half bad, although I'm pretty sure it was all soy (I spent a lot of time outgassing in the head afterward).

We had a holiday exchange; the stowage limits were pretty strict, but they told us to bring something light and fun. Team building! So I wrapped a couple of bars of gourmet chocolate in snowflake hologram paper, and I got a pair of little bottles of

Grand Marnier from Vince, he of the window panic attack I mentioned.

Mark loved Grand Marnier. The last time I'd had any was at his wake. Funny how the taste and smell of something can bring so many memories flooding back, isn't it? I couldn't sleep after the party, and I ended up in the hibernation pod racks staring down at the face of this little colonist girl who looks so much like Sofia. I just started sobbing.

Vince found me back there and talked to me a while. Turns out he's from Ohio; his folks have a rice farm. He lost his wife in the Lake Shore Bullet Train crash seven years ago; she was pregnant with their first child. He misses her so much, and it's obvious he still loves her more than anything. I feel for the guy. It was good talking to him, though.

Probably most of the crewmembers have their own heartaches. All of us live long enough, we lose someone we don't want to live without, but we have to keep going anyhow.

Love to all of you. Make sure you're hugging my niece! Can't get too many hugs at her age.

— Love, Deb

COMMLOGWALKERDEBORAH00001012055001

Hay Ma!

Hhaspy New Yaer! Hope ur having a gret time! Engneering made a still and whooooa thts some stron stuff!

Vinse sez he cn seee ghosts out th wijndows. Hes such a bobo!

— Loooooovvvvvvveeee, DEB!

COMMLOGWALKERDEBORAH00001012055002

Hi Mom,

I'm really sorry for the drunk message I sent. I haven't been that hammered in my life. Not as hung over as I expected; Dr. Cedar was handing out a remedy last night and it seems to have worked. But the dizziness is worse than ever, so I'm staying strapped in my bunk for a while.

I wanted to come clean with you about something. When I told you that I wasn't doing this because of Mark and Sofia? That was a pathetic and obvious lie. I kept hoping that if I told it to myself enough times, it would become true.

Have you ever been so sad and missed someone so badly that you thought your heart surely would stop? And yet, it never does? I feel hollow inside, and angry at God for taking them away from me. With all the medical advances we have, why do people still die from the flu? And I brought it home to them, God damn it. In my nightmares I see them in the ICU. Especially Sofia. Watching her struggle to breathe like that, fight and suffer and die anyhow … Jesus, that tore me up in a way I'll never get over. I know it about killed you and Papa too.

The first year I thought, okay, I'm mourning, I'll get over it. But I never did. If I see something that makes me smile, I'll turn to tell Mark about it … and of course he's not there. I'll do that three, four times a day. I'll walk down the street and hear a baby laugh and I'll look for Sofia … and suddenly in my mind I'm watching her die all over again.

And I still love Mark. I've tried dating, I really have. I want my family back, I want to try for another baby, but … I just can't make it work. I can't bring myself to fake it for someone I don't care about. As bad as I still want to be a mother, I just can't get past wanting Mark, and there's no way I can ever have him again.

A few months ago, I realized that the whole wide beautiful world is full of constant reminders of him and Sofia, and the ten thousandth time waking up and realizing they're gone doesn't hurt any less than the first and second.

Solution? Get off the world.

So now I'm somewhere far beyond the solar system traveling 20 million miles per second … and there are still sleeping beauties and tiny bottles of Grand Marnier out here.

But it's a whole new year, and something has to change.

> — Love, Deb

COMMLOGWALKERDEBORAH000000000000001

Dear Mom,

We hit something. Nobody knows what or how. The whole ship rattled around like a carnival ride and I got slammed into a bulkhead. I'm fine but don't know how long I was unconscious. It looks like all the auxiliary power went out for a while. But we're still in hyperspace, and all the hibernation pods seem fine, and the nav computer looks okay, but ... something's not right with the clocks. We have two atomic clocks onboard, and they should be synched perfectly but they're off by months. There should be no way that could ever happen. Nobody knows what it means. On past flights, they found some discrepancies in atomic clocks kept in different parts of the ships, but we're talking milliseconds there.

The other thing is, I'm getting an error every time I try to access my sent messages, so I have no idea if the system is transmitting properly or not. Another thing we have to troubleshoot. My head really hurts.

More later; Vince is having another panic attack I think. He is screaming complete nonsense. I better go see if I can help.

— Love, Deb

COMMLOGWALKERDEBORAH000000000000002

Dear Mom,

Vince nearly killed himself; he may still die. Dr. Cedar sedated him and we locked him in an observation room. But he woke up screaming and gouged his own eyes out with his fingers and started tearing his face off. He did a lot of damage to himself before they were able to sedate him again. He's tied down now, his face covered in blood-soaked bandages.

He's such a sweet guy. It's so terrible what's happened to him, but it's especially hard on his wife Rufina. She told me she's expecting their first baby.

More later.

— Love, Deb

COMMLOGWALKERDEBORAH000000000000003

Dear Mom,

I found Dr. Cedar dead in the hall outside sickbay. I can't get her face out of her mind. She looked like she'd been dead a month; she was all dried out and her lips were pulled back from her teeth in a horrible grin. And her eyes—oh God. You would have bad dreams forever so I won't tell you.

Her sister, the other Dr. Cedar, says it was an undiagnosed aneurysm and she was only dead a couple of hours. I don't see how that's possible, but she's the doctor, right?

I'm really glad Mark is here and we're patching things up, finally. I had so many nightmares that he and Sofia got sick and died, but she's safe in her hibernation pod and he's sitting just across the room. I really missed him, Mom.

But...I know I haven't been with him, but...I can't remember why we separated? Or when? I remember the nightmares. But it's been years ... or has it? And I feel like Sofia should be ... older now? Or is that just the hyperspace affecting my memory?

I wish I could talk to you. I wish I could talk to Vince. I feel like he'd be able to help me sort out what's in my head. At least he's still alive; Dr. Cedar says she thinks he'll pull through, but she has to keep him in a medical coma until we get to Kepler.

We're all still getting error messages when we try to access our message archives; I tracked down a couple of lines of corrupted code yesterday, but fixing them didn't help. If I didn't know better I'd think the damn program had been rewritten.

I wish this headache would go away. Dr. Cedar's meds make me too sleepy and stupid to work.

— Love, Deb

COMMLOGWALKERDEBORAH000000000000004

Dear Mom,

Sorry it's been so long since I wrote you. I had a bad reaction the drugs we've been taking for hyperspace sickness and came down with meningitis, of all things, but Dr. Cedar is getting me squared away. Finally the headache is getting better. I've been confined to quarters because I can't stand the lights, but Mark's been the best. He's been telling me all about how we're going to give Sofia brothers and sisters soon. He'll be a great dad. I can't wait.

— Love, Deb

COMMLOGWALKERDEBORAH000000000000005

Dear Mom,

Time has flown! But you know how busy it is when you're expecting. I can't believe how pregnant I am right now, and the babies are so active! Mark is one proud papa. He says I am the best mother he's ever seen. Dr. Cedar thinks there are eight babies? They all get wound around each other and it's hard to make them all out on the scanner.

Dr. Cedar and Rufina been tremendous helps in setting up the nursery. They've spun their silk everywhere; the whole room is so soft and looks like Santa's beard. Vince is in there, and most of the crew from Engineering. They will help the babies get big and strong.

I might not make it through the birth. But I'm okay with that, because my babies will live and that's what's important. It's been so long since the Kthath had a good host species and I could die happy knowing I helped save them. But I don't want you to worry— Mark and Dr. Cedar will do everything they can to make sure I can see them grow up. Mark says I'm tough and I can make it. I have a lot to teach the babies about humans and human behavior so they can fit into the Kepler colony. They'll have to take the places of everyone in the nursery, and that's hard, so I might be gone longer than I said I'd be. But it'll be fine—once my babies have had babies, we'll all head back to Earth.

— See you soon! Deb

RUMINATIONS

| RENA MASON |

RUNNING LATE to catch the bus, Luisa kicked a raised part of the sidewalk toes first.

"*Mierda!*" She winced but managed to keep her balance. She stopped, raised her leg, and massaged her big toe through her canvas work shoes. Relieved to feel no broken bones, she lowered her foot, ignored the pain, and hurried to the bus stop.

She shouldn't have tripped, but that's what happens when you're not paying attention. After walking the same way to work for the past eight months, she'd memorized every crack and weed in the three hundred eighty-six square concrete slabs from her apartment building to the covered bench where she sat and waited most days. Today, she woke up late after dreaming of the warring city, and keeping to a strict daily routine had been what saved her. The bus driver, a friendly middle-aged man named Toby, had waited for her with the door open.

"Thank you," she gasped.

Toby smiled. "Saw you coming. How's your foot?"

"It's okay. Thanks."

"Good."

He closed the door behind her and pulled away from the curb. She went to her usual spot on the bus, always empty an hour before sunrise. Nine rows back, opposite from where Toby sat, Luisa sidestepped her way to the window seat and plopped down. She pulled her hurt foot out of the shoe and examined the stubbed toe. Dark purplish blood spread out underneath most of the nail bed in the shape of a cloud. She shook her head, knowing the dead nail would eventually peel off on its own, leaving her with a raw, fragile toe. Luisa looked to the right at her reflection in the glass.

"See what you made me do?" she whispered.

Four months ago, Luisa noticed a girl who mimicked her every move in the window. The reflection looked much like her own, only younger, a girl in her late twenties maybe. She had a bleak expression and fear in her eyes. It took two weeks of experimenting to convince herself the anomaly was real and not a trick of her mind or wishful thinking. She'd taken a mirrored compact from her purse and looked into it, glanced at the bus window and back again. The reflected images differed from one another. In her compact, she saw herself as she should be: a 48-year-old widower from Guatemala, lucky to get a job at her age for financial support. A woman with two sons, both adults in constant trouble with the law and presently serving time in the California prison system. For her own good and sanity, she didn't keep in touch, disappeared from their lives. Life would've been different if she'd had a daughter.

Sadness showed on her face, but didn't compare to the young girl in the window. That girl's eyes expressed a fear she hadn't felt since first arriving in America. All the horrors Luisa had suffered through, she'd left behind in the jungle villages of the old country.

The bus screeched and hissed. It had been still for ten seconds before Toby yelled back:

"Your stop. Number twenty-two."

Her stop had come too quickly. She shoved her foot into the shoe and glanced at the reflection before rising.

"This is your fault, too."

At this rate, she might end up late to work, and that wouldn't be good. Too many others wanted her job. She passed Toby and thanked him.

"You sure you're all right?" he said. "I think that's the first time I've ever had to—"

"Yes, I'm fine." Luisa hurried off the bus.

It would be another twenty-minute walk to the Motel 8 off I-5 near Old Sacramento. Instead of thinking about the younger Luisa, she tried counting cracks in the sidewalk. After five hundred, she gave up and jog-walked the rest of the way.

This must stop. The girl in the window, I won't look at her anymore.

Luisa arrived ten minutes after seven, late for the first time since she got the job. Jan, the shift supervisor, gave her a disappointed look when she handed over the color-coded rooms schedule. Luisa glimpsed the green circular sticker on the upper right corner of the paper and held back a groan. Floors seven through ten, where they checked in most of the families with small children.

"Thank you," Luisa said, but she didn't mean it.

"If anyone finishes early, I'll send them up."

Luisa nodded and headed for the service elevator, knowing no one would come. Everyone stalled to avoid helping clean the family rooms. The coveted blue rooms schedule, where single business-people checked in, would be sorely missed today. They tended to be the neatest, with short stays, and on the first three floors. Sometimes, the beds hadn't even been slept in.

After loading up with supplies, she grabbed a vacuum and pushed the heavy cart down the hall to her first room. The door opened to a disaster area. Fast food containers with spilled contents lay strewn everywhere. Pasta noodles littered the floor next to the beds, some of them stepped on and smeared into the carpet. On average, it took thirty minutes to clean a blue room. Forty minutes into cleaning the green room, spending most of the time on her hands and knees, Luisa swore she'd never be late again.

While running the vacuum over the carpet, now clear of items too soft or wet for the machine, something black darted across the front of the window to the corner of the room. She jumped a little but kept her balance with a firm grip on the vacuum's rubber handle and continued to work. Ghost shadows often moved past her periphery in the hotel. If she ignored them, they'd go away.

The other girls often told stories about people who'd died in the hotel's rooms and scary things they saw at work during their lunches and over breaks. Luisa didn't listen to them. She kept to herself and stayed away from the gossip. Knowing too much might frighten her and she needed the job. Being isolated from their conversations came with a price, though. Other employees took it the wrong way and stopped inviting her to potlucks and parties. Sometimes, she wished they'd ask her again.

Pushing the vacuum back and forth, she could tell the black thing hadn't moved. A knot of discomfort tightened her gut. The temperature dropped, sending chills down her spine. Maybe if she glanced at it, the ghost would be satisfied and disappear. She backed toward the door with the vacuum in front of her and looked up.

It stood in the corner and pointed at the window.

Luisa crossed herself, shook her head, and prayed in Spanish.

The black thing had a human body. It took a step forward then motioned its other hand for Luisa to come.

Ottaya attempted several sleeping positions while bombs exploded far off to the north of the city. Their decoy transport had worked again, but how long would their luck continue until the rebels caught on? The old woman who'd been coming at night to join the transport caravans for shelter needed Ottaya's help, but also slowed her down. Then every morning she'd be gone again. Ottaya didn't mind showing her the way, even though she didn't quite understand why. Anybody else she might have let fall behind, but something about this woman reminded her of an important thing she couldn't explain.

When the time came to move again by day, the same woman could be seen, but only in the window glass. Ottaya thought in earlier times a different person might have looked back at her, someone younger, more familiar, but the memory remained clouded. A lot of war had happened since then, and the glass was always broken now or missing. Recently, she'd made it a point to sit in seats with more intact windows so she might learn more about the woman. But the older lady stared and said nothing.

A loud crash shattered her sleep. The transport went over something that lifted her out of the seat and she banged her head against the metal frame.

She rubbed her temple and opened her eyes.

The older woman looked at her from a glass shard.

How does she get there?

Warm blood trickled down the side of Ottaya's face, which she wiped with her filthy jacket sleeve.

"This is because of you."

"Who are you talking to?" a burly man said from the aisle, hunched over because he was too tall for the transport.

"No one," she said. Then she shouted to the driver. "What is it, Deegan?"

"Road block. They're coming on."

Ottaya rolled her eyes and pushed up her sleeve while the tall man went back to where he'd been sitting. A tattooed barcode appeared on her wrist with the numbers 12-21-9-19-1 imprinted underneath the lines—her resistance identification. Four armed, uniformed men boarded the transport and moved through the rows, checking each passenger. One soldier used a handheld scanner to inspect the barcodes, while the other three had their guns aimed at passengers. Ottaya knew the men wouldn't hesitate to fire if the reader failed to verify a code, even if it was a momentary glitch in the system. She'd seen many innocents of the resistance die this way. When they got to her, she recognized one of them.

"It's good to see you're still alive," he said to her.

She nodded.

"Don't move," he said.

The scanner's laser beam read her identification.

Ottaya held her breath and stared into his weapon's muzzle. If something happened, she knew he'd make it quick. When the green light came on, she exhaled.

"You never know," the soldier said, and shrugged—a reminder of how they'd all become indifferent to life and death.

The men moved to the next person. On their way back, the familiar soldier stood next to her and shouted at the driver. "Road bombs ahead. We'll send two cycles in front of you."

Someone in the back groaned.

"I know it doesn't always work, but if the riders stay tight and move fast enough, they could trip a bomb, ride past it and clear the way. It's all we can do," the soldier said. He looked down at Ottaya and smiled.

"Try to keep alive."

"Where is the decoy traveling tonight?"

"You know I can't tell you."

She did, but it never hurt to ask.

"You'll be safe," he said and gripped her shoulder. "We need you in one piece for the genetics module transfer." The soldier released his hold and exited the transport.

My father's memories and knowledge broken down and injected into my brain.

It would happen soon. Ottaya had been mentally preparing for it. Her mind would be a jumbled mess for a day or two, but then she'd have all the knowledge to create the genetic weapons her father had worked on before the rebels eliminated him.

The rebels and resistance had warred for millennia. They'd destroyed many places and then moved on and ruined more. Her father had discovered a way to infect the enemy on a genetic level. A way to break down the chemicals that made them up.

Ottaya looked at the woman in the glass.

"My revenge. It's coming."

Engines rattled and shook the transport as the driver put them back in gear. They'd soon be crossing terrain with hidden mines.

She shifted in the seat, feeling anxious and warm. An enormous shadow surrounded them and loomed overhead. Some of the others strained their necks to the side and leaned their heads to look up. An air convoy hovered in the sky above.

··· — — — ···

Luisa trembled, unable to move, as she stared wide-eyed at the black thing. Her focus remained on its face, and the features became more familiar—the girl from her reflection.

But why was she at the motel? What happened to her?

"*Vas*," Luisa said. "Go."

The girl from the warring city motioned again for her to come forward. The blackness covering her had once been skin. She had been burned. The char split apart like hard-caked desert floor. Red showed between the cracks—bloody raw flesh. Luisa winced. Perhaps the girl wanted to tell her what happened. Luisa's foot resisted stepping forward. Tears welled in her eyes and she shook her head.

No.

The girl didn't leave. Luisa took several deep breaths trying to compose herself. Maybe she would pass out and the vision would go away. After several minutes of feeling nothing but dizziness and nausea, she looked down at the carpet to avoid seeing the girl. Luisa continued to shake, but keeping her focus elsewhere helped. Only then did her body allow her to step toward the window.

Burnt feet and legs filled her periphery. She lifted her head and stopped. The girl pointed to the window. Luisa felt her body rise from the floor and float closer. Her body came to rest inches from the window with her feet on the carpet.

Reflections moved in the glass, but not the same way they did outside. The images differed. Cars sped across I-5 in the distance, but up close, what she saw in the window confused her. Luisa shifted her focus back and forth between the two scenes, and they didn't make sense.

The reflected landscape had been destroyed; she recognized it now—the warring city. Charred bodies and remnants of an exploded bus littered a road. A large shadow blanketed the scene. A rectangular airplane, like a floating semitrailer, hovered above the carnage. Luisa moved closer, pressed her forehead against the glass.

One of the burnt people came into focus and Luisa gasped.

The eyes! They'd been removed, but *after* the body had been burned. The sockets were nothing but dark caverns surrounded by bloody rims, their empty depths extended to the back of the girl's skull. Her brain, everything...gone. Something covered in soot and hardly distinguishable had melded into the palm of the charred woman's hand—a black bag with white stars drawn on it.

"*Como?*" she said, turning to the burnt woman for an answer.

No one stood in the corner.

"They've sent an air convoy to protect us," Ottaya said.

Two men up front turned around and looked at her.

The man in the back, who'd groaned earlier about the cycles, spoke up. "Oh yeah, I'm sure it's here for me because I dig trenches. Most valuable member of the resistance." He laughed.

His glare bore into her, but Ottaya kept quiet. Yorn had always been a disagreeable bastard, but she didn't feel like getting up and kicking his ass. She rolled her eyes at the others and they grinned, then returned to what they'd been doing. A sudden forward lurch, then back, and the transport traveled on.

Air convoys tended to be inaudible stalking shadows, loaded with weapons, explosives, and soldiers on the ready. The cycles, stripped down for speed, made a high-pitched whirring sound, but so far ahead, they'd be silent. Cyclists had one weapon—a reaper caplet—to be taken if caught by the rebels. Everything remained quiet except for the transport, which needed a new suspension and bounced and squeaked over the bumpy terrain.

A dull pop sounded from the road ahead. The transport jerked to a stop. Everyone stood and looked forward. Plumes of smoke had shot into the air. The air convoy moved forward to investigate. Deeg, the transport driver, turned up his signal receiver.

Loud static, then a voice, "Cyclists triggered mine. Sped past. Both unharmed."

Everyone clapped and cheered.

The tall man looked at Ottaya and winked.

"Stop it," Deegan shouted. "I need the numbers."

When it quieted, the air convoy's navigator relayed land coordinates for Deeg to follow in order to avoid the massive road hole left by the bomb. All fifteen passengers scrambled to find openings to look through when they went around the exploded mess.

Shadows made by the transport stretched farther across the road and crept onto the land. Soon it would be dark. Ottaya knew she'd come—the woman who reminded her of something she did not understand. Her mother had died giving birth; her father disappeared into the laboratories after that. Raised by soldiers, and other members of the resistance who cared for her while her father found a way to destroy the rebels, she knew nothing else.

At the first transport stop, and final checkpoint before leaving again for a safe place to spend the night, Ottaya saw the woman in line. She had something clutched to her chest and a look of fear on her face. The people in front of her had rolled up their sleeves, ready to be scanned.

Before the woman moved, Ottaya approached. The stranger turned to her and spoke in an unfamiliar language. Ottaya took the foreigner by the arm, leaned in, and shushed her. The woman nodded. Together, they walked away from the end of the line to an isolated area around the side of the checkpoint.

The woman whispered gibberish and reached into the bag she had a death grip on earlier. Ottaya paused, and the stranger recognized her hesitation, stopped talking, and smiled. She took something Ottaya had never seen before from a carryall—yellow, long, and curved. The woman pulled the top back and Ottaya jumped a little. This made the stranger giggle, but Ottaya didn't think it funny and would've snapped the woman's neck if she thought her dangerous. The woman peeled the sides down and took a bite, chewed, smiled again, and handed the thing over.

Ottaya took the yellow thing out of respect, smelling it. Slow and cautious at first, she took a few bites, and a pasty sweetness of exotic flavor filled her mouth. Then she devoured the yellow thing with ravenous fervor.

The foreigner smiled and appeared satisfied.

Ottaya reached into her black carryall. She'd used white stones found roadside during one of her transport trips to decorate it with stars. Drawing had always been one of her favorite things to do. Many people of the resistance had complimented her on the beautiful sketches she'd created from the ashes of the ruined cities.

The woman watched and inspected the bag.

A soldier startled both women. He'd been the familiar one. Ottaya didn't know his name, didn't want to. She'd seen too many soldiers disappear from her life, and she liked this one.

"What are you doing over here?" he said.

"Helping this woman."

"What is in your hand?"

"The skin of something I ate." Ottaya let it drop to the ground.

"It's time to go."

"Can you get us both on the transport?"

"Of course."

Ottaya looked up at the soldier in the most seductive way she knew how. "Without going through the line, I mean."

"But—"

"Please, I'm begging you. It's important. She's with me."

The woman stood silent and unmoving, waiting, as if she had done this before.

"You know I can't."

"Then I'll stay here."

"Dammit! You're stubborn."

Ottaya smiled.

"Come on, then." The soldier escorted them to the bus with his weapon pointed ahead.

"You look very official," Ottaya said. "What's your name?"

"I've seen you for years and now you ask me my name?"

"You're helping me. Yes, I'm asking your name?"

"Vinto."

"I like it. Thank you for helping us, Vinto."

"Who is she?" Vinto nodded to the old woman.

"No questions. Maybe I'll tell you after the module injection."

"You might forget."

"Then I forget. Maybe you should, too."

None of the other soldiers questioned Vinto when he escorted the two women onto the transport. Ottaya took a seat next to some window glass. No reflection appeared.

Maybe because of the darkness, maybe because she's here.

The foreigner sat next to her and smiled. An hour into the ride, the woman's head rested against her shoulder. She'd fallen asleep, and eventually Ottaya did the same.

Yorn eyed the two from the back and wondered about the strange woman Ottaya had picked up at the checkpoint. For the last few weeks, he'd noticed she had come and gone like a ghost. Perhaps the woman had been sent to further protect Ottaya. He wondered what weapons she carried.

It took Luisa into overtime to finish cleaning the green rooms. No one helped, not even Jan. During lunch, the other women kept to themselves. Luisa spent the entire day working slower than normal and thinking of the young girl. Why had she been burnt, killed— whether or not she came to warn her—or if she'd lost her mind and imagined it all?

With thoughts of the girl on her mind, Luisa almost walked past the bus stop. The deafening rattling of the engine snapped her out of the daze. The late afternoon bus drivers changed every other day. She slid her pass and chose a different seat than normal, but it didn't matter. Moments later, the younger version of the woman appeared in the glass, uncharred and undamaged. She looked happier. Luisa wondered what made her smile, and knew it wasn't her own reflection. Smiles didn't come often. Happiness was far away, perhaps in a distant past; exhaustion, for sure, but not happiness.

When she got home, Luisa reheated leftovers and ate with the television on, then showered and went to bed. Sleep came late, even though she'd been tired and would've passed out before dinner had it not been for the beeping microwave.

The warring city exploded into her dreams. Bombs and gunfire in the distance. Ruined places. Luisa waiting in line.

The girl took Luisa by the arm and walked her to the side of a building. Soldiers scanned the arms of those at the front of the line. Luisa knew she wouldn't pass. She tried to explain about seeing her burnt ghost, and thank the young doppelganger for protecting her, but in her dreams Luisa spoke Spanish. The people of the warring city spoke a language she'd never heard before.

For the first time in her dreams, Luisa brought her purse. The girl looked thin and hungry, so she'd reached in and found a banana. The girl jumped as Luisa peeled it, which made her laugh. The girl carried a bag, too, but it looked like a backpack for school: black, with white, hand drawn, childlike stars. Luisa somehow knew this girl had been deprived of a childhood, and she wanted to make it right—*the chance to have a daughter*—even if only in her dreams.

One of the soldiers approached and startled them. Luisa could tell he liked the girl, and maybe the girl had felt something for the soldier, too. He helped them bypass the line and onto an old bus with boarded windows and torn seats. In the back, a strange man watched the young girl. Luisa didn't like the way he stared.

Blaring electronic sounds jolted Luisa upright.

The dream-world dissolved as she opened her eyes.

She turned off her alarm clock, then started her daily routine. For the first time since her husband had died, looking around and counting were far from her mind as she made her way to the bus stop. The man at the back of the bus occupied her thoughts—the last bit of dream she remembered. His expression disturbed her.

"You sure you're okay?" Toby said, looking concerned.

Luisa slid her pass and a wave of vertigo forced her to grab the metal handrail.

"Give me a minute."

Luisa recovered and went to her seat, hoping to see the girl.

Stars from the vertigo blurred her vision of the window.

Stars! The backpack. The girl dies.

"Aye, *mija*," she whispered to the glass.

Tears welled and rolled down her cheeks. The thought of losing her dream daughter... She touched the cool window.

Where could you be?

She'd been asleep on that old bus before Luisa woke up. If only she could go back and warn her.

Luisa arrived at work before anyone else. Jan had still been working on the rooms schedule when Luisa went into her office.

"You're early," Jan said.

"Making up for yesterday."

"Nice job on the green rooms, by the way."

"Thank you."

Jan handed her the blue rooms schedule. "Here you go. Early bird gets the worm."

Luisa smiled, but felt disrespected that Jan likened her to a bird eating a worm. She shook her head and left the office.

Every time she'd unlocked one of the doors, Luisa looked in the windows for signs of the girl. All day she worked and saw nothing. Then, in the last room, she pulled the sheer curtains together and saw the girl in the reflection.

The scene was the same as before. A total massacre of blackened, twisted metal, an enormous blast scar toward the back of the old bus—she recognized it now—and her burnt dream daughter with her eyes and everything inside her skull removed. The image horrified Luisa. She crossed herself and looked away.

The sky rained soldiers. They fell from the floating tractor-trailer. As soon as they touched ground, one of them ran to the young girl's body. He dropped to his knees and hid his tears from the other men. His face was familiar, even through the grimace: the soldier who had helped Luisa and the girl get on the old bus. He took a vial from his pocket and popped off the lid, then poured a liquid over the charred body. She glowed bright green from head to toe, then crumpled to ash. Luisa crossed herself again. Her knees buckled and gave way. She fell to the floor and wailed.

The memories transfer injection went well. Ottaya remained groggy and couldn't recall much about the ordeal. She'd been attached to a mess of wires, while science team members spoke over one another and shined bright lights in her eyes. Even though a part of her father had been injected into her, she felt no closer to him than she had before. The disconnection made her sad, and melancholy followed her as she drifted off to sleep.

She remembered Vinto smiling down at her, telling her everything would be all right. Ottaya sensed him nearby. She forced her eyes open to the shadow of the air convoy above. She picked up on Vinto, but perceived nothing from her father's memories.

She would be happy to see the older woman again, but knew she needed rest before her arrival to help her get on the transport. Ottaya looked forward to the warmth of her body sitting next to her. The foreign woman comforted Ottaya and made her feel safe.

The next time she woke, they'd stopped at a checkpoint. Ottaya got off the bus and looked around. Relief coursed through her, and she smiled when she saw the older woman waiting at the side of the building. Ottaya neared, and the foreigner approached her with happiness. She opened her arms and wrapped them around Ottaya. Ottaya didn't understand the physical greeting. Then a look of dread came across the woman's face. As they walked back to the side of the building, the woman's incessant gibberish intensified. Ottaya stopped, placed her hands on the woman's shoulders, and in a calm, clear voice, told her everything would be all right. The foreigner relaxed, then reached into her bag and took out another one of those yellow things. Ottaya accepted and wolfed it down.

Once more, Vinto escorted them onto the transport. The old woman nudged Ottaya forward so she walked next to him.

"How long will it take to get to the lab?" Ottaya asked.

"Not long. Two moons."

"Why not suns?"

"Suns, moons, same thing."

Ottaya smiled at him.

"How are you feeling?" he said.

"Good."

"Are you ready to end this?"

"Endings also mean beginnings."

Vinto leaned over and kissed her cheek. Ottaya turned around. The old woman had a big smile across her face.

Ottaya felt weak as soon as they sat in the transport.

Vinto loaded up into the air convoy after walking them to their seats. The old woman held Ottaya close as the transport moved on.

An explosion jarred Ottaya from sleep. Chaos had erupted on the transport. The old woman stood her upright, pushed her into the aisle, shoving her to the front. Frightened, Ottaya grabbed the rails. She got caught among others fleeing the transport. Deegan's throat had been slit; blood spray covered everything.

Forceful hands pushed her toward the door. The old woman was no longer behind her. Ottaya grabbed the handrail, dug her boots into the rubber padding on the floor and held her ground. The old woman struggled with Yorn. He held a blade and brought it down into her chest. Ottaya screamed. The old woman looked back, yelled at Ottaya, and then pulled something in Yorn's coat.

The tall man back shouted, "He's got mines!"

Everyone pushed in a wave. Ottaya lost her grip and flew out the doorway.

Luisa didn't trust the man in the back of the bus. She'd awakened before the crash and saw him kill the driver. She pretended to be asleep like everyone else. He hurried back to his seat and waited for the bus to hit something and cause a commotion. Luisa knew he wanted to hurt the young girl, take her eyes and brain. She couldn't let it happen. As soon as the bus crashed, Luisa got the girl up and pushed her into the moving crowd. Then ran to the back and tackled the man, hoping he'd hit his head and get knocked out. That didn't happen.

While Luisa fought him, she felt things under his coat. They reminded her of grenades she'd seen government forces use during her country's civil war. Then the man stabbed. Adrenaline pumped so hard through her body, the pain distant. Luisa thought of the young girl. She saw her and shouted, *"Te amo, mi hija."* and pulled a pin from one of the devices in the man's jacket. His eyes widened.

Luisa pulled him close, forcing the knife deeper into her chest. She held him with a strength she'd never known. Then all went silent before bright light swallowed—

Ottaya awoke on something soft but itchy green. She sat up and moved her palm across the tips and they tickled her skin. She rolled over and saw the old woman's carryall. Ottaya lay there, admiring a blue sky that was familiar, and yet ... not quite. She wondered if it might be one of her father's memories. Tall buildings surrounded her, still intact and new: concrete flesh instead of steel and brick skeletons she'd been more accustomed to seeing.

Dark shadows took shape and descended from the clouds in a formation she recognized. Rebel air convoys filled the sky. Ottaya rose and ran with the old woman's bag clutched in her hands. She needed to find safety, and a lab where she could wait for the resistance, and Vinto—they would help her. The memories of her father would save this world.

GOOD AND FAITHFUL SERVANT

| THOMAS F. MONTELEONE |

PEERING INTO THE SCOPE of the weapon, Denek increased the magnification until the lead vehicle filled the sight. From his perch on the high-walled rock face, he had a clear view of the intruders.

"Computer," he said into his throat-mike.

There was a humming sound in his helmet as the small terminal on his backpack reacted: "Yes," said the sexless voice.

"Send this to Chicago: Intruders detected. Permission to intercept. Also, scan for any new orders."

"Done," said the machine, as it muted the helmet channel. Seconds passed as it communicated with the City.

Denek waited, while watching the three tracs advance deeper into the valley below him.

"Chicago confirms contact. Intercept. Confirm kill. And return. That is all."

Alone with his thoughts once more, he prepared to attack. *Why do they keep coming?* he wondered, as he drew a bead on the first trac. He rested his forearm and glove on the boulder and squeezed the trigger.

Bright blue light pulsed from his weapon, streaking into the valley below. The first struck immediately in front of the vehicle, but the second lanced the dome like a needle piercing a soap bubble. His scope was filled with flame, so bright he was forced to look away.

In that instant, the remaining tracs broke formation and rushed to the face of the cliff nearest him. Realizing their tactics, Denek jumped up and scurried along the ridge to get a better shot. As he stepped out into the open, the computer's voice crackled in his helmet: "Infra-red beam. It just passed over you. They have detected you on the first sweep."

He leaned back from the edge of the cliff as the words trailed off. He was wearing a man-amplification rig, giving him cat-like agility and the strength of many. It was a series of steel rods and artificial joints, fitted to his body like an exoskeleton. The computer on his back was plugged into the man-amp rig. Myoelectric sensors picked up each movement and passed it along to the computer; the movements were then coordinated and amplified. Denek preferred the rig to any kind of vehicle; small and compact, its gloves were actually gauntlets with retractable tools and weapons, and it also contained bio-connectors which fed his body nutrients and drugs, keeping him ever alert and able to do battle.

An explosion pulverized the edge of the cliff where he had been standing. The convoy's armament proved more sophisticated than he'd anticipated. He remembered the last intercept mission—three vehicles, no large armaments: it had been an easy kill.

Quickly he began scrambling over the rocks, looking like some sort of crustacean. Two more explosions ripped into the rock behind him as he scuttled away. He felt foolish, allowing himself to be discovered so easily. Denek's element of surprise gone.

Climbing up and then leaping down the wall of the mesa. He hoped to circle around and engage the two tracs on the valley floor. He ensured the computer continue monitoring for sensor sweeps as he began to creep around the wall of the cliff.

The first vehicle was within one hundred meters when he entered the valley. Extending both gauntlets, he fired. The pulses ripped into the vehicle, but seemed to be absorbed into it like smoke being sucked into a fan. They were using shields, absorbing the energy and converting it to additional power for the shield itself. Denek turned and ran from his position as the trac wheeled on its treads and ground after him. Its turbine engines emitted a high whine as it accelerated, kicking up rooster tails of the desert sand.

The man-amp rig picked up his movements and soon he was zigzagging across the sand at almost 80 klicks. Laser pulses burst around him, vitrifying the sand into glazed pools. He had no shield and was terribly vulnerable in the open.

The second vehicle began circling around to his left, and the two tracs attempted a pincer movement—each one slowly curving in to his center. As he ran, he retracted his lasers and extended a mortar. The only way to penetrate the shield was with a solid projectile. Reaching the far end of the valley, he leaped behind a pile of boulders, gaining several seconds of cover. He placed the mortar on automatic trajectory and let the computer select the azimuth. The clanking of the machinery grew closer and closer, filling his helmet with the sounds of death.

His extended hand trembled as the shell was fired. As he exhaled, he heard the explosion, and he jumped out into the open and fired a quick pulse of energy into the stricken trac. It blossomed into orange death, spreading a pollen of twisted metal across the sand. Turning on the second machine, still farther away, he saw it quickly reversing its direction, heading for an outcropping of rock. He knew immediately that the operators now wished some cover of their own, and he used the respite to reassess the situation.

Several minutes after the trac had disappeared behind the rocks, all remained silent. Could the crew be disembarking to hunt him on foot, an attempt to surround his position? He alerted the computer to the possibility, instructing it to expand its sensor sweep to include organics.

"Can you get a trajectory on that thing?" he asked as another minute passed in silence.

"Negative. The distance is too great."

"No organic readings?"

"Negative."

The face of the cliff above him erupted under a barrage of fire.

The trac laced the ledge above him with several shots and thousands of tons of rock fell toward him. He leaped instinctively from his huddling place. An ordinary soldier would have been crushed before taking more than a few steps; but the man-amp rig responded and he cleared the cascade of rock by many meters.

Out in the open again, he drew new fire from the trac, which had wheeled out from its hiding place. Once again he had to run, accelerating, increasing the distance between himself and the slower machine. The long smooth strides of the rig extended his lead, He ran almost without effort, but he couldn't employ the mortar. Retracting it, he extended the lasers once more. When he looked back over his shoulder he saw the trac fading several klicks distant. He had escaped. The wind sailed over him, sending grains of sand up to tick against his faceplate.

"Is it still coming?" he checked with the computer.

"Yes. But it is losing ground."

He continued his accelerated pace, wondering what the creatures in the tracs must be thinking of him. Surely they were impressed by his speed and power, realizing they must be fighting more than just a man. Denek smiled to himself at the thought.

When he had increased the distance to over five klicks, he slowed and stopped to survey the surroundings. He had been forced out of the natural valley into a flat open stretch of desert. The trac behind him was now just a black speck shimmering in the reflected heat.

"The vehicle has stopped," the computer said.

"Stopped? You sure?"

"I detect no movement."

Denek powered down the rig to its rest mode. He flipped down his magnifying goggles and brought the trac into focus. It remained still; he could see no one. They were both out of range of each other, yet their positions were obvious to one another. The game began, and Denek was content to wait them out.

Minutes stretched into hours. The desert sun, never clearly visible through the thick, half-poisoned atmosphere, sank deeper into the gray mist near the horizon. Denek replaced lost nutrients and eliminated wastes from his body. He was refreshed and eager to continue the battle.

Night came, changing the colorless sand into a still blue sea, and Denek switched to infrared as he continued to watch the vehicle. He wondered about the creatures inside it, plotting and figuring, wishing him destroyed.

Not allowing himself to actually sleep, he instructed the computer to dose him with enzymes to stay awake and alert. His mind churned over the events of the day. He replayed the kills, congratulating himself on his inventiveness and instinctive actions.

He wanted to finish this last one and return home. He missed the protective shell of the City wrapped around him and the others like a great cocoon. That there were forces out here wishing to destroy it struck him as unthinkable. Unnatural.

What type of beings were these intruders?

The question emerged slowly in his simple brain. Never seen, they were only known as an invading force that occasionally appeared on Chicago's warning screens. Perhaps he would someday learn more about them.

But now he stood at rest, wrapped in the armor and steel of his amplified body, waiting for one of their vehicles to make its move. He could not fail, or Chicago would be threatened. The computer continued to scan the area, ready to warn him of any movement. The night wore itself out and the dawn approached.

Which was when they chose to attack.

Flexing and testing the extensors and weapons modules, Denek poised for the engagement.

"They have dropped off two of their occupants," said the computer as the trac sped toward him.

"Where're they headed?"

"Spreading out. To both sides of you."

"Watch them. I'm going to take on the trac first."

Before either was in range, the trac opened up with a pulse cannon and it was effective. The packets of plasma vaporized the sand in front of him, throwing up a debris screen, obscuring his vision. He set up the mortar and instructed the computer to fire as soon as the target entered the lethal zone. As the enemy pulses crept closer to him, Denek stood his ground, waiting.

Suddenly the mortar coughed out its first missile and as quickly as he could reload, it fired again. The first one exploded to the right of the trac, but the second shell pierced the defensor shield, ripping the left tread to pieces. Helplessly spinning, the trac was an easy target. He extended his arm and fired three rapid laser bursts into it and it disappeared in a bright orange fireball.

He ran forward, dodging, and skipping toward the two intruders on foot, being wary of their weapons. The one closest to him opened up first, anticipating his movements.

One of the bursts burned past Denek, passing through the rig's steel rods along his left forearm. The heat of the contact seared his skin, causing it to ripple like chicken flesh. Pain short-circuited his senses and his hand and wrist were inoperative. They were locked into the gauntlet of the rig and he could not move them. He had the computer inject him with something to block the pain.

Still running toward the intruder who had wounded him, he raised his good arm and fired. Several bursts missed before a final one he cut the figure in half.

Seeing the fate of his companion, the other intruder pulled back and ran from Denek, diving for cover behind the smoking husk of the vehicle. He fired a quick pulse into the wreckage and it exploded once more. In the midst of the shrapnel rain that followed, the body of the intruder bounced and rolled across the sand.

"Computer. Contact Chicago. Confirm kill. I'm coming in."

The computer hummed as it followed instructions. Denek rubbed a steroid ointment over his burned forearm, being careful not to touch the still glowing tips of the steel rods.

Turning away from the wreckage, his peripheral vision picked up slight movement in the distance. His final victim—still alive? To have survived the concussion was impressive, and his enemy's toughness made him wary. When he raised his weapon, an odd thought struck him and he paused, lowering it. He had never had a chance to see an intruder up close. No one ever had. The only thing he knew about them was that they were treacherous, murderous beings who would destroy the City if given the opportunity. Denek had learned everything he knew from Chicago, but now considered the chance to learn something for himself. Perhaps he would even be rewarded if he could discover something new about the enemy?

Retracting his laser, he studied the crumpled figure, weaponless, one hand grasping at the hot sand, attempting to move, failing. An organic sweep and heads-up display by the computer indicated a low ebb of life forces. Denek flipped up his goggles and selected a slow jog, heading toward the body. He wondered what sort of creature he would find. Anticipating the worst, he kept his weapons gauntlet activated in case the computer's readings were not wholly accurate.

As he stood over the figure, his shadow fell across it, giving it a darker, more foreboding appearance. Denek huddled down, extended steel-reinforced fingers, and grabbed the creature's shoulder, rolling it over, face upward.

It was human.

Young. Feminine. Denek drew back his hand and stood up. Confused, almost disappointed he didn't find something else, he felt his hands shaking slightly within the gauntlets. He had never imagined the enemy to be like himself. Chicago had never suggested that it may be so.

To him, the intruders had always been faceless alien bipeds wishing to destroy the City. But now, something did not fit into place. He turned over the alternatives, the possibilities. There were things he wished to know; he could not yet destroy this female.

He looked down at her again, noticing that she was barely conscious, with several deep cuts on one arm and shoulder. He tore off a piece of her jumpsuit, wiping up the sand-caked blood, and tying it over the arm. Her face was light, unburned from the fierce sun, there were several wisps of blond hair along the edge of her helmet. Long eyelashes. Thin lips. Sharp features. Angular, harsh, but somehow attractive anyway.

His pulse quickened as he noticed her eyelids flutter. He shook her and her mouth opened as she gasped for breath.

"Where're you from?" he asked.

No answer.

Denek kicked her. "Speak. Where are you from?"

Keeping her eyes closed, wincing from the blow, she spoke slowly: "The City of Angels."

The words were like bursts from a weapon, shocking him. "You speak our language?"

A pause, then: "Of course...why wouldn't I?"

Denek did not understand what this woman meant. "What is this city of angels?"

Her eyes closed, her breathing labored as if just talking proved a great effort. "Where I came from."

"I want the truth...there is only one City."

"I'm telling the truth."

There was no fear in her voice nor in her expression as she opened her eyes to see Denek towering over her.

"Where is this 'City' you say you come from?"

"A long way from here. We rode for many days."

"There is only one City," Denek said with the conviction of a true believer.

Neither spoke for several seconds before she asked: "Why do you want to kill us?"

"Because you're intruders," said Denek, almost laughing at the absurdity of her question.

"Intruders? What do you mean?"

"You approach the City. That can't be done."

"We only wanted to contact your people and—"

"You wish to destroy us," said Denek sharply.

"No! That's not true. We are just like you. We speak just like you, don't we?"

"This can't be so. You're lying," he said, but somewhere in his simple mind, he was not so certain. She spoke with an inherent honesty in her voice.

"Look, I'm telling you ... all we wanted to do was contact your City ... your people ... see how you had survived." Her voice grew stronger as she began to shake off the effects of the explosion. Denek marveled at her toughness, in spite of her frail appearance.

"Explain what you mean." His curiosity grew in spite of his instructions and training.

He gave her water, waited for her to gather some strength. Finally she spoke.

"There were stories ... legends, I guess, that there were other places like our own. Once in a while men went looking. They didn't find much, but the stories continued. Some of the parties that came out this way never returned, so we came to check it out."

Her words seemed true to him, at least the part about other groups of intruders. He knew this because it was he who had destroyed some of them.

"They were unarmed," she added.

This was also true. Denek remembered how easy it had been to pick them off. He nodded.

"You?" she questioned, noticing his affirmation.

"Yes. It's my duty. Chicago demands it."

"You sound like the City's alive," she smiled weakly.

"It is. Chicago tells us all we need to know."

She didn't answer, continuing to stare into his eyes. Her gaze was uncomfortable and he was forced to say more: "Chicago is the giver and taker of life. Without it, we are nothing."

"Like a god or something," she said softly. She paused, biting her lower lip. "Well, I see ... I'm sorry ... I didn't know all that.

Forgive me, please."

Denek didn't understand her, especially the odd word she used: forgive. He almost asked her about it, but somehow he was intimidated by her. It was an odd feeling, since he could crush her skull beneath his steel glove in an instant. Yet he could sense the power, the assuredness within her.

Several minutes passed in silence before she spoke again: "What're you going to do with me?"

Her words jarred him. She was so direct, so open. "I ... don't know. I have been ordered to kill ... all of you."

She looked over to the burned-out trac. "Yes, I know. You're very efficient."

Her words would normally have been a great compliment, but somehow they sliced into him. The female was so utterly helpless and yet she was not. He could not kill her.

Seeds of uncertainty were sprouting within him.

"Perhaps Chicago would be interested in seeing you,"

She frowned. "From what you've told me, I'm not so sure."

"Explain."

"I could tell you were surprised we could talk to each other? It's like something you don't want to think about too much."

Denek considered this, his slow mind churning over the words. If she was truly alien, how could he understand her at all?

"Maybe ..." he said haltingly. "Maybe your people ... they learned our tongue ... to deceive us ... to lull—"

She laughed.

Denek understood her disarming reaction: "I'm wrong?"

"If we can't even get close to Chicago, how could we 'learn your tongue'?"

She had a point, he thought. "Still, there must be a reason. Chicago would know."

"Oh, I'm sure it does ..." she said, grinning, looking more attractive than ever. "But I don't think it wants to tell you."

"What do you mean? Explain."

And she did.

The desert burned away the hours as she recounted the recent history of her City. She told him of the olden times when the men who had built the cities had actually controlled them, of how the cities were once swollen with humanity and of how men fought among themselves, killing and maiming each other. She told him of the drugs, of how the men who controlled their City learned to control the people within it by pumping drugs and enzymes into the drinking water, releasing spores into the contained atmosphere. She told him of how her ancestors had rebelled and overcome the controls, taking away the power of their City, returning control into the hands of men. Her City functioned to serve her; not the converse. Denek challenged her many times, seeking clarification of a word or an idea, but always she had the correct answers. Her logic was unassailable. Heresy, yes. But still he could not help but almost believe her.

He dressed her wounds and gave her some of his rations. She refused to use any of his drugs, saying that they were not part of her culture. He deferred, attempting to understand everything he could about her.

As night came, wrapping them in the sudden coolness of the blue sand, they huddled closer together. Their talk drifted away from the cities and the ideas and the laws by which they lived. Instead they talked about themselves. He told her of his years of training in the City's militia, and the isolation of being a guardian out on the perimeter.

She told him of her own years, of freedom and of curiosity. She had been free to learn and love and live. Denek had never been very aware of this idea of freedom until she spoke of; but it permeated her entire being. Her speech was clear and precise. Each word seemed carefully selected, yet she spoke without hesitation.

He felt clumsy and awkward as he sat by her in his rig.

Later, they prepared to sleep, and he watched her take off her helmet, stretching out on the sand. Her long hair danced lightly in the breeze. He reached down and released the pins in all the articulating joints in the rig until he was free of the device. She sat watching him in the darkness, silent and waiting.

"You aren't supposed to do that, are you? Remove it, I mean."

"No," he said. "I'm not. How did you know?"

"Because you look very awkward and unsure of yourself."

"I ... I am never without the rig."

"So why did you take it off?"

Denek puzzled with this. He was not at all certain why he'd done it. This female was making him feel things he'd never experienced, thoughts he'd never had ...

"I ... I don't know."

"I can tell you. But, better yet, I can *show* you." Her voice was calm and controlled as always.

He nodded and she moved closer to him.

"What are we doing?" he said.

"Following our instincts."

When it was over, she slept; but Denek lay beside her, looking up at the brightest stars through night mist. Their joining had been a strange and alien thing to him. She had been so receptive to him, so full of movement. It was an odd, almost apocalyptic thing. The suddenness of it lingered in his mind.

And he felt utterly naked, exposed. Helpless. The feeling filled him with terror, and he eased away from her as she slept. Denek quickly refitted the rig to his body. He still thought of her as he did this; but when he had locked the final joint-pins into place and felt the weight of the computer on his back, he could feel his true life and mission rush back to fill him.

Chicago.

He should have been returning by this time. He hoped the City had not tried to contact him while he had taken off the rig. These were his thoughts as he instructed the computer to inject him with a sleep-zyme.

The heat of the awakening desert danced on his faceplate and he was awakened also. His eyes fell on her, still asleep, looking even more attractive than the night before. He stirred slightly and the rig picked up his attempted movements. A metallic joint creaked and the sound awakened her. Opening her eyes, she looked up at him and smiled.

"Hello," she said.

Before he could answer, he felt his right arm point toward her even though he had not initiated it. He tried to fight the movement but the arm continued to straighten. Knee and pelvic joints locked so that he could not take a step; he was helpless as he watched the weapons module click forth from the gauntlet.

Panic. Dread. The sensations dizzied him as he stood immobile and helpless.

He started to scream out a warning to her, but the bright beam had already swept over her, slicing through the center of her skull. He continued screaming as he could only stare at her cauterized remains.

And then the computer's voice hummed in his ear: "Denek... be silent."

He felt a slight twinge in his left arm as the rig injected a muscle relaxant into his tense body. Soon he stopped screaming, and his body went limp in the steel cage around him.

"Why?" he asked. His mouth felt dry and thickly coated. "What happened? How did that happen?"

"The mission required completion. Something you had not yet done."

"But... I thought that..."

"No, Denek," the computer cut him off. "Chicago was aware of everything. You did wrong."

He waited for more, but the machine was strangely silent. Then the rig began to move once more. The elbow and knee joints reversed themselves and he fell over on his back. Knowing suddenly what was happening, he fought against the slow, inexorable movements. "Why? Please tell me!"

"Knowledge always comes with a price."

And that was all the computer had to say.

The rig continued to move, and his legs and arms bent back at horrible angles, tearing away the connective tissue. The pelvic and shoulder girdles bent closer together, shoving his helmet toward his stomach, and the snapping vertebrae made popping sounds. Ligaments tore, bones cracked, and internal organs ruptured as Denek screamed as the rig folded itself into a compact cube.

In a final brief flash of sentience, he thought he understood what the City was telling him...

Performing one final organic scan over the pulpy mass it now enclosed, the computer, satisfied, turned itself off.

TWELVE KILOS

| PATRICK FREIVALD |

BRIGHT RED BLOOD squirted between blazing orange polyfiber strips, and Darren's stomach growled. He twisted the mop again and cursed every droplet that escaped the bucket, destined for the rusted metal grate in the floor. Two, maybe three milliliters spilled per job. Sixteen jobs a day, seven days a week didn't add up to much, but it did add up. A liter a month might move his family to a higher level, farther from the heat of the core. But this month he wouldn't even keep his family from the tithe, and he had no one to blame but himself.

Jacelyn heaved the last body onto the autoloader and wiped her red-stained hands on its shirt. He hid his envy. Damned meaters never had to worry about spillage. Meat wouldn't flop down the drain, wouldn't soak into clothes and mops and hair. One, maybe two meaters a month didn't buy out their tithe. A life of luxury.

The body flopped over onto its back, and Darren sighed as he recognized its face. Hal couldn't have been more than sixteen, and he and Darren's daughter Felicity had been friends of a sort. A kid that sloppy never should have been a harvester in the first place; lost a kidney last week, a good six feet of intestines the month before, and that's no way to buy out. A matter of time, this.

His stomach rumbled again.

Jacelyn's smile distracted him from his reverie, rotted teeth behind pale lips in a face that might once have been pretty. It held more pity than scorn, and he didn't need a meater's sympathies, no matter how well intentioned. Sure, blooding came hard, and harder still to those with mouths to feed, but an honest day's work took effort, and let it never be said that he didn't try his best. To break her gaze he pulled his lunch from his pocket, tore open the pouch, and squeezed the gelatinous contents into his mouth. The vegetal, hydroponic slime drowned out the iron tang of blood-stench for two gulps.

His muscles strained as he lifted the bucket onto the hover lift, and he held his breath in anticipation as he swiped his finger across the barcode. He knew, but he didn't want to.

"Thirty-nine point four kilograms," the mechanical voice read, dispassionate in its pronouncement. The lift disappeared into the ceiling and he turned, shoulders slumped. The priest emerged from the wall, a tangle of wires and tubes in a parody of humanoid form, three yellow glass eyes glowing too bright from clusters of internal LEDs.

He bowed his head in fear and shame, and shivered as the cold metal fingers ran through his hair. It took his mother's voice, as it always did, but none of her tone. "Blooder Darren, your monthly tithe is fourteen thousand four hundred kilograms. The counters tally fourteen thousand three hundred eighty-eight kilograms. Do you acknowledge the discrepancy?"

He licked his chapped lips. "There weren't enough bodies brought—"

"Do you acknowledge the discrepancy?"

"I do," he blurted.

"And you accept the responsibility of failure?"

"I do."

"Then pray."

They said it together, his exhausted rasp mingling with his long-dead mother's dulcet monotone.

"May the World-Machine forgive my inadequacies. As we sacrifice, so does It, that in Its eternal hunger and torment it might keep us from the Pit Eternal. Amen."

The priest continued. "In reflection of Its pain, return to your home and prepare."

He kept his eyes closed as the priest withdrew. He opened them to Jacelyn's, bright and blue and centimeters from his face. She kneeled in front of him, work suit soaked with sweat.

"How bad?" Her warm breath reeked of onion and rot.

"Twelve kilograms."

She hissed in a breath. "The tithe, then?" It wasn't a question, and he didn't respond. After a moment she stood, and the bloody smears on her knees mocked him. "Maybe they'll—"

"Just don't." He took her offered hand and let her drag him to his feet. "I've missed quota three times in five years, but never by more than five. Twelve? They won't forgive that."

"They might. You're a good worker, one of the best blooders I've ever seen. They have to see that—"

"No, they don't. The World-Machine knows no compassion or love or virtue or vice—"

"—only hunger and sacrifice, that it might keep us from the Pit Eternal," she finished. "Amen." Her hand on his shoulder left a red-brown streak. "You're right. I'm sorry."

He left her there, frowning after him, as he punched out and showered before the trip home. Hot water cascaded down his face when the claxon sounded the arrival of another trainload. He'd toweled off before the gunfire began, and wondered which lucky blooder had taken his place.

Ona's heart broke when she met him at the door, eighty minutes early from a ten-hour shift. She didn't say anything, but he saw it as he brushed black ringlets from her pale face, wrinkled and tight but still beautiful even with tears she couldn't afford to shed filling her eyes. And then she said nothing, and neither did he, even when Felicity broke down in tears and ran to hide in her room.

He kissed his wife, first her cheek, and then the stub of each hand as she brought them to his lips, the daily gesture a reminder of his unbroken promise those many years ago. *As the World-Machine protects us, I will protect you, to the end of all days, to the edges of the*

Pit, forever and always.

A lesser man would have abandoned her after the accident sixteen years prior. A man of his talents could have had anything; an apartment near the surface where the air came fresh through the purifiers, where shimmers of sunlight might reflect down the shafts to warm his face. He did the work of three, and could have anything that would pay for.

But he wanted only her, and their daughter, and that meant buying out three tithes. Three tithes at one hundred sixty kilograms a day, seven days a week. Fourteen thousand four hundred kilograms a month, fourteen thousand forty-eight liters of blood—depending on iron content. His mother told him he couldn't do it, up until the moment she stumbled naked and crying from the train car. His father told him he couldn't do it, but loved him for trying.

But he did it. For sixteen years he'd bought out three tithes, twice or more what any other blooder could manage. He'd killed seven men and four women in fights for the largest puddles, and even with the forfeiture of their blood he earned the right to live, the right for his family to live. His daughter, the spitting image of her mother decades past, his loving wife, and himself. Now one of them had to die.

He never should have picked up that bucket. Flush with morning's energy, he'd filled it too full, and in his haste he'd slipped. It hit the ground in a geyser, showering him, showering Amy, who laughed and licked it from her lips. She never saw the energy beam that vaporized half her head for her blasphemy, and they'd docked Darren's tithe as if he'd killed her, five-point-three kilograms on top of the fourteen he'd spilled. His appeal had fallen on deaf ears, and though he'd worked as hard as he could those last few hours, he couldn't make up the difference.

"My love?"

He shook off his thoughts and tried to smile. Ona hugged him, and whispered in his ear.

"We knew this day would come. You've given me so much

time, so much I wouldn't have had. It's time to let go."

He shook his head. *No, no, no, never.*

Behind him Felicity echoed his defiance, amplified it. "No. We can run. We don't have to do this."

They turned together, mouths open in shock.

"Honey," Darren said, "you can't defy the World-Machine. It protects us from—"

"No. It doesn't protect anybody. It feeds on us, uses us. It's nothing but a—"

He slapped her, and slapped her again when she opened her mouth to continue. "Where did you hear these blasphemies?"

She shook her head. "No, I won't say."

"But you'll repeat them." Ona's soft rebuke did what his slaps could not.

Felicity's eyes blazed, but she cast them downward. "I will repeat them. And repeat them and repeat them, until you understand. There is no Pit, or if there is we live in it. The resistance—"

Darren grabbed her shoulders. "The World-Machine is all that stands between us and the Pit. It can't survive without us, so we do as we must to feed it. If we fail, all is lost. The resistance is work of the Enemy."

Eyes down, a hint of a sneer crept to her lips. "You feed the Enemy."

He stepped back. "What?"

"The surface is clean, pure. Anyone can live there."

Ona shook her head. "Sweet daughter, they've fed you lies."

"I've been there."

His hand stung as he backhanded her to the floor, and he cried out as he kicked her. "You will not blaspheme in my presence, daughter."

Huddled on the floor, arms wrapped around her legs, she whimpered. "I've been there, and it's beautiful."

He reared back, and Ona stopped him with a touch. He closed his eyes and fought to compose himself, and dropped to his knees.

His wife spoke for him, knowing his mind better than he did. "Explain yourself, daughter."

"Liam resists. I've traveled with them, beyond the high levels to the surface itself. The sun doesn't burn your flesh, there is no radiation. Animals cavort in gentle sunlight, plants—green plants!—flourish under blue skies. And rain! You wouldn't believe rain, even if I showed it to you. Fresh water falls from the sky to nourish the land below. You wouldn't believe."

Darren opened his mouth, but Ona cut him off. "You swear this? On your life you swear this?"

"I do."

"Then tell us how to get there." He and Ona locked eyes over their daughter.

But Felicity shook her head. "You'll betray us. I know you, father, and I know you, mother, and I know you're too loyal, and that you have to see it first to believe. We live in the Pit, and your lives are dedicated to keeping us there."

"Daughter," Darren said. "I warned you."

Ona kissed his cheek, and he fell to her calming warmth. "Let me talk to her," she whispered.

The girls went into the bedroom, the only other room in their tiny apartment, and while they talked Darren slept as an acolyte should. Energy controlled everything they did, every shred they used for themselves a selfish denial of the World-Machine, every Joule a sacrilege to the agony It suffered on their behalf. He woke when footsteps intruded on his dream.

Ona bowed her head, eyes cast to the floor. "She's sleeping."

"As is right," they intoned together.

He brushed her cheek with his fingertips, an electric thrill even after all these years. They'd chosen.

They cried together, and made frantic, desperate love on the floor, and cried again and again. And then he opened a channel. His mother's voice answered.

··· — — — ···

He jostled awake and brushed his daughter's hand from his shoulder. "What time is it?"

"An hour before morning claxon. Let's go."

He stumbled to his feet, still in his travel clothes from the day before. He stepped toward the bathroom and his daughter shoved him toward the front door. "There's no time! Just go."

He paused at the front door.

The turn of a knob, and his daughter would feed the World-Machine. A step into darkness, and his family would die. Would Ona's love die with their daughter? Would his?

He turned the handle and stepped outside, running his tongue over gritty teeth. The lights would come on only at claxon, so darkness consumed everything. "Fel, we're—" He breathed a sigh of relief as three yellow eyes blinded him from everything else. "Come, daughter. It's time to go."

Agony wracked him, more than he thought possible. *Despair is a sin*, he thought, but the thought didn't save him. It took an eternity to realize the pain wasn't emotional, wasn't spiritual. Three yellow eyes dimmed, disappeared, became two. Green, not yellow. Liam's. His daughter's voice accompanied him to the afterlife.

"It's okay, Dad. It's okay."

He woke to an alien world. Blue blazed above him, an unrelenting brightness that penetrated to the core of his being. He turned from it, tried to see in the unrelenting light, could just make out humanoid shapes in a sea of soft green.

The priests have come.

A step forward, then two. Something tickled his feet, a scattering of tiny strips like his mop, green instead of orange. Delicate, they crushed underfoot. He breathed deep, and couldn't describe the joy contained in that air. Life, hope, happiness, he'd never known an aroma so rich.

A silhouette filled his vision, black curls and pale skin, delicate hands in a blue dress.

"Hi, papa. Welcome to the surface."

He grabbed her, pulled her to him. "What is this?"

"This is truth. Our life underground, that's the lie."

"No." He shook his head and buried it in his daughter's shoulder. "My whole life, the things I've done. It needs me. It needs us."

"No, Dad. It used you. It used me and your mother and everyone you've ever known. The World-Machine is the Pit."

He cupped her cheeks and dropped his hands to her neck. Her pulse quickened under his callouses, a desperate flutter unhinged from reason. He squeezed.

"Liar."

She clawed at him, raked nails across his hands, drew precious microliters of blood but didn't, couldn't, diminish his purpose.

"You want me to give up my wife. You want me to live a blasphemy. I cannot. I will not. I. Will. Not."

"Darren!

He turned at his wife's shriek, almost let go of their daughter. Her struggles weakened, and he squeezed harder.

Something large and pale filled his vision, then his head exploded in pain.

On his knees, he struggled to regain his feet. Another explosion of light and pain, and he lay on the green strips.

Grass. This is grass.

His mind plucked the fact from somewhere, childhood movies from before the Scouring or fairy tales from his father.

That's impossible.

"Yes, father," Felicity said, and he realized he'd spoken aloud. He looked up, and found his daughter holding hands with their neighbor, the sandy-haired boy Liam. They smiled at him, sad and hopeful. "It's impossible. But it's real. Everything you've known is a lie. When we go back—"

Darren shook his head. "No. We can't go back. I've betrayed you. You and Liam. They're going to take you for the tithe. If we go back, you'll die."

Liam's smile held no warmth. "We know. And it's too late to do anything about that. But you can do something. You can bring it down. Save humanity from the Pit."

"No, it doesn't have to be like this. I can—" A sharp pain stabbed into his neck, and the world swam, then went dark.

Darren shook the cobwebs from his head. A cacophony filled his ears—gunfire and screaming and laughter—and then only laughter. He rushed forward, mop in hand, bucket handle tucked into his elbow, as he'd done a thousand times.

The first body lay face-down, a sandy-haired man, too lean, too young. Another lay next to him, her mangled, naked body twisted into a parody of human form, but still she held his hand. Jacelyn tore them from one another, and he refused to see their faces. He shoulder-blocked Curt out of the way with a feral snarl, smeared the polyfiber strips through the wet, red liquid, and squeezed it into the bucket.

The priests had given him another chance. They'd given him new life, new purpose. Thirty days, nine thousand six hundred kilograms.

And yet...

01101110 00100000 01101001 01100110 00100000
01110111 01100101 00100000 01100001 01110010
01100101 00100000 01110100 01101111 00100000

BREATHE YOU IN ME

| MASON IAN BUNDSCHUH |

YOU ARE DYING in a Las Vegas hospital.

As your memories break away from the animal protein of your synapses like spores released from a mushroom, we collect and collate them. They are every scene of your life and we will remember them as you. Knowing them, we will be you.

Your dying thoughts flash in endless, inane, succession:

A small simian hand clasping yours—a juvenile of your kind, with trust in its eyes.

A scurrying quadruped, linked to your concept of ownership, rubbing itself against your legs.

A room with unprotected windows open to the day filled with others of your kind laughing, shoving mutilated organic material into your mouths to rip and tear.

A plate of glass showing a reflection of yourself with your illusory self-image distorting what you actually see; a memory of putting on the clothes you wear like the pupae of insects.

We see a face, coarse and rigid on account of the underlying skeletal structure, yet you called it beautiful. You remember this face turning to you, baring its teeth and its body to you, evoking an emotion called love.

Your emotions, like your memories, are chemical reactions. These memories are the exhalation of your humanity. We are breathing you in, consuming you, taking our fill, even as we recreate you in our image.

We, who never forget, shall reconstruct your entire life from these disjointed, disordered fragments of your dying brain. There is time. Always there is time. Waiting has been ours since the beginning. We wait now for your frail body of sinew, meat, and oxygen rich blood to be reconfigured.

We recognized the memory of when you came to us.

To you the tunnels are forbidding and immense. You feel fear, the primordial instinct to which mammals are slave. Claustrophobia, you call it claustrophobia though you can scarcely touch any side. Your logic is flimsy, but see how you wield it to push away the fear. You believe in reason like your ancestors believed the thunder spoke to them.

You fear the dark under the city. But it is not *you* who feels cramped by the sewers. It is not *you* who have outgrown your home.

Your memories flow and are assimilated. We assemble all that you have ever known, whether or not you were aware of it. All of these memories are here, in you. Now, in us.

Here, now, sparking up from your meat brain, is the instant you first stood on our threshold. We taste what you tasted, smell what you smelled. We know all that you perceived through your pinched and unevolved senses.

You were there with a man. The words you thought for him were 'transient, homeless, poor, junkie.' You pitied him, hid revulsion from him, but we know that this ragged man is one of the Children. Dirty, feral, full of unquestioning needs and appetites; no ideals or pretenses or nuance. Such are the subjects of the New Kingdom. The New Dominion.

You sought him out to show you through the hollowed out bones of Las Vegas. You imagine that he lives deep underground like the hundreds of others who live in the city beneath the city. But we know that no human lives deep—all of your kind live only on the edges. *We* know the meaning of deep.

Your life is relived in our memory.

"Don't worry," he's saying to you as you stand outside the viaduct entrance down by Dean Martin and Trop. "Ain't nobody gonna mess with you 'cause you're with me."

You do not entirely believe him. Not these days. That's why you're carrying the snub-nose in your pocket. And the pepper-spray.

But the gun is new.

In all the years you've been a reporter you've never had a real problem with the local indigent population (apart from that meth-head in North Town when you did a piece on squatters in fore-closed houses), but things have changed with Husk on the scene.

Your exposé on Krokodil a few years back, that flesh-con-suming cocktail of codeine and gasoline, had been hailed as presci-ent. But Husk… (You've heard the DEA call it Penny. They claim it's because it's cheap, costs pennies on the dollar. You think the DEA is not as creative as it used to be.) Husk makes ole Krok look tame as Molly.

Husk didn't leave open sores. Husk users walked around look-ing as healthy as any normal user right up until they turned up mummified along I-15. That's the other thing; they never were found in some flop house, or in an alley. Always along the freeway, sometimes miles outside of town. But always the same symptoms. You'd seen the coroner's reports. You'd even pulled favors to be a fly on the wall during an autopsy (but that would have to remain privileged information.) In your notes you'd described the effect of the drug as dry rot from the inside out; that the desiccated junkie looked like a pumpkin left on a porch too long. That was right be-fore you threw up. You remember it with shame.

You know there's a big story in it. And you know Husk is coming from right here in Vegas, right from the cavernous storm drain system under the Strip. You know it. You feel it.

Prescient.

And so you refound Chaz. He'd been a source a year back. A battered indigent who'd bounced in and out of shelters and streets, but who had that perversity of character that *wants* to show off the ruin of his life to journalists like you.

He stands with you in the stark sunlight. Before you is the

black maw of the sewers. You remind Chaz to tell everyone below that you carry no money, neither are you with the police nor any of the charities or shelters.

He grins, showing meth-rotten teeth. "No one here would go to no shelter. They don't let you use."

You don't let on that you're feeling the gun in your coat pocket.

"I'm just here to *see*," you tell him. "The world deserves your story."

It is a line you use often. Egos are so easily stroked.

He leads you from the light of day to the cold slap of shadow.

You have come to us.

As your eyes adjust you see a few crude pallets in alcoves. They are empty. You know that daylight is for crawling out on the surface and begging, or stealing. But you also know there are those who live deeper where the police never go, who rarely venture to the surface. The true citizens. Our Children.

You tell Chaz, as you penetrate deeper, that the DEA is looking for any excuse to come down here and clean it out. And you know it's true. Even for a city so image-conscious as Las Vegas— which has always turned a blind eye to the homeless living piled on one another in the sewers, considering it a win-win for everybody (one casino owner even confided to you, "and as a bonus, every year the flash floods do a little Spring-cleaning")—things changed once Husk turned up.

Chaz is several steps ahead. "I know why you're here."

He doesn't stop or turn and you suddenly realize there are no rats. You expected rats. The gun is heavy in your pocket. You control your breathing.

Chaz slips around a corner. "You want to know about Husk."

You follow. You are much deeper now. Garbage sticks to your feet. Broken milk crates are stacked along the walls, almost covering the blind graffiti. Your flashlight is a fragile bulwark against the pressing tons of concrete and glass overhead.

"Husk," you repeat. You tell him you believe it comes from

here. Not from over the border, not from cook labs in the desert.

"All you daylighter folk worry that it'll come up top. But don't you know there's too much light up there? It don't want to be no closer."

You know this is junkie-talk. You've heard it so many times on assignment. But here, underground, in these trash-strewn tunnels, you have the gun in your hand now. Hidden, but there. The automatic physiological function of sweat betrays you.

"I just want to know," you tell him. That is the curse of the journalist. The need to know.

He laughs and it is ugly. Rotten.

He leads you into a side tunnel. All along the walls are patchwork wooden bunks raised inches above the fetid trickle of slimy water. You've seen this before. You remember the hundreds of glassy eyes peering from filthy beds.

But things have changed.

"Where is everyone?"

You wonder if they heard you coming, scattered like roaches. But you know that is absurd. Junkies do not bolt. The denizens of such places do not run; they do not flee in their own domain.

"Oh, they all left. Steppin' out." Chaz's silhouette in the shaking light is indistinct. "We gotta seed elsewhere. It's too dry here. Not like it used to be before the mountains rose."

You wonder if you remember the way out. There have been several turns, and it would be easy for someone to come up behind you and...

"We gotta keep moving," Chaz says. He walks to the back of the tunnel-dorm. There is something on the walls. Mold thick as fur. "Gotta move. Spread out. It's a big world. A big world."

You are now in a sloping tunnel. Chaz is far ahead now. You wonder how deep under the dead alkaline they dug these sewers. But these walls do not have the symmetry of human engineering. There is water running down past you. The uneven floor is slippery. Small bones crunch underfoot with a wet sound. You can scarcely see them, covered as they are with diaphanous mold and fungi. The walls, too, are thickly carpeted with sheets of musty growth. You realize the air is a different kind of foul than that of unwashed bodies and urine, and for the first time you sense *us*, even if through a thick veil. You wonder if some disease had overtaken the homeless population. You cover your mouth with your hand as if that could stop the spores you've already breathed in.

Breathe us in. Feel us in you.

You cough.

"Where are you taking me?" you ask.

"You got that flight to Portland soon," Chaz says. His voice isn't right.

"How do you know that?" Your primate fear kicks in. It is purely chemical, yet you cannot fight it. You will go no further of your volition. We are here to carry you now.

"Portland is nice and wet," says Chaz, and then he hunches over in the muck, pulls a tuft of matted growth to his lips, his nose.

He grunts and convulses, begins giggling.

"I see god," he says.

You curse at him, yell, step back. The gun is in your hand and you aren't even aware you've pulled it out. You realize there is a soft green cloud of mold already growing on your exposed skin. You rub at it and it smears. But it's there on your other hand too. And of course on your face. In your nostrils.

Breathe us in.

Chaz answers your whispered question, though he could not have heard it. "This is Penny, this is what you were looking for." His emaciated arms fly out to the sagging walls, the ruinous liver spots of decay growing in the unbroken darkness.

You are screaming. You echo in our throat as we coat yours.

"Nice and wet," the thing that had been Chaz says as his flesh sloughs off, unneeded now that we have you to carry us. "We've been sleeping under the destroying sun for so long. The world is so big, so wet, and now that we're awake we're hungry."

You don't hear his last words; this is part of our memory. Just as you are now us.

You do not remember how you were found on the surface by other humans. You only remember waking up in the hospital, feeling good. You feel so good. You tell everyone. They were worried. But they don't need to be worried anymore. Whatever illness you had has passed. You feel very good.

You feel ready to travel.

Ready to seed.

01100010 01100101 00100000 01110011 01100001
01110110 01100101 01100100 00100000 01100001
01110100 00100000 01100001 01101100 01101100

18P37-C, AFTER ANDREA WAS ARRESTED

| ELIZABETH MASSIE |

I WAS THE LAST OF MY KIND to be free, and oh, how the researchers salivated and clapped their pudgy, scientifically-purposeful hands when they stole me away from my home and imprisoned me in their silvery-clean lab. As they prodded me, probed me, and forced from me samples of hair, skin, blood, and semen, I could see the other faces of my kind, pressed to the bars of their cages, watching, their brows furrowed and their eyes dulled with depression.

I cannot live this way, I thought. Then I thought again, harder, *I cannot and will not live this way. Are you with me?*

But of course none of them could read my mind. They had not been taught to pick up such signals as Andrea and I had. And so, even though I was among my kind for the first time in my life, I was alone in my misery.

It was a snowy day when the City Protectors, in their cheerful blue suits and jaunty red caps, slammed their way into Andrea's home on a tip from someone, a neighbor maybe? A family member? It matters little now; the deed is done. The snow was impressive and beautiful as seen through our living room window, but not beautiful as judged by most humans, for, unlike rain, snow is something they cannot yet control, and this snow was inconvenient and angry, hurled from above as if from a spiteful deity. In they came in their bright blue coats and pants, tracking melting snow on the floor, already enraged at having to be out in the weather, their weapons at the ready in case Andrea resisted.

One Protector grabbed Andrea by the neck, spun her about, and slammed her face into the wall. "How dare you defy the law!" the protector growled as her fellow officer jabbed a shackle-shot into her shoulder. "We'll see how the courts will deal with you!"

And so it was that Andrea was drugged and dragged from our little house at the edge of the city and taken away in the human-cage vehicle as I was drugged and dragged from our house and taken away in the animal-cage vehicle.

I have not seen her again.

I may never see her again.

I am now imprisoned at RCHIA—the Research Center for Human Intelligence Advancement, its acronym pronounced "rich-EE-ah" if you care to say it aloud, though if I could speak I would find it most foul on my tongue. The room is cold, almost unbearably bright, and smells of metal tools, sterile gauze, human bodies scrubbed with antiseptics, and simian despair. There are thirteen of us caged here. One is pregnant with a future experimental subject. Our cages line the walls, and steel tables sit in the center. At any one given time, day or night, one of us is strapped down and our skulls are opened up by the "Bright Eye" surgical machine overhead. My first few days I watched what was going on.

I don't watch anymore.

I have a new name, given me by the technicians. I am no longer James, but am 18P37-C. It is tattooed on the palm of my hand and in a chip under my skin.

Here is how it all came to be, this state of affairs. Thirty-three years ago, all that remained of my kind, a scant twenty-seven of us, were rounded up in central Africa, crated, and brought to RCHIA. The American government had paid the officials of those once-forested, drought-ravaged nations well, and the leaders were more than happy to trade us for water, food, drugs, and weapons.

Since then, chimpanzees like me have been bred in captivity and used in brain research and for selective brain and spinal cell transplants into humans who have suffered major head trauma, brain diseases, or cord injuries. Even though current medical technologies make most of these transplants archaic, there are always a few wealthy humans who fear such implants ("It will pervert our thinking! My dear cousin will never be the same!") and demand living tissue—our tissue—that has been stolen from us, reconstituted in micro dishes, and made a suitable match for humans.

Through these sad years, humans have maintained a particular sense of morality when it comes to their own kind. People should be healed, fixed, restored at all costs. The technicians look at us with eyes too shiny with their own superiority of position and imagined superiority of purpose.

At RCHIA, my kind are trained from birth to complete various tasks, understand and show an understanding of complex concepts, and to communicate in sign language. Young babes who reveal no promise early on are discarded; the rest are given various mind-enhancing medications and education (both aversion therapies and positive reinforcements such as trips to the compound's tree-dotted campus) with the goal of increasing their mental powers so they will be useful down the line to donate their brain matter. A fine crop of brilliant chimpanzees to be used at the pleasure of the scientists and frightened trillionaires. In apprehension that some might learn to speak audibly, all of the chimpanzees have had their vocal cords removed as a precaution. It is a very quiet lab, this one.

Brilliant, they are. But brilliance succumbs to melancholy and repeated procedures and so after years of this the chimpanzees are worn out and hopeless. The "Bright Eye" takes a few more samples from them and then, like the hapless, average babies before them, they are disposed of.

There is always a new crop in the making.

There has been no major outcry from the wider human population, not even from those who claim to care about species other than their own. To pacify the masses, zoological parks across the country have created quite realistic chimpanzee bio-trons that amble and gambol about the large grassy enclosures to the thrill of visitors. Angela told me about these places; she has visited them. "Chimpanzees in Their Natural Habitat," the signs cheerfully proclaim. People laugh and point and hold their own children up to see the tiny, infant chimpanzees clutched to their mother's breasts and the curmudgeonly old patriarchs pouting in the shadows. Knowing that the true natural habitats of my kind are long gone—clear-cut, poisoned with toxins, and claimed by powerful warlords as their own personal kingdoms—it is accepted by the majority of humans that living in parks is better than having no chimpanzees at all. People are happy that these lovely creatures, so smart and charming, have been saved from extinction and are now protected for generations to come.

Of course, this leaves those in the lab free to do as they will do for the betterment of a small, wealthy portion of humankind. The work unfettered, unrestricted, and inspected by higher-ups who have similar sympathies to those who run the lab.

Andrea worked at RCHIA when she was younger. A trainee, trusted, put to work with two other technicians in the vaporizing studio. Animals that died or were euthanized were sent to them for final erasure from this world. Menial work that paid a pittance, but jobs are scarce. Andrea, all of nineteen, did her work dutifully until the studio received two dead chimpanzees, and one, Andrea discovered, was carrying a fetus that had reached a viable stage of development. Andrea was surprised that the scientists had not noted the fetus, or had decided to ignore it, even though it would have been quite easy to keep the mother in a state of suspension long to bring the fetus to term.

But when Andrea inquired about the fetus she was 1.) told that the mother had died of an accidental overdose of a particular chemical which would have quite seriously and negatively affected the brain development of the fetus and 2.) told that she needed to keep her questions to herself; her job was to get rid of dead bodies, period, not second-guess anything or anyone.

With a scalpel she rescued the tiny being—me—and spirited me to her home at the edge of the city. I remember very little of my first months, except that I was warm, tenderly cared for, and safe. Andrea explained to me later that finding me was a startling moment in her life, a time of epiphany. She could no longer work in the service of death. She left her position at RCHIA, and began painting wild, bright, and glorious landscapes from her imagination, lush and vivid as might have existed in the 20th or 21st centuries. Many people found her art to be trivial, delusionally fanciful. But there were enough who found her fantasy paintings to be appealing or at least entertaining. Those were the patrons who helped Andrea make a living, even if that living was minimal.

During the first months of my life, Andrea taught me sign language (I was in no way brain damaged from my mother's overdose) and games of strategies. I quickly came to understand her spoken language as well as her signed language, and we became the best of friends. She named me James.

Over time Andrea developed a passion for ancient religions and mystic spiritual traditions. She immersed herself, and read to me many nights the teachings that most impressed her, passages from revered texts that moved her soul and mine. She embraced the concepts of compassion that were the core of these religions. She chanted and sang; she blessed other beings she encountered from one day to another. She practiced the art of controlling one's breathing and heartbeat with the power of the mind, and became quite skilled at this for it brought her into stillness and quiet. With great patience taught me the same. Some evenings, after tea, we would sit silently on the floor, and become nothing for a minute or two. When we returned, we were refreshed and at peace. We even trained ourselves to catch portions of each other's thoughts when focused enough on one another.

I was safe with Andrea. I observed the greater world through her window and through the readings we shared. At times I felt a faint genetic longing for the wild, but was satisfied with the cloistered life I had been given. Andrea's art shifted from landscapes to sky-scapes and what she imagined could exist out and beyond what we knew for certain through so many years of far-reaching exploration. I tried my hand at painting, but not every soul can express itself outwardly through art. My artwork was laughable, but I enjoyed the laughing.

And then I was discovered, Andrea arrested, and I was caged at the RCHIA lab.

Voiceless despair, hopelessness, and dread.

There is no sound quite so horrible.

The first one I was able to reach was 17P24-C, whose cage is next to mine. She is twelve years old and newly impregnated, with dry, drooping lids and lackluster fur that had come out in patches where she has repeatedly and furiously groomed herself. Using the sign language we both understood, I told her it was time to resist. I saw in her eyes a hint of soured bemusement, and she turned away. It took another several weeks to get her to understand what I meant, and for her to admit I was right.

Patiently, and in time, she convinced the others, though several were very resistant until the full impact of our plan dawned on them. Then, we became of one mind, one heart, one purpose.

With hand signals and spellings, I taught them, as Andrea had taught me. The technicians didn't follow our communications, for I was careful and subtle as I signed through my bars.

And we practiced.

Even as we were taken out and cut and stitched and returned to our cages, we practiced. Even as some of us lost bits more of our mental faculties, the portion of the brains that remained were able to focus on the plan.

We practiced. Becoming nothing, returning with a new sense of what peace might mean.

The technicians worked. Feeding us, tinkering with the "Bright Eye," experimenting and cutting, complaining as they always did, gaining nothing that could even smack of peace.

This morning, 17P24-C began to sense the fetus within her, moving, stretching, and told me immediately. The baby was not yet viable, and we knew time was of the essence. I alerted the others. They were ready. All thirteen of us exchanged knowing, relieved nods through the bars of our cages around the room.

We have reached the moment to act. Practice is over. We are ready.

We wait until the technicians are standing by the counter near the door, drinking coffee and rambling on about some sort of sport on which they had all placed bets. Arguing over which team was fastest, strongest, most clever. Laughing, scratching, stomping about in their little white shoes.

I look at those of my kind, their eyes prepared for surrender and happy for it. They look at me. I give the sign, a simple hand gesture, a finger pointing ceiling-ward. Sky-ward. I think of Andrea.

We focus on our breathing. It slows. We focus on our heartbeats. They slow. We will become nothing.

And this time, we will not come back.

Peace.

Peace.

00101110 00100010 00100000 00101101 00100000
01001001 01110011 01100001 01100001 01100011
00100000 01000001 01110011 01101001 01101101

NO FIXED ADDRESS

| GARY A. BRAUNBECK |

"It is the little rift within the lute,
That by and by will make the music mute,
And ever widening slowly silence all."
– Alfred, Lord Tennyson

"$\Delta p \Delta \geq h$."
– Werner Heisenberg

1

Fur-clad hunters tracked shaggy mastodons across the ice sheets to the steppes beyond, and some kept going south, seeking better hunting, more hospitable territory, and then the ice crashed into the sea and the hunters dropped into the waters, pressing hands over their ears as ice filled their lungs.

In death, it was not the icy waters that took them first, but the sound. Such a piercing sound none had ever heard before, nor would they again.

It was then the First LayerSpace Plane rippled near the corners of perception and the two Progeny emerged, quite by accident. After having been separated for so long, their excitement at finding one another made them reckless; they had been engaged in a sine experiment between the Tenth and Eleventh LayerSpace Planes when the perception ripple occurred; caught by surprise, delighted at this unexpected result, they had moved closer to the aperture in order to calculate its dark-mass ratio and found themselves inexorably trapped in its drag when the corners began to correct their positions.

They barely had time to call out as the force pulled them away from one another.

Upon emergence, each found itself to be alone, and without the other to give the Entirety necessary for an attempt at Re-Sounding, remained where it emerged, waiting for the time when they would be rejoined, Entirety achieved, and the solution to this new problem found.

To silence the fear in their core—a fear born of being separated from one another for the first time—each concentrated their efforts toward finding some trace of the other's sine-signature.

But this world beyond the ripple was not the same as theirs, and though both knew the possibility of multiverse travel, neither had truly believed, until this moment, that it could ever be achieved in such a tangible manner.

And so, as they searched for each other's sine-signature, each calculated hypotheses for how to duplicate the phenomenon.

The planet spun, ages passed in instants, races were born, thrived, and fell to the dust of extinction, and as this world evolved, there were those whose curiosity about it led them to explore it, to dig beneath its surfaces, to climb its highest mountain peaks, dive the depths of its oceans and, through this exploration, some of these curious ones eventually found the two Progeny (though these explorers, these divers, these climbers and discoverers, had no idea what they were), in time depositing them in places where they were viewed as curiosities or exhibit pieces consigned to antiquity.

But in this stillness of antiquity, each found the other's sine-signature.

How long it had been since they had last spoken neither knew or cared to remember; all that mattered now was their having found one another again.

And so, after millennia of fear and loneliness and deep thought, they achieved Entirety once again, and began what each knew to be the most important conversation they would ever have, spoken not in words but multidimensional equations. For centuries this conversation continued until, at last, they sensed a single, invisible, vibrating string of another consciousness that—though far less evolved than their own—somehow managed to create a sine-signal so similar to their own that both thought for a moment perhaps a third Progeny had been sent to find them, to help guide the rest of their race to safety.

They knew, then, that they must follow this vibration to its source; perhaps the answer to their problem could be found there.

In this way the matter was decided and their exacting preparations begun.

2

When I was six years old I fell down the stairs of our house and cracked my spine. Had it been one centimeter deeper I would have been paralyzed for life, but as luck would have it, the injury required only two surgeries followed by months of bed-rest, during which I could only move my arms or have my head propped up on pillows when it was time to eat. I read hundreds of books during those months, learned how to play poker from my mother, and drew so many pictures my father threatened to wallpaper every room in the house with them if I didn't stop. To save both paper and his nerves, he devised a contraption with hooks and pulleys that enabled me to raise or lower a small blackboard above my bed, allowing me to lie on my back (I was supposed to remain flat as often as possible) and draw pictures with the dozens of pieces of different-colored chalk he purchased at an art supply store. I thought of it as my blackboard sky. Some of the chalk was of the glow-in-the-dark variety, and every night before I fell asleep I would draw a picture of a guardian angel so that if I woke up in the middle of the night, frightened, I had only to look above to see my glowing angel with its luminous wings, and I'd know that I was all right, I was protected, someone was watching over me. Eventually that guardian angel lost its wings and gained a space suit and helmet—its disguise. To me it was the goal of all goals—not just that I someday be able to get out of the bed and walk on my own, but that of knowing that any one of a thousand-thousand fates were waiting out there for me in the world, and the one that would claim me was among them, wandering, searching, no fixed address, always moving closer.

If it weren't for that, if I'd not had my blackboard sky on which to depict glowing guardian angels disguised as astronauts and the dreams of all I planned on doing once I could walk again (flying to the moon in a rocket ship was right at the top of the list), I think my head would have started ticking like a bomb on a subway train, and I would have gone stark, staring crazy by the time I was seven. I still have that blackboard, and every so often I take it out of the closet and spend a half-hour or so drawing on it, just to remind myself that at least I had an outlet as a child when one was so desperately needed.

Or, rather, I *used* to. I *used* to do a lot of things, look forward to things, plan for things, and hope for things. And then came the story of the Boy in the Box Tower.

3

The first part was jammed between pages 93 and 94 of a used paperback edition of Anton Chekhov's *The Party and Other Stories* on a stained piece of notebook paper that looked as if someone had spilled coffee on it and then, in anger, crumpled it into a wad and thrown it away, only to have someone else later find it, smooth it out, and write on it. The handwriting (printing, actually) was that of a child—perhaps 7 or 8 years old—and if the spelling, punctuation, and grammar were any indication, not a particularly bright child; but I stopped thinking about those things by the time I reached the end of the first paragraph:

The boy In the boxTower

befour he was calld the boy in the Boxtower his name was vincent. he was not like everyone else. he was difrent. he had a special gift for distruction. vincent could distroy anything just buy looking at it when he was upset. he hated it but didn't no what he could do too stop it. it was resess and all the forth-graders went outside too play. vincent walked too a corner of the playground and sat alone. he didn't hav friends. everyone thought he was a freek. vincent wasn't intoo math or science

or reeding or righting or history. he was intoo horror and ghosts and creetsures and aleyans frum
space in books and movees. he yousd to watch
horror movees with his dad befour his dad got all
sad and killed himself. that was why vincent was
always depressed. he never reelly talked two people or got along with anywon. he was always alone,
even when he was home with his mom who was
always drunk and on the fone with her sister asking four monee to help with the bills. a kid was
walking to vincent, a big kid.

"hay, freek!" the kid shouted at vincent. then
he hit vincent in the face hard. vincent fell back
but then got up. vincents nose was bleeding and
his left eye began to twitch.

"you would not bee like this if yore dad wasn't
mean and hit you all the time," said vincent to the
big kid.

"well at leest my dad is alive and not some
psycho who killed himself!"

vincent grabbed a big rock and beat the kid in
the face with it. the kids face all bloody. vincent
stood with tears in his eyes. the twitch in his eye
went faster. he felt very hot inside. all the heat like
fire heded to his eyes. vincent stared at the kid
with the bleeding face. with his eyes he made the
bleeding kid go on fire all over. the big kid started
screeming reel loud. vincent cryd harder and took
off running until he reechd the big tower of card-
bored boxes.

it took him 7 hours to climb to the top of the
tower where there was a room for him to hide.
noone new where he went, but they started looking four him. but vincent was not alone in the box

tower. the device was there with him. the device
always found him. the device was his only friend.

"*That* is seriously fucked-up," came a woman's voice from behind me.

I started, nearly knocking over the stack of books I'd been in-
ventorying, and turned to see that Claire, who worked one of the
cash registers, was standing there reading over my shoulder.

"Jesus, Claire! Have you been taking some kind of ninja training on your days off? I never heard you."

"You were so engrossed, I just *knew* it was something odd."

I tilted my head and grinned. "You were hoping it was another
twenty, weren't you?"

"Can you blame me?"

I'd once found a twenty-dollar bill inside a well-read copy of
Love Story. Claire and I—along with the other volunteers who'd
been working that night—had used it to order a pizza.

The place where we work is called, simply, BARGAINS. It's a
second-hand store, not unlike those run by Goodwill and the Salvation Army, where people who can't afford to shop at regular
department stores come to buy clothes, furniture, household appliances, televisions, VCRs, DVD players, and assorted other electronics ... and, of course, books. I volunteer on Friday nights and
Saturdays, and am in charge of the electronics and books sections.
(I'd taken the day off work on this particular Friday because of a
too-long doctor's appointment, and had decided to come into the
store early.) I make it a point to always go through every box of
donated books that comes in and remove anything left inside. Over
the years I have found concert tickets, bank receipts, condoms still
in sealed packets, phone numbers, addresses, photographs of people whose names I'd never know, money, candy bar wrappers ...
people will use the damnedest things as bookmarks, and then forget to remove them before tossing the books into the large metal
BOOK DONATIONS bin outside the store. I'd once suggested that

we request people leave their names when donating books in case something of value was found inside, but the store has no computer to create such a database, and even if it did, cataloguing who donated each book would soon become a full-time endeavor; so, instead, I go through each book before placing it on the shelves.

"There's more on the back," said Claire.

I turned over the page and there, in the same childish handwriting, was this:

> the device was sending him a message, so vincent listened very carefully. he almost never understood what the device was telling him but it was nice to have someone talking to him and not yelling at him or ignoring him.
>
> "The wavelength in the waveguide is: $\lambda g = 2\pi/\beta$, which is always greater than the free-space wavelength of $\lambda 0 = 2\pi/k$—except for the 00th mode, where $\lambda g = \lambda 0$ applies as frequency decreases, the guide wavelength increases until it becomes infinite, at a cutoff frequency of:
>
> $$f_c = \frac{c}{2}\sqrt{\left(\frac{n}{a}\right)^2 + \left(\frac{m}{b}\right)^2} \quad [s^{-1}]$$
>
> "—where 'c' is the speed of sound. Below the cutoff the propagation constant β becomes imaginary, and the mode decays rapidly instead of propagating without loss. So the 00th mode has a cutoff frequency of zero."
>
> vincent smiled at the device and said, "thank you, C'haill-ol-i."

"What the *hell?*" I said.

Claire put her hand on my shoulder and leaned closer. "Got any idea what that is, Mr. Wizard?"

"Some math equations that are way beyond me—and please stop calling me 'Mr. Wizard.' I teach 6th-grade science, not quantum physics."

"So maybe it's just something the kid made up?"

"Probably." I found it hard to concentrate with the touch of her hand sending waves of heat down into my chest. "Probably," I said once again, folding the page and moving to place it in the stack of other items I'd found left in today's books, but Claire was faster and yanked it from my hand.

"C'mon, Patrick! You're actually expecting me to believe that this doesn't interest you in the least? Look at it! All of a sudden, when 'the device' starts talking to Vincent, his grammar and spelling are fine—okay, his capitalization needs work, but otherwise..." She waved the page in front of my face. "*Tell* me this isn't the most attention-grabbing thing you've encountered all day. *C'haill-ol-i?* What kind of word or name is that?"

I just smiled and shook my head, amazed as always that this lovely, vibrant, so *alive* woman showed any interest in me at all. I knew she thought of me as a friend, and I kept hoping things would turn into something more, but I was too afraid to make the first move. Besides being ten years younger than me, Claire was far too vibrant to weigh herself down with a man who had to use a set of canes to walk around—an after-effect from my childhood injury. Although the crack in my spine did eventually heal, it left quite a bit of nerve and muscle damage behind, enough that decades of twice-monthly physical therapy has done little to improve. I can walk short distances without the canes—say, from my living room to my bedroom or to the kitchen—but for anything farther, I need the canes. When I'd talked briefly to Claire about how frustrating it sometimes became, she'd laughed, cupped my face in her hands, and said, "Yeah, but you get the best parking spaces." How could a guy *not* fall for a woman with a sense of humor like that?

I found myself suddenly full of courage and decided to ask her out for a bite to eat after the store closed, but when I turned fully around to face her, her face had drained of color.

"Claire? What's wrong?"

Saying nothing, she pointed toward a row of television sets a few yards away; all were tuned to the same local channel where the noontime news was just starting with a breaking story.

A solemn-faced reporter stood at the edge of a school playground that was swarming with police, EMTs, several teachers and parents, and a lot of crying, frightened children. The volume on all of the televisions was set at low so it was difficult to hear everything the reporter was saying, but the words "two young boys," "fight," and "fire" came through loud and clear.

Claire touched my face and made a beeline for the nearest set, turning up the volume, though by that time there was no need; I think we both knew what had happened.

Two young boys from a local 4th-grade class had gotten into a fight during recess and the boy who'd started the altercation had somehow been set on fire. The boy he'd hit had run away during the confusion and still hadn't been found. The names of the boys were not being released yet.

I was still trembling when Claire came back to the sorting area.

"When were these new boxes of books brought in?" she asked me in a thin, quavering voice.

"This morning, right after I got here." I picked up the copy of the Chekhov paperback. "This was in one of the bottom boxes."

"So it would have to have been dropped in there either last night or sometime this morning before the store opened, right? I mean, there were other boxes *on top of it*, right? So that book and this piece of paper had been there for a while, right?"

I looked up at her. The color had still not returned to her face. "Right," I whispered.

She unfolded the sheet of paper, staring at it as if it were something diseased. "Please don't say this is a coincidence."

"I wouldn't insult your intelligence like that."

She stared at the page and tried to smile. "Good. I probably would have hit you. Oh, God, Patrick—" She took hold of my hand. "—what're we going to do?"

"We could go to the police and show this to them, but my guess is that someone would think we were trying to ... I don't know ... *pull something* on everyone. That we'd made this ourselves and were using it as a way to draw attention to ourselves."

She gave a slow nod of her head. "They'd think we were either a couple of scumbags or a couple of crazies. Or both."

I squeezed her hand. "I didn't want to be quite so blunt about it, but yes."

She stared at the page for a few more seconds and then released a breath that seemed to take everything out of her. "Jesus Christ—look at it now." She threw the page down on the table.

In the last two minutes, the story had been continued:

$$\Omega hd = |\psi hd|^{2} = |d\Theta/dz|hd$$
$$\dot{x}(t) = x(t-2) + J{-}1[F(x(t) - x(t-2) + \Omega) - x(t) - x(t-2) + \Omega]$$
$$\partial\partial t\_v\theta R\_$$

$$-$$

$$B0s$$
$$4\pi\varrho 0R2$$
$$\partial$$
$$\partial s$$
$$(Rb\theta) = 0 \, ,$$
$$i(V)dA = {}_iA + d\mathcal{L}$$
$$i(V)dA = 0$$
$$A = L(r;v;t)dt + p\pm(dr \, {}_i \, vdt)$$
$$h(x) = h_0 \sin(2\pi x / \lambda),$$" said the device to vincent as he lay down his head to rest.

"yes," whispered vincent. "they're coming for me. but they won't find me right away. And when they do, they'll have to come over the bridge."

"$\Omega hd = |\psi hd|^{2} = |d\Theta/dz|hd$," said the device again.

"I will," replied vincent. "i'll make sure to do it right."

"Patrick, I swear to you, *I swear to you*, I didn't do that."

"I know," I said, this time struggling to my feet and taking hold of both her hands. "I was looking at you the whole time. I know you didn't add that."

"Then...how?"

"I don't know."

We both looked at the page on the table, and then Claire said: "Patrick, when the store closes later, I want to come home with you. I don't want to be alone tonight."

"I think I'm even more scared than you are."

She tried to smile but couldn't. "That's why I like you so much. You don't have a false-macho bone in your body. That's a *good* thing, in case you were wondering."

"You can sleep in my room and I'll take the sofa."

She shook her head, never taking her gaze away from mine. "No, I want to sleep next to you. I don't want to fuck or anything like that, I just want to fall asleep feeling safe." And then she kissed me full on the mouth; not a quick, we're-just-friends kiss, but one with deeper affection behind it.

"I figured you'd never work up the nerve," she said, starting back toward her register. "And, yes, I've known how you feel about me for a while now. It's mutual."

My heart should have soared, but I was suddenly terrified that I wouldn't be able to keep her safe from...whatever it was that was happening.

4

The world from which the Progeny came was a dying one, one that lay far too close to the place where the expanding universe began to contract. For this reason, all of their efforts were directed toward finding another place where their race might be able to sustain itself and, eventually, prosper.

Progenies were not born, however, they were created by the pupils, and it was a time both exciting and frightening to young pupils, and the pupil C'haill-ol-i knew that his destiny lay in the fulfillment of this most important task.

As time passed, C'haill-ol-i achieved high status; not yet a Seeker, but already a Sentient, and he created a Progeny Device to search for other life among other stars in other galaxies, unseen but known. The Progeny Device passed near the Ninth LayerSpace Plane and back as it was programmed, but in the messages it sent were uneven waves that emerged as streaks of clashing colors, mud-gray splotches, even a black spray that swelled and shrank, appeared and vanished. With regret, the Seekers who were C'haill-ol-i's teachers declared it Undone. The fountain of multihued lights that recorded the Device's existence dimmed and faded. The messages ceased. A second Progeny Device, this one much altered by C'haill-ol-i, was dispatched but did not send any messages after its passage through the LayerSpace Plane; instead, a column of blackness marred the fountain of lights. This black column did not waver, nor did it grow—it shifted; first here, then there, moving from point to point without traversing the space between. The black column persisted despite all of the Seekers' efforts to remove it; even after a Seeker declared it Undone, the column of darkness continued to lash within the fountain of lights.

Seekers were appointed to examine the work, test the equations, study the methods; they could find no flaw, yet the fountain of many colors remained disfigured and hideous, marred by darkness that had become the darkness of ignorance, and then the shadow of fear. "We can find neither Progeny," said one Seeker at the review hearing, in a voice composed of the complex mathematical equations that were the core of their language. "Once they passed through LayerSpace, they were lost to us. We know they still exist somewhere. We know they seriously flawed, perhaps fatally flawed. Both pose a problem, perhaps even a threat, to any life form. Neither has responded to the self-destruct command. It is beyond our ability to stop it or to correct it. We have tried to no avail."

The two Progeny Devices were now forever stranded wherever they had emerged.

The Seekers gazed at the marred fountain of light, a pale, sad flicker here and there the only visible reaction among them.

"Sentient C'haill-ol-i," the Seeker of Seekers said, *"the pursuit of knowledge is to our race the highest order of intelligence, second only to love and respect for intelligence itself. You have brought dishonor to this pursuit, and a threat to life. However, in doing so, you have also alerted us to the dangers of unknown hazards that lie beyond LayerSpace. We thought ourselves ready to travel among the stars in search of Absolute Unitary Being, but find instead that we must be resigned to roam no farther than the reaches of our own star system until we have solved the problems your Device has revealed. This knowledge is most precious to us, for we now know that our race is doomed to die here, so we must now concern ourselves with preserving our knowledge and casting it to the stars in hopes some worthy race will discover and interpret its meanings. But there still remains the matter of your failure.*

"Because the good you have brought to your own race is overshadowed by the evil that you may have brought to other life forms, it is the decision of this review panel that you must complete the project you have begun. Until the lights of the Device fade, you will monitor them, for however long the Device continues to exist."

C'haill-ol-i's own lights dimmed and flickered. *"May I,"* he asked in a low voice, *"continue to work on the Device in order to try to solve this mystery?"*

"Yes, Sentient C'haill-ol-i. That is the only task you will have for as long as we continue to exist."

5

The boy who had been set on fire did not die; to everyone's amazement, his body sustained only first-degree burns. He would be hospitalized for a week or so, but he would be fine. His name was Eugene Oberfield. The boy with whom he'd had the fight, Vincent Martin, had still not been located by the time the 11:00 p.m. news began.

Claire and I sat next to each other on the sofa, holding hands and watching the newscast, hoping for something that would help us make sense of everything.

The television screen showed a tearful little girl, her teacher kneeling by her side with an arm around her shoulder. The little girl was talking to a reporter: "… an' then Vincent, he was all bloody and crying, he … he looked up at Gene and his eyes … Vincent's eyes … they were *red*, I swear it, they were red, an' then Gene, his … his shirt started to burn an' the next thing he was all *on fire* and there was so much *noise* in my head, it hurt *so much* …"

Claire picked up the remote and muted the sound after that. "I'm sorry, I can't stand to hear how scared she was—hell, she probably *still* is scared. All those kids are going to have nightmares about this for the rest of their lives."

Every witness—most of them children—had described something that could only be classified as spontaneous combustion. The local news had spoken with a handful of so-called "experts," all of who offered different explanations for how this could have occurred. None of them sounded as if they believed their own words.

"Why do you suppose your friend hasn't called back yet?" said Claire.

I checked the time. "It's only 8:20 in California. He's probably just now checking his personal e-mail."

Once we'd gotten to my house, I'd copied the equations from the page and scanned them into my computer as a jpeg file and sent it to Derek Trial, a friend of mine from college who now taught physics at UCLA. I'd tried to be blasé in my explanation, telling him it was something one of my students had found in an old textbook, and if he had the time, I'd appreciate him letting me know what the hell it all meant so I could put the student's curiosity—and my own—to rest. I'd given him my phone number and told him I'd be up very late, so he shouldn't hesitate to call. I was starting to worry that maybe I'd been *too* blasé about it and he'd figured it was nothing that needed his immediate attention.

Claire scooted closer to me, slipping her arm through mine and resting her head on my shoulder. She'd showered and changed into a pair of my pajamas, which were far too big for her and made her look ten times as beautiful. "Thanks for letting me stay tonight."

"You're welcome," I said, kissing the top of her head. She surprised me by turning her face up to mine and giving me a deep, passionate kiss, her tongue slipping briefly into my mouth.

"You're a pretty good kisser," she said after that.

"I practice a lot when I'm alone."

And for the first time in hours, she laughed, *genuinely* laughed. "Oh, God, you're a Woody Allen fan, too! *Love and Death*, right?"

"Right."

She put her head on my shoulder. "I'm so glad I know you."

"Tell me that the first time you have to help me with my back brace."

"You wear one of those?"

"Not all the time, but every once in a while I have a bad patch and it's the only thing that helps. That, and a lot of Percocet."

"How did you hurt yourself, anyway?"

I told her about the accident, about the months in bed, and about my blackboard sky.

"Do you still have it?"

I nodded. "It's in my bedroom closet. It still has what's left of my guardian angel-forward-slash-astronaut in the bottom right-hand corner. I never erased it. I have to touch him up every so often—glow-in-the-dark chalk doesn't last forever."

"Nothing does," she said, looking back at the television. "Do you think Vincent wrote that himself? Do you think he *knew* what was going to happen before it did? That he was going to hurt that other boy just by *looking* at him?"

A slight chill went through me. "I can't help but think of what Sherlock Holmes said. I don't remember the exact wording, but it was something like, 'When you've eliminated the impossible, whatever remains—"

"—however improbable, must be the truth,'" said Claire. "Oh, God—you're a Conan Doyle reader, too!"

"Guilty as charged, my dear Watson."

"I'm feeling a little better now."

"Good." I turned to kiss her again. Just as our lips met, my cell phone began ringing.

Claire's entire body went rigid. "Oh, boy—I bet I know who *that* is."

I gave her a quick kiss. "Here's where we find out something… I hope."

"Your lips to God's ear."

I answered the phone. Before I'd even finished saying hello, Derek was practically shouting at me.

"*Bull-shit* a student of yours found this in an old textbook, Mr. 6th-Grade Science Teacher."

"Great to hear your voice again, as well."

"Sorry, Pat. I didn't mean to raise my voice, but—do you have *any idea* what this is?"

"I was hoping you could tell me."

"It wasn't an actual question, I was—aw, *fuck* what I was trying to be. You were always faster with funny comebacks than me."

"Well, I had to practice something between ballet auditions."

"Pat, please—where did you get this?"

"I found it in an old book at a used bookstore. The paper it was written on was pretty old, as well, but it seemed interesting and I figured you were the man to go to."

"The book and paper might have been old, but…"

I felt my back tensing—never a good thing. My back stays tense for too long, it's hello-medieval-torture-brace time. "But what? C'mon, Derek."

"Okay. At first I thought it was just a random assortment of basic sound-wave equations—I mean, the business where the propagation constant β becomes imaginary, and the mode decays rapidly instead of propagating without loss, so the 00th mode has a cutoff frequency of zero, pretty basic stuff, but the more I examined the patterns—what is it?"

"Uh, nothing, sorry—I took a drink and it went down the wrong way." Which was the best lie I could come up with to explain the sudden gasp I'd released. Derek had used the exact same words as Vincent had written in the story. "Please, go on."

"Have you ever heard the term 'entrainment'?"

"No."

He was talking in a rapid, deadly cadence now. "It's been proven that externally-imposed sound vibrations can have a profound influence on human physiology. Say you're sitting in your kitchen trying to balance your checkbook and you begin to notice that your shoulders are hunched up and your back is tighter than normal. Suddenly the refrigerator snaps off and you heave a sigh of relief. Your shoulders drop, your back loosens up, and your whole breathing pattern changes. What do you think just happened? Certain biological rhythms have unconsciously "entrained" themselves to the 60 cycle hum of the refrigerator's motor. External sound vibrations temporarily altered your physiological makeup."

"Okay…?"

"The basic theory of entrainment has been applied in Cymatics and proven to be successful. Sound and vibrational waves can be used to heal the human body."

I was getting dizzy. "That still doesn't tell me what all this means. What the hell did I find?"

"It's a theoretical equation set for the organic production of a very powerful torsional wave. You know what I'm talking about, right?"

"Galloping Gertie," I replied, looking at Claire with my best I-need-a-little-privacy-but-it's-nothing-personal look, then standing up and walking a few feet away. My legs were wobbly and my back was starting to hurt like hell. "The Tacoma Narrows Bridge, right?"

"You got it. There's no way to test this equation without going back to Hans Jenny's research and cross-referencing its equations with these, and even then you'd probably have to go back to the work in early Cymatics, but… *Jesus*, Pat! Even the *idea*…"

"Tell me one thing, will you?"

"If I can—this is really freaky stuff."

"If—and I mean *if*—this was more than theoretical, what would we be talking about?"

After a long moment of silence where I swear I could hear his brain cells crashing into one another and creating sparks, Derek said, "We'd be talking about something that would be able to organically employ Cymatics and entrainment to force anyone or anything in its focus to vibrate at its natural frequency and achieve resonance."

"In simpler words…?"

His voice was thin and tense. "You'd have a human being whose sheer *will* could affect and alter—if not outright *destroy*—the standing vibrational waves that hold all matter in place."

6

C'haill-ol-i's people launched a life-ship into LayerSpace, one containing records of all their knowledge, all their art, science, philosophy, everything that had made them as they were.

C'haill-ol-i continued to monitor the fountain of lights with the blackness of evil at its core. He calculated exactly when each Progeny Device emerged from each of the Eleven LayerSpace Planes, and when they suddenly altered course and reentered, teasing him like a child playing a game. He could not know what they did in the intervals. He no longer saw the multihued lights; all he could see was the blackness, the evil.

C'haill-ol-i often gazed at the glowing heavens, with the three pathways of stars that looked like ribbons, and his own lights beat in harmony with the gently pulsing lights from above. Those nights his shame drove him to renew his efforts to find the evil he had launched, the ugliness he had injected into such beauty. Each time he was able to determine where and when each Progeny Device had emerged from LayerSpace he prayed that this time it would be destroyed; they had both been winding and twisting through the Planes without direction or purpose, as if each were confused, or mad. In charting the emergence of each Device from LayerSpace, he was also charting planetary systems, more than anyone had imagined, could imagine—no race could explore them all; one might as easily examine every grain of sand on an infinite beach.

But then something changed. The fountain of lights with the unquiet black column was glowing one second, and then it flickered, dimmed, and faded. For one millisecond, contact with one of the Progeny Devices had been established, only to be lost again. The Seekers turned to C'haill-ol-i for an explanation, only to find him gone, as well.

Now in LayerSpace, C'haill-ol-i flared with laughter. Folds, he thought; of course. Space did not fold by itself, one had to fold it; in the brief moment of contact, C'haill-ol-i had folded himself into the First Progeny Device and brought with him all the knowledge of his race, as well as their genetic codes.

How little it had changed, he marveled, centered in the midst of the ever-rising, ever-falling torrent of light that ranged the spectrum of color. How beautiful it was. How could something this beautiful spread such darkness, such evil? C'haill-ol-i had done his work well, better than he had known. But he had not programmed the Device to be self-repairing, so how...?

He did not know, but the Device had that capability, as well as many others it had learned, assimilated, or taught itself throughout its journeys. In the Device's sine-wave memories was a dead creature being probed by the photoscan, another creature that walked without grace through the darkness that was the core of its primitive heart, one weighted down with sadness as much as rage. This creature was alive, but tired...and so alone...

...C'haill-ol-i touched the creature, and knew at once...

...The Device...

... The Device had been gathering its own knowledge, sampling genetics from other races, merging them with its own organic structure to create a new being, one descended from C'haill-ol-i's original Device yet very much its own. The evolved Device had learned to create organic life and instill that life with knowledge.

C'haill-ol-i looked beyond and found himself outside the Device, surveying the world it had been probing; a lovely planet, with clouds, seas, obviously with an intelligent life form. C'haill-ol-i knew he could fold space/time again, if he chose, and have enough time to explore the galaxy and still return to learn everything there was to know about this planet, but then the Device sputtered, and there was a mini-nova in C'haill-ol-i's mind, and he knew that the Device had

*proven itself superior to its creator, perhaps even equal to the Creator of Abso-
lute Unitary Being (thought of as "God" by this new life form the Device had
chosen); C'haill-ol-i was now forever trapped within the Device he had created.*

*And both the First and Second Progeny Devices were in the hands of a
human child, a small boy named Vincent, who was tired of being picked on,
beaten up, mocked, hungry, and lonely, a boy who was so very, very angry at the
world...*

7

"Slow down," said Claire, cupping my face in her hands and kissing
me hard on the mouth. "There, hold onto that for a moment, okay?
I'm not going anywhere, I don't think you're crazy, and I *know*
something's going on here that we can't explain to anyone else and
not wind up in straightjackets. So—look at me, Patrick. There you
go. Now, I was following you just fine until that tonsorial wave
business or whatever—"

"Torsional wave," I said. "It's a vibrational wave that's not only dispatched vertically, but twists in a wave-like manner, as well.
Listen to me, Claire: 'Galloping Gertie' was a nickname given by
engineers to the Tacoma Narrows suspension bridge in Washington State in 1940. They called it that because of its frequent and
unusual undulating movement. All bridges vibrate to some extent,
but Gertie was unique; motorists who had to cross her every day
often compared it trying to drive a car on a roller-coaster track.

"On the morning of November 7, 1940, four months after the
bridge opened, the wind was blowing at exactly 42 miles an hour.
This wind hit the solid girders of the bridge deck and caused the
deck to vibrate back and forth just as it had been doing every
morning since the bridge opened for traffic, so at first no one
thought anything of it. But then Gertie began twisting and undulating like a piece of soft taffy in a pull before it completely collapsed.

"The wind caused the bridge to vibrate at its natural frequency
and create a torsional wave that helped the bridge achieve reso-

nance in two orientations: one over the length of the bridge, causing the undulating movement, the other from side to side, causing the twisting motion. The damn thing was toast once that happened. Resonance occurs when the frequency of a wave achieves a standing vibrational wave with maximum amplitude and—"

"Calm down, you're losing me again."

I closed my eyes and took several deep breaths. "I asked Derek to give it to me in the simplest terms possible."

"Simple would be good," said Claire. "I like simple. It gets me hot." She tried to smile at her joke but didn't make it.

"There's a lot of evidence to back up the theory that everything in nature is held together by sound waves. Don't ask me how, but somewhere out there tonight is a little boy—a very hurt, angry, and probably lonely little boy—who's been given the power to alter the physical and the physiological by manipulating those waves."

She stared into my eyes for a moment, then said: "He can change or destroy something with sound just by looking at it?"

"He can change or destroy *everything* just by *willing* it."

She began shaking. "How do you know?"

I nodded toward my computer desk where I'd placed the sheet of paper I'd found in the book. "While I was talking to Derek, I went over to my desk to look at the page. Go see for yourself."

She looked at my desk, then back at me. "I'm really starting to freak out here, Patrick. I don't want to look. You tell me. You tell me and I'll believe it."

"Will you help me put on my back brace? We need to get dressed and get out of here."

"But what about—?"

"The one page has now become five, and it's all in Vincent's handwriting, and it's probably the first genuine record of extraterrestrial contact ever written, and no one will believe a word of it because the race who contacted us—who contacted *Vincent*—no longer exists . . . except in Vincent himself."

"How do you know where to begin looking for him? Jesus, the

news said that there must be a hundred people in a bunch of different search parties looking for him. How can we hope to—?"

"Because Vincent *told* us where he is."

"The tower of boxes...?"

"The tower of boxes near a bridge."

It only took her a few seconds to figure it out. "Oh, my God—the recycling plant."

I nodded. "From the freeway you can see that enormous pile of boxes they let stack up during the week."

"And the 11th Street Bridge is the only way to get there until they finish with the roadwork."

I pulled her toward me and kissed her. "I *knew* you were the girl for me."

A tear slipped from her eye.

"Oh, Patrick—that *poor* kid. Can you imagine the way he's been treated all his life, to want to...to...?"

"Don't finish that thought," I said, struggling to my feet. "We need to get out of here."

"Right beside you all the way."

"You do know that I've been a little bit in love with you for a long time now, don't you?"

She smiled. "So I guess it's only fair you should know I've been a little bit in love with you since this afternoon. I hope we get a chance to enjoy it."

"Me too."

8

By the time Claire and I reached the 11th Street Bridge, it was all over the news; all of the children and teachers who had been witness to the fight between Eugene Oberfield and Vincent on the playground were now hospitalized and under heavy sedation because of auditory and visual hallucinations that had terrified them and sent many into fits of violence.

"Entrainment?" asked Claire.

I nodded. "Vincent is testing his power. He's lashing out at everyone he thinks has wronged him. Except instead of hitting them with his fists, he's attacking them on the physiological level. If he can maintain this, then he'll figure out pretty soon that he can do more damage."

Claire put her hand on my leg. "I'm sorry that neither one of us had the nerve to act on our feelings before now."

"You and me both."

"Do you think he'll ... do you think Vincent will listen to us? That he can still be reasoned with?"

"Look at me, Claire. I've got this goddamned Spanish Inquisition torture device strapped to my back and I stumble around on two metal canes. The kid's going to take one look at me and know I haven't had the best of times, either. The trick is going to be how long I can hold his sympathy once I've gotten it."

We took the 11th Street exit and drove across the bridge toward the entrance to the recycling plant. The plant had gotten a lot of criticism in the last several months because it dumped all cardboard items—especially the numerous boxes—from both residential and business clients into one large pile that it took care of once a week in order to save energy. Some weeks, the pile of boxes was so high it towered over the fence surrounding the plant.

Once over the bridge, Claire and I could see the top of the "box tower." It rose easily twenty-five feet above the ground.

Claire covered her ears with her hands and winced. "Oh God—*can you hear that?*"

I'd slammed on the brakes and covered my ears, as well. All I could do was nod my head and look in the rear-view mirror. Claire did the same, and a few seconds later we both turned to look out the back window.

The 11th Street Bridge was twisting and rolling and collapsing in on itself, its metal girders and concrete braces becoming rubber, the entire structure undulating like a piece of soft taffy in a pull.

It took less than forty seconds for the entire structure to crumple and give way, crashing down in a burst of dust and debris.

The unexpected pressure that had jammed its way into our ears and skulls subsided at once. Our heart rates returned to normal. We could see clearly again. And the sudden internal heat we'd felt in our chests evaporated.

"He knows we're coming," I said.

"Do you think he wants to hurt us?"

I shook my head. "No. If he wanted to hurt us, he would have destroyed the bridge while we were on it. This is a kid who's learned how to fold time, space, and all the matter that exists within and without. You can't sneak up on someone like that." I was almost laughing at the absurdity of it all. "He destroyed the bridge because he wants us to have some privacy. It's his way of saying, 'Come on in.'"

Claire squeezed my hand. "I hope you're right."

I put the car in gear and continued toward the recycling plant. It didn't surprise me to find that the entrance gate had been twisted inward and everything lying between the car and the tower of boxes had been parted like the Red Sea. We were able to drive right up to the tower.

Claire got out first, then came around to my side and helped me get out and to my feet. Instead of the canes, this time I'd brought the metal arm-crutches that braced around my forearms. I did not want to fall or stumble.

We started toward the tower of boxes, and as we neared, it began to re-shape itself; boxes that had been broken down and flattened were made square and firm again; others that had been soaked with rain or sewage crackled as they dried; and as every box was re-made, the shape of the pile became more and more tower-like, with windows at various points around its circumference and even gables at the top. Claire and I entered through a set of tall swinging doors and found ourselves looking at a great winding staircase leading up to the top.

It was no longer a tower of cardboard; it was now solid stone.

"There's no way I can climb those stairs," I said.

"You don't have to," said a voice from behind us.

I turned around, saw a small shape standing in the shadows.

"Patrick," whispered Claire, grabbing my arm. "*Look.*"

She was pointing toward one of the windows. We were at least a hundred feet above the ground. A sudden wave of vertigo caused me to grab onto her to keep my balance as I looked down and saw the seemingly endless staircase winding down, down, down.

"Hello, Vincent," said Claire.

"Hi," said a child's voice as Vincent stepped into the light.

I had never seen such old eyes in a child's face; in them were memories of loneliness and sadness more profound than any adult ever knows by the age of fifty. His clothes were dirty and old, not hand-me-downs but the type of clothes people bought at our store, people too poor to afford even the basics. He walked in a heavy heel-to-toe fashion as if he feared the ground might open up and swallow him before his next step. One look at him and my heart broke in a thousand places but didn't make a sound; the heart never does when its cracks.

"We came to help you, Vincent," I managed to get out. "And C'haill-ol-i, too."

"He told me you'd be coming," said Vincent. "He said you'd be my friends."

I moved closer to him. "He was right."

"I know."

I glanced around the bare room.

"You're looking for the Two Progeny," said Vincent.

"You wrote so well about them, I...I wanted to see them."

Vincent unbuttoned his shirt and pulled it open to reveal the longest, ugliest wound I'd ever seen running down the center of his chest. It was pink and moist, still fresh, but in the light it also looked slightly metallic, as if the surgical site had been soldered closed instead of stitched.

"C'haill-ol-i told me it has to be like this," said this broken and frightened little boy. "He said that my ... my flesh had to be re-made. Hey—I got something to show you, Patrick."

Before I could ask what, he tore off his shirt and lifted his arms as a pair of wide, luminous wings unfurled behind him, wings that were both flesh and machine, and shone with incandescence that seemed almost holy.

My breath caught in my throat, and for a moment I was six years old again, flat on my back, looking up at the guardian angel I had drawn with glow-in-the-dark chalk, the guardian angel, not yet an astronaut.

"Do you like it? I thought this was the way you drew me."

"It's perfect. You got it just right. Thank you, Vincent."

"You're welcome. I wanted to have an astronaut suit but I wasn't sure what one of them looked like."

He turned his head toward the window as a sound in the dis-tance began to come closer; the sound of dozens of angry voices.

"My story didn't have a good ending," he said, folding back his impossible wings and walking toward the window. "It ends like that *Frankenstein* movie with Boris Karloff. All the villagers come with torches and burn the castle to the ground."

In the distance I could see the bright flickers of dozens, maybe hundreds of torches, the flames snapping against the night.

"I think I'll make them all crumple up like a piece of paper."

"Please don't," said Claire.

He stared at her, his face expressionless. "Why not? C'haill-ol-i and the Progeny showed me how. I can turn them into anything I want. I can make them nothing. Nobody was ever nice to me. Only my dad, and he killed himself because he was so sad all the time and the doctors couldn't do anything to help him."

"We'll be nice to you," I said. "Just give us the chance, okay?"

Vincent looked at my crutches and the way I was standing, stooped over and shaking.

"I'll bet people made fun of you, didn't they?"

"A lot of them still do," I replied. "But I don't let it hurt me anymore."

Claire put her arm around my waist and held on tight.

"Could you maybe show me how to make it not hurt? C'haill-ol-i and the Progeny, they're inside me now, and they kinda have to do what I want. They showed me everything, told me everything, they gave me *powers*. It's weird but kinda cool. Kinda scary, too. Hey—did you know that C'haill-ol-i and the Progeny, that their world is all gone?"

Claire nodded. "Yes. We read your story."

"Did you like it? Was it a good story?"

"Oh, yes, yes it was. Very exciting, but also very sad."

His face brightened. "You really mean that, don't you?"

"I do, hon. Really, I do."

I looked outside; the torches and angry voices were even closer, much closer than I thought they'd be. Jesus Christ, were we suddenly back in the witch-hunts of the 1800s? Torches? Seriously?

"I don't have the … the folding part down too good yet," said Vincent. "Sometimes I make things happen too fast, or at the wrong time. That's how come you kept finding the story getting longer. I'd write it in my head, but then I'd cause things to fold and the words were just … just *there* on the paper you had."

"It's a neat trick," I said. "Will you show me how you do it?"

He smiled. "Sure. Maybe—hey, maybe you can tell me what I'm doing that's not right. C'haill-ol-i and the Progeny keep trying to tell me, but I don't understand a lot of the words. I will, though. I think I'll understand them when I'm a little older." He looked out the window once again and glared. "They've never been nice to me. Why should I be nice to them?"

"Because I'm asking you to," I said. "As a favor for me. As a favor for your new friend."

He turned to face Claire and me, holding out his hands. "C'haill-ol-i and the Progeny said that if you were telling the truth, then you wouldn't be afraid to touch me."

Neither one of us hesitated. It took me a moment to untangle myself from the forearm braces of the crutches, but as soon as I did, I took hold of one of Vincent's hands, Claire took hold of the other, and then she and I joined hands.

As soon as all our hands were joined, the walls within the tower began altering themselves, filling with glowing spheres that shone not any single color, but all colors, one bleeding into the next until it was impossible to tell the difference between gold and red, red and gray, gray and blue, and with each burst of color and combinations of colors there came musical notes. The first was a lone, soft, sustained cry that floated above us on radiant wings, a mournful call that sang of foundered dreams and sorrowful partings and dusty, forgotten myths from ages long gone by, then progressively rose in pitch to strengthen this extraordinary melancholy with tinges of joy, wonder, and hope as the songs of the other spheres and colors joined it, becoming the sound of a million choral voices raised in worship to the gods, becoming music's fullest dimension, richest intention, whispering rest to our weary hearts as the light moved outward in waves and ripples, altering our inner landscapes with every exalted refrain, voices a hundred times fuller than any human being's should ever be, pulsing, swirling, rising, then cascading over our bodies like pure crystal rain; then suddenly the rain, the music, all of it was *inside* us, assuming physical dimensions, forcing us to become more than we were, more than we'd been, than we'd ever *dreamed* of becoming; the sound grew without and within us, and we became aware not only of the music and the colors and whirling spheres, but of every living thing that surrounded us outside the tower; every weed, every insect, every glistening drop of dew on every blade of grass and every animal in deepest forest, and as the sounds continued rising in our souls, lavish, magnificent and improbable, we saw the Earth and the Moon as they must have looked to the Progeny as each moved through the cold, glittering depths of the cosmos and LayerSpace; the dry, pounded surface of the moon, its craters dark and secretive and dead as an old bone.

Just beyond was a milky-white radiance that cast liquid-gray shadows across the lunarscape while distant stars winked at us, then a burst of heat and pressure and suddenly we were below the moist, gleaming membrane of the bright blue sky, Earth rising exuberantly into our line of sight. We marveled at the majestic, swirling drifts of white clouds covering and uncovering the half-hidden masses of land and watched the continents themselves in motion, drifting apart on their crustal plates, held afloat by the molten fire beneath, and when the plates had settled and the rivers had carved their paths and the trees had spread their wondrous arms, there came next the People and their races and mysteries through the ages, and in our minds we danced through some of those mysteries, holding hands as we stood atop places with wonderful and odd names, places like Cheops' pyramid and the Tower of Ra, Zoroaster's temple and the Javanese Borobudur, the Krishna shrine, the Valhalla plateau and Woton's throne, and then we started dancing through King Arthur's castle and Gawain's abyss and Lancelot's point, then Solomon's temple at Moriah, then the Aztec Amphitheatre, Toltec Point, Cardenas Butte, and Alarcon Terrace before stopping at last in front of the great Wall of Skulls at Chicén Itzá. The skulls were awash by a sea of glowing colors, changing shape in the lights from above, their mouths opening as if to speak to us, flesh spreading across bone to form faces and then—

—and then we were One, all of us, we were the first to find the state of Absolute Unitary Being that C'haill-ol-i's world had perished in pursuit of.

We were un-made and re-made, all of us.

And we knew everything; that no one thing was true.

It was all true.

And it was all so … fragile.

We are in here with Vincent, with C'haill-ol-i and the Progeny, and we know, Claire and I, why the actions of the Progeny were perceived as evil, and why Vincent's anger at the world is still a very dangerous thing. We strive every moment to teach them about understanding, about acceptance, about love.

But we also share their fury, their desire for destruction, and look upon the world and the multiverse with equal parts compassion and contempt.

And we draw on the blackboard sky of the multiverse, creating new worlds, new races, new possibilities, always knowing that at any given moment, on the flash of a nearly-ruined child's anger, any or all of it can be erased.

We draw on the blackboard sky of the multiverse, and yet still hold a special affection for Earth and those who walk upon it. But this special affection walks hand in hand with a special hatred, that born from the beaten, half-broken spirit of a child who did not deserve neither the pain inflicted on his body nor the affliction now carried in his soul.

We have a special eraser for this particular place on our blackboard sky, for if and when it is decided that the Earth no longer has a place in our state of Absolute Unitary Being. Every so often, just for fun, we do the math. So far, the equations balance out. But numbers can change, waves can alter, feelings can be hurt beyond repair.

Sometimes, Vincent smiles down upon the Earth and says, "They'd better be nice."

So far, the equations balance.

So far.

Still, we keep the eraser within easy reach.

For like my dreams and goals of childhood, when I lay prisoner in my bed wondering which of the many possible fates out there would find me, the final moment of destruction of this world and all worlds, all matter, all time, all space, all potential, *everything*, is still out there, wandering, searching, moving toward a destination not yet found, a transient, lost but still moving, with no hurry, no pressure, and no fixed address.

EOT

| ␄ |

01101111 01110110

Made in the USA
Charleston, SC
11 April 2015